Mavis's Shoe

SUE REID SEXTON

**WAVERLEY
BOOKS**

For Moira

This edition published 2011 by Waverley Books,
144 Port Dundas Road,
Glasgow,
G4 0HZ,
Scotland

Reprinted 2011

ISBN 978-1-84934-105-9

Also available as an eBook
  ePub format ISBN 978-1-84934-113-4
  Mobi format ISBN 978-1-84934-145-5

A catalogue record for this book is available from the British Library.

Printed and bound in Poland

Some reviews for Mavis's Shoe

'Sue Reid Sexton doesn't flinch from giving her readers a gritty and sometimes heart-rending account of the trials confronting her young heroine … This is ultimately a story of courage and survival as well as a highly readable and vivid account of one of Scotland's worst wartime disasters.

Esther Read, *The Scots Magazine*

'This haunting, beautifully written blend of fact and fiction captures the strength of humanity, the courage in adversity and the heartbreaking loss caused by one of the most tragic episodes in our nation's history.'

Daily Record

'Sue Reid Sexton's work with war veterans gives an insight into Scotland's most devastating wartime event.'

STV's 'The Hour'

'A moving new novel about a child living in Clydebank during World War 2 … Sue Reid Sexton's work with war veterans gave her plenty of resources to draw upon when it came to capturing the feelings of survivors of war.'

The Sunday Post

'*Mavis's Shoe* reveals the shared trauma of war from Clydebank to Baghdad.'

Sunday Mail

'A remarkable story of a young girl's survival of the aftermath of the 1941 Clydebank Blitz.'

BooksfromScotland.com

'This is the first book to be simultaneously published in Braille in Scotland. And it's a great book. It's also good that it isn't in dialect – Glaswegian – it is Lenny Gillespie talking, so folk all over can understand it.'

Allan Balfour,
Head Editor and Braillist at the Scottish Braille Press,
who transcribed *Mavis's Shoe* into Braille

'Captures wonderfully well the community spirit of the time, and is a heart-warming illustration of family loyalties.'

Raymond Young, Education and Lifelong Learning,
Clackmannanshire Council

'Great subtly in the writing, which made the story all the more moving. If all of Sue Reid Sexton's and Waverley's novels are going to be of this calibre, I can't wait to read them.'

Moira Foster, Waterstone's Review

'The book took me right back, I felt just as lost as the wee girl in the book during the bombing.'

Isa McKenzie, Clydebank Blitz survivor

'I recommend this book – I thought it a really moving story – fiction based on the facts of those terrible nights of 13 and 14 May 1941.'

J Peel, Amazon review

'This book is important. It is moving and well researched, and should be read by everyone.'

J Wilson, Amazon review

'Just to let you know how much I enjoyed "Mavis" – twice! I cheated the first time – couldn't resist starting at the bit when Lenny arrived at Carbeth, then went back to the beginning, and the next day read it all again in the right order! It really conjured up the whole atmosphere, and the intensity of Lenny's feelings was conveyed so well. I'm sure it will do very well indeed and will sustain interest over the years as it's so evocative of that nightmare period.'

Marlene Macowan, who was evacuated from
Clydebank to Carbeth in March 1941

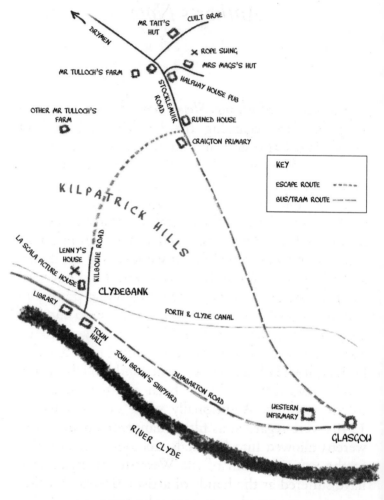

Lenny's journeys

Author's Note

As the author of *Mavis's Shoe* I have strived to ensure all particulars regarding the Clydebank Blitz and other historical events and circumstances are correct and true. However, all the characters are my own invention and not based on real people, apart from three notable exceptions: the first is Allan Barnes-Graham, the owner of the Carbeth-Guthrie estate; the second is Miss Read, the teacher at Craigton about whom I know nothing but her wonderfully apt name; and the third is Jimmy Robertson who I did not have the pleasure of meeting but who by all accounts did live in a bus which also functioned as a shop and had a tree growing through the middle of it. My apologies also to the owners of the tearoom which used to stand beside the Halfway House pub and which would surely have featured had I been aware of it earlier in my research. Additionally while children in the 1940s were regarded as filthy, dangerous beings who weren't allowed into hospitals, apologies are also due to the war-time staff of the Western Infirmary who have suffered at the hands of artistic licence. Further apologies are owed to anyone who feels that they or their experience has been misrepresented, but this is a work of fiction and no offence is intended.

I would also like to take this opportunity to thank all those who helped in my research who are too numerous to mention by name. Special thanks are due to Marlene MacGowan and Kevin Morrison of the Special Collections section of Glasgow Caledonian University, the library group of the Royal College of Surgeons and Physicians especially Bill Reid, Pat Malcolm of West Dunbartonshire Libraries, and Tommy and Jane Kirkwood, May McGregor and brothers Dennis and Jimmy Cairns of the Carbeth huts, and Isobel Douglas for her invaluable help on children who have experienced trauma. I would also like to thank Anne Nicholson, Karen Sullivan, Moira Salter and others for historical advice and for reading this book at various stages, and Liz Small and Penny Grearson of Waverley for their tireless help and attention to detail. Lastly, I would like to thank Jim without whom this book wouldn't have happened. All these people and more made my research not just interesting but a very positive experience despite the sadness of some of the subject matter.

Sue Reid Sexton

Chapter 1

For those of you that don't know, this is my story of the bombing. There was trouble before it even started.

The March cold was biting hard. I was soaked through and my knickers had begun to chafe. I pulled my cardigan double across my tummy and peered into the station entrance, called up the closes. No Mavis.

I stuck my hand in the pocket of my dress. The house key was gone! Boy, was I in for it when my mum got home. Dripping wet, no key, no coat, and no Mavis. I stood and trembled, partly from cold but also from fear. I could already feel her hand on my backside.

As I turned the corner into our street the sirens went off and I started to run then for no good reason, thinking it only a precaution and having nowhere to go. We had no shelter and I had no key to the house. I shouted for Mavis as I ran, and peered down closes and over garden walls.

'Mavis!' I shouted. She was only four. She shouldn't have run off.

We'd had such a good day, me, my mum and Mavis. It was the 13th of March 1941 and the sun had been shining, my mum had earned a good bonus in the factory the night before and she'd met a 'nice young man' who'd asked her to the pictures. We spent the day at the park, the three of us (when one of us should have been at school) and we went window-shopping in Kilbowie Road. The day was bright and clean and full of hope, but we were tired from the air-raid sirens. Every night for a week they'd been and all false alarms. Off we went every time knocking on someone else's shelter or into the flat at the bottom of our close, and then back up later when the all clear sounded, sometimes minutes later, sometimes hours. We were extra tired too, Mavis and I, from walking and laughing and worrying about my mum. We never knew when she'd change and you wanted to be ready to duck when she did.

But I want to say, in case you're wondering, that she wasn't always like that. She didn't used to be. It was only since my dad wasn't coming back. She would never have kept me off school before and she would always have been with us, safe in the house. She was patient when I lost things and told us stories about 'home', her home which wasn't Clydebank, when we lay in our alcove bed with her between us, all snug and warm, or she hummed tunes and made me recite my times-tables as if they were tunes too.

But after the park and the window-shopping, she sent me and Mavis home with a clip round the ear (I was being nosey and wanted to know who her nice new friend was) and money for chips, enough for a whole bag. I pinched Mavis in the chip shop so Mr Chippie gave us a pickled onion for her tears. Then we wandered down to the canal.

We spoke different from everyone else, being not from there, so on the way down we practised speaking, like we sometimes did, so no-one would know. We rolled up our tongues and pulled back our lips.

'Rrrrr,' I showed Mavis. Some sounds were rrreally difficult.

'Rrrrr,' she went, or something like it. Of course, four year olds aren't very good at that sort of thing.

'A rrright good seeing-to,' I said, like Miss Weatherbeaten at school, or that's what the kids called her; a good weatherbeating is what you got for talking, or for not talking rrright, but then I'd go home and get a hand across my backside for not talking proper English.

But now I had so much more to worry about.

'You lost Mavis?' said the woman next door. 'You'll be in for it now, Lenny, pal. Where's your mum?'

'Gone to the pictures with a nice young man.'

'A nice young man?' She laughed lightly.

'Yeah. Said she wouldn't be late tonight.'

'Hmm … .' She shook her head.

'You don't have a spare key do you, for our house? It's just … I lost mine,' I said.

'Christ, how did you get so wet? Fall in the canal again?'

'Yes … no … .'

'Mavis didn't fall in did she? Your mum'll kill you. Look we've got to get into the shelter. You better come in with us. We can just about squeeze you in. There's not much of you is there?' And she laughed again and pinched my arm.

'Thanks, but I've got to find Mavis. Mavis!'

'Someone else'll take her in. You'll get her later or in the morning. Don't you worry. You just look after yourself, seeing as no-one else round here is going to.' And she glanced at our house.

'No, I can't, really I can't. I've got to find Mavis.'

'Well, you know where the shelters are. Make sure you get in somewhere.'

'Yes. Thanks,' I said. 'Mavis!'

I was running again now. The sirens were going but I was the only one running.

'That'll be the blitz then!' laughed the old lady at the corner, to her daughter. 'About time too!' They waved goodbye to each other and she disappeared into the darkness of the house on the corner.

All around me people were pulling the blinds down in their windows. Darkness was falling but there was a big beautiful full moon, as plump as you like. 'Mustn't let the Gerries find us,' my mum used to say, every night at the same time, when she was there, or I'd say it to Mavis, and Mum would say 'Who'd want us anyway?' But there was no hiding in that light, a light that bathed us all in silver, and picked us out from the shadows.

I went round all the closes in the street and shouted for Mavis. I even went into the one at the top of the street. An old man lived there, a man who kept a stick specially for naughty kids like me. I whispered to her in there but I stayed there the longest and even went up some of the stairs. The cold whistling through the close made my bones shake. The baffle walls didn't help the draught a bit. They'd been built outside all the closes, front and back, to stop bomb blast, and to give us something extra to bump into in the black-out.

'Mavis!' I whispered, wanting to be heard and not heard.

Out in the street, people had been going to shelters

slowly, taking time to gossip on the way, but their steps quickened now, and I heard muttering, tiny snippets of conversations.

'Germans over the Clyde Valley ....' People were moving faster. The woman next door was there again dragging her little girl through their close on the way to their Anderson shelter. I followed them.

'Get in here now, quick,' she said to her daughter, 'and stop your nonsense. Where's your brother? No, you can't go back for your dolly. It's too late now. Oh, and I've left the tatties on the boil. Oh, you're back, Lenny. Did you find Mavis?'

'No,' I said.

'Well, you better go and get into your shelter then. Where's your mum?'

'We haven't got a shelter,' I said.

'No, neither you have and we've no space left in here either. Look, there's too many already.'

'No, I didn't mean that.'

'Don't be silly, woman, she doesn't take up any room,' said someone at the back of the shelter.

There was a rumbling sound, like the engines at the factory, or a car, only louder, but it was up in the sky, then a screech like a whistle or a scream. It seemed to last a long time. We looked up frozen in not knowing. Then the most almighty explosion shook the ground underneath us and everyone screamed.

'Get in here then and shut the door,' said the woman.

'No! No! I've got to find Mavis!'

She reached out to pull me in but I shook free of her and slammed the door shut. I could hear them arguing inside. The door burst open again.

'Lenny get in here now or I don't know what … !' she said.

'I've got to find Mavis!' I said. 'Mavis! Maaa-viiis!' I backed up the garden and headed through the close. The shelter door clanged shut and the rise and fall of voices went on behind it.

There was a shoe like Mavis's by the close mouth. I picked it up and turned it over in my hand. The baffle wall was hot at my back. I wasn't sure the shoe was hers. I tried to remember her feet, her shoes, like mine only smaller, her shoes that had once been someone else's. I stuck it in my pocket, where the key should have been.

There was another of those long whistling sounds, a pause and then a boom, then again, another whistle, a pause and a boom, and again, and again, and a strange crackling noise, like wee bangers on bonfire night. The ground shuddered and shook and rumbled like in the boat to Rothesay last summer, and I began to shake too. I wrapped my hand around the shoe in my pocket and stepped out from round the baffle wall that covered the view from the close, and looked all about me.

The tenement building over the road had gone, or most of it had, and what was left was burning. I'd never seen flames the size of these, leaping and gobbling everything up. This made no sense to me. I searched my memory for something I could compare this to but there was nothing, just like there was nothing left of this building, only a hole where something indestructible had been. The sky was on fire too and the road was a sea of broken glass, rising and falling. Looking to the right, I saw a parachute drifting gently over the hill, silent and beautiful, but when it landed it made the ground under my feet shake again and another building exploded, one I couldn't see. The world was back to front, the wrong size and inside out.

Through the smoke I could see the old lady with the bag at an upstairs window in the corner tenement over the road. The window was broken. She was still holding her bag, clutched to her chest as if her life depended on it. Mrs … Mrs … what's-her-name? Then she vanished and with the sound of crunching and the crack of split wood, the floor she had been standing on appeared in the window below. Suddenly it was engulfed in flame, orange hot flame. A whoosh of heat smacked against me. I screamed and stumbled back behind the baffle wall and into the close where I'd been standing.

'Mavis!' I muttered over and over and turned in several circles, coughing.

The smoke seemed to follow me in but there were other smells too, like a mixture of all the things you don't want to smell, singeing hair, whisky like my dad, gas, burnt rubber like when I left my shoes too near the stove, poisonous stuff of one kind or another, and above my head I thought I heard whimpering; someone was up there who should have come down to a shelter.

'Get down!' I shouted into the din.

Smoke and dust flew about, caught in a hot swirl, filling the air, filling my mouth and my eyes. I coughed and spat. My eyes burned and watered. My heart was beating so fast I thought it would burst right through me and I gulped for air.

I ran back through the close, crossing the drying green with my knees banging into each other and my stingy eyes half-closed to see through the smoke. I was just about to knock on the shelter when I heard loud singing coming from inside.

'We're gonna hang out the washing ... .'

I looked back at the building I had just run through and saw that it was on fire, its walls black against the orange windows. I fell against the shelter and felt the heat of the blaze in its metal burning my hands and I saw above the burning building that there were other parachutes, parachutes which I knew now were not lovely things but carried bombs big enough to tear apart the mountainous tenements that were my town. And all around me the sky was filled with still more drops of fire, little drops flying all around, caught in a whirlwind as if the very sky had come to life, and all the laws of nature and gravity that I had learnt at school, had all been lies and were of no use now.

The noise was deafening. I couldn't hear the chorus in the shelter any more, only the thunder of engines and explosions. I think I stood there for some time but I don't know. My face felt tight, as if my skin had shrunk, as if the fire was trying to get right inside me, right into my head, so I turned away and covered my face with my arms. But when I looked again, this time over the back, it was even worse. Behind me, behind the shelter, behind the houses, beyond, there were flames bigger even than the flames over the road, reaching right into the sky, so much flame it was like there wasn't room for it all down below. It lit up the whole sky and all the buildings. There was nothing hidden.

The Gerries had found us and we were laid bare-naked, and I had lost Mavis.

A sudden blast brought me to my senses and I saw that next door, our own tenement was in darkness and shrouded in smoke, giving nothing away.

'Mavis!' I shouted, though my throat hurt like there was glass in it, and I started quickly towards our home, falling over things that shouldn't have been there. I raced in through the back close and banged as hard as I could at the downstairs neighbour's door, panic and hope all tangled up together. It was meant to be safer there than upstairs during an air raid. Maybe Mavis had made it back home after all, maybe she was in there with the rest of them, safe with a neighbour.

'Mavis!' I shouted. 'Are you in there?'

'Lenny! Where have you been? Where's Mavis and your mum?' said the woman at the door. A row of faces lined the candlelit hall.

'Is Mavis here?'

'No, love, she's not here,' said the woman. 'Come in and close the door. Look at the state of you.'

'But I've got to find Mavis,' I told them.

'You have to come in here with us, Lenny darling, you can't go back out there. Move along you two and make a space for her.' The twins from the top floor keeked round at me. Their faces gleamed wet in the candlelight.

Bangs and cracks and booms shook the ground and split the air.

I began to back out of the close. 'None of you've seen her? Mavis?'

They shook their heads.

'Come back here now, Lenny, don't go out there. Come back!'

But I was already gone. Shaking like my bones didn't fit any more I picked my way across the pile of glass and debris in the street, squinting through the smoke which pricked at my eyes like needles. Someone called after me, 'Lenny! Lenny, come back here!'

But it wasn't Mavis and it wasn't my mum so I kept on going.

I was going to try all the shelters and all the closes, but I had to try home first, so after they stopped shouting and they'd shut their door, I went back into the close.

There were no lights, because of the blackout, so I could see almost nothing and had no idea what I was going into but I could taste the smoke that was billowing all around me, clinging to everything, clinging to my nose and tongue, the dust on my lips and in my eyes, catching at my throat. I took three quick steps up the stairs, then two more. The noise all around was so huge and booming that I couldn't hear anything else, not even my own voice. I felt the tremor of the bombs in the walls as I made my way upwards feeling with my hands and when I came to the first landing I saw the orange glimmer of fire in a fanlight, a pane of glass, above the middle door. Trembling I ran past it and up the next flight, keeping my eyes on it as long as I could. At the second floor I pounded on our door with my two fists.

'Mavis! Mum! Open up, it's me. It's Lenny! Please, open up!'

I banged harder but they didn't answer and my hands began to sting with the heat of the door, and there was a cracking sound behind it like big rashers of bacon being fried as if my dad was home. I kicked the door hard, and nearly fell.

'Lenny, is that you? Get back down here. Come on! Get down from there and into the house.' It was the man from the other flat downstairs.

I stepped back from the door and looked at it hard. 'Lenny!'

Our fanlight was dark. Our house was alright! A hiccoughing laugh got out of me. Maybe Mum had gone home for a sleep and didn't know what was going on. Sometimes she slept so heavily we could clean the fire and bang the kettle on its metal and she wouldn't waken. I raised my fist to bang the door again and the fanlight exploded with a neat 'pock' sound and threw its shimmering glass all about me. The blackness of its glaze was replaced by red, rippling fire.

I screamed and slid and fell back down the sooty stairs, slithering on shards of glass and stumbling over the first floor landing where a door had fallen in and flames licked the corners of the door jambs.

'It's all on fire, you've got to get out!' I shouted at the man at the bottom, the one who'd been shouting at me. 'My mum wasn't in and I lost the key.' He was standing just in the doorway of his flat, dimly lit from behind by candles. He stared at me and said nothing, didn't move. Never was a one to talk, as my mum would say. He watched me, following me with his eyes until I was back at the close mouth.

'Lenny … ,' he said feebly. 'We need to get you seen to. Come in here. Lenny!'

A right good seeing-to, I thought. There's always someone wants to give you a right good seeing-to, and I nipped round the baffle wall, then came back and shouted at him as loud as I could, 'You've got to get out! The whole building's on fire! And I have to find Mavis! And my mum! It's all on fire up there.' I pointed upwards.

I didn't wait to see more. I didn't want to stay in there with the glass and the smoke and no mum or Mavis and the ceiling about to collapse, but then I thought of the bad boy's old granny, the bad boys who'd been at the canal when I lost Mavis. Their granny lived in our close and gave me sweets when she was well enough, and I stood, engulfed by this thought, like I'd been welded to the pavement, and I thought about the floor above landing on her bed and her in it, like the other old lady, Mrs … Mrs … from over the road, and I thought about that happening to my mum.

But while I was thinking all of this I noticed another parachute, over to my left and a bit down the hill, above the buildings. It was lit up in the sky and with my heart squeezing the air from my lungs I hurled myself in the other direction, over rubble, over broken wardrobes and crockery, and glass, like a wash of unlucky mirrors, glinting up at me everywhere, winking and crunching under my shoes. The blast propelled me forwards and I was face down in something wet and stingy that stank of whisky and cat wee. I wrenched myself round straightaway, in time to see a fountain of debris fly into the air, straight up as if it was on sticks, then it curved in big arcs towards the ground, like the fountains I'd seen in books in the library. Bits of stone and shrapnel, splinters of table, a frying pan, torn curtains, crackled through the air with dust and grit through it all and everything landed in hard ripples and bounced in all directions, hot dust raining on my head, blistering up my nose and down my throat and I blinked and blinked so I could see.

But I was lucky I only caught hot dust. The nearest miss was a piece of window frame that rattled and bounced like a stone on water past my head, and once I'd cleared my eyes I saw metal girders sprouting out of the ground like the twisted trees in the graveyard, swaying and creaking. Stumbling and crying now, retching for breath, I got up and kept on going up the hill, tripping over dark things I couldn't see, peering with stingy eyes through the dust and stench and lifting myself up each time I fell, my hands and knees cut on whatever was down there, until finally I was on a rise clear of the burning buildings and in a park. There were other people there too, wandering about, or standing looking, or running. I stopped to gaze back through the smoke at the great orange glow that spread over everything I could see.

I saw black buildings with red windows fiercely burning, row upon row, and I looked for the church spires but couldn't see any. Again I checked my memory but I had no way to make sense of all this. There were flames so big the wind took them sideways, it was light when it should have been dark, and noisy in the quiet night-time, the roar and drone of unseen engines overhead like giant killer bees. Things I'd known for two whole years since we'd come to live in Clydebank were suddenly gone.

And I'd lost Mavis.

Chapter 2

I felt sick, like I'd eaten too much, and the stuff I'd eaten was bad. I felt as if I was going to explode, me, myself, going to explode with all the bad things that were so hard to understand, that were filling me up so I couldn't make sense of any of them.

Why did Mavis have to run off that day of all days? And why did my mum have to go to the pictures and leave me in charge of her? Where had they got to and how was I ever going to find them when, although I knew I was in Boquhanran Park, everything round about it was upside down and on fire?

A woman ran past where I was staring. She was screaming and had no coat, like me. One of her arms was hanging by her side and flashed red in the light from the bombs. I watched her go up the hill. The smoke was not as thick in the park but the smell of it was in my cardigan as I wiped my face with my sleeve. I gagged and shook because I was so afraid that there was a bomb inside me and it was exploding in there already. I was so scared because even the thought of Mavis didn't feel right, the very thought of her. And when I started retching I stuck my hand in my pocket for the shoe that might have been hers and pulled it out and squeezed it hard with both hands until it hurt and prickled, and I looked at my hands and saw through my tears that they were glistening as if they were covered with diamonds and dark with blood.

I looked up again because another bomb had landed not far off. I hadn't been watching the sky and there might be another one, with my name on it, as my mum would say, although not usually about bombs. There was a man in a dark uniform coming towards me.

'Get into the shelters everyone!' he shouted. He was an ARP warden I noticed and, also, he was the man from the chip shop, Mr Chippie we called him. Why would Mr Chippie be wearing an Air Raid Protection warden's uniform? Who was looking after the chips? Perhaps his wife was there all by herself.

'Hello,' he said, squatting down in front of me, where I sat on the grass. He spoke so quietly I could hardly hear him.

I looked beyond him at the sky, turning my head all around. I had to watch for bombs.

'You should be in a shelter,' he said. 'You can't sit here with nothing over your head.'

I put my hand on my head. It felt odd. My hair seemed to have shrunk and there was sticky stuff like jam over my ear. It didn't feel like me. I didn't understand so I kept checking the sky, but most of the parachutes seemed to be further away now.

'We need to get your head seen to,' he said.

He wore a helmet which was reflecting the little stars of light that were streaking across the sky as if they were sliding around on top of his head. He had a torch which he turned on and pointed at my face.

'Oh!' he said suddenly, giving me a fright. I

wondered if he'd been hit by a bomb. 'You're Lenny. You were in my shop.'

I looked into his face. The strap under his chin was too tight and his face was dirty, not like if he was in his shop. He was always very clean in his shop.

'Where's your mum and your wee sister, what's-her-name?'

'Mavis. Have you seen them? She ran away from me down at the canal while I was fishing out her shoe.' I waved the shoe at him.

'No, I haven't seen them, but I'm sure they'll be safe in a shelter somewhere, where you should be. Come on and I'll take you somewhere you can get patched up.'

'I don't need patching up. I need to find Mavis, and my mum.'

'Lenny, I have to go and see to other people too so you must come with me now. Okay? Right now. If you like I can carry you, or if you can, you can walk. We have to go out of the park and down Kilbowie Road to the picture house. You like the pictures, don't you?'

I leapt to my feet.

'My mum might be in there with a nice young man,' I said, 'but I haven't got Mavis. She'll be angry because I lost Mavis and she'll give me a r ... .'

'If your mum is in there,' he interrupted me, 'she'll be chuffed to bits to see you, with or without Mavis.'

'But I've got to find Mavis. I can't go into a shelter because then she won't be able to find me either, if I'm in there. Honestly, you don't understand.'

'Okay then, I'll take you to the picture house and then I'll go and find Mavis for you. You see, I've got this hat on to protect me.' He tapped it twice with his knuckles. 'You don't have one of those so you should be indoors where it's safe. And look, I found you, didn't I? Now, let's go before it's too late.'

'Okay,' I said. I wasn't sure because my mum said I shouldn't go with strangers and he sort of was one, but he was an ARP man too and I had to take his word for it that my mum would be 'chuffed to bits' to see me, with or without Mavis.

'Where do you live?' he said.

I told him, and I told him that I couldn't go home because the building was on fire, and he said yes, he knew.

'Can I hold your hand?' he said. 'Is it sore?'

'No, I mean yes … ow!'

'In that case, I'll hold your arm here.' He put his big hand around the top part of my arm.

'Ow!' I said.

He tried the other one very, very gently and it was alright. I looked up along the length of his arm, up towards his big dark shoulder and somehow the bombs inside me seemed to have stopped crackling so much, though they were still fizzing away, and I wished my dad wasn't missing presumed dead.

Mr Chippie smelled of chips, of smoky chip fat which clung to your nose and made you want to wrinkle it up, but only while we were still standing on the hill, in the park. As soon as we left the park the billows of smoke came all around us, and some other horrible stink that I couldn't name covered the smell of fat completely. We both coughed and coughed and when I looked at him a few minutes later when he was wondering which way to go I saw that he was crying, although he only looked serious, not sad. He wiped the tears away with a dirty rag from his pocket, and took hold of my shoulder again.

We picked our way through the blazing streets, dodging falling stone and watching the sky. That was my job because he said he could see how good at it I was, checking the sky. He was checking the houses. That was what he was good at but he must have been checking me too because every time I looked at the houses or round about me he told me to concentrate and leave the buildings to him.

We passed my school, big and solid, quietly dignified in the flickering shadows, and I felt less sick. Then we heard the whiz of a bomb behind us and ran for cover in a nearby close. His free arm pulled me into his stomach and I smelled the chips again.

'Phew!' he said. 'That was a close one! Shame you don't have eyes in the back of your head like my wife.' I felt his grip tremble on my arm and after we seemed to have been there a long time and there was no more debris flying about I said, 'We better get going then.' I didn't know what to call him. 'Um, Mr ... Chippie? My arm?'

So we got going, but what a sight we saw: the whole row of houses, as far as I could see was on fire, gigantic flames billowing out from the windows four floors high, at least a hundred feet, mountainous spikes of flame creeping over the roofs, and all across the street there was glass and bits of people's homes; and despite the noise of the blaze and the drone overhead I could hear things exploding inside the houses, like the explosions in my head, like I could hear the inside of my stomach. I held on tight to his coat with my sore hands and he held on to me.

'Watch the ground, Lenny,' he said. 'Nothing else … well, okay, the sky too, but make sure you know what you're walking on.'

Glass is what it was, sliding together like bits of ice, and stones and bricks, and broken furniture sticking up at angles waiting to catch us. Pressed close to the buildings on the side of the street that wasn't burning, we made our way down the hill, running from close to close, taking shelter in each as we went. He held my arm tight, his great bulk shielding me from the heat and he rushed me down the street so fast my feet flew over the debris. Great booms and bangs burst somewhere close by and fires seemed to start up everywhere.

'Annie! Annie!' he called suddenly. 'Annie!'

We'd stopped just inside another close. My back was against the wall.

'Close your eyes, Lenny,' he said, 'and stand there and don't move.'

I looked at him, amazed.

'Close them!'

I closed them, though it didn't seem like a good idea. Who was going to look at the sky now? He was holding my shoulders.

'Now, don't open them whatever you do until I say so. Alright?' His voice had gone hard but I could barely hear him. I nodded. He let go of me. The whistling of the falling bombs seemed to have made its way inside my head and got stuck. I didn't like having to close my eyes with that noise in there and I began to feel sick again. I heard small explosions beside me like doors banging and somebody brushed past me. I couldn't hear Mr Chippie any more. I was adrift in a sea of fire and debris.

I opened my eyes. There was a lady lying on the ground in front of me. Her face was black, as if the soot had fallen down her chimney but it was shiny soot and she was asleep. She must have had a leg tucked up behind her because I could only see one. Her dress was torn and I wondered how she could sleep in the middle of all that. I was going to waken her when Mr Chippie came back.

'Lenny, don't touch her!' he said, quickly as if it was all one word, and he grabbed my hand. And I understood what I wanted not to know – that this lady was dead and that her leg had come off, and there was red blood on the grey paving stones of the close floor.

'Annie, will you take wee Lenny with you to the Scala while I get the others out.' He wasn't speaking to me. I had been staring at the dead lady and when I looked up I saw another lady dressed like my mum in a grey coat but with no hat. She was a bit younger than my mum and had a baby wrapped in a blue blanket in her arms. They both had streaks of dust down their faces. I looked at her. I wanted Mr Chippie.

'I'll stay with you,' I said to Mr Chippie.

'Go with Annie. I need to stay here just now.'

'But … .'

'Go quickly, Lenny. There's no time,' he said, 'and I have to find Mavis.'

'Promise,' I said, telling not asking.

'Yes, now go!'

He put a hand on Annie's shoulder and then on mine and pushed us out onto what was left of the pavement and turned back into the close.

Annie didn't hold my hand or my shoulder. She

held her baby and glanced back at me a couple of times to make sure I was still there. The heat was so intense it was making me see things funny and my face felt tight again. I couldn't hear her over the noise when she finally stopped and turned and spoke to me, but I saw her point down to a break in the burning buildings. It was a road and she wanted me to go through the fire with her. I shook my head: I wasn't going down there to be killed but she frowned back at me then grabbed my cardigan and pulled the back of it up to my head, indicating I should cover my head, then she took a firm hold of my hand and pulled me forwards with her.

Another window frame crashed behind me and I took a big breath of courage and hurried on so that she could let go of me and together we stole through the gap in the wall of fire, her back bent over the baby, me with my grey cardigan pulled about my face. I watched the ground, glancing only momentarily at the buildings, forgetting the sky for the moment.

And then she fell. I didn't notice at first because I was up ahead of her and when I glanced around I was alone and the heat was making everything ripple and move, like when leaves get caught in a corner. But I saw something I guessed was her on the ground and ran back.

She was on her side, her back still arched round the baby and there was a big piece of stone over her legs. She was squealing like a pig in my uncle's yard. It made a pain start in my tummy and I couldn't move. Then a huge bang in one of the buildings nearby woke me up. I pulled and shoved to get the stone off her, but she seemed to scream all the more and nothing happened; it wouldn't move. She caught my grey cardigan in her hand and pulled me down to her.

'Get someone!' she said, her eyes big and wild and staring at me. She'd stopped squealing now and was whining like a dog. The baby was still, like the woman in the close. 'Take the baby,' she said.

As I looked about me for someone to get, three women and a string of kids from my school came into the street the same way we had come, all covered in blood, clothes torn and black faces.

'There's a woman down here! There's a woman down here!' I said and I waved my arms about my head.

'Take the baby!' said Annie. I lifted her arm off him. The arm was limp and so was the baby.

'Here he goes,' I said. 'I've got him. Don't worry,' and I tried to smile but it hurt because of the heat on my face, and because he seemed very dead.

'Take him now. What's your name? Lenny? I thought you were a girl.'

'I am a girl,' I said. 'Leonora.'

'Thanks, Leonora. Bye Davie.'

Why would she think I was a boy?

Two of the women were trying to lift the stone that was on Annie's legs when I left. I pulled the baby tight into my chest as if to squeeze some life back into him. He wasn't like other babies I had held, the lady next door's or Auntie May's when she visited last summer, all bursting with life, solid and warm. He hung over my arm as if he wanted to slide to the glassy ground, as if he'd had enough and didn't want to go any further. I didn't like carrying him. I was angry that I had to. What about Mavis?

There was another bang behind me, the slow rumbling bang of a building falling, like the big anchor chains at the dockside, and then I caught up with the kids from my school who, like me, were picking their way lightly over the hot debris.

And just along another few yards there rose the big white building that was the La Scala picture house.

Chapter 3

The La Scala was just about the most exciting place in the whole world to me at that time. I loved going to the pictures and I saw *Gone With The Wind* there, and *Fantasia*. I was scared of the sorcerer in *Fantasia* and I still don't like brooms. My mum cried in *Gone With The Wind*. Sometimes we had a big bag of soor plooms, sticky boiled sweets that were too big for my mouth so I couldn't help making a noise and dribbling. We didn't always go to the Scala picture house. There were other ones that cost less, but it was the best treat ever to go to the Scala. I wanted nothing more than to sink into those velvety seats and watch Mickey Mouse or Shirley Temple doing a little dance routine.

But this was different. The doors of the picture house were broken, all three of them which actually made six because they were double doors. Their elegant glass peacock pictures were broken at the neck and squeaked under my feet on the hard floor as I followed the other kids inside. There were people in the foyer and dust everywhere, even on the fancy mirrors on the walls and the counter. The brassy rails that were usually so shiny and perfect were grey and grimy. The comforting warmth of the dark brown wood was dulled and a smear of blood led through the glass from the outer door to the inner, like a red carpet for a film star.

I tiptoed over it with baby Davie slung awkwardly over my arm and went up to the pay booth. It had a big sign over it in white on black that said 'PAY HERE' and a perfect circle cut into the glass to speak through except it was too high for me. I had to speak through the money slot at the bottom, but there was nobody there.

I didn't like to go through the next set of doors; I had no money to pay. The kids from my school had somehow vanished while I was taking all this in – and I felt very alone and sore, and so cold all of a sudden that I began to shake again. A group of grown-ups were talking all at once close by. I don't know who they were, and then a boy a few years older than me suddenly shot out the door. He stood on the steps for a few minutes before darting off into the cloud of dust.

'Stop!' I shouted after him. 'Don't go out there!' I stepped into the bloody glass to call to him. It was horrible.

'It's alright. He's a message boy,' said a woman. She was wearing a thick red jumper and a rough tweed skirt. She reminded me of Miss Weatherbeaten, my teacher. 'We need help here. He's gone to get help.'

'But he'll be killed!' I said, panting. 'He hasn't got a tin hat like the one Mr Chippie has.' The tears started to pour down my face and it hurt terribly. I was shaking and shivering. The woman in the red jumper put her arm round me.

'Now, don't you worry,' she said. 'He's had lots of training. He knows how to get a message through.' But her arm was shaking across my shoulders.

'The buildings are all on fire and there are bombs dropping everywhere!' I said. I felt very sick again. A shudder ran through me as if I'd been picked up like a rag doll. The dead baby seemed to be very heavy now and I began to lose my grip.

'Oh, dear, I'll get him. What's his name?' I let her catch the dead baby, although I couldn't hear her properly, and I put my sore bleeding hands to my face.

'Ow!' I whined. 'Ow!' My face hurt terribly, especially when I touched it.

'Don't touch!' said the woman in the red jumper. 'You'll only make it worse.'

'Ow!' I said in reply.

'Don't!' she said again, louder this time, to make sure I'd heard. She took my wrist and pulled it away from my face, but my wrist hurt too. Everything seemed to hurt.

'Ow!' I whined through my tears. 'I lost my wee sister Mavis!' I sobbed a big sob, and I drew my hand across my face and patted my sore wrist where she'd held it. A stabbing pain shot across my cheek.

'Don't … .'

'Is my mum here?' I said, glancing at my red hands, ignoring the pain in my cheek. I started towards the inner door, ticket or no, Mavis or no. 'He's called Davie,' I said, nodding at the baby and pushed the door open. 'I think he's dead.'

But the door was too much for me, or it was locked or someone was standing against it, because I couldn't get it open. I tried the next one then another woman appeared from amongst the people there. She was wearing a big fur coat and under it a big shiny handbag over her shoulder. She came over to me and bent down so that our heads were close together and I couldn't get round her and she spoke very loudly. I heard every word.

'Stand still!' she said. 'Now, stop crying!' I gulped, drew myself in, and kept very still, as ordered. 'Tell me your mum's name.'

'Peggy Gillespie,' I said.

'And what's your name?'

'Lenny.'

'Okay then, Lenny Gillespie, I'm going to take you into the Ladies and get you cleaned up.'

'But … .'

'Don't interrupt! It has to be the Ladies if I'm to come with you,' she interrupted. Then she continued, 'This lady here is going to look for your mum.' She pointed at the lady in the red jumper. And then she went on talking to the other grown-ups in the outer foyer, 'And I think we all need to move further inside the building as quickly as possible. Come on everyone.' The back of her fur coat tickled my knees as she turned first to them and then back to me. 'Now,' she said, 'can I take your hand?'

I shook my head, even though this was clearly a lady who had to be obeyed, and I pointed to the bit of my arm Mr Chippie had held. She led me through the glass doors to the inner foyer and over to the sweetie kiosk. I stopped her there.

'But I lost Mavis too,' I half-whispered. I couldn't bear to think it.

'Oh, dear,' she said. 'And who is Mavis?'

'She's my wee sister and she ran away from me … and Mr Chippie said he'd find her.'

'Oh, dear,' she said again, and she crouched down

beside me, this big lady with the fur coat and it tickled me about the ankles and the glass scrunched under her feet. 'I bet your Mr Chippie does find her, but we'll have a good look in here too, just in case. Now, stop crying.'

We went into the Ladies. There were other people in there too. Some of them were complaining that the toilets weren't working. There was a strong smell of sick and the floor was wet. I hung onto the fur coat. Her hand lay across my back. Suddenly I needed to wee too, but I couldn't bring myself to let go of that fur, so for a minute I jiggled about, shifting from foot to foot and hoping no-one would notice until finally the big fur lady did and her big hand across my back directed me into a cubicle.

When I came back out, embarrassed to leave what I had done behind me unflushed, I saw a boy about the same age as me right there in the Ladies. He had scruffy black hair and his face was filthy and there was blood by his ear. His cardigan was torn and his arm was bleeding, and he glistened all over like diamonds in amongst the dust and soot. He stood there looking at me for some time, cheeky thing, and I wondered who he was, and then a big lady in a fur coat appeared beside him, just like the one beside me. She pulled me over towards her.

'Now, young Lenny,' she said, 'I'm going to start at the top and work my way to the bottom. You have to sit very still and try very hard not to cry, even though it might hurt a bit. You have to be a big boy, brave and manly, just like your dad. I bet he's brave.'

I didn't like the sound of this.

'But … .'

'And what happened to your trousers?' she said.

'I don't have any trousers,' I said. 'I'm not a boy. Why would a boy be wearing a dress?'

And I looked for the first time at my clothes and realised that the only part of my dress left below my waist was the strip of material that held the pocket, and the shoe that I was clutching within it. Hurriedly I pulled my hand out and yanked my cardigan, what was left of it, down over my bottom. And while I was beginning to worry about the boy I had seen and wondering whether he was still there and had noticed my nakedness, the fur lady reached down and lifted me up onto a black Formica space beside the sink. As I flew through the air in her able arms, I realised the boy in the mirror was me.

I twisted myself away from her, transfixed by this boy whose eyes were wide and white in the blackness of his face and I looked at my transformation. I looked for myself in his hair, his forehead, the curve of his black face, the collar of his shirt and peering over the lip of the mirror I saw the pocket and recognised his hand, like mine, was hidden in its shallow depths, fumbling with the shoe. I took my hand out and held it up to the mirror and the boy waved back. He looked as scared as I was, as pleased to be me as I was to be him, and I wondered if he'd lost his wee sister and his mum too, and whether he felt sick. He had lines down his face where he'd been crying, white smears, and another from the bottom of his nose across his cheek and there were flecks of blood here and there on his cheeks. His hair was long for a boy and grey on top like an old man. But he wasn't an old man. He was young like me. He was me.

The lady in the fur coat appeared behind him.

She had a pair of tweezers in one hand and a lace-trimmed handkerchief in the other. What would she need those for?

And then the lights went out and we were plunged into a darker darkness than I had ever known. I was never scared of the dark but in that moment I felt sicker than ever and someone started to scream. I think it was the boy, I wasn't sure but it was someone very close because it was right in my ear, right inside my head, then the fur lady's fur coat brushed past my cheek and I felt myself lifted back onto the sticky wet floor. She took my sore hand.

'Stop that noise!' she said, and the screaming stopped, and she led me out of the Ladies, banging my head and my elbows and knees on the swinging doors as we went. Other people were trying to squeeze past us, and when we got into the foyer again the beautiful green carpet that I loved so much with its swaying fronds, like in the canal, was strewn and scrunching with glass from both the inner and outer front doors.

We stumbled over someone sitting against the wall. The only light was from the blaze beyond the doors, the inferno that was still raging outside, and in its flickering glow I could make out shadow-like creatures moving across the foyer, hurrying to and fro.

And the noise was stupendous, as my dad used to say, but in a funny voice. Stupendous! But there was nothing funny about this. I had somehow forgotten the noise while we were between the deadening walls of the Ladies, buried as it was beneath the stairs. It hit us now like a sudden storm. There in the foyer beside the sweetie kiosk and the sweeping carpeted stairway, dust fell soundlessly from the ceiling, while the bang, crackle and rumble of exploding buildings hammered and roared all around us. The planes, the killer bees, were too far distant for us to hear now, blanked by the screams and shouts of people and the boom-crash of their deadly cargo. More people were arriving, stumbling in the doors, or what was left of them. The lady in the fur coat raised her voice.

'Keep moving to the back of the foyer!' she said. 'There are sofas and space there! Do we have medical people yet?'

For a minute there was no reply and I wondered if anyone had heard her. I was just about to say that I didn't think so (perhaps she was only talking to me) when a lady's voice on the far side of the kiosk said, 'We have a nurse. Just one. She's over here looking after this baby.'

'I'll be there soon,' came a muffled cry from the other side of the foyer.

The fur lady still had a grip on my sore hand and holding on tight she pulled me towards the back of the foyer. It was a long room with sofas along the walls but it was pitch-dark now that the lights had all gone out.

'No!' I shouted. 'No! No!'

She dragged me along anyway and then suddenly let go of my hand and, like Mr Chippie not long before, she said, 'Stand there and don't move!' She didn't tell me to close my eyes thank goodness because I don't think I could have done it, even though it made very little difference having them open, and I didn't fancy having to disobey such a big fluffy commanding person all by myself without even Mavis beside me.

Mavis.

After a very long time, although it may only have been couple of minutes, a door on the opposite wall opened and the cool rays of a hurricane lamp seeped into the foyer. A man in a suit was holding it over his head and peering past it into the crowd. Mrs Fur came back, her face lit like those of the people around me, by a ghostly chill. She took my sore hand again, for which I was grateful even though it hurt, and she pulled me in beside her.

'More lights are on their way,' she said loudly to anyone who would listen. 'And there's plenty of room further back, if you could all move further in. Perhaps someone could check the kitchen for a broom. There's glass all the way back here. Do we have a kitchen?'

As I've said, I don't like brooms. It wasn't going to be me. I did my best to hide in her fur.

A boy ran in the front door and pushed through the crowd. He handed her a slip of paper. She let go of my hand to hold it and read. I put my arm around her back and gripped the strands of her coat, shrinking into the darkest shadow behind her.

'Well done!' I heard her say, and, 'Tell them ... .'

I couldn't make out the rest. Tell them Lenny is here and will wait until Mavis and her mum come for her. I'll be in the downstairs foyer with the creamy walls and the green fronds under my feet. There's a big fluffy lady holding my hand, and can I have a new dress?

The fur began to move.

'Where's Lenny? Where's that girl gone?' she said. 'Oh, there you are, now come along and don't waste time. We need to get you seen to.'

A right good seeing-to.

She took my hand again and I found myself at the back of the foyer on a dark-green sofa. Everyone was very busy. There was an argument going on over by some small doors on one wall but it didn't last long. Two ladies, one in a black uniform, the other being the lady in the red jumper, disappeared through a door which said 'STAFF' on it in white letters on black, like the PAY HERE desk. They reappeared shortly afterwards carrying brooms and buckets and dish towels.

'Did you find my mum?' I asked. 'And Mavis?' But the lady in the red jumper didn't seem to hear.

More hurricane lamps appeared and were hung from the electric-light fittings. A boom on the other side of the wall (we were by now at the very back of the building) made everybody scream. Mrs Fur sat down beside me on the sofa and took me quickly by the shoulders.

'Sit down!' she said rather unnecessarily. I had already sat down. I nearly stood up again so that I could sit down again specially for her but thought better of it. Once more she brought out her tweezers and her lace handkerchief and laid them down on her lap. Then she changed her mind and put the handkerchief back in the pocket of her huge coat. There was a cut-glass ashtray on a small table nearby which she balanced carefully on my knees.

'Now, my darling,' she said. 'You've been very brave so far. Can you be brave a bit longer?'

I nodded and squirmed. I didn't want to be brave.

'Right then, here goes,' she said. 'It may hurt.'

It hurt alright. As the bombs fell, and the buildings fell, as more people fell into the foyer, some quite literally landing in a heap on the floor, the fur lady picked her way in sharp little pricks from the top of my head to my ankles until there was enough glass in the glass ashtray to make another ashtray altogether. My face was wet, and when I touched it my hand was red with blood but also washed with tears, and I was scared to move anything at all but most especially my face. It was like my skin was humming, if I could have given it a sound, humming with stinginess that was like pressing a bruise if I moved it. Yet she had been very gentle. I looked into her face all the time she was doing it. I followed the lines under her eyes to see where they went. She looked very worried and very old, older than my gran who came with Auntie May last year.

'Well,' she said finally, with a great puff of her lips that made the hair above her forehead jump, 'I think I got them all.' She smiled a big smile and some of her wrinkles disappeared. I couldn't smile back. 'You are the bravest little girl I have ever come across in the whole of my life!'

I tried a little smile then.

'Aw, now don't you smile if it hurts, you poor darling,' she said.

Her hand disappeared inside her coat pocket and the lacy handkerchief reappeared. She mopped my face, very gently with it and then handed it to me with a frown. Then she produced a pair of tiny scissors, embroidery scissors I think, from her big shiny handbag under her coat. Very quickly she glanced at the door where the man with the first hurricane lamp had appeared, which said 'MANAGER' on it in white on black, then she whisked the green chair cover from the top of the sofa (what my gran calls an antimacassar). She was so fast I wasn't sure I could believe my eyes. It was a green square, the same colour as the rest of the sofa, put there to keep hair grease off the sofa itself, very posh. She cut it in several places then tore it into strips. I glanced over at the kitchen door. She and I caught eyes, conspirators in a terrible deed. She picked up another antimacassar and began to wipe around the cuts and then tie strips of the torn one around my hands and arms.

'Now what are we going to do for clothes?' she said.

I shivered at the reminder of how ill-clad I was and looked at my legs which were bare but for smatterings of blood. I leant forward and laid both arms across the tops of my legs.

The furry lady thought for a bit then she took off her fur coat and hung it over the arm of the sofa and in doing so she instantly shrunk to normal size, a bit bigger than my mum and a lot older, but kind of normal anyway.

'Stay there!' she said sternly and disappeared back towards the front door. When she came back she had a lady's slip in her hand which she handed to me and told me to put on. 'No, no, no,' she said. 'Take off your shirt, I mean your dress, first. That's it. Mmm, bit long isn't it?'

The slip was so long in fact that it hung all the way to my ankles and folded onto the floor. She tied the straps into loops on my shoulders. I put the remaining top half of my filthy torn dress back on over this snow-white garment and immediately its perfect surface was ruined. I smoothed down the front of my old dress and took care to check Mavis's shoe was still in the pocket. There I stood, apparently dressed in Victorian fancy dress, just like last Hallowe'en and surrounded by gigantic bonfires.

'Do you think the bombs will land here too?' I said.

She looked up at me. She was on the floor now on her knees in front of me with her head on one side, looking at the bottom of the slip.

'What?' she said.

'Do you think the bombs … ?'

'No,' she broke in. 'We're safe as houses here.' And then her hand flew to her mouth, and this time I couldn't help but smile although it wasn't really funny. 'Oh, dear,' she said. 'Yes, of course we're safe here. This is a big solid building made of brick and stone. Even the roof's made of stone.'

I didn't believe her. It was nonsense, of course, but I didn't mind her lying, not really and I knew there wasn't much point in asking about Mavis and my mum but I thought I would anyway, even though I knew she'd fib.

She took a long time to answer but that might have been because she had taken her scissors out again and had started to cut the slip around my knees. It was a plain slip which bumfled up under the arms beneath my dress. There was another great bang the other side of the wall. We both ducked.

'Tell you what, I'll go and find out if there's any news of them. You stay here.'

She'd finished her cutting now and the scissors were back in her bag. She stood up and put her hand on her fur coat, stroking it like I had done when I was hiding behind her in the foyer. Then she lifted it and draped it gently over my shoulders.

'Sit there and keep warm,' she said. Her big shiny handbag swung under her arm and she disappeared again towards the front door and the great stairways that wound up to the upstairs foyer, on either side of the PAY HERE desk.

The coat was still warm from her body and very, very heavy. I pulled it around about me and sniffed it. I closed my eyes and succumbed to its warmth, and let my bruised arms be held in its embrace.

The noise continued to rage, and people fell over my legs or crossed the foyer weeping or shouting. Names were called in the darkness and for a while I joined in. 'Mavis!' I called. 'Mum!' But I couldn't bear not hearing them call back. 'Lenny!' I imagined them saying, Mavis and my mum, in all the ways they said my name: 'Lenny!' that angry way; 'Lenny!' the glad-you're-there way; 'Linny!' which was Mavis's baby way; 'Lenny', just me. I'm just here, just here by the wall on the dark-green sofa.

A lot of time passed, or I think it did, and my eyes got used to the gloomy dark. I'd already scanned the foyer many times for Mavis and my mum. Now, I wondered if I knew any of these other people and realised suddenly that I did. The kids from my school were in a huddle by the stairway, and a few feet along from me were the two bad boys, two boys a bit older than me, at least eleven or twelve and better fed. They were shivering against the wall. It was their granny who gave me sweets and who might have a ceiling on her head now. I pulled my own head down into the fur and peered at them over the row of shadows between us. The big boy was crying. His head was bobbing up and down on his knees and his brother was close up beside him. They both had dust in their hair and their clothes, like everyone else. The younger one was staring hard towards the outside doors.

Not scary at all now.

Not like before. Not like earlier that day … .

After we'd left my mum and got chips from Mr Chippie, me and Mavis had been eating our chips by the canal sitting on a lock gate while the sun began to set. Then Mavis had dropped her shoe in the water – kicking it against the side – and quickly taking off my coat I'd climbed down the metal steps to get it. But the water under the gate kept nudging it away from me and reaching for it I'd lost my grip and fallen in. It was very, very cold but I'd managed to grab the shoe and fling it onto the canal bank, spraying dark water across the gravel. A dog had come and sniffed at it then jumped up at Mavis and taken our last chip, nearly knocking her into the canal after me.

'Stay on the gate,' I'd shouted, but she didn't listen. And it was then that the bad boys had come. They'd kept shoving me back into the canal with a stick until I thought I'd have to swim to the other side and come back by the lock gate. But I wasn't going to leave Mavis.

'Come on, wee sprat,' said the smaller of the two.

'Hello, Mavis,' said the other.

'Leave her alone!' I said. The smaller one's stick caught in the dip in those bones at my throat. I fell back in, coughing.

'Looks just like her ma … ,' said the big one.

'Leave her alone!' I said, back at the surface.

'Cat got your tongue, wee yin?' he said.

Mavis had been silent, a storm brewing on her

brow. She'd stood facing this boy, a boy we both knew to fear, and kicked one foot against the other. She'd glanced at me sideways beneath her scraggy shock of hair. Her hands were fidgeting behind her back. She'd lifted her face again and stuck her tongue out at him.

'Oh, cheeky little madam then, are we? We'll see about that then.' He'd made a grab for her but she stepped back just in the nick of time and flung a small handful of dirt in his eyes that she'd been hiding.

'Filthy wee bastard, dirty scumbag! Christ!' He'd danced from foot to foot, edging blindly to the side of the canal, rubbing the dirt into his red running eyes.

The other boy had stopped poking me with his stick and turned from where he was crouching by the water's edge to lunge at Mavis. He took hold of her by both shoulders and shook and shook and shook her until she screamed, but the moment he stopped she'd whipped out her other hand and flung a handful of dirt in his face too. Then she'd taken off down the towpath faster than you could whistle.

'We'll get our dad to you, filthy wee shites!' they'd shouted.

Both blind now, they were easy. I was freezing cold, but, back on dry land and feeling gallus with a tummy full of chips, I'd shoved the smaller one and he'd fallen into the water. The other fell after him without any help from me. I'd wrung out my dress and hurried down the towpath after Mavis, squeezing water and weeds from my cardigan as I went, and forgetting my coat.

But Mavis had gone … .

'Mavis!' I said, suddenly back in the Scala. The boys looked over. 'Mavis!' I said again. I pulled myself to my feet, the fur coat dragging along the floor behind me and stood uncertainly in front of them. Four big white eyes stared at me from sooty faces. I felt sick and didn't get too close.

'Sorry about … ,' I started.

The older one waved his hand vaguely in my direction. There was another bang and smoke flew in sharp clouds across the room. Their four big white eyes blinked and gazed towards the front door.

'Have you seen Mavis?' I said. 'Mavis? Remember?' They shook their heads.

'Mavis,' I shouted, thinking they might not be able to hear me. 'She was with me down at the canal.' I didn't want to enlarge on this. 'The canal … ?'

They looked at me now.

'I look a bit different,' I said, patting the fur with my bandaged hands. 'My hair was about this length,' I said, indicating my shoulder, 'and my dress was blue, and attached. To the rest of it. And I was in the canal?' I took a step back, just in case. 'Mavis is like me only she's four. Her shoes are like this one.' I drew it out of my pocket with great difficulty, the fur coat was so heavy. 'You know my mum,' I added, although I didn't want to bring my mum into this.

The big girl sitting next to them turned to face me now too. I recognised her from one of the baker's shops on the main road. She looked me up and down, which I hate. Why do grown-ups do that? And then she nudged the older boy hard with her elbow. They both winced.

'Sorry,' he said, to me, or I think that's what he said. His mouth made a 'sorry' sort of shape, then it smiled. I couldn't smile so I nodded and hoped he understood. I was very surprised to see him say sorry. I didn't think bad boys said sorry.

And then while I was standing there thinking about this I got very cold and shivery even though I was still wearing the big fur coat, so I pulled it round about me again, right up to my neck and over my ears so that I didn't have to hear the noise outside so much, just my heartbeat. Being in the picture house was like being in a cave, the one we went to when we were on holiday in Rothesay, when my dad wasn't missing presumed dead and Auntie May was there with the baby, and being inside the coat made my heartbeat echo loudly about my head. It felt nice, even though the hair of the coat went up my nose. After a bit I was forced to come out for air.

The bad boys and the big girl had forgotten about me so I wondered where the owner of my fine coat might have got to and whether she, or the lady in red or Mr Chippie had found my mum or Mavis. I know I should have sat still, like I'd been told.

On the other side of the foyer there was an area slightly back from the bit where people were milling about. It had two doors off it which both said 'PRIVATE'. One of them was open and on the other side there was a short corridor lit through a small window without glass by the flickering of the fire outside. On the floor of the corridor there were people lying asleep in a row, asleep of all things, in all that noise and clamour when there was an emergency happening and all the buildings were burning! The flickering light fell on their closed faces without even a pane of glass between them and the danger. I looked at them and wondered how they could do

41

that and a panic got me by the throat and I wondered who was watching the sky and whether I should go out there and watch it for them. Somebody had to, but they were so ordered in such a neat little row that I thought somebody must have told them to go in there and be already watching the sky for them. They were very still and that cold feeling I'd had not long before came back.

And then I saw that one of them was wearing a grey coat like my mum's and my stomach leap up into my throat. I murmured her name, 'Mum.'

Something kept me hovering at the door, unable to step in there, unable to step back, barely breathing with my head sinking back lower and lower into the folds of the huge fur coat. She was not moving, and while it was true that my mum didn't move much when she was asleep, and as I've already mentioned, she slept the sleep of the dead, as my gran said last summer, I knew she wasn't asleep. I don't know how I knew from that distance and with all that noise, but there was no doubt in my mind at all.

There was a long strange silence and then a whine somewhere up in the sky, like a firework – a Guy Fawkes rocket screeching off up into the distance – only I could tell this one was going the other way, heading fast towards the earth. And like the rocket the whine stopped and in its pregnant pause I waited for the bang, holding my breath then throwing myself down in a big fluffy heap between the door jambs.

'BOOM!' it went, and something smacked hard off the wall outside, like hailstones on a classroom window, and a puff of grit flew through the small window and landed on the sleeping people. No-one moved. When I was sure nothing else was on its way in I stuck my head fully above the fur coat and stood up.

'Mum!' I said in a loud whisper, a stage whisper my dad would have called it. 'Mum!' I said, urgently, in the way I would if she was busy and hadn't noticed there was someone at our front door.

Her face was turned away and she'd lost her hat. I felt a hot breeze flow past me between the window and the foyer at my back. At last I tiptoed into the abyss, holding my breath, heart banging in the confines of my chest, my throat dry from more than debris dust, and my eyes wide.

Step-by-baby-step I edged forward as if I was on the high brick wall near the factory my mum works in. The flickering light faded. I waited. It grew again and I edged forward until I saw that her ear was not the same and the curve of her cheekbone had gone. Bolder now I strained my head round to see, the heavy fur coat shaking my balance, and just when I thought I'd fall and land on these poor souls I saw the face of Annie thrown carelessly to one side as if she really didn't want anything to do with the world any more, Annie who had led me through the wall of fire and had fallen behind me. Annie and her baby, Davie. Annie not my mum. Annie who'd entrusted me with Davie. I was so grateful to her for not being my mum! Not my mum! Absolutely not my mum!

A smile cracked my face and the tears smarted to my eyes. My shoulders shook and I breathed heavily in shudders of relief. Big wet tears ran down my chin and slithered onto the beautiful coat. Snotters slipped over my lip and salt was in my mouth. My hand was in my pocket and I thought if I could just stand still long enough then time would wind itself back and we'd be in our house, on the edge of the bed, with dinner on our laps listening to the radio and Mum dancing across the room, like she did before Dad wasn't coming back, before Mavis's shoe fell in the canal, before I lost her and Mavis.

And then I felt sick again, and scared and cold, and I backed out of that little corridor a lot more quickly than I went in and stood in the doorway with the fluff of the fur coat at my nose, watching the shadows of the flames ripple across the shoulders of the sleeping dead. I drew my hand across my face and wiped it on the remains of my dress.

I had to find Mavis. It was crystal clear.

I turned to the foyer, but first, just out of the corner of my eye I noticed a bundle by the door. I bent to look. It was baby Davie, still wrapped in his blue blanket. He was a little way off from the others and his cheek was cold. His mum, Annie, was looking the other way.

'He's over here, Annie,' I whispered. 'Davie, your mum's just over there, not far away.' My voice seemed loud, like when you put your fingers in your ears and speak. I knew they couldn't, but I waited for them to move. They'd say 'Thanks Lenny!' and Annie would coo the way Auntie May did.

But it was very quiet in there, and I realised suddenly there were no killer bees overhead, no great booms, only the crackle and roar of the blaze outside.

'Sorry,' I whispered into the gloom, for no particular

reason and went to leave. If the Germans had stopped bombing us the lights might come back on and then I could find Mavis and my mum. I had to get a move on.

But I hated to leave them like that, so I went quickly back in and lifted baby Davie, awkwardly in my strange clothes, and took him to Annie and laid him beside her under her chin and along the front of her body so that they could sleep the sleep of the dead together.

'Sorry,' I whispered again, and went to the door.

''Scuse me,' said a man who was backing towards me in the dark.

He and another man were carrying a woman by the legs and shoulders. I got out of their way.

'You shouldn't be in there,' he said. 'Go on now. Don't be hanging about here.'

They shoogled past me with their awkward burden, bumping me out of the way with their backs. The woman's hand fell from her lap and dunted the fur coat, sliding quickly down its length, stroking its lovely softness. Her head was slumped to one side, like Annie's. They disappeared into the little corridor. There was a muffled thud and a murmur of voices. I had taken my arms out of the sleeves of the big fur coat and pulled it around my ears again.

'It's quiet now,' I heard one of them say, 'but you never know. Let's hope this is the end of it.'

They pushed past me again and disappeared into the smoky crowd.

I had to find the lady with the fur coat but it was hard because I had the fur coat and although I'd looked right into her face when she was taking the glass out of me I wasn't sure I'd know her. I moved about the foyer, a big puff of fur with a head on top, peering into the gloom at all the people sitting against walls or stumbling about. The bad boys were still there, but the big girl had gone, and the lady in the red jumper was nowhere to be seen, never mind Mr Chippie.

Figures appeared in front of me, lit now by candles as well as hurricane lamps, a yellowy glow bringing pink to their ashen faces. Their voices seemed louder, all louder than each other, calling names out, calling for quiet, calling for help, calling. I tapped a man on the arm.

'Have you seen … ?' but he didn't hear me. I could barely hear myself, even though it was true, the bombs had stopped. Perhaps I had some debris stuck in my ears. I tried someone else but no-one seemed to hear me. Maybe they had dirt in their ears too.

The killer bees had gone away at last. I could go and find my mum, because although I'd lost Mavis, Mr Chippie was right that she'd be happy to find me and she might even be looking everywhere for me right then, just like I'd been looking for Mavis.

So I kept my eye on the doors of the La Scala in case Mavis or my mum might come walking through them.

But as I was watching, I saw the message boy who had gone out earlier. He ran up the steps to the ladies with the hurricane lamps and gave them a piece of paper then he ran back out again. And just as he disappeared into the smoke, there was a drone overhead and the whistling, the waiting and the boom-crash as it all started up again and the bombs fell once more. Everyone screamed and ran inside and

I went to a wall as far back as I could and slid down against it and pulled the big fluffy coat over my head and around my hunched-up knees and held on tight to the shoe in my pocket, waiting for the ground to stop shaking.

Chapter 4

A very long time later, I don't know how long, the killer bees left and the boom-crashes stopped. I poked my head through the top of the fur coat and looked about me. The smell hit me again, whisky and sick, and smoke hovered in the foyer and pierced my eyes making them run again. There were more people lying down too with other people kneeling over them. There were two ladies at a table with paper and pencils and a hurricane lamp and three people were talking to them, one holding a wee kid. Another hurricane lamp was hanging from the chandelier in the middle of the foyer making it glisten like newly polished silver. I recognised a girl from my school with her mum and dad. Her arm was in a sling made from a scarf and one of our teachers was there too. A man was lying asleep further down the wall, sleeping the sleep of the dead. There was red blood on the green swirling carpet underneath him.

The two bad boys were crouched a little further along the wall. They were whispering to each other and glancing in my direction. I shrunk back into the coat but kept my eyes above the surface, just in case.

And then I saw Mavis.

She was coming in the middle of the three outer doors. Actually what I saw was the left-hand side of her except for her head which I only saw the back of because she was talking to the person she was with. She had on the same grey cardigan as me, the same blue dress, the same sock and the same shoe and she was filthy like me too. I only saw half of her because someone was in the way and my neck wasn't long enough to reach up, but I was off the floor in a flash and dodging the crowd as if I had wings on my feet.

'Mavis!' I shouted.

Another person went past carried by the two men from the back corridor. They were blocking my view. I dodged one way then the other. A fat lady was bending to a child. An old man was leaning on the pillar.

'Mavis!'

She was standing with Mr Chippie. She had her back to me and Mr Chippie was bending down to hear what she was saying. I couldn't see his face for his hat, but I knew it was him.

'Mavis!' I said again.

Something wasn't right.

Mr Chippie looked up and saw me there in my big fur coat. He didn't smile. He just looked.

'You found Mavis!' I said again.

A look of sudden recognition came over his face. He turned to Mavis but I couldn't hear what she said. I bent to throw my arms round her. She shook her head and turned round to me.

Mavis had no eyebrows and she had no fringe and she had big blue eyes instead of big brown ones. She had both hands in the pocket of her dress and there were stripes of wet tears through her blackened face.

Mavis wasn't Mavis, or not my Mavis. We stood looking at each other for what seemed like ages. I think I was waiting for her to turn back into the right Mavis. I heard Mr Chippie, and it was Mr Chippie, saying something to somebody else, to another grown-up somewhere over our heads, and then her face crumpled, this strange Mavis. It just folded in on itself and she began to sob. I think I sobbed too and I fell onto my knees so that I could put my arms around her and we hugged each other. I hugged Mavis with my arms out of the sleeves of the big coat which fell about us, and she hugged her big sister. She smelled of whisky and rubber and something else I'd never smelled before, and I hoped that when I stopped hugging her that she would be Mavis again.

We hugged for a long, long time but when we stopped, her eyes were still blue.

Mr Chippie wasn't talking to whoever he'd been talking to any more. He was standing beside us with his forehead all crinkled.

'This isn't Mavis,' I told him, standing up.

'I know,' he said. 'It's Rosie. You know her?'

White lines had appeared above his eyes where the crinkles had been.

'No, not really.'

'Not really?' he said

'Not at all,' I said. 'Not. No.'

'You don't know who her grandparents are or an aunt or uncle that she could stay with?'

'No. Sorry.'

I thought about this. Poor thing. She must have lost her mum and her sister too. I wondered if her dad was missing presumed dead. She was still holding my hand and was half inside my big fur coat which I'd lifted from the floor.

'I have to go back out,' said Mr Chippie. 'Will you stand here and give the ladies her name when it's her turn?' He nodded towards the ladies with the hurricane lamp and the bits of paper.

I stared back at him.

'I'm still looking for Mavis,' he said. 'I just haven't found her yet. It'll be daylight soon and … .'

A siren rose in a wail above us. He stopped what he was saying. So did everyone around us, and then cheers went up from all sides of the room and everyone stood up, those that could. They seemed to be clinging to each other, the shadows etched into their faces by the simple light of the hurricanes. They were all the same colour, the colour of dirt and debris, as if they themselves were just dirt and debris thrown up by a great explosion.

A small crowd was gathering by the front doors, peering into the smoky inferno beyond. Rosie had wormed her way right inside my coat and Mr Chippie had disappeared.

'Have you seen my mum and dad?' said Rosie. 'And my gran and my auntie?'

I shook my head.

'My big sister?' she said.

'Sorry, no. We can ask these ladies here,' I said pointing at the ladies at the desk with the hurricane lamp.

The bad boys were still against the wall but they were standing now, very close together, not looking fierce at all with their mouths hanging open. The siren had changed everything but I wasn't sure what to do so I just stood there with wee Rosie, watching everybody moving about.

After a bit the big girl came back and she and the bad boys huddled together, all hugged up tight as if they only had one body between them. Then it was Rosie's turn with the ladies with the hurricane lamp and the paper.

'Her name's Rosie,' I said when she wouldn't speak.

'And your name?' asked one.

'Lenny,' I said. 'Lenny Gillespie. Did you find my mum, Peggy Gillespie?'

She looked down a list of names and shook her head.

'No, sorry darling.' She looked sorry.

'Or Mavis Gillespie, my wee sister?'

'No, no Gillespies.'

'Oh.'

She asked lots of other questions, mostly about Rosie, but I wasn't really paying attention by then. I was trying to figure out what to do next and waiting for someone to tell me. Daylight was peering through the smoke outside like the mist that had been there a few days before only hot, and I still hadn't found Mavis or my mum. The thought of going outside was very scary. What did hot mist feel like, and what would I find?

Rosie was pulling at my dress.

'Rosie says you're not her big sister. Is that right? Lenny?' said the lady.

'No, I'm not her big sister. I'm … .'

'So she's no relatives that you know of?'

'No,' I said. 'Rosie, where did you last see your

mum and dad? Have you got any aunties or a gran or anyone?'

She shook her head and stood still as a statue, as my mum used to say, then her little hand flew out of her dress pocket and pulled at her earlobe, again and again and again.

'My dad took me to the shelter first,' she said, 'and when he didn't come back with Mum and Gran and … I looked out and ….'

Her mouth was hanging open and she'd have pulled her earlobe right off if I hadn't taken hold of her hand and held on tight. The lady with the hurricane lamp was still as a statue now herself and her mouth was hanging open too. I felt an ache in my stomach and I tried again to will wee Rosie to be Mavis so that Mavis could be safe and sound with me, and something really awful wouldn't be true. But Rosie didn't feel like Mavis. Rosie was taut like a frightened cat and every part of her was sore and hard against me.

'They might have forgotten me,' said Rosie. 'Are they here?'

The two ladies seemed to have forgotten her too for a minute and were talking to each other instead. I glanced over at the bad boys but they were gone and for some reason this scared me witless and I felt my body go tight like Rosie's and there wasn't enough air and I twisted this way and that, straining myself to full height to find them amongst the shifting crowd. And people were coming from other parts of the building now, mostly heading towards the doors. I knew that I knew the bad boys' names but I'd never used them and I couldn't find them in my head just when I needed them most, and I couldn't move to hunt for them because Rosie was so firmly attached and because of the big fur coat, so I stumbled and thrashed about and frightened myself even more until finally I screamed, 'Stop it!'

I wriggled out of the coat and out of Rosie's grip and squeezed with my skinny body and my lack of decent clothes, just a slip and half a dress, through all the people between me and the door until I found the bad boys and the big girl tiptoeing on the brink of outdoors. They looked at me in surprise. I was surprised too.

'Where are you going?' I demanded, in a fury, breathing heavily despite the stench out there.

They looked at me uncomprehending but I was as baffled as they.

'Where are you going?' I demanded again.

The bad boys looked at the big sister.

'Where are we going?' said the older one to the girl. I noticed she had the same eyes as them, dark in their dirty faces, and scared.

'Home,' she said at last. 'We're going home. And we'd better check on Gran too, I suppose. Got to find Mum and Dad.'

'Wait there,' I said. 'I'm coming with you but I've got to give back the coat first.'

I nearly fell right over the top of Rosie on my flight back inside. She'd been standing right behind me. And when I got back to where I'd dropped the coat, it was gone. I asked the hurricane lamp ladies but they didn't answer. They were talking to someone else. I searched the faces in the crowd as it flowed on towards the doors, then I slipped into what spaces I could find, fighting upstream to the foyer on the first floor and into the picture house itself.

'Mum!' I shouted. 'Mavis! Peggy Gillespie!' I watched all the people shifting about in the gloom, silent and drawn, my eyes darting from face to face, and behind them on the big safety curtain that I loved so well I could just make out the picture of the *Queen Mary* liner coming into dock in New York Harbour, as on a cold quiet night, oblivious to the grim reality beneath her.

'Your mum wasn't here, Lenny.' It was Miss Weatherbeaten, from school who wanted really good 'r's. 'I'd have seen her if she was. Sorry. Try the librrrarry.'

'The librrrarry?' I didn't think she'd have gone to the library. She didn't read.

'Or the Palace. Or maybe she went to the Rrregal.'

'Rrright then!' I said, and squeezed and slipped once more through the people. The Palace, not the Regal, which was too far, and certainly not the library.

But when I finally got back to the front doors without Mavis, my mum, the lady in red, the fur coat lady or even the fur coat, the bad boys and their big girl sister were all gone. But Rosie was still there, standing on the doorstep staring at a brick that lay there. I was overcome with fury again.

'Where did they go?' I demanded of poor Rosie. 'Why did you let them go?'

Now that it was daylight I could see that she wasn't remotely like Mavis apart from her hair which was probably the only bit that might have been very like Mavis's except that she'd singed off the fringe and both her eyebrows. Her little face crumpled again and she began to sob.

'I want my mum!' she wailed, angry now, like me,

and I wanted my mum too, my mum who should have known all this was going to happen and gone to the pictures with her nice young man another night, and then we'd all be standing there and I wouldn't have been left in charge and lost Mavis.

'Where do you live?' I snapped, after all of this had hurtled through my head.

She started to pull at her earlobe again.

'Okay,' I said with a sigh, giving in. 'It's okay. We'll find them. We'll find them all. Just don't cry again.'

'Where's my mum? I want my dad and my nan.' She was trying hard not to cry. 'Where's my big sister?'

I took her by the wrist and led her back inside to the ladies with the hurricanes.

'Stay there,' I told her firmly. 'They'll look after you. I have to go and find Mavis. Excuse me,' I said to the ladies who were busy with someone else. 'Excuse me!' They didn't hear.

'Stay here,' I said to Rosie again and left her there pulling her earlobe with her little face all crumpled.

Chapter 5

I stepped out of the doors of the La Scala picture house as if I was jumping in at the deep end of Hall Street Baths like I did with my dad last summer. I suppose, too, I thought that once the bombers had gone it might all magically go back to normal, the buildings would be in their places and people would walk about, all the shops open, Mr Chippie in his chip shop. But the wall of fire that I had run through was still there although it had sunk to smoke and embers now, and the row of tenements in Kilbowie that once had been as solid as a cliff at the seaside was full of holes and the holes were full of smoke.

I passed the spot where Annie had lain and picked my way through the fallen rubble, coughing all the way. There was a gigantic hole in the main road with twisted tramlines reaching up to the sky and men down in it working. A small river was flowing from its lower end from a burst water main, which ran down over the sides of the road towards the railway. I'd never seen underneath a road before and might normally have been tempted to stop, but I had more important things to think about.

Over towards Singer's factory, where my mum worked making sewing machines and guns, the timber yard was still ablaze, hot, huge and orange. I'd overheard people talking about it but now I saw for myself. It was unimaginably big, like hell itself, spread out over a vast area. Perhaps that was what brimstone was like, just as the minister said once in church. He had fearful, angry eyes which he raised to the ceiling. An uncomfortable silence had followed. But then perhaps we were all 'damned to hell' like he said when he brought his head back down. He glared first at the stone slabs on the floor and then at us, and then out the door which would have been, now I thought about it, roughly in the direction of Singer's yard. He may have mentioned a way to avoid hell's blaze but fear blocked my ears. Too late now.

As a result of the fire in Singer's timber yard, smoke lay thickly over everything, a clinging, cloying smoke that stank to high heaven, as my dad used to say, and hurt your eyes and nose. Great billows of it rose from Singer's and hung there preventing any clear view of much else, but even so, I could see from the road which rose over the railway bridge that the Palace picture house had been hit, the Palace where I thought my mum might be. One of its domed towers was gone and black smoke was bursting out of its roof.

I was gripped by that sickness again, that sick blow like I'd been winded, and my legs were shaken by the need to fold. I stood as still as I was able and wiped my nose with my smoky cardigan.

'Please make her be alright,' I whispered. 'Make it alright. Make her be at the Regal. Or the library.'

A gust of wind made the smoke from the Palace judder first to the left and then to the right, as if even the wind was shocked and didn't know what to do, and a cool sun was trying to push through. I told myself my mother never went to the Palace, or hardly ever; why would she go there last night? I don't know how long I stood there on the bridge. People passed me, making their way down towards the town hall and the river.

Then a voice beside me said, 'Lenny? Is that you? Mavis? Did you find Mavis? Oh, good!'

It was a woman's voice, one I knew and couldn't place, but was sure I'd heard not long before. I turned and saw Miss Weatherbeaten, my teacher, bending down towards me, and there beside her was Rosie, not Mavis.

'Rosie!' I said. 'What are you doing here? I told you to stay with the hurricane ladies! It's not Mavis, Miss Weath … Miss. It's Rosie. She can't find her family but the ladies at the Scala know.'

'I see,' she said, and she looked Rosie up and down. Rosie sniffed.

'I didn't want to stay there,' Rosie said at last. She glared at me as if it was all my fault. 'I want my mum!'

'Of course you do and of course you didn't want to stay there,' said Miss Weatherbeaten, taking Rosie's free hand, the one that wasn't pulling on her earlobe. 'Where are you going Lenny? You've been standing here a wee while.'

Normally when Miss Weatherbeaten asks me a question I answer straightaway. I couldn't, however, just then. Nothing came out of my mouth. I looked at her. She was wearing an old-fashioned tweed coat with a fluffy collar and huge buttons and I realised I'd never seen her outside before. There were black smudges below her eyes which were more than shadows and not made by smoke.

'Well?' she said. This is what she always said if you were slow but not how she usually said it. 'Lenny?'

She was either very kind or very tired, probably both, because she sighed and it made all the air rush out of me too and it let the trembling in my legs take hold again. I looked at the Palace picture house. It had been her idea after all.

'Ah,' she said, and 'Hmm,' as if she'd understood.

And try as I might to stop it, my face folded up just like Rosie's and I felt the sooty snotters run from my nose, and I coughed a kind of sob-cough that felt like barking so that I had to put my hands over my mouth to stop another one escaping, which didn't work. Soon I was barking and sobbing and retching and shuddering and holding the railway bridge wall to stay upright, and without a coat to hide in.

Miss Weatherbeaten didn't touch me, or not straightaway. Somehow in the midst of my crying I heard a whine, like the whimpering of a dog that's been left behind and which turned out to be not wee Rosie, but Miss Weatherbeaten. As soon as I was able I wiped the tears back so that I could see her weeping into the faded silk scarf that had been around her neck. She put her arm lightly around my shoulders, not big and warm like the fur-coat lady because Miss Weatherbeaten was thin like my mum and wore no lipstick, except that I could see she had worn red lipstick like the one my mum had been wearing for going to the pictures. She hugged me lightly and then wiped her face.

'I'm sure everyone will be alright,' she said, quietly, as much to herself as to me.

Rosie meanwhile was crying in that tired breathless

way, like a baby about to sleep, exhausted by grief. I took her free hand, the one that Miss Weatherbeaten wasn't holding and gave it a squeeze. Miss Weatherbeaten completed the circle by squeezing mine. After a bit we all seemed to calm down enough to speak again.

'Right then,' said Miss Weatherbeaten, suddenly becoming a teacher again and letting go of our hands. 'This is what we'll do. We'll go down to the Palace and see who we can find. And if we've no luck there we'll go to the library.'

'The library?' I echoed. So did Rosie.

'Yes, and the town hall,' said Miss Weatherbeaten. 'The library is the control centre and the town hall, is, well, the town hall.'

'The control centre?' I said, and Rosie tried to say it too. 'The town hall?'

'But first the Palace,' she said.

'First the Palace,' I said after her.

'Lenny,' she said.

'Yes, Miss Weather … ?' I said.

'Be as brave as you can,' she said. 'There's a good girl.'

Those shudders were threatening to start up again but I fought them hard and didn't think about my mum being missing presumed dead, or Mavis. Miss Weatherbeaten took our hands again but in a teacherly way this time, so Rosie and I had to let go of each other, and we all started down the road towards the Palace.

The people at the Palace were very nice but some of them were dead; I saw them on the pavement. I had to have a good look too because I couldn't stop myself and because I wanted to be absolutely sure they hadn't made a mistake when they said my mum hadn't been there. I was very glad but also not glad because I really wanted to find her.

Miss Weatherbeaten had a look at the dead people sleeping on the pavement too. I think she knew one of them. She gasped and fumbled with her silk scarf again and told me to take Rosie a little way down the road and she'd catch us up. It wasn't easy because of the mess, and Rosie was only wee, and I wasn't sure she was going to come after us at all, she took such a long time about it.

And when she did she talked briskly about stuff we had done at school, about the weather and how the weather was bright that day, if only we could have seen it above the black smoke, and what the reasons for that were, and to tell you the truth it didn't sound much like the lesson we'd had and she didn't sound much like a teacher, but her grip on our hands was very familiar and mine was sore. Rosie was having trouble not falling over, the ground was so mixed up, and because Miss Weatherbeaten kept pointing at the sky, even though we couldn't see it.

I didn't want to look at the sky, even though sometimes the smoke cleared and it was blue, not any more. I didn't want to see any killer bees. I didn't really want to look about me at all the mess and people, but I really, really wanted to find my mum and Mavis, so I had to look, in fact I had to peer and try to see things that I didn't want to see, though my eyes felt like sandpaper.

Rosie just kept asking for her mum and dad, over and over again.

When we got to the town hall at the bottom of the

road there were so many people and they were in such a state I wondered whether we'd ever find anyone, and then we discovered there was a queue to give your name and to ask questions, so we went and found the back of the queue and stood there. We weren't at the back long. Lots of other people joined us, and other people came past and searched through the queue for people they knew, so after I bit I asked Miss Weatherbeaten if I could do that too. We both told Rosie to 'stay there' but somehow she just couldn't, so in the end she came with me and we wandered in the crowd looking into everyone's faces.

I found school friends and people I'd seen in shops. There was noise and silence, people crying, and most of us filthy and grey. A lady fell over suddenly and an old man too, and someone helped them over to a wall to lean on. But no-one had seen my mum or Mavis, and Rosie was as silent as the grave, as my gran would have said: just looking, not seeing.

When we came back it was Miss Weatherbeaten's turn to go and look and when she came back she stood there with us for a while longer and then she said, 'Your weather report was very, very good, Lenny. Well done!'

Even though I hadn't slept and was filthy, sore, scared and hungry, I blushed and tried a smile, although given the state of my face she wouldn't have known. I'd spent a lot of time looking at clouds for the sake of that report. It was strange to be reminded that she was my teacher again and not the kind lady who had cried with us on the bridge by the station.

'Just thought you'd like to know,' she said.

'Thanks,' I said.

We stood a while longer, edging slowly towards the desk, and then she said she needed to go and find someone, or find out if her house was still standing, I'm not sure which because all either me or Rosie heard was 'Stay here.' I think she also said, 'I'll be back soon.'

So we two huddled together because, being a bright spring day meant it was cold, and we hadn't slept or eaten, and some ladies came round and handed us sandwiches and hot tea which I burnt my lip on but didn't care. They gave me a dress too, a green one with long sleeves and velvet on the collar, and a coat like my own dark blue coat, and a blue dress and coat the same for Rosie. I put my old dress, what was left of it, over the new one because I needed somewhere to keep the shoe, and I was cold. I helped Rosie on with hers.

We seemed to be there forever. I decided three times to leave and find Mavis and my mum myself and then changed my mind, and then suddenly we were at the desk. I didn't recognise the lady there.

'I'm Lenny Gillespie,' I told her and I explained that I'd lost both Mavis and my mum.

'I see, and who's this?' she wanted to know.

'That's Rosie,' I said. Rosie stared at her over the desk.

'Hello, Rosie,' said the lady.

'I've lost my mum,' said Rosie, very slowly. 'And my dad, and my gran and my sister and … .' She was pulling at her earlobe again. I took hold of her other hand the way Miss Weatherbeaten had.

'Oh, dear,' said the lady kindly. 'Where do you live?'

Rosie was pulling hard at her ear and staring at the papers on the table. The kind lady asked her question again and after a bit Rosie shook her head. The kind lady sat back in her chair and sighed.

'She was in the shelter and the others were on their way there,' I said. I had started to explain but Rosie put her hands flat over both ears, closed her eyes and said loudly, 'I want my mum! I want my mum!'

I tugged at her wrist but she wouldn't let me take her hands from her ears, so I said to the kind lady, 'Mr Chippie, I mean the ARP man, he only brought her.' I shrugged.

She nodded that she had understood, and swallowed hard.

'Ah,' she said.

We both looked at Rosie. Her eyes were open but she still had her hands over her ears. She was looking at the kind lady.

'Oh, dear,' said the lady. 'What's her surname?'

'I think it's Thomas or Tomlin or something like that. I can't remember.'

I got down in front of Rosie and gently pulled her hands from her ears.

'Thomas or Tomlin?' I said.

'Tomlin,' she said.

'Rosie Tomlin,' said the kind lady. 'What a nice name.' She checked down a list in front of her, then lifted her glasses off her nose and looked very worried. 'Well, Rosie Tomlin, you had better come behind this desk here and sit with me.'

Rosie looked at me crouched on the floor in front of her, her hand still in mine, and she glanced just briefly from me to the kind lady and back again, uncertain what to do. She shifted on her feet until she was squared up to me and stopped there, stock-still.

'No, Rosie,' I said. 'You go with her. I have to find Mavis and my mum.'

The kind lady persuaded her by saying there was another little girl who would be staying with her too and that her grandchildren lived next door and it would only be for a while anyway, but they had jam in the cupboard and a new baby over the road.

'And if you like,' she said, 'Lenny here, can come and visit you.'

'Will my mum be there? And my big sister?'

The kind lady looked worried again. She didn't answer Rosie's question. She just shifted over in her seat and patted the cushion beside her.

'You come and sit here,' she said.

After a bit Rosie decided this was alright and let go of my hand and went and sat on the edge of the kind lady's seat.

Again, just like in the La Scala I was overcome with some strange kind of fury. It felt like I was angry with Rosie but how could that be? I felt angry and sick again when I thought about my mum and Mavis, but I couldn't be angry with them – how could I? And I felt as if I'd been shrunk to the same size as Rosie, the same size as Mavis, and my stomach churned as I stood there looking at Rosie and the kind lady on the same chair at the other side of the desk.

'Now, Lenny Gillespie,' she said as if memorising my name, 'what about you?'

I was just about to reply, my mouth was open and everything, but a boy came into the room with a piece of paper and handed it to the kind lady, who read it and checked it against her list of people in front of her on the table. She looked up at me and back at her list.

Her finger ran down a column of names, once then twice, then a third time. I tried to read the upside-down writing but it was too squiggly and there were lots of smudges.

She asked me if I had relatives anywhere nearby, any neighbours, had I been evacuated at the beginning of the war, anywhere I could go, anyone I could stay with, at least for a couple of days?

I told her I didn't know, I just wanted my mum and my wee sister, and she said, 'Your mum has been taken to hospital.'

The air seemed to be sucked right out of me and I thought I was going to be sick suddenly. The top of my head prickled with heat.

'She's going to be alright,' she said, 'but she was caught under a building. Where did you say you lived?' She glanced at her list again. 'She was just around the corner, not far from the canal. They got her out about five a.m. I'm not sure which hospital it will be. I'm sure they'll send word back when they know themselves.'

'Was Mavis with her?' I said.

I wanted her either to say it wasn't true, just kidding, or to say it all again because I knew I couldn't remember it all. But worst of all, Mavis wasn't with her.

'Which hospital?' I said.

'I don't know,' she said. 'They'll let us know as soon as they know themselves.'

I got her to tell me everything again and then she said she had to get on with the next person and why didn't I go to the school? There were buses going to be leaving from there evacuating everyone that was left, just in case. In case of what? In case it happened again. Happened again? How could it happen again? Rosie was looking at me now.

'I can't take you home too, Lenny,' said the kind lady. 'I'm sorry but I can only take the really wee ones. You have to go and find a bus to get on.'

Now I was really furious.

'But what about Mavis!' I shouted. 'I can't leave Mavis!'

'Shouting is not going to help anyone,' said the kind lady sternly, and I knew she was right, only I was still feeling the same size as Rosie and Mavis. 'When they find her they'll bring news of her here,' she said quietly.

The people behind me were still waiting and she looked over my head at them now.

As I made my way through the crowd I looked back at Rosie. She watched me until I couldn't see her any more and probably for a bit longer too. I stood on the steps of the town hall and saw that the library had been hit and books were scattered all over the road. Some men in clean suits and coats were going up the steps, oddly bright without the grime that covered the rest of us. It was the control centre. Looking at the broken door at its entrance it seemed a funny sort of thing to call it.

The day was bright but a heavy haze of smoke sat on the still air, unmoving, as if trying to hide us all, and made it dark. I stood as I had on the steps of the Scala and, like last year with my dad, I jumped off at the deep end and strode purposefully through the crowd and the debris, down the road past the library with its broken books, past broken tenements and broken people, checking their faces one by one, but seeing no-one I knew. They had budgies in cages and crockery in prams and great big bundles on their backs. Most of them were heading the same way as me, going west, out of town. A strange silence hung over them like the hovering smoke and I wondered whether something might explode if anyone disturbed it.

Inside me I felt those explosions, like the explosions of a little engine driving me on with all my strength until I came to the canal underpass and passed under and up onto the tow path by the green, green canal water and began to retrace the steps Mavis and I had taken, and shortly after, it would seem, my mum. As I got closer to home I found people I knew.

'Lenny,' said the scary man from up our street, the one whose close I'd looked in for ages for Mavis, and who had a special stick for naughty kids like me.

I'd only seen him once before and he looked smaller than I remembered and dirty of course. He was wearing a brown jacket and trousers and a brown tweed cap. He wasn't carrying his stick but I wasn't taking any chances and kept well back.

'Lenny, did you hear about your mum?' he said. 'They've taken her to the hospital.'

'Did you see her?' I said. 'Is she alright?'

'She was under there a very long time,' he said. He made a funny noise with his lip and looked at me sideways. 'Are you alright? You got burnt I see. Your hair is all gone.'

I touched my short, frizzy hair.

'Under where?' I said.

'Under there.' He pointed to the smouldering building beside us, what was left of it. 'But I saw her when she came out. Her legs were in bad shape and she didn't want to go in the ambulance because she didn't know where you two were, but she was talking. She's alive.' He smiled at me. 'She only stopped in the close to shelter a minute. I saw her running up the street. But where's Mavis?'

'Don't know.' I was too scared to tell him I'd lost her, even without his stick, so I tried a smile so he'd think everything was alright.

He nodded slowly and pursed his lips the way I'd seen the headmistress at our school do, and his face seemed to wrinkle up as if he was an old, old man, which I don't think he was, only old, or older than my dad anyway.

'Someone will have her,' he said. 'Don't you worry. Ask at the town hall.'

An old lady hobbled over to us. She came out of the building opposite carrying a big bundle tied in a grey blanket with a brown belt and some string. It was almost the same size as her. She dropped the bundle at our feet, nearly knocking me over.

'Mavis was in our back court,' she said, breathing heavily. 'You're Peggy's girl aren't you? Peggy Gillespie?'

I tipped my head. Peggy's girl, yes I'm Peggy's girl.

'Poor Peggy,' she said, still breathing heavily from her bundle. 'And I wondered about Mavis being out on her own when I saw her from my window. She was with the girl downstairs, and when the siren went she jumped up and ran off saying she had to find Lenny. That's you isn't it?'

'That's me, Lenny,' I said, my voice not much more than a whisper now.

'She went that way,' she said, pointing up the street

where most of the buildings were burning. There wasn't much street to see because of the debris.

'That way?' I didn't like this.

'Yes,' she said. We all three stared up the road.

'No,' I said.

'Yes,' she said. 'I saw her with my own eyes, don't you say otherwise. I saw her. One of her shoes was wet. Must have stood in a puddle.'

I put my hand in my pocket.

'It wasn't a puddle,' I said. 'It was ... .'

'Don't you tell me what I did and didn't see!' she said. 'Don't you tell me I'm wrong! I saw what I saw. Don't you tell me!'

'That's not what she meant,' said the scary man with the stick. I wondered if he still had his stick and whether he ever used it on old ladies.

He touched my shoulder and turned me away from her. He smelled of smoke like we all did but he didn't smell like other men, all sharp and sweet and not clean: just smokey. I didn't want to go with him but I didn't want to stay there either, and while the old lady was trying to get her bundle up onto her back he touched the side of his head to indicate she was mad.

'Don't mind her, Lenny, and don't mind Mavis either. She'll have gone into one of the shelters up that way and be absolutely fine. Ask at the town hall but get down to the buses as soon as you can and get yourself out of here. Have you no family? No, of course you don't. They'll all be too far away, won't they? Why don't you stick with me a minute and I'll take you down to the buses? That's where I'm going.'

He had a soft voice that I liked, but he had a stick for naughty kids like me too, so I said, no thank you very much, I wanted to go home to see if Mavis was there yet and I told him there was a kind lady at the town hall who was going to take us both to stay with her. This was a lie of course, but sometimes lies are alright; my mum said so.

'Cheeky wee midden, just like her mother!' screeched the old woman as she went past, heading back the way I had come.

'Don't mind her now,' said the scary man with the stick.

I thanked him and, taking another gulp of not very clean air, started further on up the road Mavis had taken.

It was a strange thing not knowing whether to be wildly happy because Mum wasn't dead and lying in a corridor without us beside her, or terrified because her legs were bad, like Annie, who was lying in a corridor. And I had the same discomfort about Mavis, except I had no idea at all about her and didn't know what to think of all these grown-ups telling me she was bound to be alright when so many people were absolutely not alright. There was no way of knowing who was going to be alright and who wasn't.

I didn't know what to think at all so I tried very hard not to think about anything, but it wasn't very easy.

Chapter 6

It wasn't much further to our street from there but it seemed to take forever. When I got there this is what I saw.

First of all, and most importantly, there was no Mavis, not that I could see much because of the smoke that was still hanging around, but I did ask the men that were working in the rubble, once I'd got their attention. I had to lie and say my mum was just down the road because they wanted to take me away. They didn't think it was safe. Well, I knew that, but I still had to find Mavis.

They were working on the house on the corner, the one where I'd seen the old lady with the bag fall from one window to the other then disappear in a guzzle of fire, so I told them about that, and then they asked what else I'd seen and I told them about the people in the bottom flat in my close, and the bad boys' granny.

Although the street was so different, all black and hollow, everything all mixed up together, it was strangely familiar too; it was my street after all, even though the windows were all over the road and you could see the sky where the roofs should have been, and I felt suddenly very heavy as if I'd been given a whole sack of coal to carry all by myself.

I was cold and hungry too. It seemed a long time

since the sandwich and tea in the town hall and my tummy had started growling and it hurt. I wondered where everyone was, and a shock went through me, like when I touched the electric wire at school by mistake, because I thought I might find Mavis, but I might find her broken and hurt, or lying all flung about like she lies when she's asleep, only she might be sleeping the sleep of the dead. And suddenly I didn't want to see Mavis at all. I stood there with the glass scrunching under my feet and the noise of big stones falling and the smoke up my nose, and I closed my eyes so that I didn't have to see anything, least of all Mavis. But somehow I still saw her because she was in there already, right inside there where I couldn't get her out even if I wanted to.

And that shuddering came over me again like the bomb inside me was about to go off and I pulled every part of me in around my heart, my eyes pushed into my head, my head inside my neck, my legs pressed hard together, my shoulders around my ears, my fingers knotted together, my elbows in my tummy, and I held on with all my might so that nothing would escape. But it didn't work. I still had to breathe and when I finally let go, because I couldn't hold it forever, it came out in a big gluey moan which I didn't recognise and which scared me all the more. I gulped it back in but that didn't work either and my face hurt from the salt tears in my cuts.

A noise startled me in the crunching glass and I jumped back and opened my eyes. A dog was staring up at me. It was a fawny-brown dog with a black wiry back, big pointy ears and a tail that curled all the way round in a circle. It belonged to one of our neighbours and lived to sneak into people's houses and steal their dinners. We looked at each other for a minute and then it barked the loudest bark you ever heard and gave me such a fright that I screamed and screamed and it was all I could do not to fall into the splinters and the glass at my feet.

The dog barked again and then somebody whistled and the dog stopped to follow the sound, and just where the entrance to our close should have been I saw the two bad boys and the big girl who was their sister. And further up the street I saw Miss Weatherbeaten, of all people, climbing over a pile of building with her hair all loose about her shoulders and blowing about gently in the breeze that wasn't there.

The dog barked again but I couldn't see it through my tears so I didn't know what it was, just explosions in my head that wouldn't stop, and I couldn't see Miss Weatherbeaten any more but I knew I was falling over backwards and might go under the window frames and the stone, just like my mum had been for hours on end with the fires going on all around her and no-one to save her. And I could still hear my shouts coming out of me as if they were someone else's, shouts like my mum when she came for us in Ayr, like my dad when he was last home, like the lady in the street who had a fit and wet herself, and in the distance there was the boom-crash of a delayed action bomb.

This is it! I thought. I'm going over!

It didn't hurt but it did knock the last bits of breath out of me and I thought for a minute I'd been lucky and landed on an armchair like the one I'd seen on my way there, sitting at a squinty angle on a garden wall, but it wasn't an armchair. It was one of the rescue men. He caught me and lifted me up as if I was a wee thing like Mavis and he carried me to where the bad boys were with their big sister. He didn't put me down straightaway even though I was far too big to be carried, but it was just as well because I don't think I could have stood up anyway.

'You need to go and get onto buses down on the main road as soon as possible,' he said. 'These buildings are not safe. If you know of anyone stuck in there we'll do what we can, but you need to get out of here.'

It was Mr Chippie!

'Mr Chippie!' I said. 'It's you!'

He looked down at me. I wiped my nose on the sleeve of my new blue coat.

'It's … it's … ,' he said.

'Lenny,' I said. 'I lost my hair.'

'I know, I remember,' he said. 'I haven't forgotten, and I haven't forgotten your sister.'

'Mavis.'

'Yes, Mavis. I haven't forgotten her. But we did find your mum. She was … .'

'Yes, I know,' I said. I didn't want to hear. I didn't want the bombs to go off again.

'Yes,' he said. 'Yes.'

The bad boys and their sister were standing very close together, like when they were in the Scala. They weren't scary now at all.

'Did you … ?' I nodded towards the tenement that had been ours.

'Was anyone … ?' said the bigger of the bad boys. It was his granny who lived in the bottom flat and couldn't move; the man there was probably his uncle.

'Most of them got into a shelter,' said Mr Chippie. 'Anyone left won't be alive.' We didn't want this news. 'Have you been to the town hall or the church to check?'

I nodded and so did they, but I hadn't seen them there so I thought they must be lying.

Then, with a crunch and a tumble, Miss Weatherbeaten arrived.

'I thought you'd be here,' she said. 'I told you to stay at the town hall. Did you find Mavis?'

I shook my head and a little bomb went off in my stomach.

'Hello, Miss Wetherspoon,' said Mr Chippie. 'Sorry about your friend.' He put me down on a big piece of stone so that I was nearly the same size as Miss Weatherbeaten. 'You've got to get this lot out of here,' he went on not waiting for her reply. 'It's not safe and I have to get back to work.' And as if to prove his point the ground was shaken by a building in the next street collapsing and sending a new cloud of dust all over us. We put our hands over our ears, the bad boys and me, and I fell against Miss Weatherbeaten who was suddenly beside me. I was as big as the big boy because of the stone, but I felt much smaller than any of them. Miss Weatherbeaten put her arm round my shoulders.

'I was looking for Lenny,' she said. 'I'm going to take her on a bus if there is one but I heard there's a big queue of people and no buses.'

'I can't go. I haven't found Mavis,' I said to her, incredulous. 'I have to stay and find Mavis.' I'd told her that already, and her a teacher too!

'Lenny, Mavis is most likely safe somewhere,' she said.

'But I have to find her. Most likely isn't enough.' I was surprised by my own boldness.

And then they all joined in, even the bad boys and their big sister, telling me she was probably safe but that we weren't and we had to get moving soon. They seemed to be all talking at once so that in the end I couldn't hear anything, just rumbles and thumps and the grating sound of lorries and bricks. I watched Mr Chippie go back to the building he was rescuing in and I said, 'I can't.' I said it over and over again, half to them and half to myself, and I wished Mr Chippie would come back and carry me home again, but I *was* home so he couldn't, and I wished they'd all stop talking and not listening.

'Kids!' said a voice behind us. It was the scary man with the stick. 'Stop arguing and get into a shelter.'

'We're going to the bus,' said Miss Weatherbeaten, whose hand I had grabbed. I was off the stone that Mr Chippie had put me on and was up against her coat.

'There aren't any,' he said. 'They're all full.' He looked like he too was carrying a sack of coal all by himself, but all he had was a small brown suitcase. 'And the Germans are coming back. We have to find shelter now. My shelter is big enough for all of us. And look, it saved my life.'

We all looked at him with his saved life. He didn't seem very big, for a man, and he was swaying slightly. He put his suitcase down on some bricks, took off his brown cap and mopped his head with a clean white handkerchief. The black smoke from the row of blackened tenements seemed to sway with him and he glanced back down the road towards the sunset that was gathering there beyond them and beyond the rubble and the ARP men and the gaps further down where the buildings were gone.

I felt sick again and Miss Weatherbeaten squeezed my hand, but I don't think it was on purpose. I felt her tremble the same way I did. We all looked at each other through the dust. The Germans were coming back, and I wondered if the bad boys knew about the scary man's big stick as well and decided that if anyone knew about it those boys probably did.

'When are they coming?' said the big girl in a hushed voice. She and the boys huddled even closer together, merging in a mass of grey.

The light was fading behind her and I realised it was about that time of day, the same as the day before when I had pushed the smaller of the bad boys into the canal and lost Mavis. I calculated that meant we had not much time at all.

'Soon,' I said, before the scary man could reply, and I looked at the bad boys to see if they were thinking the same thing as me, that time was not on our side, like my gran had said last summer. It was hard to tell. Then they both talked at once, and everyone started to fidget, as if they had ants in their pants.

'We've got to go, Izzie,' they said (like Lizzie but without the 'L'). Her hair was sticking up around her face. 'Mum and Dad said we've got to go!' And they started off.

'We'll never make it in time now but at least we'll be out of here,' she said, quickly following.

'But where are you going to?' said the scary man.

'We're going to Carbeth,' said Izzie, calling back. 'We have a hut there, my uncle has a hut there too.

But we need to go now or it'll be dark and we won't find the way.'

'What on earth are you doing here, then?' said the scary man.

'My gran … ,' and she threw her head towards the tenement, their granny's and mine, but I didn't want to think about that so I started hopping from one foot to the other. Then Miss Weatherbeaten took my hand again and we turned to follow Izzie.

'Rosie!' said Miss Weatherbeaten. 'I told you to stay at the town hall!'

There was Rosie in the same coat as me standing on a broken heap of furniture. She was hopping from foot to foot too and pulling on her earlobe.

'Rosie,' I breathed. Rosie, a pretend version of Mavis, right outside our own front door. I felt a surge of annoyance with her for running off, just like Mavis, and then turning up where Mavis should have been. 'Rosie,' I said. She grinned white teeth through her dirty little face.

'Well, it's too late now,' said the scary man. 'We all have to get into a shelter or go wherever we're going. Now, can somebody find me a stick of some kind to help me get over this pile of rubbish?'

Miss Weatherbeaten started looking about. Rosie stayed where she was. I kept a firm grip on Miss Weatherbeaten's hand which made her search for a stick more difficult. And I didn't want to have to search and find something I didn't want to see, like Mavis.

'Take Rosie, and follow the boys,' she said in a voice that couldn't be questioned, so I did, even though I didn't want to.

'They said I had to go to Edimburry,' said Rosie.

'I don't want to go to Edimburry.' She sniffed loudly and pulled the back of her hand across her cheek. 'I want my mum.'

'Edinburgh. You should have gone, Rosie,' I told her. 'Now the Germans are coming back and we'll have to go into a shelter with that scary man with ….' But Rosie didn't know about the scary man with the stick and she had enough to worry about with the Germans.

We caught up with the others and we all waited for Miss Weatherbeaten and the scary man near the top of the road.

'How far is Carbeth?' asked Miss Weatherbeaten. Her face was flushed and her eyes were red and bloodshot.

The two bad boys looked at each other, two faces alike in the dirt.

'About ten miles over the hills, up Kilbowie Road,' said the biggest.

'Then go!' said the man.

'Ten miles?' said Izzie with a snort. 'Two at the most.'

'Seven,' said the smaller boy. 'Let's go!'

'Alright, three,' said Izzie. 'Up Kilbowie Road, along Cochno and then over the hill. There's a path over the hill and stiles over the walls and then along the main road and turn right at the Halfway House, that's the pub. Maybe four.'

I looked back down at what was left of my street, nearly dark now.

'How far is a mile?' I said.

'Not far,' said the man with the stick. He had a real stick now, made out of a fancy piece of wood, like a banister from a stairwell, or a piece of a bedstead like the one in my friend's house.

'Here's home,' he said, 'what's left of it. Just as well it's at the end of the row, so we can go round the side or we'd never get to the shelter.'

I looked at his stick. I didn't want to go into the shelter with him and his stick.

Izzie and the bad boy brothers started to leave.

'What's the hut like? How big is it?' I said. 'Who else is there? Where do you sleep?'

'In the hut, of course,' the smaller bad boy called back. 'There's bunk beds. It's not very big but it's bigger than a normal hut. There's a rope swing right next to it and rabbits and a lily pond and other kids and huts and a river we dammed for fish and … .'

'Can I … ?'

'Yes, come and visit us sometime. There's always space, if you don't mind the floor.'

'She's a girl!' said the bigger one.

'No, I mean now,' I said. 'Can I come now? Or as soon as I've found Mavis?'

'Lenny, come on!' said Miss Weatherbeaten from the corner of the building. It was dark now, as dark as it was going to get, as dark as the big fat moon was going to let it, which was not very. We were all lit up again like the night before, picked out from the shadows for the Gerries to see, for the Gerries to put us in their sights and rain down their bombs on us all over again. Rosie was on ahead, her dark hair glinting like jewels set in silver, her hand in the hand of the scary man with the stick as he led her to the shelter, and I knew I'd have to go with her because Miss Weatherbeaten might not know what his stick

82

was really for, for beating naughty kids like me, and like Rosie who didn't stay where she was told to stay, and like Mavis.

I wished I could go with Izzie and the bad boys, even though they were bad. I grunted goodbye at them and went round the building to the shelter, thinking what about Mavis and what is going to happen to us?

The door of the shelter was hanging off. Miss Weatherbeaten and the man with the stick went to find something to fix it and Rosie and I went inside and sat on a bench, Rosie with her feet swinging, her toes gliding over the puddle that had formed on the floor, and me next to her. She quickly tucked her arm through mine. She had a grizzly big snotter from her nose to her top lip. I was so thirsty I even thought about scooping up the puddle.

'My mum will be missing me,' she said.

'Were there any other girls like you in the town hall?' I asked her. I didn't want to think about the bombing that was going to happen soon.

'Yes,' she said.

'Anyone called Mavis?'

She nodded. My heart leapt and I tried to stand up but she held onto my arm so I sat back down. My feet landed in the puddle, and one shoe got soaking wet.

'What did she look like?'

But the girl she described was nothing like Mavis, too big, too fat, too blond.

'Anyone else?'

It was hard to tell. Rosie was only four. How was she going to know?

'Where were they all going?' I said.

'Edimburry, to stay with that lady. But one of the other ladies said she didn't know where we'd end up,' said Rosie.

I wondered whether some other girl in another shelter was holding Mavis's hand. Mavis was as cute as could be. She'd get a piece at anyone's door, as my mum always said. She had straight dark hair, like mine, and healthy red cheeks, not like mine, well perhaps my cheeks were red at that precise moment but they certainly weren't healthy. She had big brown eyes that you couldn't say no to, even if you were told to by my mum. I hoped there was a girl looking after her in a shelter. Better still, I hoped she was a million miles from there and not in a shelter at all.

But one thing I suddenly knew for certain was that there was nothing I could do for Mavis at that exact moment, absolutely nothing, and while that filled me with horror, it made things easier too. The same was true for my mum who was as safe as she could be in a hospital now. So while the scary man and Miss Weatherbeaten were trying to lift some fallen masonry to jam against the door to protect us I had a good think, sitting there in the dark. I peered out at them in the silvery light, with the wisps of smoke and that terrible stink. We needed dinner and water and sleep and air without smoke, and we needed to be away from there.

'Stay here a minute will you?' I said to Rosie and climbed out of the shelter, both feet now wet from the puddle. The back of the scary man's building had a piece missing. A lot of it was on the ground. There was a glow I didn't like inside a downstairs window. I heard men shouting out in the street.

'Miss Weatherbeaten ... ,' I said.

Miss Weatherbeaten was bent over. I saw them from behind. They didn't hear me. The scary man had his arm around her shoulders and was murmuring to her; I couldn't make out what. I heard her sob, and just like I had done, she was retching, and then I heard her voice but it was too quiet to hear properly. Their faces were close together. Something urgent was being said. He held her in front of him. He was holding her by the shoulders and talking to her and even in that silver light which made them look like two ghosts, I could see her listening to him and nodding, and then he listened to her, even though she was still crying as she spoke, and then he nodded too.

Although he wasn't a big man he had to lean down to see her because she hung her head so low, then he lifted her chin with his finger, so that she had to look at him again. And I saw how kindly he was looking at her, even though he had a stick, and I wondered whether my mum had been wrong about him after all.

Then the sirens went and they looked up and saw me and barked at me to get into the shelter straightaway, and I could see there was something they were trying to hide from me, near the back of the building.

I wondered if it was Mavis, sleeping the sleep of the dead.

'Is it Mavis? Where is she?' I said, trying to see round them.

'No, it's not Mavis,' said the man with the stick, and he raised the stick that they had found for him and waved it at me, so that he was scary again.

'Please go into the shelter, Lenny,' said Miss Weatherbeaten in a shaky but teachery voice, so I turned to go back in and nearly fell over Rosie again. She had followed me out.

'I don't want to go in there!' said Rosie.

'I don't want to go in there either,' I told Miss Weatherbeaten and the man. 'I don't want to stay here. I want to go to Carbeth with those boys and Izzie. We can come back tomorrow. We can't stay here. I can't stay here. Please.'

The sirens had stopped now. Rosie took my hand. I held hers tight. The possibility of trying to find Carbeth, just me and Rosie, danced through my mind until I realised I was scared of doing that too.

Miss Weatherbeaten glanced behind her.

'Carbeth,' she said. She was thinking about it. 'How is your bad leg, Mr Tait?' The scary man with the stick had a name: Mr Tait.

Mr Tait leant on the fancy stick and shook his left leg.

'Carbeth is a very long way,' he said, 'and we've almost no time to get out of town. Rosie is too wee and I can't carry her, and poor Lenny here hasn't slept since yesterday no doubt, or eaten. None of us have.'

'I can carry her,' I said. 'And we had a sandwich and some tea at the town hall.'

'No, Lenny, I'll carry her.' Miss Weatherbeaten was sure, I could tell. 'Can you walk, Mr Tait?' she said. 'I'll take responsibility for these two. We only have to get to the hills.'

He looked about him, and fidgeted with his buttons, and took off his cap and scratched his head. Then he gave his leg another little shake and put his hat back on.

'I'm staying,' he said. We all stared at him, surprised.

No-one said anything, and then suddenly everyone started talking at once. Mr Tait went into his shelter and pulled a piece of corrugated iron in front of the door but not before Miss Weatherbeaten had hugged him and they had another conversation that I couldn't hear properly. Funny how adults all seem to know each other.

Then Miss Weatherbeaten took Rosie's hand and I still had her other one and just at that moment we heard the distant rumble of the killer bees, like a tiny hum, and for a second we listened to it grow and then ran round the house.

But I looked back and saw what they didn't want me to see.

There were bricks and blocks of stone, great big pieces of wood, a chest of drawers and a gas cooker, and in the middle of all this was a face, a face I thought I half-recognised, floating in this sea of debris. It was the face of a woman, youngish, probably not much older than Izzie, with brown hair, silver in that light, hair that was pulled back in a clip over her ear. I saw her collar, blue with white flowers, and the blood that had flowed down onto it from her mouth. Her lips were dark with it and her eyes were not quite shut, like she was very tired, and not really sleeping the sleep of the dead, tucked up in a bed of bricks.

I was pulled round the corner so suddenly that I nearly fell over again and then I couldn't see that face any more, and something sank in me right down to my soggy wet shoes. The noise of the German planes was louder now and we hurried as best we could over the mess on the road. My legs were like lead, as if they had grown and were fat cylinders of metal like the bombs and I thought I'd just have to stop. But behind me the engines roared and then the bombs started to come down again, boom-crash, boom-crash, and sometimes the awful screech first, the ground shaking beneath us and grit and stones flying past our heads and some of it hitting us, and not being able to see for the smoke and the burning in our eyes as if the fires had set light to them. And the heat! It was so hot I could hardly breathe and everything looked wibbly-wobbly as if the buildings were made of putty and were being melted.

Miss Weatherbeaten was up ahead of me with Rosie on her hip, trying to hurry in a place where no hurry was to be had, and Rosie was bumping and flopping against her, holding on with both arms tight around Miss Weatherbeaten's neck.

I scrambled on and I wondered why the Germans were back. There was nothing left to bomb. The houses were all down or torched and the distilleries and Singer's burning still from the night before. They'd already got my mum, who'd said 'Who'd want us anyway?' Well, I wanted to change that. Who'd want to kill us more like? Why would anyone want to kill us? Us of all people? What good was that going to do?

Miss Weatherbeaten came to an abrupt halt and turned sharply towards me. Her eyes were flashing like beacons in her head and her mouth was trembling, as if she was trying to say something but hadn't quite decided what, which wasn't like her. Her hand held the back of Rosie's head so that she couldn't turn round.

'Promise me,' she shouted above the din. 'Promise

me you will look at the ground and nowhere else. Rosie you must close your eyes and keep them closed NO MATTER WHAT. D'you understand? No. Matter. What. It's very important. More important than staying in the town hall, MUCH more important. Lenny, the ground only.'

'Can't I look at the sky?' I said. 'Someone's got to look at the sky.'

'Well, alright, the sky and the ground under your feet. Nowhere else.'

I tried hard not to look. There were people lying in a row where someone had cleared a space, people who were a funny colour and had torn clothes, burnt clothes and no hair and pools of dark blood around them. They didn't really look like people but I knew that's what they were. Some of them had bits missing, like a leg or a foot, and close by there was a collection of those bits. I saw an arm, a hand, a leg.

'Lenny, the ground!' said Miss Weatherbeaten fiercely.

But it was too late.

I don't remember much of our escape through the streets after that, just the noise, the endless drone of the killer bees overhead and the relentless boom-crash, the roar of fire and the shouts of other people trying to escape, and all I saw was the ground beneath my feet and the people sleeping in death, separated from their feet or their hands, no longer whole, unable to complete themselves. I wondered what my arms would look like without my hands. I watched my bloodied hands clamber over the debris with my feet close behind them, and I watched Rosie's feet swing round Miss Weatherbeaten's back and her fat little hands grasp Miss Weatherbeaten's coat, and I wondered if my mum still had her feet and hands attached in the hospital or if she'd lost her hands that were so much a part of her, a part of me.

And then suddenly I realised I was walking on a real road with hardly any bricks or glass and I ran ahead to where Miss Weatherbeaten and Rosie were and we walked all together now as fast as we could up the hill. Rosie was on the ground walking but only for a while to give Miss Weatherbeaten a rest.

We crossed the big main road, Great Western Road. There were other people walking there too. Some of them had bags and budgies in cages. There was a huge woman in several coats but others had nothing, just themselves: a man in only a shirt, trousers and bare feet; a boy with blood down his face and front; a goat leading a little old man, a woman pushing a pram with a baby in it, running with another child running beside her. A lady fell. I don't know if she got up. People may have shouted but they were drowned out by the noise. Some were well-dressed and fat with layers. Others were ragged and burnt.

And then we came to fields and, being March, the fields were damp and the grass dead and stringy to catch at our feet, but my feet were already wet from the puddle in the shelter and my new dark-blue coat that the lady at the town hall had given me was thick and warm against the bushes and bracken. The air was cleaner. There was less smoke because of a breeze, so we could breathe better. We were going more slowly now. Rosie was being carried again and we knew we were out of the worst, being away from the town, but bombs were still crashing all around us in the hills and the killer bees were still scudding overhead. We could see them clearly circling over our heads through the moonlit air.

Chapter 7

When we came to a big flat stone as wide as a road which was pushing up out of the grass, we climbed up onto it and stopped. There were other people on the stone too. They were watching the sky and watching Clydebank, shouting about what was happening.

'That's Yoker distillery,' said a woman, pointing. 'The bastards! Our James'll have been down there!'

When I stood there and looked back towards Clydebank, all I could see was a huge orange glow over the whole town and reaching up into the sky, and I felt a pang for Mavis because she was still lost and I hoped the fire hadn't gobbled her up like the big scary dragon in her book. She wouldn't have stood a chance in there.

'We have to go back,' I said.

'What?' said Miss Weatherbeaten, turning suddenly to look at me. Rosie burst into tears.

'I still haven't found Mavis. I don't know why I came here.'

'We'll find Mavis tomorrow. We can't go back,' she said.

'But I have to find Mavis!'

She let go of Rosie and put an arm around me and tried to pull me in towards her but I threw her off and jumped down from the rock.

'Lenny!' she shouted.

'Lenny!' screamed Rosie.

And I lurched to a halt.

'I shouldn't have come here,' I muttered, gazing up into the orange sky. I pulled Mavis's shoe from my pocket and rubbed the leather between my finger and thumb. What was I thinking? Poor Mavis! And my mum. Why didn't I stay? I can't go on from here. Where's Mavis? Where is she? Why did I think I could leave her? She's probably under a building right now calling for me, calling for me and trapped … .

A killer bee appeared from nowhere and roared over my head. I threw myself onto the ground. Behind me, on the rock, there were screams, then a mighty explosion and we were all showered with mud.

'Mum and Mavis, Mum and Mavis, Mum and Mavis … ,' I said over and over under cover of my arms which were wrapped tightly around my head.

Rosie screamed a scream that would cut you in two. 'I want my mum!' It was as if she was tearing her own throat out. 'I want my mum!' she screamed and I heard it because it's what I wanted to scream too. 'I want my mum!'

Another plane, and another, and another, the bombers roared above us, ripping through the air, like God being angry, shouting down at us and tearing everything to pieces, even the trees and the hills, the grass torn from the ground and the bare rocks exposed in the moonlight.

Mum and Mavis, Mum and Mavis, Mum and Mavis; am I dead yet? Mum and Mavis, Mum and Mavis … .

I leapt like a cat when Miss Weatherbeaten laid her

hand on my shoulder. Miss Weatherbeaten's words ran over me in a fog of noise and her hand trembled against me. She was on the ground beside me and Rosie was there too. Miss Weatherbeaten picked me up and hugged me on her lap and unfolded my arms from over my head and my legs that were up at my chin, stiff and hard as if I'd been all nailed together. She was shaking all the time she did it and Rosie was against her shoulder and then under her arm. We all three rocked as if we were one scared little kid in the corner of the playground.

'We're going to be fine,' she said. 'There is nothing we can do about anyone else just now, only ourselves, and we have to stay together and be sensible and carry on over the hills because no-one can possibly go back in there. Just keep going and stay with me. Oh, my goodness, stay together whatever we do, and let's not look back any more, just hope and pray that everyone will be alright.'

It was like the words were tumbling out of Miss Weatherbeaten's mouth into my ears, but then I cried and she cried and I could hear Rosie shivering beside us, shivering and hiccoughing like she'd been drinking fizzy juice, but she hadn't, and we all shook trying to find our breath between crying.

And then Miss Weatherbeaten took us to the burn that was running not far off along the side of the path and she cupped her hands so that we could drink some water. Then I drank and I drank some more with my face in the water, I was so thirsty. We washed our faces in it too and we washed Rosie and drank some more because the only drink we'd had all day was the drop of tea at the town hall.

Miss Weatherbeaten said it was true, we didn't know what had happened to Mavis and that it was quite possible she had not survived, but far more likely she had and was somewhere safe and warm right then at that precise moment. She said the best thing I could do for her now was to look after myself and keep myself alive so that I could look after her better when we did find her. She said a lot of other things that made me feel very tired.

It struck me that Miss Weatherbeaten was not at all like the Miss Weatherbeaten I'd known at school who would have banged her ruler on my desk and told me to stop crying IMMEDIATELY or she'd give me something to cry about. She'd have told me to go and wash IMMEDIATELY if I'd been dirty or she'd have promised me that right good seeing-to that she was always on about. It struck me too for the first time that no-one I knew had ever had a right good seeing-to from Miss Weatherbeaten.

When we went back to the big flat rock, Mr Tait was there with his small brown suitcase. He must have followed us after all and I couldn't help being pleased, even though I couldn't decide whether he was a bad man or good one. Miss Weatherbeaten wasn't as surprised as Rosie and I were. Rosie crawled up into his lap and fell asleep straightaway, even though the killer bees were still dropping their bombs, and we sat on the edge of that rock in a little row, me squashed in between Mr Tait, the not-quite-so-scary man with the stick, and Miss Weatherbeaten who was looking very weather-beaten indeed, but whose shoulder was comfortable anyway.

I suppose I must have drifted into a half-sleep,

sleeping the sleep of the living, because I heard them talking but couldn't understand. Broken sentences drifted over my head.

'... very basic, but needs must ... ,' she said.

'... what if there's no room?' he said. 'We won't be the first.'

'... can't surely turn us away?' she said.

'... right thing to do in ... ,' he said

'... no sanitation or water ... ,' she said.

'... safe where we can stay for a few days ... .'

'... bring Rosie back ... ,' she said.

'... no bombs ... no fire ... no bodies ... no danger... .'

Miss Weatherbeaten's shoulder shifted slightly.

'... my closest friend in all the world ... ,' she said. 'All I had.'

'I'm so sorry,' he said.

'... nothing left to lose,' she said.

'Oh,' he said, 'it may not seem like it now but there's always something left, something that's still to come.'

I wondered what he meant. I knew that if I lost my mum and Mavis, I mean really lost them, forever, then I'd want to be dead too, and then I wished I hadn't woken up to have that thought. I opened my eyes and there was that orange glow over the whole town and in the sky I saw the outlines of the planes, like moths fluttering at a candle. On the path that skirted round about us, the white moonlit faces of other Clydebankers floated past us, trudging slowly and methodically up into the hills.

Miss Weatherbeaten carried Rosie a little bit of the way after that until she'd woken up properly. Mr

Tait carried his small brown suitcase and his stick. We crossed fields and moorland, climbed gates and snagged our coats on briar. There were sheep hiding against walls and cows huddled against the farm buildings not far off. The hills rose up, solid, silent and surely indestructible, and trees shifted by the path – pictures of a quiet country life of hard work and peace, a life my dad always wanted but couldn't persuade my mother, a life disturbed now by killer bees.

The path started down the other side of the hill. We stopped and put our backs to a big tree (a beech, Miss Weatherbeaten couldn't help telling us) and Mr Tait opened his suitcase and pulled out some cheese and a loaf of bread which he ripped into pieces and gave to us. Nothing ever tasted so good!

But while we were sitting there, one of those big black killer bees growled right over our heads nearly deafening us all. We ducked. The tree shook angrily and the plane passed on up the valley into which we were peering, our valley of hope. How could that be? It never occurred to me that the Germans might follow us here, that bombs could land in Carbeth too.

'So where can we go now?' I wailed to everyone and no-one.

'To Carbeth, though Lord knows what we'll find there,' said Miss Weatherbeaten. 'All I know is it won't be bombs even if that one did go down there.'

'Will my mum and dad be there?' said Rosie. She was shivering again, almost as much as me. No-one answered her so she had to ask again. Still no-one spoke. Finally Mr Tait told her we had to go to Carbeth for safety. We'd find out about her mum and dad later. Rosie gazed back at the orange sky above Clydebank and tugged at her earlobe.

Mr Tait groaned as he pulled himself upright with the aid of his stick. He seemed to be limping now which I hadn't noticed before, but we needed to move to keep warm. Perhaps he had difficulty with the steep downhill we were on.

A burn was now running along beside us, murmuring quietly to itself but no birds sang in the trees at its edge, and at the bottom of the hill it ran under a bridge which carried a road. I remembered what the smaller of the bad boys and Izzie had said: Kilbowie Road, over the hill, over the stiles, along the main road and turn right at halfway. Halfway to what? I couldn't tell, but we were at a main road so we could go 'along the main road', and off in the distance up ahead we could see another bedraggled little group with bags and bundles shuffling along just like us.

I wondered again how big a mile was and felt sure we had passed many, many miles already. The thought that we might have missed the way began to creep slowly into my mind and gave me something new to think about.

I tried to think about how good it was going to be to get where we were going. There was a rope swing for a start. There was also a rope swing where we went to stay in Ayrshire at the beginning of the war, evacuated without my mum, but I was only on it once because I fell off. They said I was too wee to be on it in the first place. But I knew I could do it. Then my mum had come and taken us back to Clydebank because we weren't clean or properly fed, so I never went on the swing again.

And there was a lily pond at Carbeth. I'd never seen a lily pond but I couldn't help thinking it sounded beautiful. I imagined sunlight sparkling on water, reeds swaying, grasses full of little wild flowers, and lilies like big daisies only pink, or maybe yellow sticking out of the water. I'd never seen lilies, even in books, so I wasn't sure.

And rabbits, he said there were rabbits. My friend had a pet rabbit, a chocolate brown one with black ears. I liked rabbits.

But most of all I thought about how excited the smaller bad boy was when he told me about Carbeth, how he didn't look bad any more at all and it was hard to believe he was the same bad boy who had poked me back into the canal with a stick.

The big moon spread its eerie brightness, lighting our way and glinting on the road. Although we could still hear the boom of the bombers and sometimes they flew over our heads, they didn't drop their bombs on us, only on home. We could still see the orange glow of Clydebank above the hill filling the sky all around, but a certain quietness was there too and the sound of our feet on the hard road, the shuffling of our coats, our sniffs and sighs all took on gigantic proportions.

I began to feel a new kind of tiredness, a tiredness that expects no end. I could feel my bones banging together, crunching at the knees and elbows, fleshless bones, bones that magically held themselves up without muscles, thwack, thwack on the road. Perhaps we were dead after all only we didn't know it. Perhaps we had died and gone to hell but then God had changed his mind and rescued us and we were on our way to heaven. Our faces were blue, and the trees were blue, Mr Tait's brown jacket and trousers were blue, and his small brown suitcase. The fur on Miss Weatherbeaten's collar was blue, and my coat and Rosie's were both super blue, because they were blue to begin with.

I wondered whether to tell Miss Weatherbeaten that we had missed our way and I sang to myself, just quietly so as not to disturb the others, while I wondered. 'Run, rabbit, run, rabbit, run, run, run, Don't let the farmer catch you with his gun.' I wondered if there were any real rabbits there by that road. I couldn't see any but perhaps they were in bed where I should have been or too scared to come out of their holes.

And while I was singing and walking I remembered coming up into the hills with my dad. I suppose it must have been those same hills and it must have been just after we arrived in Clydebank because he left as soon as the war started. We saw rabbits that day, and deer. I wondered if the deer were hiding too. We'd had a picnic by a river and went paddling. Mavis was too wee, I suppose, so it was just Dad and me. He had chocolate and sandwiches and beer and it was sunny and warm, just me and my dad who's missing presumed dead.

And then I remembered the old lady with the bag in the house on the corner who appeared in the downstairs window and was gobbled up by the fire. It was her who said 'missing presumed dead' and she said it about someone else, I think, her husband or son, and not about my dad, and that gave me a warm feeling, that perhaps he was only missing and not actually dead. My mum had been missing and she wasn't dead. Maybe Mavis was the same. 'On the farm, no poor rabbit, comes to harm, because I grab it! Run, rabbit, run!'

A plan was starting to form in my head. We would go to Carbeth and find a hut and then I'd find the hospital my mum was in and bring her to Carbeth and while I was at it I'd find Mavis, probably at the town hall. I'd bring Mavis out here too and we'd stay there in a hut safe from the bombs and Mum would get better. Mavis and I would catch fish in the river and play with the other kids, and we'd find ourselves a proper house and stay forever, and my dad would come home and bring lots of medals and presents for us all. We probably wouldn't go to school either because we'd all had such a terrible time, except perhaps Miss Weatherbeaten who could live with us and teach in the school they had out there, Carbeth school probably. The sun would shine of course, so we'd be happy every day and eat bananas seeing as we hadn't had any since the war started. No-one would ever mention the Germans because we'd have forgotten all about them. We'd all be far too busy being happy.

Apart from my singing, no-one uttered a word for ages, so when Miss Weatherbeaten said she thought we'd arrived it gave me quite a fright. I think I may have been sleepwalking, just on and on and on, and I found it hard to get any words out, just like coming out of a dream.

There was a low stone building by the side of the road and a track running away from us alongside it. The track was full of shadows, dark black in contrast to the brightness of the moon and I was blinded for a while. Rosie started to snivel again at the thought of going up this track so Miss Weatherbeaten and Mr Tait left us at the bottom with Mr Tait's small brown suitcase. We leant against the end of the long low building. It was warm to the touch. There must have been a fire on the other side of it. Rosie and I crouched down into the darkness and I put my arm around her and we slumped onto the grassy verge and fell asleep.

A short while later we were woken by the sound of a giant killer bee buzzing right over our heads. We looked up and saw its blue-grey underbelly soaring over us, over the long low building and through the blackened silhouettes of the trees, and then we heard a deadened BOOM as it dropped its cargo over the hill and another fainter one a few seconds later. We leapt to our feet.

'Miss Weatherbeaten!' we shouted. 'Miss Weatherbeaten!' and Rosie shouted 'Mr Tait! Mum!' (For my part I still wasn't sure about him and his stick, even though he'd been very kind to Miss Weatherbeaten.) We screamed and shouted and nearly started up the dark and shadowy path after them, but not quite. Fortunately Miss Weatherbeaten came running back down the track to us with Mr Tait hobbling a good way behind her.

'It's alright, I'm here,' she said, holding both of us in close and tight, which actually hurt a bit because of all my cuts. 'We've found a hut that's open just up this hill.'

Just up this hill? Grown-ups will tell you anything to get you to do what they want. That hill was the worst hill I ever climbed in the whole of my life. My legs, which had been bones without flesh not so long before, became pure jelly, like the stuff around my mum's meat loaf (which didn't have much meat by the way). It was a steep hill with stones all shapes and sizes to trip you up and it went on for ever and ever. I remember a fence, a little gate, a door that made a squeaky sound like the oven door at home and I remember a foosty sort of smell, a smell I know now as moss on wood, and I remember the candle being lit, the flame sputtering at first and throwing out tiny white sparkles and then the yellow glow that grew and took the blueness from our faces that were gathered all four around it.

There was an old battered sofa against a wall with a crocheted blanket over it. Rosie and I sat down on this until Miss Weatherbeaten told us to get up again and put the blanket over us. We sat side by side with the crocheted blanket tucked under our chins while she and Mr Tait lit another candle and looked about the place. My eyes were closed before I knew it and I fell asleep to the sound of the stove being filled, and I was back in our single end room in Clydebank with the bang of the kettle on the ring and my mum's snores beside me in the bed.

Chapter 8

So we had arrived in Carbeth at last, wherever that was and whatever that meant, so for those of you who're not local perhaps I should explain what all these huts are about. This is what Miss Weatherbeaten told me.

After the last war the landowner allowed some soldiers who came back to build temporary homes on his land. Gradually more came to be built by workers from Glasgow and its smelly factory towns (like Clydebank) so they could have somewhere nice to go at the weekends and for holidays. They were not permanent homes, only escapes, but escape was exactly what we and many others needed. We were neither the first nor the last to arrive. There was no organisation organising us. We were dependent on the charity and goodwill of strangers, and of each other.

When I woke up the following day it wasn't actually the following day, as it turned out, it was the day after that, or very nearly and I think I only woke up because I was starving hungry. It was dark outside and I'd been dreaming of voices whispering and the crackle of fire.

'Welcome back,' said Miss Weatherbeaten.

I had been lying on the old sofa, my back to its back and my arm cradling Rosie who lay alongside me. My head had been in Miss Weatherbeaten's lap and my neck was stiff and sore as a result. I rubbed it and pulled myself upright at the other end of the sofa.

'It's still dark,' I said.

'You missed the daylight,' said Mr Tait from the other side of the stove. He was rubbing his hands over its warmth, and although I had on my old dress, the new dress and the coat the lady at the town hall had given me, and the cut-off petticoat from the fur lady at the Scala, I was jittery with cold. The crochet blanket fell back over Rosie and a tiny hand came out and yanked it jealously in.

'Come over by the fire, Lenny, and have some bread,' said Mr Tait.

I thought about this. He still had his stick and I didn't know where I was. It was dark outside and I wanted the daylight, I wanted to see things. I wanted my mum and Mavis, and I wanted my dad too, come to think of it. What about my dad? Wasn't it about time he got here? I knew he wasn't coming, of course I knew that, and neither were Mavis or my mum, but it's still what I wanted, and I was cross with them all for not being there.

So I didn't answer and Mr Tait didn't ask again. I looked round the room so that I could make up my mind about it.

The first thing I have to tell you is that it was pretty fancy for a hut, so to begin with I thought we were in the wrong place. I thought huts were small brown affairs with thin walls made of strips of wood with only a tiny window for light or no window at all. I thought they were full of spades and flowerpots and jam jars filled with nails, like my uncle's hut when we went to visit him, and hammers and saws and screwdrivers hanging on hooks from the walls. So it didn't seem much like a hut to me. It had more than one room for a start. There was a door over in the corner and another one beside it, although the shadow was too thick to be sure. The stove was small and pot-bellied which meant it had a round door with curved glass in the front. It sat to the left of the sofa where I was. Its door was open and inside there were logs burning and hissing and sighing as if they too were glad they'd finally arrived there. Mr Tait was at the other side of this stove swaying in a wooden rocking chair. His stick was on the floor beside him and beside that there was a three-legged stool like the one in the cow byre at my other uncle's farm that I'd forgotten about completely until then.

Mr Tait tapped the stool with his fingers by way of an invitation to join him, but I wasn't finished looking round the hut, if it really was a hut.

Beyond Miss Weatherbeaten, who was smiling and watching me, there were thick heavy curtains which might have had big green leaves on them except they were past their best, like my mum said she was, and had rips in them and threads hanging down at the bottom. There must have been a window behind them and a bit further along there was another door with a large wooden handle on it, the front door through which we must have come in whenever that must have been. My eyes strayed back to Mr Tait in his rocking chair. He had a brown china teapot in one hand, just like ours at home, and a large cup in the other.

'Tea, Lenny?' he said.

I nodded.

The gurgling of the tea landing in the cup filled the heavy silence of the room. He put the teapot on top of the pot-bellied stove and held the cup out to me. I sat exactly where I was so he put it on the little three-legged milking stool then pointed a round wrinkly finger at it and raised his eyebrows in a questioning sort of way.

I nodded again. Miss Weatherbeaten leant forward over the space between her and him and picked up the tea. I half-expected a row for not having better manners but she handed it to me with a smile. I would almost have preferred the row and then I would have known the world was still in some sort of order, but I took the tea which was lukewarm and strong, just how I like it but without milk, and nodded my thanks.

'It's somewhere around midnight, Lenny, and we haven't heard a squeak out of the Germans so I don't think we need to worry about them any more,' said Mr Tait. 'Not tonight anyway.'

'That's good isn't it, Lenny?' said Miss Weatherbeaten.

I was just about to nod when I noticed a flapping sound like paper in the wind and my eye was caught by a drawing hanging on a single nail above the pot-bellied stove. It was a loose sheet of paper with a line drawing of a horse crossing a field. It swung loosely on its nail, galloping without a rider.

There was a knock at the door.

I looked at Mr Tait and then at Miss Weatherbeaten. Rosie was finally roused. We all four stared at the door as it opened. A boy of about five burst in and came to a sudden halt next to the three-legged milking stool. He ran back to a girl who'd come in behind him and buried his face in her side. I don't think he was expecting us.

'Mrs Mags said to tell you you're welcome to a brew if you'd like to join us,' said the girl, 'and there's a bit of food too if you'd like. We didn't want to wake you before.'

And then with a sharp intake of breath she drew me a look that made my face burn. Her eyes roamed from the top of my head which, let's face it, with most of my hair missing wasn't the head of a girl any more, all the way down my coat, the sticking-out bit of pocket with Mavis's shoe in it, the new dress underneath that, the bit of cut-off petticoat which was sticking out beneath that, and all the way down to my shoes and grimy socks, both of which were mercifully now dry and crispy.

'Are you a boy or a girl?' she said.

I felt my jaw drop. I could almost have said the same to her. She was wearing a pair of men's boots, dungarees of all things, and a thick Aran sweater.

'We'd love to come,' broke in Miss Weatherbeaten, 'if you could just tell us where?'

The girl gave us directions and then, with a final look at Rosie, who was now upright on the sofa with no eyebrows or fringe to cover her sleepiness or confusion, she left taking her small brother with her. A puff of smoke shot out of the pot-belly and unfurled itself towards the ceiling as she closed the door, and the galloping horse swung wildly in the wind.

'Well, that was friendly enough,' said Mr Tait.

I shot him a look.

'Mostly,' he smiled.

'They can't put us out at this time of night, can

they?' said Miss Weatherbeaten. 'Not with these girls, surely?' She had wrinkly bits on her face I hadn't seen before.

'No, of course they won't put us out,' said Mr Tait, but he looked extra wrinkly too. 'They're offering us food.'

I didn't want to go, not a bit, not even a tiny bit but Miss Weatherbeaten said we had to meet the other people there. She pointed out I'd be scared in the hut if I was left by myself, and hungry, and when that didn't work and I still wouldn't stand up to go she stopped being the new Miss Weatherbeaten and went back to being a teacher and told me in no uncertain terms that I was to get up IMMEDIATELY and think of others.

So I did, even though the others I was thinking of probably weren't the ones she meant.

The other hut was quite different from the one I'd woken up in. It seemed to be a lot smaller for a start but that might just have been the number of people crammed in between its wooden walls. There was no floor space at all as far as I could see which wasn't far because Rosie and I were in behind Miss Weatherbeaten. I was hoping the shadows would hide me completely.

There had been a great hullabaloo going on when we'd listened outside the door but it dwindled to a murmur like the shoosh of our fire when we went in. But not for long.

'Move along there, George, Dougie,' said a woman in grey woollen trousers and a jumper that was too small. 'Come on in. John shift the wee one onto your knee and let these poor souls have some room.'

She waved a hand at all these people and a space magically appeared on a bench. We sat, three in a row with Rosie on Miss Weatherbeaten's knee. I, myself, was directly opposite the stove and fully lit by two large candles attached to the wall on either side of it. No shadows for me then, so I hung my head.

Mr Tait, remembering his manners stood up again and offered his hand to the woman, glancing round the company for anyone else's hand that he should shake. There was an old man hidden in the corner, where I wanted to be, in an old cap, a grubby shirt buttoned to his neck and dark-red braces. Mr Tait leant over to him and shook his hand.

'Mr Tait,' said Mr Tait.

'That's my father-in-law,' said the woman, and 'Stop it, you two!' she said, not to the two men but to some little kids who were having a carry-on behind the sofa. They stopped and their faces appeared over the heads of the people sitting on it.

'That's Mr MacInnes,' she went on indicating the old man in the shadows. He smiled and shrank back to where he'd come from.

'This is my son, Sandy,' she said, and a cheer went up, then she went round the room, naming everyone and I started to sweat. It was warm in there with so many bodies, and each time she called a name, every single one of them stared at that person, so-and-so's sister, uncle, brother, neighbour, friend, and they began to cheer and whistle after each name, and soon it was going to be my turn. As the circle swung towards me I hung my head still further and crept into Miss Weatherbeaten's shoulder.

'And there's Mr Tait,' she said, and her voice rippled

round the room. There was a pause. I was next to Mr Tait. 'And Bella from next door, and our Izzie on the other side of our guests ... .'

Izzie?

I stole a glance. It really was Izzie, on the other side of us, two along from Miss Weatherbeaten. What about the bad boys? I stole another quick glance. Yes, they were there too. Miss Weatherbeaten was talking now. I heard 'Rosie' and 'Lenny' and 'Miss Wetherspoon'. Then Mr Tait said he was Mr Tait, which he'd already said, and I wondered why he would do that.

'Well, Mr Tait, Miss Wetherspoon, Rosie and Lenny,' said the woman. 'I'm Mrs MacInnes or Mags. Mrs Mags is what everyone calls me. You are all very welcome here. Someone give them all a toddy.'

I forgot most of the names straightaway.

The general uproar wound up to full volume again and the tiny floor space next to Mrs Mags was filled to bursting by two girls. One was Bella from next door who'd come to invite us over and the other looked just like her and must have been her sister. They were arguing over a kettle and some jam jars and after a minor tussle we were all of us handed a jar, Rosie included, with steaming hot toddy in each of them. Whisky! I couldn't drink that, my mum would kill me, and anyway, it tasted so ... well, I'd no idea how it tasted!

'Extra honey for the wee one,' I heard Mrs Mags say, and a teaspoon clinked round the jam jar.

While I was being handed my steaming brew I became conscious of eyes on me, not staring but sneaking glances, and the two behind the sofa were making very little pretence about it either and were whispering loudly together. Who were all these kids? Surely they didn't all belong to Mrs Mags? I sipped the hot golden liquid and let its whisky slip up my nose and make my eyes water.

Over my head Mr Tait and Miss Weatherbeaten were talking to Mrs Mags about our hut, which of course wasn't ours but somebody else's, somebody who was completely unaware of our presence there. Mrs Mags didn't seem to think that was a problem, for the time being anyway, which was a big relief.

I didn't really want to talk to anyone so I looked at the drawings that were pinned on nails all around the wall. They were like the one over the stove in our hut, which wasn't ours, except that they weren't all horses, just some of them, with the result that cows, sheep, ducks and deer were also galloping round the walls in the heat and the draft caused by so many people in such a wee small space. There was a drawing of a girl's face, directly over the stove, so that her chin bobbed up and down as if she was talking. She was smiling, in her eyes as well as her mouth, and I realised it was Izzie, the bad boys' big sister. People look so different when they smile, and she was smiling now, chattering to the two bad boys, and in her portrait she was chattering away to the whole room.

A bowl of hot rabbit stew and dumpling was thrust into my lap with a twisted fork stuck in it halfway up to the handle. I muttered my thanks and downed the last of the whisky so that I could eat, which made my eyes water all over again. The jam jar was whisked away. We all moved up so that Rosie could have her plate on the bench as a table.

'There you go, darling,' said Mrs Mags.

Rosie looked up at her in the same new dress that I wore with the same dark hair that I had only mine was mostly gone. Then she turned to the bowl and ate with great seriousness until nothing at all was left.

The rabbit stew tasted fantastic, with carrots and onions through it as well as the dumpling.

'No-one slept much last night or the night before so there was too much sleeping today. No-one's tired,' said Mrs Mags. 'I'll come over with you and see that the hut is alright and you've found everything.'

The smaller of the two bad boys from the canal came and took our plates.

'You made it,' he said to me, meaning I'd made it to Carbeth, not that I'd made the stew.

I nodded.

'You didn't find Mavis.'

I shook my head. He didn't say any more, but he stayed there with the dirty plates wobbling in his skinny arms until the forks landed on the floor with a clunk and a clatter.

'Dougie!' said Mrs Mags, with kindly exasperation. 'Deary me!'

I tried a smile but my face hurt.

Mrs Mags was clapping her hands now and chasing everyone out or into bed, I don't know which, but some people disappeared through a door at one end of the room and I could hear the thuds and clumps of elbows against the wooden walls and squabbles over blankets and beds. Others, like Bella and her sister and the two little kids behind the sofa, disappeared out the front door with cheery 'Goodnights', so they didn't all belong to Mrs Mags.

The hut fell quiet.

Mrs Mags took Rosie's hand and we all went out into the cold night, our feet whistling through the long grass, the dew soaking into my socks, wet feet again. She had brought a large green jug of water with her which she set down on a chest of drawers I hadn't noticed before. She lit the candles and opened a door.

'You didn't sleep in the beds?' she said. 'You must sleep in the beds, of course you must!' She held up her candle so that she could peer at us.

'We just fell asleep,' said Miss Weatherbeaten.

'Yes, I bet! Well, there's a double bed in here for you and bunks for the kids in this bit.'

There wasn't room for us all to go through to see but I could hear Mr Tait trying to explain.

'We're not married,' he said.

'No, sorry, of course you're not,' said Mrs Mags. 'Silly me!'

'We're neighbours, some of us,' said Mr Tait. 'We found each other wandering about.'

'Wandering?'

'Rosie was supposed to go to Edinburgh with … who was she going with?' said Mr Tait. His voice was soft. I tiptoed to the door to help explain.

'She lost everyone,' he whispered. 'Everyone. All dead. So the ARP said. I'm not even sure where she lived but so many of the streets are flattened. You can barely get along most of them. The place is on fire. I mean everything. You've seen the orange sky. Shocking, shocking.' He was shaking his head now and I heard a rasp escape him, that I hadn't heard before and he put his hand to his mouth, like I did, I suppose to stop the explosions coming out. Perhaps Mr Tait had bombs inside him too.

Mrs Mags put an arm on Mr Tait's back and so did Miss Weatherbeaten.

'I'm Lenny's teacher,' said Miss Weatherbeaten. 'I lost … I lost people too.' There was a pause while we all waited for her to explain. 'My friend. My closest friend. She was almost family to me. We did everything together. Except that night. She went to the pictures with some other friends.'

'How awful, you poor things!' said Mrs Mags.

'Lenny's mum's legs were crushed so she's in hospital,' said Mr Tait, 'but we don't know where yet.'

There was a pause. Miss Weatherbeaten and Mr Tait seemed to be sniffing. I listened waiting for them to go on. The story wasn't finished.

What about Mavis? I thought. No-one even mentioned Mavis.

And all my sadness and my fury came right up from my toes, like that bomb was going to go off no matter what I did, it was going to catch me right there when I wasn't ready, and I thought of all the terrible things that might have happened to Mavis and how it was all my fault for not looking after her properly, for not keeping her safe from the bad boys, for not running after her fast enough down by the canal. And I thought that no-one even cared.

A gulp of a sob got out, and then another one, and another.

'I want my mum!' said Rosie quietly beside me. 'I want my mum. Where's my mum?'

We both started to wail. I was vaguely aware of the adults standing looking at us, but I felt like my insides were being wrenched out. Finally I yelled 'MAVIS!' at the top of my voice. 'What about Mavis?' And Rosie was yelling too.

'MUM!' she shouted in that voice wee kids can cut the air with, and pulling at her earlobe till it bled.

There were footsteps and suddenly I felt my face being hit and I fell sideways onto Rosie, knocking her flat and landing on top of her. We lay there knotted together in a sodden heaving heap, while Miss Weatherbeaten shouted at us. I don't know what she was saying. I was too busy sobbing, and pulling poor whimpering Rosie out from under the debris that was me.

Mr Tait took Miss Weatherbeaten through to the other room with the double bed, and I heard them both talking at once, then Miss Weatherbeaten said, 'I don't want to live. What's the point?'

Mrs Mags helped me and Rosie untangle ourselves and get up. We were both crying like tired babies, all shuddery and shaky, and Mrs Mags poured water from her big green jug into a bowl that was there and helped us wash our face and hands. She cooed just like my Auntie May who'd come to stay last summer and she took us into a room with two sets of bunk beds and a very small space in between, just wide enough to walk. At the back of the room was a door to outside with a window in it. Right opposite that was another very small hut which was the toilet, or the cludgie. It had a love heart carved into the door for light which didn't make much difference, and a shelf for a candle. She promised not to go away while Rosie and I took our turns, but Rosie wouldn't shut the door, or let us out of her sight, so we had to stand there and look the other way, with the wind blowing through us.

Then Mrs Mags took us back into the hut and closed the door behind us.

'Tomorrow we can try to find your mums and whoever else,' she said. She tucked us both into one of the bottom bunks, kissed us both goodnight even though she didn't know us at all, and left. Then she sneaked back in and said, 'Come over tomorrow and I'll give you some fat to put on your burny face, Lenny.' Then after a bit she said, 'Try to be patient. The grown-ups are upset too.'

I didn't reply. How would she know? She hadn't lost Mavis.

Chapter 9

I slept badly in the same narrow bed as Rosie. She kicked and wriggled when she was asleep, like Mavis did, and before that she whimpered for ages and kept asking about her mum. I couldn't tell her the truth. She must have heard it anyway, surely? Why did she have to keep asking? She wasn't going to believe me. So I said yes, we'd go and find her in the morning, though I knew I was lying. Sometimes that's alright, my mum said.

When she'd finally gone to sleep I started to cry again. It was too quiet now apart from the murmuring of the grown-ups through by the stove and the unfamiliar noises outside the window, and the creaking and moaning of the hut. Too strangely calm and scary at the same time. I was tired of it all. It was time for all this malarkey to stop and everyone to come out and say it was over, it was just a game and look there's your house and your mum and your sister. But no-one did.

I tried very hard to think about the rope swing and the lily pond and how I was going to bring Mavis and my mum out here and we'd all be happy, and my dad would come, but every time I closed my eyes to try to imagine it, all sorts of other things got in the way, and every time I fell asleep I saw things I didn't want to see, things I'd been told not to look at, things I'd only myself to blame for seeing, and for seeing again and again in the dark.

So I kept waking up just as I was drifting off to sleep and once when I woke up I saw Miss Weatherbeaten in the other bunk bed. Her head was sticking up above the covers and her lips were dark, her hair tied over her ear with a clasp and her eyes weren't properly shut. I got out of bed to shake her but instead stood over her peering to see if she was breathing. The only light we had was a glimmer of moonlight through a small pane in the door. She didn't seem to see me, even though her eyes were half-open.

I was still upset with Miss Weatherbeaten for slapping me, even though she was a grown-up and a teacher. Only my gran who came last summer ever did that, apart from my mum and that's different, and my mum nearly slapped my gran back. I was scared Miss Weatherbeaten might do it again, but I also wondered if she was sleeping the sleep of the dead, like the lady in the sea of bricks, so after a bit I gave her a little poke and she sat up and nearly bumped her head on the top bunk. She wasn't happy about that but she didn't slap me again. I got back into bed with Rosie feeling better now that I knew Miss Weatherbeaten was alive.

The next time I woke up Miss Weatherbeaten was gone but I could hear her in the stove room putting coal on the fire and sniffing. Mr Tait must have been in the big double bed. So I went back to sleep and dreamt about Mavis and my mum buried in bricks or with their hands off, or my mum's legs lying on the road, crossed like when she's in bed, but with blood on them. When I woke up that time Miss Weatherbeaten was back in the bunk bed, looking just like she had the last time so I had to tell myself she was alright over and over again, over and over again.

The next time I woke after that I smelled smoke and whisky, and I had to get up and check round the whole hut to make sure it was alright and no-one was going to fall through anything or be gobbled up by big orange flames. I had a good look at the door to outside with the little pane of glass, just to make sure it was still there. Miss Weatherbeaten was awake too when I went back to bed. She smiled at me but I was too busy tucking myself in, and Rosie was crying again. I couldn't smell the smoke and whisky any more. Maybe the smells were just in my head.

In the morning the room had changed. It was full of sunlight which danced in little splotches in a square on the floor. There was a faded rag rug in blue and brown and yellow and under that it was wood. The walls were wooden too but painted white and the bunk beds were white too. The bed Miss Weatherbeaten had slept in was empty, its covers flung back against the wall, whitish sheets crumpled where she had lain. Rosie was gone and I was cold even though our new blue coats were piled on top of the blankets on top of me, cold without Mum or Mavis. There was a funny smell, like the inside of Mr Tait's shelter, dank like dungeons, a mouldy wet smell even though the room looked as fresh as daisies, as my Auntie May would say.

Through in the stove room the grown-ups were talking again. I could hear them say Rosie's name but not Rosie, and I could hear the wind outside and guessed there were trees nearby, perhaps the one with the rope swing. Something thudded against the outside wall, a little thud, perhaps the size of Rosie, but then Rosie reappeared beside me from the stove room, so it couldn't have been her.

She was swinging from one foot to the other. She had her new blue dress back on and her dark hair was sticking out at either side of her face like my dad's sidies (that's sideburns in case you didn't know). She was fiddling with her earlobe again and had another big snotter bulging down from one nostril.

'Can we go and find my mum now?' she said.

'Rosie … .'

'I need a wee.'

'Good for you.'

'You have to come with me.'

'No, I don't.'

'Yes, you do.'

'Ask Miss Weatherbeaten. Miss Weather … .'

'I don't like Miss Weatherbee.'

There was another thump against the outside wall. We held our breath to listen.

'What's that?' she said in a loud whisper, a stage whisper as my … .

'What's that?' she said louder now, pulling at her earlobe.

'Stop it, Rosie,' I said. 'You're scaring me. It's only other kids playing.'

'What are they playing?'

We listened again.

'War,' I said. 'They're playing war. Get back into bed Rosie. It's cold.'

'I need a wee,' she said.

Resigned now, I got out of bed and pulled my new green dress over my head, over the cut-off petticoat that I'd been wearing. My shoes were by the stove, along with my socks, too far away to be of use. The rag rug was soft under my naked feet and cold, but not half as cold as the dewy grass between the little door with the pane of glass and the cludgie. We checked left and right to make sure it was safe, no killer bees or gypsy moths, no Gerry invaders. The sounds of boyish war raged on from distant trees and huts.

'Hurry up!' I said, once Rosie was up on the throne, which is what our neighbour called it. 'Hurry up!'

She whined and kicked the door.

'Come on!' I said. I didn't want to think about the neighbours at home.

'Rosie!'

Two boys suddenly appeared round the corner of the hut, their arms outstretched like wings, engine noises spewing from their mouth, then 'ack-ack-ack-ack-ack!' they went, with nasty mean looks on their faces. They screeched to a halt beside us. Rosie was on her feet and decent in double-quick time.

'Well, look who's here,' said one of the two. It was the older bad boy from the canal, the baddest bad boy. The other, Sandy, I recognised from Mrs Mags's hut the night before.

'Sorry,' said the other one. He had sandy-brown hair and was tall, once he'd stopped stooping to be a plane. He looked at me and Rosie, standing in the wet grass holding onto each other. 'Sorry!'

'Don't be sorry,' said the bad boy. 'That's the girl who pushed me into the canal, only now she's a boy so we can hit her if we like … .'

'Shut up, George!' said the sandy-haired boy.

George the bad boy drew out a pretend machine gun and blasted us away, 'ack-ack-ack-ack-ack!' and ran off round the hut again. I had been going to point out that I hadn't actually pushed him in the canal. It was his brother I'd pushed. He'd fallen in all by himself, with no help from anyone.

The sandy-haired boy stared at me. I must have been a sight, and I know he didn't mean any harm and was trying to be nice but I wished very much that he would go away, or at least look at something else.

'Sorry,' he said again.

'You can't help being stupid,' I said, before I could stop myself. He looked stung and immediately I wanted to say sorry but he'd already said too many sorrys and I thought he might think I was copying him if I did, but I heard it inside my head. Once he was round the corner I could hear his bomber bee plane start its engines again. Yes, stupid. I was right.

Rosie tried to insist on the cludgie door being wide open while I went to the toilet but settled finally for it being open about as wide as my hand. I let her watch me so that I couldn't disappear. Then we went round to the front of the hut.

This is what we saw.

Green.

Green, pale green and lots of it but some brown and brownish-yellow and a bright-blue sky with white wispy clouds overhead as if nothing had happened.

There was grass everywhere, short winter grass, green but winter yellow too, not like the stuff in the park at home. Some of it was thick and long as if it would tangle itself around your ankles if you tried to run across it and it was sprinkled with big juicy drops of dew. There were trees all around the edges of the field, trees with just the beginnings of their new spring leaves twittering in the wind as if they had been shocked awake by the day. Berry bushes raged like fires blown in the lightening breeze, shaking off their last rotting berries, or reaching out to the new sunshine for its tiny bit of warmth. Yellow broom gathered in thickets here and there between the huts.

The huts were green too, but a different green. They were green like window frames, green like park benches, green like my new green dress, and they were sprinkled across the field all any-old-how, this way and that, and in between them were other newer huts, some half-built with jagged bits of wood sticking out, and sky where the roof should have been. These new huts were different colours, the softer colours of wood, some old and some fresh, some with words on them that I couldn't make out over the distance. One was an old bus and not a hut at all, but it had curtains in the windows and a chimney on its roof.

Away up at the top of the hill and over to one side was a big wide tree, looking like the one we'd leant against on the way over from Clydebank, a beech probably. There were huts on either side and kids like me all around it. The tree was shaking at one side and I realised it was the rope-swing tree!

Voices drifted across, shrieks of delight and fear. I so wanted to run across that yellow tangly grass and leap onto the rope and swing from one side to the other, and to have all those kids shrieking for me because I was going too high, higher than all the others, higher than all of them, right up into the branches and then down to the ground and back up again. But they'd all laugh at me, a boy in a dress who couldn't hang on to a rope to save her life, as my dad used to say.

'Brruumm-brruumm-brruumm!' The boys came round the hut again and some others flew down the hill towards them. Rosie and I collapsed in a little heap, boom-crash against the front door, hearts pounding. 'Brruumm-brruumm-brum-de-brum!'

The door opened and we fell back inside.

'How did you get out there?' said Miss Weatherbeaten. She helped us up while I waited for my heart to be still. It hurt to beat so hard and I felt silly for being scared of two stupid boys.

'Stupid boys!' she said as if she'd heard my thoughts.

'Stupid boys!' said Rosie in her wee girl's voice, fumbling for my hand.

Mr Tait got up out of the rocking chair by the fire, and came over.

'Lenny,' he said. 'Rosie. How are you this morning? What did you find out there? Anything interesting? Apart from stupid boys, I mean. Rabbits? Anything?'

An adult doing his best, I suppose. He was trying to be friendly but he still had his stick. I could see it next to the chair where he'd left it.

'No, nothing,' I said.

'Nothing?' he said.

Miss Weatherbeaten laughed, but only for a second.

'What did you see out there, Lenny?' she said.

'It's sunny.'

I went back into the little bedroom with the bunks and put my cold bare feet on the soft rag rug.

'Lenny,' said Miss Weatherbeaten.

She'd followed me in there. She was too tall for that room. She shouldn't have been in there.

'Lenny,' she said again. 'I know this is hard but there's no need to be rude to people.'

'I'm not being rude.'

'Well, actually you are.'

'No, I'm not. Leave me alone.'

'Don't you dare talk to me like that!' she said.

'I'm not at school and you're not my mum.'

Mr Tait appeared over her shoulder. Miss Weatherbeaten straightened up with a sharp intake of breath. He tapped her gently on the arm and she left the room with a snort. I could hear her talking to Rosie. Worry prickled at my neck.

Mr Tait stood there a minute or two.

'What a nice little room!' he said after a bit. 'Where does this door lead to?'

'What? I mean, pardon?' I said. 'The cludgie.'

'Well, that's handy!' he said in a cheery voice. 'I thought you had to go out the front and round. Can I open it?'

I nodded. He opened it. The door had a brass, oval door handle with a string bag hanging from it that I hadn't noticed before. It squeaked a little when he turned it. A blaze of sunshine burst through and lit up the white walls so that I was suddenly dazzled. His shadow was like balm on my eyes as he moved into the light and then he slipped through and the brightness hit me again.

'You didn't tell me about the bench,' he said.

What bench? I thought. I didn't see a bench.

'Bit rough and ready but very comfortable.'

There was a big gust of wind in the bushes and some dry leaves floated past the door.

'Oh, dear, I left my stick,' he said. 'I'll never get up again.'

No stick?

'You didn't tell me how lovely it was out here. How lucky we are to have such a beautiful day!'

The drones of the far-off killer boy bees came closer again. I sat on the edge of the bottom bunk and leant on my hands. I put my fingers in my ears. I didn't like that sound. It was making me feel sick and I didn't like to feel sick like that. I had to listen really, I knew I had to, just in case, but I had to not listen too, so it made a whirlpool in my stomach and I put my head down onto my knees and my palms flat over my ears and when that didn't work I put both thumbs onto the little extra flap bits at the front of my ears and pressed hard right inside until all I could hear was my breath, fast breath, fast and shallow, and in my breath I could hear the squeaky seesaw in the park at home and that made me feel not sick again.

When I took my thumbs off my ears again I could hear Mr Tait talking to someone outside.

'Perhaps you could play something else, just for now?' he was saying. 'Would that be alright? What about cowboys and Indians? It's just the girls, you know … .'

'What's that got to do with us?' It was the big bad boy, George. I didn't like him and he didn't like me.

'Well, quite a lot actually,' said Mr Tait.

'Yeah?'

'Shut up, George.' It was the other boy, Sandy.

'Oh, now, shut up is not very nice either,' said Mr Tait. 'How old are you two? Eleven, twelve? And I thought you were about fourteen. Deary me, Mr Tait, you are losing your touch!'

'I don't care,' said big bad George. 'You shouldn't be in there. It's not your hut and they'll be back here next weekend and you lot'll have to be out.'

'Shut up, George,' said Sandy.

'Shut up, yourself!' said bad George.

Then the swish of the tangly wet grass told me George'd left.

'Oh, dear, what a charmer!' said Mr Tait.

'Sorry about him, sir, Mr Tait,' said Sandy.

'Why?' said Mr Tait, in his nice steady voice. 'You don't need to apologise for him. You didn't do much wrong, only a couple of shut-ups. Apart from that you seem nice enough. His parents are still in Clydebank, so he's bound to be a bit anxious.'

'He's always like that.'

'Would you like to join me on this bench?' said Mr Tait. 'Lenny won't come out. She thinks I'm a bad man with a big stick. So I have to sit here all by myself.'

How did he know I thought that? I kept very still on the bed, crouched because I couldn't sit straight because of the top bunk. I pretended I wasn't there.

'She thinks I'm stupid,' said Sandy.

'Well, perhaps playing Gerries and Brits wasn't the brightest thing to do, today, here. They've been through a lot.'

'Lenny looks as though she's been through a hedge backwards,' said Sandy. 'I thought she was a boy.'

'She's got the grit of a boy,' said Mr Tait. 'She's tough like her mother but she's seen things no-one should ever see. She's run through fire, that girl, and walked on glass, and starved for a day-and-a-half, and then walked over the hill through the night. You should ask her and maybe she'll tell you what else she did, how else she kept herself alive to tell the tale. What's the point in surviving to tell the tale if no-one bothers to ask you?'

I didn't really want to be asked. I just wanted to know when we were going to go and find Mavis and my mum. I didn't want to have to tell some stupid boy, but I liked Mr Tait saying I had grit, even though it hadn't felt like it at the time and I certainly didn't feel like it right then.

'She's the bravest little girl I've ever come across, to tell the truth.'

I liked being brave, but I wasn't sure about being the bravest little girl he'd ever come across. And after all, I wasn't little, I was big, too big to be so scared right there on that bunk bed miles from any Germans or bombs or anything.

'I don't think she'd want me to ask,' said Sandy.

No, you're right, I didn't.

'Well, perhaps not today, but some day soon, if we're still here. You don't want us to leave before you've got round to it, do you? And then it'd be too late, unless we can find a way to stay longer.'

'You can ask my dad when he gets here at the weekend,' said Sandy, 'or go and see Old Barney. He's given us some more ground to build on, over the hill, in that direction, or you can stay here on this bit, Paterson's Ground. It goes right up to the fence and down to the pub and a bit over that way too.'

'Old Barmy? Not a name that bodes well,' said Mr Tait with a laugh.

'Not Barmy. Barney, like on a farm, like an owl, a barn owl,' said Sandy. 'He's the gaffer.'

'So you don't own the hut?'

'Oh, yes,' said the sandy boy. 'We own the hut, everyone owns their huts, we built them after all, with anything we could find. I put the roof on the kitchen lean-to on ours. With my dad.'

'But Barmy Barney owns the land, or this man Paterson owns this bit?' said Mr Tait.

I got bored after a while. It was all too complicated, this hut business, with Patersons and Barmys, so I drifted off to consider whether anything I had done was as brave as Mr Tait had said it was, but that took me back to the things I shouldn't have seen, things that it was my own fault that I saw, and that made me sick again, so I tried extra hard to listen to them again, and wished Mavis was there to look after.

'So it's your granddad, is it?' said Mr Tait. 'Well, I think they're lovely. I must congratulate him on his expertise. I think my favourite is the one over the stove. Is that your cousin?'

'Yes, that's Izzie,' said Sandy.

'I do a bit of painting myself,' said Mr Tait.

That was a surprise. He didn't look like the sort of person who would paint pictures and get all messy.

There was a pause while no-one spoke. I wondered if they could hear my breathing. Some distance away I heard killer George in his pretend plane.

Then I heard Sandy taking his leave, and then it was just me and Mr Tait.

'Oh, there's a rabbit!' he said.

I half-jumped up to go and see before I'd realised and stopped myself. I sat back down, my stomach all churning. The wind breathed through the bushes.

'Actually my favourite is the one of the horse above our stove,' he said. 'Looks like it's galloping in the wind. Which one's your favourite?'

Chapter 10

I didn't reply, of course I didn't. But I did want to see the rabbits and I was getting hungry. I had no idea what time it was, or even whether it was morning or afternoon, but I knew I was ravenous. He must have heard my feet.

'Lenny, if you're going through to the front perhaps you could bring me my stick. It's beside the rocking chair. This bench is a little low and I'm having trouble getting up.'

Again I didn't reply.

'Lenny?'

I'd heard him but I was halfway gone.

Rosie and Miss Weatherbeaten were sitting on the front step of the hut. There was a little overhang of the roof with enough room beneath it for two chairs. But there weren't any chairs so they just sat on the step. They had jam sandwiches in their hands and were sitting together but with a distance of two feet between them. Rosie was watching Miss Weatherbeaten intently over the top of her sandwich. She had jam on the end of her nose.

'There's a sandwich for you on the dresser,' said Miss Weatherbeaten.

I went back in for the sandwich.

'Take Mr Tait his stick first, Lenny. That's his bread you're eating,' she said.

I was so hungry I'd eaten most of the sandwich before I got back to him. I handed him the stick.

'Lenny … ,' he said, before I could escape.

'When are we going to find Mavis and my mum?' I interrupted him.

'Could I please have a sandwich too?' he interrupted back.

I looked at the crust in my hand. Mavis. She always made a fuss about crusts and I had to show her you just had to eat them.

I had just stepped out the back door and given him his sandwich when there was a bang, and then another, and then another and before I knew it I was back inside the mouth of the door, back against the wall with my heart thumping, just like it was a close mouth on Kilbowie Road. I heard a thwack against the side of the hut from roughly where Mr Tait was sitting, followed by, 'Ow!'

While I was still standing there he appeared in the doorway rubbing the back of his head with his hand.

'What was that?' I breathed.

'Oh, my goodness!' he said. 'What a fright!' He laughed and hung onto the door and patted his chest. 'Are you okay?'

'What is it?' I said.

'It's the sound of a sheet of wood being dropped on another sheet of wood, or something like that.'

There was another sound, one which I recognised as a hammer, bang, bang, bang, on a nail, bang, bang, bang, on wood. I'd heard that sound at my uncle's house when he and my dad were building the hen coop. I wondered if there were hen coops here. We hadn't stayed long enough to see my uncle's hens, and then the war started and they both went away. I didn't mind that sound once I knew what it was, but my heart thumped anyway.

'Lenny, will you come and sit with me on the bench, please?' said Mr Tait.

I didn't reply.

'Please?' he said. 'I want to tell you something that's really quite important.'

The funny thing about Mr Tait was that despite being a scary man with a big stick for naughty kids like me, he had a very soft voice, a very kind voice, and he had given us all his food from his little brown suitcase, even though he didn't really know any of us, and he'd walked over the hills with us in the middle of the night when he could have stayed at home in his shelter, though to be fair, his shelter was horrible and dark, his home was destroyed and it had that woman's face in the bricks.

And when he said he had something important to tell me I didn't really want to know because important things might be things about Mavis or my mum that weren't the things I wanted to hear. They might not be the good news that they were alright and were on their way to Carbeth. What a lovely thought that was, Mum and Mavis walking over the hill on their way to here!

So I stayed right there against the wall at the end of the bunk beds while Mr Tait shuffled about at the back door. Finally he slid down onto the doorstep and made himself comfortable there with his back to me. I looked at the top of his head while he spoke. I could actually see the top of his head and not just his hair. The skin there was white, whiter than his grey hair and it was full of grit, and I wondered if that was what I had inside me. It certainly felt like that sort of grit that was inside of me, as if the bombs and the noise had gone right through my skin and inside my very flesh so that I couldn't get it out. It wasn't the kind of grit I had hoped he'd meant.

'I just wanted to tell you not to be scared now,' he said, 'and whenever you get a fright, like that fright that we just had, just keep reminding yourself that you're safe now. Look at this lovely place! How could we be anything but safe here?'

George, the killer bomber, puttered away in the distance. I listened to his drone until it died. Of course I'm not scared, I wanted to say, not of the killer bees, not really. But I was scared of him and of Miss Weatherbeaten and of the bad boys and Bella who thought I was a boy. I was scared to think certain things; I was scared of what I saw when I closed my eyes. I was scared of … .

I looked at the top of his head again. I was scared of not having grit. I was scared of being a jelly that couldn't stand up. I flexed my knees to make sure, my back still flat against the white wooden wall.

'I'm not scared,' I said.

'No,' he said, and I thought he might be secretly laughing at me. 'But when you get a fright like that just remember that all this will pass, this jumpiness and f … and worry.'

'I'm not scared,' I insisted. Wasn't he listening? What was the point in talking if he wasn't going to listen? 'I'm going to walk back over and find Mavis,' I said.

I hadn't really thought about this; it just came out,

and then I suddenly remembered something odd that he'd said earlier on.

'How do you know I'm tough like my mother?' I said.

'I work at Singers.'

'You know my mum?' My back came off the wall.

'Yes.'

I didn't know what to ask him then so I stood there with this strange piece of news and let my mouth hang open in readiness.

'Oh, look, there's those rabbits back again,' he said.

I nearly looked out the door, so nearly, but I stopped myself just in time.

'So you know my mum,' I said, still trying to understand.

'Yes,' he said. 'It was me who identified her when they pulled her out, remember?'

'No!' I didn't want to hear it. I didn't want to see it.

'And I know your dad is gone,' he said. 'Lenny, come out here and see the rabbits. Don't be hiding in there. They seem to have a burrow somewhere over there. Come on. Come and have a look.'

He stood up from the step and I saw him wobble and grab the door jamb to steady himself, so I had to go and look, and he was right, there really were four little brown rabbits in amongst the grass, only about ten feet away, their little white tails bobbing in a sea of green and pale yellow so you couldn't lose them in the shadows. They were different from my friend's rabbit, not so brown and their ears weren't black, but as soon as I came off the doorstep they ran leaping into the bushes in a great panic. Run, rabbit, run, just like in the song, except I didn't have a gun.

'How was she?' I said. I was back inside the door again. He was leaning on the wall outside.

'She was drowsy and couldn't speak very well,' he said. 'That's why I had to tell them who she was, and her legs didn't look very good, but the rest of her was fine I think. I don't know. But she's in safe hands.'

'So she's … ?'

'She's alright. We'll just have to wait and see.'

'She's not going to die?'

'I don't think so. We need to wait and see. You know this is Sunday? Perhaps we should say a little prayer for her.'

'So she didn't say anything about me, or Mavis?'

'Only that she wouldn't leave without you and Mavis. Not at first.'

I felt like my throat had been torn out. I couldn't speak. Then he said what I already knew, 'We don't know which hospital she's in but there aren't that many hospitals and that's what the communication centre at the town hall is for. They'll be able to tell us where she is.'

'That's where I'll have to go then. Today,' I said. There was a pause. I noticed his hands were trembling a bit. Perhaps it was the cold breeze.

'What about a little prayer then?' he said, and although I knew my mum didn't really like prayers, I thought any little bit would help, which is what my gran says, any little bit helps, and anyway I was sort of praying already, only it was more like wishing extra hard and promising to be good and to never let Mavis out of my sight ever again once I'd got her back.

So I didn't reply and he started to pray, right there at the back step leaning against the wall, and his voice went softer than anything, softer than the wind that was tickling my neck, softer than the hair on a rabbit's back, softer than Rosie's whisper in the night.

'Dear God,' he said (like he was writing God a letter). 'Dear God, please make sure Lenny's mum and Mavis are alright and bring them safely to us here as soon as possible. Amen.'

It was like he'd heard the wishing inside my head and I looked down and saw my tears make little wet dots on the rag rug so that the grey-blue was purple and the yellow-brown was orange, and I sniffed back the snotters and wiped them on the sleeve of my new green dress.

The shoe! Mavis's shoe! I didn't have my old dress on so I didn't have her shoe.

'Oh!' I cried and started pulling at the covers of the bed where Rosie and I had slept. Mr Tait's shadow fell over it. 'I can't see! I can't see! Out of the way!' I said and I pulled at the blankets until everything was all over the floor. Tangled up in the sheet I found the torn remnants of my dress with the shoe still in its pocket.

I looked up at Mr Tait who was in the room now to the side of the door so the light could get through. It was the first time I'd actually looked at him. He was a bit blurry because I still had tears in my eyes and he looked at me, then looked away, then looked at me again. This wasn't his room. It wasn't mine either. I pulled the shoe out of its pocket and waved it at him by way of explanation.

'Mavis's?' he said.

I nodded.

He seemed to be going to say something but it was me that spoke first.

'It's very quiet. Where's Rosie?'

I didn't wait for him to answer; how would he know anyway?

They weren't on the front step, or anywhere I could see from the front step. I still had my ripped-up dress in my hand with Mavis's shoe in the pocket. I wrapped my hand round the pocket and squeezed and squeezed. I didn't want to go out there, but I had to find Rosie, so I stood on the little creaky front doorstep and shouted.

'Rosie!' I shouted. 'Rosie! Come back here now! Rosie!' I didn't shout very loud to begin with because I didn't want anyone but her to hear me, but when she didn't come, when no-one else came except Mr Tait who I could feel standing behind me with his stick, I shouted a bit louder.

'Lenny,' said Mr Tait.

'Rosie!' I said, louder still. 'Got to find Rosie,' I told Mr Tait, in case he hadn't realised. 'Rosie!'

I stepped out onto the little muddy bit by the front door so that my shouts would carry further.

'Lenny, she's fine,' he said, as if I was listening. 'She's with Miss Wetherspoon.'

'Rosie,' I shouted again. That sickness began to rise again and I thought I'd lose my jammy piece that I'd just eaten. Bang, bang, bang went my heart, and my ears were hot. Bang, bang, bang went the hammer on the fallen pieces of wood. Boom-crash went the bomb, and I fell back over the doorstep onto the bit where the chairs should have been and landed on my bottom. I banged my elbow on the hut wall on the way down.

Mr Tait and his wobbly legs bent down to help me back up. He took me inside the room and sat me on the old sofa then he went straight back outside with his stick and started shouting for Rosie. I was scared for her, scared for her being out there on her own, and scared for her being with Miss Weatherbeaten, so I crept over and watched him through the window, the same window that had been behind the dark-green leafy curtains with the threads hanging down the night before. He went over to the big beech tree with the rope swing, still calling her name, and hobbling very badly with his stick. There were people there that I hadn't noticed and they pulled back to let him through, and just for a second I saw her.

I saw Rosie.

She was on the rope swing, her new blue dress all puffed out by the wind as she glided forward and then sucked back along her legs as she swung back. Her hands gripped the rope as tight as could be and her face was flushed with delight. She was flushed with delight even though I knew her whole family was dead, and she just wouldn't hear it.

Miss Weatherbeaten was hovering about, ready to catch Rosie if she fell off. She had on her coat with the furry collar. There was still dirt all down it, as if she hadn't even shaken it, waiting for the wind to shake it for her I suppose. She was smiling too. Didn't she care that she'd lost her very close friend? Didn't it matter? Maybe the friend wasn't important after all but still I was annoyed with her for smiling like that and with Rosie for going off without telling me and for going with Miss Weatherbeaten, and to the rope swing of all places, which I was dying to have a go on but couldn't!

Mr Tait stayed where he was, perhaps the ground was too rough for him to go any further, but he waved first at Miss Weatherbeaten and then at Rosie, and some voices drifted down the hill and through the open door of the hut and right into the room where I sat watching by the window.

' … flying … ' I heard Rosie say.

Other voices I didn't know made those stupid whooping noises people always make to little kids.

Mr Tait started coming back down the hill towards me. I went and sat back on the sofa where he'd left me. The horse over the stove was galloping in the wind from the door. The glass on the stove door was black. Mr Tait was taking a very long time. I looked at the glass door and it began to worry me. It was very dark and I thought I'd better not get too close, just in case it blew out like the glass in our fanlight at home, so I got off the sofa and went and sat on the floor by the dresser so that I could look out from the shadows over the grass and up to the big tree with the rope swing and all the people gathered round it. Mr Tait was nowhere to be seen.

There was no ticking clock in that hut like there was in our house, even though there were three-and-a-half rooms in there and we only had one, and I wondered how anyone knew when to go to school or to work (I didn't know the huts were only meant for holidays and weekends), and I wondered for the first time about the people who lived there, the people whose hut we had broken into like thieves. What if they just arrived right there and then and found crumbs on their floor and their beds all slept in and unmade?

Mr Tait and Mrs Mags, from the other hut, suddenly arrived and startled me.

'Oh!' said Mrs Mags, who was startled too. 'I didn't see you there in the corner.'

I didn't reply.

'Lenny, Mrs Mags is talking to you,' said Mr Tait.

I stood up.

'Lenny,' said Mrs Mags, turning my name over in her mouth. 'What's that short for, then?'

I didn't answer.

'Lenny?' said Mr Tait, egging me on.

I hugged the shadows.

'It's short for Leonora, I think, isn't that right, Lenny?' he said.

How did he know, nosey parker? It's none of his business what my name is. He's not my dad. Lenny is my dad, short for Leonard. Leonard Gillespie. Lenny. Like my dad. Missing presumed dead. Missing.

'Mrs Mags has kindly boiled some water for you to have a bath in,' said Mr Tait in his soft voice.

Was he mad? I didn't have time for a bath. It must be at least lunchtime and we still hadn't set off to find Mavis and my mum.

'I was going to bring it over here,' said Mrs Mags, 'but your stove's gone out so you'd better come over to ours and we'll close all the curtains. Mr Tait and I will make sure nobody disturbs you.'

I imagined Mr Tait standing guard outside the door with his big stick, waving it at George the bad boy.

Rosie and Miss Weatherbeaten arrived in the doorway, throwing more shadows over me.

'How kind!' said Miss Weatherbeaten to Mrs Mags when she heard about the bath plan, and then they got more and more excited, or so it seemed, at the idea of getting our stove warmed up and of filling a proper tin bath in front of it and putting me in it and then putting Rosie in it, and I squashed myself up against the wall in the shadows behind the dresser where they seemed to barely notice me again, and I closed my eyes and stuck my thumbs back in my ears so that I couldn't hear them talking or the bang, bang, bang of the hammer further down the field.

So it gave me quite a jolt when I felt Rosie slip her arm around my back, and before I knew it I'd hit her on the head, a big whack over her ear. I don't know who was more upset, Rosie, me or Miss Weatherbeaten and, as if I was doing everything I possibly could to make things worse, I shouted at Rosie to never run away from me again, ever. I shouted it really loud so that I cut through all the friendliness of the grown-ups and a great big silence came crashing down on us.

Poor Rosie's eyes filled up and she ran back to where Miss Weatherbeaten was standing by the stove and disappeared into her big coat with the old-fashioned furry collar. They all stared at me in horror, Miss Weatherbeaten, Mrs Mags and Mr Tait, so I came out of the shadows and pushed past them all, bouncing off Mrs Mags's big round tummy and ran into the little bunk room at the back and hurled myself onto the bed Rosie and I had slept in. I pulled the covers around my ears so that I wouldn't have to listen to them being angry with me, and I wouldn't have to listen to Rosie sobbing again, especially seeing as it was all my fault.

A strange silence fell.

A little while later Miss Weatherbeaten came

through and shut the back door with a snap. I heard her stop by the bed then move on back through to the stove room, and when I stuck my head over the blankets I could smell coal being lit in the stove, a wisp of smoke hanging between the bunks. The sun had stopped beaming in the little window on the door and the room was cold, even though I was under the covers. I got scared again because no-one had come to give me a row for hitting Rosie and shouting at her, which is what they should have done because it was a terrible thing to do to poor Rosie who'd lost all her family, all dead and gone, when all I had to worry about was Mavis, missing presumed dead, and my mum's legs.

It had gone very quiet through there. No-one was moving and I think Mrs Mags must have gone. Miss Weatherbeaten had a louder voice than Mr Tait, quite high and piercing, especially when she was being a teacher, but Mr Tait's voice seemed to carry right through the hut, even though it was soft, so that I could hear what he said better than I could hear her.

'She's right, you know, Rosie,' he was saying. 'You must always tell us where you are. Most especially you must always tell Lenny where you are. She'd be so upset to lose you.'

'But Mr Tait, she was with me. She was perfectly safe,' said Miss Weatherbeaten. 'Surely as long as one of us knows where they are … ?'

'Yes, but Lenny didn't know she was safe. Perhaps just for now we should always tell each other where we are, all four of us, even if we're only going outside for a little sit, or to the … the back,' he said. The cludgie is what he meant.

'I'm not sure Lenny deserves such consideration,' said Miss Weatherbeaten. She was louder now so I could hear her. I wondered if it was deliberate. My Auntie May does that too when she's annoyed with you. 'And now she's hit poor Rosie. You'd think she'd have a bit more understanding.'

'And you hit Lenny yesterday,' said Mr Tait.

There was a shocked silence. Nobody moved, not a floorboard creaked.

'That was different,' said Miss Weatherbeaten, after a while. 'She was hysterical.'

'She's nine,' said Mr Tait. 'She's seen things no-one should ever see. She doesn't know where her sister is or even whether she's alive. She doesn't even know where her mother is. I don't think she deserves to be hit.'

There was another long silence.

'I know how hard your loss is,' said Mr Tait.

The covers were down from my ears now, ears that were straining to get back through the bunk-room door to hear more, but Miss Weatherbeaten didn't reply. When Miss Weatherbeaten did start talking again it was in such a quiet voice I couldn't make her out at all. Then there was a loud bang, bang, bang as someone tapped the side of the stove with the poker or something like that which made my heart jump and race all over again. I tried to remember what Mr Tait had said about what to do if you get a fright like the one we had this morning, but I couldn't remember anything, my heart was beating so fast. I even forgot what I was trying to hear and why it had been so important, and then I got very tired and slumped back down under the covers.

After a bit I realised Rosie was standing at the

doorway. She was pulling her earlobe, of course, so I was instantly cross with her, which I didn't mean to be. I didn't mean to be so mean.

'Rosie,' I said. 'I'm sorry. I didn't mean to hit you, and I didn't mean to shout.'

Rosie didn't say anything, but she sprang like one of the cats in our back court, and sat down on the bed beside me. When she'd been there for a whole five seconds she wriggled down and stretched out beside me and put her arm around my middle. I put my arm round her too and hugged her in tight, wishing she was Mavis.

'Sorry,' I said again, grateful for her warmth.

'That's alright,' she said. 'Mr Tait told Miss Weather we're going to go over the hill to stay in a tent. I've never been in a tent.'

'What hill? What tent?' I said.

'I don't know. Don't be angry!' she said.

'I'm not angry!' I said, angrily. 'I don't want to go and stay in a tent, and the only hill I want to go over is the one back to Clydebank to find my ... .'

'Me too,' she said, before I could finish. 'Then we could live in a tent after that.'

I shook my head, and held my breath. Someone was going to have to explain things to Rosie. Someone had to make her listen. I didn't want it to be me; I'd no idea how to say what needed said, but I thought I might ask Mr Tait to do it.

'What time is it,' I said after a bit. 'We need to get going or it'll be too late.'

But she had taken back the arm that lay around my middle and was fiddling with her earlobe again.

'Rosie, you have to stop pulling at that ear of yours,'

I said, like a proper big sister. 'You're going to make it bleed again.'

My outburst of sisterliness didn't make any difference so I decided we had to get up instead.

'Come on,' I said, and shoved her over a bit so she had to get up. I took hold of the hand that was at the earlobe and led her back through to the stove room.

'I'm sorry for hitting Rosie,' I announced, still holding Rosie's hand as evidence.

'Of course you are,' said Miss Weatherbeaten drily.

'You never meant to do it in the first place,' said Mr Tait.

No, I didn't. But how did he know that? I wondered if he'd ever hit anyone with his stick without meaning to.

'I didn't mean to be rude to Mrs Mags or you or anyone either,' I said.

I said a special sorry to Miss Weatherbeaten, not because she deserved it but because I knew there was something I didn't understand and it seemed like a good idea. She and Mr Tait exchanged glances, then she slapped both palms on her knees twice, like I'd seen her do at school when she was about to give us instructions. Her mouth tightened up, she licked her lips and straightened a stray hair.

'Thank you, Lenny,' she said. More glances flashed across the room. 'And ... I'm sorry too, for slapping you last night. I think we're all a bit upset, don't you?'

'I'm sorry you lost someone,' I said, feeling brave now.

'Oh,' she said.

That's all she said. I thought she might say more, like what her special friend's name was and why, if she felt like a sister, she went to the pictures without her that night. She didn't have a real sister of her own, poor Miss Weatherbeaten. But she didn't say anything and her mouth that had been tight, wasn't tight any more, in fact she looked as if I had just slapped her.

'Thank you,' she whispered. She reached into her coat pocket and brought out a rag and wiped her eyes with it. It wasn't a rag. It was the silk scarf she had been wearing when I first saw her in the La Scala.

'I didn't mean to make you cry,' I said. It was true. I'd much rather she hadn't. Rosie, who was still holding my hand, gave it a big squeeze and moved right in beside me, standing on my toes, so I think she felt the same. I was worried now. Perhaps I shouldn't have said anything.

There was a knock at the door and then almost immediately Mrs Mags stuck her head round to say the water was ready and that someone whose name I can't remember was just rinsing out the bath. Why didn't Rosie and I just come over now?

Miss Weatherbeaten slipped out the back into the bunk room, embarrassed, I think, by her tears. I decided I had to take charge of things.

'I'm sorry but we haven't got time for a bath today,' I said as politely as I could. 'You see, we have to go over the hill to Clydebank to find out where my mum is, and Mavis.'

Mr Tait stood up from the rocking chair.

'Lenny,' he said. 'It's too late to go down there today.'

'No, it's not,' I said. 'It can't be. We have to go today, now, right now. I have to find Mavis.' It seemed like a simple fact to me, not complicated or hard to understand at all.

'We have no way of getting there,' he said. 'I'll go in the bus tomorrow.'

'No, we have to go today,' I said, getting cross now. 'I have to find Mavis.' How many times had I said that and still no-one listened?

'Thank you Mrs Mags, we'll be over in a couple of minutes,' he said.

I tried to smile at Mrs Mags as she was leaving but my face was still sore and I didn't really feel like smiling.

'Miss Wetherspoon, why don't you go over first with Rosie?' said Mr Tait.

Miss Weatherbeaten appeared, red-eyed, from the other room and nodded.

'I don't want to go!' said Rosie.

'What an ungrateful pair you are!' said Miss Weatherbeaten. 'I came back through all that mess in the town to find you, Lenny, to make sure you were safe, even though I told you to stay in the town hall and you didn't, and all you can do is be rude, and shout.'

'I didn't ask you to come back,' I said.

'You … !' she said and I saw her hands twitch while she was speechless, so I took a step back.

'And I didn't ask for a bath.'

'You … !' She looked as though she was going to explode. She had bombs too, I could tell, but different ones from mine. 'You're filthy. Of course you need a bath. Now get out that door and say sorry and thank you to Mrs Mags right this instant, IMMEDIATELY!'

'No!'

'Yes! How dare you say "no" to me!'

'No!' I said again.

Rosie started up crying again only this time she was really screaming, making as much noise as she possibly could, and in behind all that while we were shouting at each other about being selfish and losing Mavis and all the rest of it, I could hear Mr Tait's steady voice saying things like 'Now, ladies' and 'Would you both please calm down and be sensible' and 'Lenny, I think you should stop' and 'Miss Wetherspoon, that's really not fair.'

And suddenly I got very scared. The noise was so violent somehow, bouncing off all the walls of the big hut, that I thought the ceiling was going to come down on my head or the stove was going to explode through its glass door, and it felt as if all the windows were shaking and the floor was rumbling under my feet and that the world was about to end. Mavis is what I was thinking, Mavis. So I shoved past them, just like I had done earlier and I opened the front door and rushed out onto the front step where it was still bright and sunny. There were people outside, not close but close enough to see me if they looked.

I didn't want them to see me, not in the mess I was in with no hair and my old filthy dress which I'd flung over my head with the shoe in the pocket. The tears were running down my face again, salty in the cuts, so I took off down the hill behind the hut where I hadn't looked before and I couldn't see anybody, just more huts, lots more huts. I ran on down the steep hill through the long dead grasses until I came to the road, and there I straightened out my clothes and wished I had my coat. I set off towards Clydebank, along the road we had come, or so I was hoping although I wasn't entirely sure.

Looking back I saw the long low building which was the Halfway House pub where we had turned in, and over to my right across the fields, stood a farm and behind the farm shone the big yellowy sun. It was a fierce golden yellow with no heat and it threw its light over the hills beneath it, making the shadows of the cows stretch out in gigantic lines; a yellow glow like the orange one that had hung over Clydebank.

Chapter 11

I walked on with steps of anger and fear, whispering to myself in time with my feet. Mum. And. Mav. Is. Slap, slap, slap, slap. I hit the road, hard as hard, until I was close in under the shadow of the hill where the sun couldn't reach any more and it was even colder still. Mum. And. Mav. Is. Mum. And. Mav. Is.

Mum.

I clapped my hands in time with my feet and my words, and soon I was clapping loud and hard. I began to think about all the things I had done wrong in the last few days. There seemed to be a lot of them and I hit my hands, which were sore already; I hit them together extra hard each time I thought of another thing and especially hard when I got to that particular day.

I stopped walking along the road. I just stopped and stood there and thought about that day and how I'd tried to be nice to Miss Weatherbeaten but instead ended up being horrible to her, and I'd been rude to Mr Tait and ignored him when he was talking to me and now I'd run out on Rosie too and I hadn't said sorry and thank you to Mrs Mags. I wanted very much to say sorry to everyone again. The problem was I wanted to find my mum and Mavis much more than I wanted to do any of that.

My hands hurt and were bleeding again where the glass had been, so while I was standing there with the goose pimples taking hold of my legs, I tried to wipe some of the blood away with the pocket remains of my dress.

When I looked back up at the road, a horse and cart was coming towards me with a man at the front of the cart and huge milk churns at the back. He stopped just before he reached me. He was a big man high up on his cart, with a knitted hat and an old coat. A little triangle of shirt glowed dim in the twilight.

'You alright?' he said, as I set off along the road again.

'Yes, I'm fine,' I told him, which I wasn't. I forgot for a moment what a sight I was.

'Do you mind if I ask where you're off to?' he said.

'I'm going to Clydebank to find my mum and my sister,' I said, stopping to be polite.

'Ah, now there's a place to be going,' he said and he nodded his head.

I wasn't sure what he meant.

'I lost them. We had bombing,' I said, in case he hadn't understood me either.

'Yes, I know,' he said. 'I heard it. How were you planning on getting there?'

'I'm going to walk over that hill. It's on the other side.'

'Not of that hill it's not.'

'No?'

'No, that's just farmland and moor. It goes all the way to the middle of nowhere. You don't want to go there,' he said.

'No,' I said. I stuck my hand in my pocket for the

shoe and looked up the hill I thought I had come down with Mr Tait, Rosie and Miss Weatherbeaten. It was dark and shadowy now and the trees were starting to creak in the wind.

'The path you want is by the school, by Craigton school, up the burn beside it, about another mile further on,' he said. 'But you don't want to be going over there tonight. It's going to rain and it's nearly dark already.'

'But I do want to be going over there tonight,' I said.

'You may want to,' he said leaning down towards me, 'but whether you actually can is quite another matter again.'

'But I have to try,' I said. 'What else am I supposed to do?'

I looked at him, up there on his cart. The horse shifted its footing and the whole cart shook, jangling the milk churns. He seemed to be thinking about this problem of mine, but instead of giving me the answer he gave me another question.

'Where have you come from?' he said.

'Back there,' I said, pointing along the road.

'Back there?' he said. 'Won't someone back there be worrying about you being out after dark?'

I didn't answer.

He seemed to be thinking again.

'Do you know what I think you should do?' he said. 'I think you should go back where you came from and plan what you're going to do about your mum and your sister. You can't just set off without having a plan. It's no use going over the hills at this time of night and it'll be dark over there in Clydebank too. That's no use either. You need to go back to "back there" and have a good night's sleep and get on the bus in the morning, if you've got any money, or start walking as soon as you're up and have had a good breakfast.'

'Do I? Is that what I should do?' I said.

'Good breakfast's very important,' he said. 'And when you find your mum and your sister you can bring them to me at that farm over there.' He pointed at a farm I couldn't see. 'I'll tell them how hard you tried to find them.'

'Will you?'

'My name is Tulloch,' he said. 'Mr Tulloch. Now, are you going to get up here so I can give you a lift back to "back there" before we freeze to death in this wind or would you like to think about it a bit longer?'

So Mr Tulloch gave me a lift on his horse and cart which was something I'd never done before, sat on a cart with a horse clip-clopping away in front of me. At any other time I would have been excited beyond belief, but I couldn't be because of Mavis and my mum. He helped me up there with his big rough hand, rougher even than mine, rougher even than my dad's. I sat beside him on the seat at the front and he flicked his reins just a little and said something like 'Goan', which was probably meant to be 'Go on', and the big old horse started to move and the milk churns rattled behind us. To be honest it was very uncomfortable and the swaying this way and that, caused by the horse, made me feel as though I was going to cut myself in two about the middle.

But I was warmed up in no time and I felt heat wafting back on us from the horse too, though I may have imagined that. The horse smelled strongly of old grass, and steam was rising from its back. Its big round bottom rolled right in front of us and the ears on its head turned forwards and backwards, listening.

We'd only gone a very short way when through the dark I saw something dive into the bushes beside the road. I knew what … who … it was instantly.

'Rosie!' I said, and I asked Mr Tulloch if we could stop.

Mr Tulloch stopped the cart and I ran to where she was.

'Come out right now. I know you're in there!'

She didn't come out immediately.

'Sorry,' she whimpered, eventually stepping out in front of the horse. 'Sorry. Don't be angry.'

'What are you doing here?' I said, knowing the answer.

'I want my mum and … '

'Rosie, your mum's … ,' but I thought better of it, just in time. This was not the moment.

'What?' she said. 'What about my mum?'

'Nothing,' I said.

'Girls, I'm in a hurry here,' called Mr Tulloch. 'The light's nearly gone.'

'Coming!' I said. Then to Rosie I said as quickly as I could, like gunfire, 'We can't go over tonight. It's too dark. We'll go over tomorrow, I promise. We'll get Mr Tait to come with us. Tonight we have to go back.'

I could see she wasn't happy with this.

'Come on,' I said and I took the hand that was pulling at her earlobe and led her back to the cart. 'Look, we're going on a cart. I bet you haven't been on a cart before, have you? Isn't it big?'

She still wasn't happy but I shoved her up there

anyway and put my arm round her on the seat at the front. She was cold and shivery, still taut like a cat and she wouldn't look at Mr Tulloch.

Mr Tulloch said 'Goan' again and the horse and cart creaked forward into the falling darkness. Rosie fidgeted beside me the way she had before she fell asleep the night before. Mr Tulloch started humming to himself, but it was a tune I hadn't heard before. It came out in time to the horse's walking and Mr Tulloch rocked his head along with its feet. His shoulder squeezed warm against mine with the rhythm of the tune and he smelled of work and warm milk.

Just before we got to the long low building that was the Halfway House pub, he asked where 'back there' was.

'Here,' I said. 'It's just here.'

'I'll leave you at the door then,' he said.

'No, not here,' I said. 'Back there.' I pointed with my thumb over my shoulder. I didn't want to go past the Halfway House pub and be seen by anyone.

'So "just here" is "back there" is it?' he said, and he called to the horse and it stopped.

He told us to be careful and not be wandering about after dark. He offered to walk up the hill with us to wherever we were going but I grabbed Rosie's hand and hurried over the road.

'Don't forget the planning,' he called after me.

'I won't,' I called back. 'Thanks for the lift!' And Rosie called too.

Neither of us was sure what to do next. We waited until the noise of the cart had faded before we tried to think. I tried to think. This is what I thought.

I thought Mr Tait was probably alright, even

though he had a big stick, but I'd gone right off Miss Weatherbeaten. She was even worse than when she'd been my teacher at school. All the nice stuff had stopped. I figured it was only a matter of time before I got a right good seeing-to from her. I didn't trust either of them because they said we could go and find my mum and Mavis and we didn't. They hadn't even told Rosie she'd lost her family, not properly, not in a way she would understand. I didn't want to go back to them. We needed somewhere to sleep, a hut with a stove and preferably a tin of beans. A couple of jammy pieces were just not enough for a growing girl, as my gran used to say. In the morning we would have had a good night's sleep and a good breakfast, just like Mr Tulloch said, and off we would go.

I put my plan to Rosie and she nodded in agreement, but now, faced with the hill to climb and a hut to find, it didn't seem quite such a good idea, especially in the dark.

Things take shape in the dark, not the things you want to see and not the things you'd expect either, just things that shouldn't be there. Even things that should be there, like tree branches and huts, seem closer so you pull back thinking they're going to hit you. But it's the things that don't belong there at all that are the worst and it makes no difference whether your eyes are open or shut. You see those things anyway. I saw smoke billowing in the trees and close mouths in the angles of the huts. I saw bricks and debris in the chairs and tables beside them, and arms and legs in the twisted woodpiles at their doors.

I don't know what Rosie saw but she gripped my hand until there was no blood in it and all the fingers were numb. Many times I wondered whether this was such a good idea after all. Perhaps we should have gone back to Mr Tait and Miss Weatherbeaten. But all I knew was I had to get to Clydebank the next day and this staying on our own seemed to be part of the plan. So up we went one step at a time, gasping and snivelling and sweating in the icy wind which was growing stronger the higher up the hill we climbed. At each hut we stopped and listened, and in each hut we heard voices, and in those we didn't we felt the chimney or the end wall for the heat of a stove in case there was someone in there, but sleeping.

Finally we found one. It was hidden in the trees so we would have missed it altogether if there hadn't been white edging round its windows. This hut was different from the one we had been in before, and different from Mrs Mags's hut too. It had only one door, no overhang from the roof with a space for chairs that weren't there, and it wasn't very clean. There were cobwebs everywhere and for a second I thought we couldn't go in because I was scared of spiders. But I had more important things to be scared of than spiders, so I went on in through the unlocked door pulling Rosie in behind me.

It was absolutely, completely and utterly pitch-black dark.

Chapter 12

It may have been absolutely, completely and utterly pitch-black dark in there but it was also quite a bit warmer than it was outside so we shut the door against the wind and started to fumble our way about inside. I could smell coal. 'See if you can find a candle,' I said. 'And some matches.'

But Rosie's grip on my hand hadn't loosened so I suggested we swapped hands so that I could get some feeling back. We inched forward, my free hand waving before us. There was a chair; we banged our knees off it, and a wooden box for coal; we banged our knees off that too, and a stove. The stove wasn't lit and it wasn't warm, but it wasn't cold either, not stone cold like when we haven't had coal for a few days at home, and, given that it was so cold outside now, I wondered perhaps if someone had been there for the weekend and had gone home again. Perfect! There were a few small lumps of coal in the wooden box. I set them in the stove. Matches were what I needed next.

'Rosie, you'll have to let go,' I said. 'I can't look for the matches if you have to come with me and I only have one hand. If you look about too we'll find them twice as quick. Or you could sit in this chair and I could explore a bit.'

'I can't see,' she said.

'I know that, silly,' I said. 'I can't see either.'

'No, but I really can't see,' she said.

'I know. I can't see either,' I said. 'What if I kept talking to you and you could sit in the chair.'

'I don't like this place,' she said.

'I don't like it much either but it's all we've got and it's only for tonight.'

'I don't like it,' she said, only in a whisper this time.

I gulped back the panic and I shook my head to get the pictures out of it, but I kept seeing the lady with the leg missing when I was with Mr Chippie in the close in Kilbowie Road, the first time I was supposed to keep my eyes shut. Well, I had my eyes shut now and I could still see her. In fact I had my eyes wide open and I could see her just as clearly.

I shook my head again.

'What are you doing?' Rosie whispered.

'Nothing,' I said.

'Yes, you were,' she said.

'No, I wasn't,' I said.

'Yes, you were,' she said.

'Okay, I was shaking my head,' I said.

'Why?' she said.

'Because ... ,' I said, breathlessly, 'because ... .'

But I couldn't tell her why.

'Because I don't like it either.'

'I saw my mum,' she said.

'Your mum?'

'Yes, she's over there.'

I couldn't see her arm pointing, and I couldn't see what she was pointing at. A rush of chilliness crawled up the back of my legs. It felt like dust from a blast so I rubbed it to be sure.

'Your mum's not here Rosie,' I said. 'In fact, your mum's not anywhere.'

'Yes, she is,' she said.

I could feel her body shake as she pulled on her earlobe with her free hand, and I knew I couldn't tell her about her mum being dead.

'I just mean that she's not here,' I said.

'But I saw her,' she said.

'Can you see her now? If you look really hard is she there?'

She sniffed and I waited for her. The wind was making a lot of noise in the trees now and a clock was ticking. A branch thwacked suddenly against the side of the hut making us jump and throw our arms around each other. I knew exactly what it was but it made no difference.

'It's a tree,' I told her.

'I know,' she said.

'Only a tree.'

'I know.'

We stood locked together like that for what seemed like ages, and then somehow it seemed funny and I started to laugh. I don't know why it was funny, I just know it was. There was a tree outside, lots of trees. I liked trees, and I liked the noise they made. Trees didn't hit you on purpose in the dark. They didn't even hit your roof on purpose. They didn't drop bombs on you. They stood between you and a cold wind, and sometimes bits of them kept you warm in the fire. Trees were good. I don't know why it seemed so funny.

Rosie pulled back from me when I started to laugh, but she didn't let go.

'What's wrong?' she said, in a worried little voice.

But I couldn't speak for laughing, like a different kind of bomb inside, so after a bit she gave up asking and laughed too and we went on like that throwing our heads back and banging them together by mistake and laughing all over again, for ever and ever and ever.

'The tree!' I said, uncontrollable now, like my gran said.

But all the time we had one hand linked, still in a vice-like grip, like the vice in my uncle's hut, as if for dear life, tight and sore, while our other hands flew through the air, slapping our thighs and patting our chests, as we gasped until our tummies hurt.

I don't know when it happened but somehow we were crying again, sobbing, wailing, and howling into each other, me dripping rivers of tears on her neck, snotters in her hair, and her making wet teary patches on the front of my old dress.

The branch bumped the roof again, and then again, and again, until I started to listen for it, to wait for the next one, guessing when it would come, listening to the gusts of wind blowing around us and through the branches and the grasses.

'Listen,' I said.

She was shuddering now, struggling to breathe properly, her little sobs caught in her throat.

'Listen, Rosie,' I said. 'Listen to the trees.'

I told her what to listen for, the big gusts that made the branch hit the roof hard, and the little ones that stroked it, and I told her why I liked trees so much, and she said she thought trees just stood there. But she'd stopped crying by then, or she wasn't crying so hard. All her strength was gone, except for the hand which held mine.

I noticed that I didn't see so many things in the dark as long as I was talking. So I kept on talking to Rosie about the trees and how they made nice homes for the birds and the squirrels, ('What are squirrels?' she said) and how they make nice homes like this one for people too, and all the time I was talking I was feeling my way around the stove trying to find some matches or a candle or a hurricane lamp like the ones in the La Scala. Then we shuffled past the chair and another box and I found a door, so we edged sideways through it, not because it was narrow but because Rosie was still holding onto my hand which she had in both of hers now.

I thought I would run out of things to say about trees pretty quickly but it seems there was quite a lot I knew about trees that Rosie didn't, being only four, like there were different kinds of trees with different shaped leaves, trees that went to sleep in winter and others that didn't.

My hand found some shelves.

'Miss Weatherbeaten told us that,' I said. I stopped talking so that I could think about Miss Weatherbeaten. I got the feeling she liked trees too, and I wished she hadn't slapped me and lost her temper. I was just beginning to worry about not going back to the other hut when Rosie tugged on my hand again.

'Why have you stopped?' she said.

'I don't know,' I said and went back to searching the shelves I had just found, and telling her about squirrels and field mice.

No matches but two apples, last year's so they were

a bit wrinkly but they were still apples. Further along there were three more and a carrot, then another carrot, then a few potatoes. I passed an apple to Rosie who sunk her teeth into it immediately.

'There's a bed,' she said, through her apple. She pulled away from me but without letting go and I heard the rattle of springs. 'Very bouncy,' she said, and after a pause, 'loads of blankets!'

So we got the apples and the carrots down from the shelf and put them on the bed. It was indeed a very springy bed, though some of the springs went almost through the sheet. I had one last go at the shelves for matches then gave up and we climbed into the bed which was the same size as our bed at home in the alcove, and we ate our booty.

The tartness of the apples made our mouths smart and the carrots were bendy and tasteless but it was a meal even so. The bed smelled funny, like my dad when he'd been working (beer and tobacco) and it was cold and damp but we squirmed down into it anyway, grateful to be there.

Being bedtime I asked Rosie what her favourite bedtime story was, so I could go on talking, and keep my head clear. Rosie didn't have a favourite so I picked the first one I could think of just so I could keep talking. But there was a problem: all kids stories have scary bits and neither of us felt like scary bits. So we changed the stories. The three little pigs built a sensible brick house, each helping the other, in a town with no wolves. Jack went up the beanstalk and found a friendly giant, and Goldilocks woke up to breakfast in bed, perfect porridge, not too salty, sweet or hot and with honey on top, all made by the cheerful and welcoming bear family. Rosie liked that the best so I told her it again with extra bits like a whole jar of sweets by the bed, a radio with 'Run, rabbit, run', and two hot-water bottles with soft knitted covers, one for her feet and one for her tummy. For the third telling she wanted her mum to come and make friends with the bears, and her sister to be in the bed, and her dad to be waiting to take them all home.

'Go on then,' she said, eager to hear more, so on I went.

But this seemed like a bad idea and when it was time for Rosie's mum to make friends with the bears I stopped and wondered if I ought to explain that her family were all dead, but Rosie was snoring quietly beside me, snuffling her way through her dreams, so I carried on in a whisper. There was a golden car outside with leather seats and chocolate bars and my dad was in the driving seat. My mum helped me inside and there was Mavis, cuddled up with a big plump teddy bear. We sat, the three of us, in the wide back seat of the car and watched the people go by the window.

And so I must have fallen asleep.

The next thing I know there's another boom-crash and my arms are around my head. Rosie's hanging onto my sides. She thinks she's hanging onto my dress but she's got my sides as well. I can feel my heart beating hard against her fists, and I'm listening for the falling of buildings and the crackle of fire and the drone of the killer bees, and for a second I can't figure out where I am because it's so dark and I can't remember how I got to wherever I am. And even though nothing changed whether my eyes were open or closed, I knew it wasn't a dream. I knew I was awake, but things were missing, the noise especially, only the bumping on the roof that was right above me where the ceiling and the upstairs flat should have been. And then I knew where I was. But I didn't know what the noise was, so I kept waiting for the bombs to fall again, like at the beginning after the siren had stopped and before the bombers first came.

'Shhh!' I said, in case Rosie spoke.

I could feel cold air drifting in from the doorway. I heard a footstep, then a scrape, then the boom of the outside door shutting, then the shuffle of a foot on wooden floorboards.

Rosie and I kept very still. I reached out and pulled the covers over our heads.

The rasp of a match fizzed and was gone.

'Candles, candles, where … tsk … tsk … ? Damn.' It was a woman's voice.

She was in the room now and fumbling, as I had, at the shelves. I held Rosie tight so she couldn't move. No light came through the covers, so the match had died.

A dish wobbled in a slow hollow murmur. The woman's feet scratched along the floor. It was a witch, I was sure of it, like the one in Hansel and Gretel, looking for a match to light the fire to boil the cauldron to cook us up for dinner.

She started humming to herself, like my mum does when she's happy and busy at the same time, only the witch was quieter and her tune unhurried, dawdling along. I began to wish she'd hurry up. We couldn't keep still under the smelly covers forever. But what if she undressed right there at the bedside and climbed in beside us! She probably had a stick for naughty kids like me too, a broomstick, and I told you I didn't like brooms.

I could feel bombs fizzing up inside me, fizz, fizz, fizz, and Rosie's fingers were fiddling about trying to get to her earlobe. The witch was fiddling too, fiddling about at the shelves to get to a match. There was another 'Tsk' followed by a long silence, then she sighed a sigh that would have emptied a room, and the floorboards creaked with her footsteps as she went back through to the stove without closing the door.

I made an air tunnel in the blankets for us to breath and we listened to the footsteps in the next room. Something heavy was dragged across the floor.

'Damn,' she muttered again.

I wondered if it was a body. It sounded like a body, and now my head was full of all those things I shouldn't have looked at, and I wondered whether she had been to Clydebank and brought back something to add to the stew. I knew she wasn't a witch really but it got stuck in there, inside my head and I couldn't get it out. A leg, like a bone for a dog, a hand, a foot with purple toes like my gran's, or a whole person, the whole lot in one, and if it was small, what if it was – and this hit me like a fist in my tummy (like a certain boy at school) – what if it was Mavis?

I had to see. I had to brave the witch and make sure it wasn't Mavis.

But Rosie wouldn't let go. I fought to free myself.

'Don't!' she whispered. 'Don't!'

And then the shifting about next door stopped and we were stuck half-upright out of the blankets like statues, mid-tussle on a bed with creaky springs, on a freezing winter's night with no fire. We waited for the dragging noise to start again, but there was only the wind in the branches shooshing, as if we didn't already know to be quiet.

'I've got to see!' I whispered.

'Please don't!' Rosie said. 'What if she gets you?'

'Don't be silly, it's not a ... .' But I didn't know what to tell her. 'Lie down,' I said. 'Let's lie down. Slowly!'

We set about lowering ourselves back into the bed and suddenly there was a gigantic 'BOING' of a spring and I knew we were in trouble. The noise seemed to bounce off every unseen corner of the room and come back to us twice as loud. We dived back under the covers in double-quick time.

'Your nails are digging into me,' I told Rosie. She didn't let go. 'Rosie!'

We waited for the witch to fling back the covers, my tiny moment of bravery gone. I lay there, the cowardly jelly I didn't want to be, reasoning with myself that it couldn't possibly be Mavis through there, and this witch wasn't a witch, and that she must be deaf or she'd have heard the spring and us whispering. But me, I wasn't deaf. My ears were working so hard my brain hurt and I couldn't tell what was real and what I had made up.

Then a new shooshing began, the gentle breathy sound of sleep, like my mum's sleep before she snored and I wondered if it wasn't a witch at all but my mum, not in a hospital but out looking for me and Mavis, and here she'd found me at least and didn't even know. And every time I moved Rosie grabbed me tight again, though she was half-sleeping, and I ached with longing for Mavis and my mum. I tried to pretend it was my mum having a quiet cup of tea before bed, the teapot on the hob and the cup tapping on the wooden arm of my dad's chair, the tick-tock of the clock, Mavis flinging her arm over my chest and rolling in beside me.

And so I must have drifted off again.

The rain against the window was like the birds that sometimes tapped when we left crumbs for them on the ledge, and I wondered why my mum didn't laugh and lift Mavis to see them, and then I realised it was the fanlight and the crackling of a great fire that was waiting to gobble us all up and then BANG, the fanlight burst and I woke up.

A branch was battering on the roof and so was the rain, but I listened extra hard again to make sure that was all it was and wished there was some light to take away the things in my head, things I didn't want to see and it was all my own fault were there. But the rain was like a blanket covering all the other sounds so I told myself some stories and I thought about Mr Tulloch with his horse and cart and I tried to remember what he'd said. Something about planning, so I began to plan what I was going to do in the morning but it all got too complicated and finally I fell asleep.

Chapter 13

It was the silence which woke me, and the daylight blazing in the window from a truly blue sky, reaching over us to the shelves that had no matches. Drips jumped from the roof past the rain-spattered window, the inside of which was thick round the edges with spiders' webs that stretched along the wall and across the slatted ceiling, heavy with bluebottles.

I pulled my collar tight around my neck and checked Rosie's breathing like my mum did when Mavis was a baby. My hand rose and fell with her back where she was coueried into me, and I stared up at the ceiling.

I wondered if this was all I'd ever have, just Rosie, and that I'd never see Mavis again. And it felt like dying but without dying because I still had that pain inside me that made me not breathe. So I lay as still as still and the tears ran from my eyes past the top of my ears and through what was left of my hair onto the bed and I wished I could be smaller and smaller so that I wasn't there at all and didn't have to feel that way. What if … ? I thought, What if … ? like a huge hole that was swallowing me up and I didn't care any more if there was a witch next door who wanted to boil me up for dinner.

A bird sang suddenly like a hammer on metal and

the room darkened quickly to shadow then burst alive again as if someone had just passed by, but it was only a cloud. My throat hurt with all the coughing I had done and with holding on. I lay a while longer and tried to keep breathing, then eased myself out of the covers and crept to the door.

In the room, there was a pile of blankets on a sofa and a square little stove which matched the bruises on my thighs. A box of matches sat on a shelf amongst some books. A pair of glasses sat up there too with an inch of candle lying on its side. Small, black hand prints were on the door jamb.

But no witch, just trees and more trees beyond the window and bright, bright sunshine.

Today I will find Mavis and my mum, I told myself. All this nonsense will be over. I will walk over the hill and go to the town hall and tell them who I am and they will tell me where my mum and Mavis have gone. Then I will get on a bus and go there too.

My plan got stuck at this point. I had no money for a bus, and there was Rosie.

Then I saw a rope swing dangling from the cross branch of a big tree. At the bottom of the rope a piece of wood glinted in the sun and slanted towards the ground, inviting me to step up. I went back to the bed to get my shoes. Rosie had woken up and was about to yell, so before she could I said, 'There's a rope swing, Rosie. Come and we'll have a shot.' So she didn't yell but got out of bed instead and came with me.

Obviously I had to test it first to make sure it was safe but I didn't feel like swinging or talking so once she'd uncrossed her grumpy little arms, I helped her on beside me and we rocked lazily back and forth, tripping our toes across the mud below.

It was a shock when Miss Weatherbeaten arrived and a confusion too because I was so pleased to see her and didn't want to be, but ashamed at the same time for running off.

Miss Weatherbeaten didn't seem to notice any of this because she was too busy crying into her silky scarf, and then she was laughing and crying all at once.

'Look at the state of you!' she said. 'Just look at your hands! They're still bleeding!'

This was something I hadn't noticed but was true.

She had a lady with her in a pink scarf and hat who said she'd found two little girls asleep in her bed, like Goldilocks. Her name was Mrs Wilson and she didn't look anything like a witch.

'I used to be a nurse,' said Mrs Wilson, 'until I got married and had my family.' She had a look at my hands too. 'That must hurt,' she said.

And when I came to think of it, it did, but not as much as losing Mavis.

'Oh, how silly I am!' said Miss Weatherbeaten, dabbing at her eyes. She helped us off the swing (even though we could do it ourselves) and crouched beside us to check my hands, kind again. Mrs Wilson said she had first aid things in the hut and went to find them.

Like Mr Tait at the back door I could see the top of Miss Weatherbeaten's head. There was no grit in her hair and the hair itself was clean and browny-red with little strands of white and tied neatly back with a piece of brown string. I started to explain that we had just been having a little shot at the rope swing and then we were going to Clydebank over the hill.

'Well, you can't go like that,' said Miss Weatherbeaten. 'What on earth would your mother think of me?'

I told her my mum would be happy to see me whatever state I was in (like Mr Chippie said), but she wasn't really listening.

Mrs Wilson came back with a bottle of iodine and a rag and dabbed at my hand. The iodine was the same colour as Miss Weatherbeaten's hair.

'Ow!' I said.

'Sorry,' said Mrs Wilson. 'Bit nippy, isn't it?'

And I wondered whether she wasn't a witch in disguise after all, until she gave us both an oatcake from her pink pocket.

'Mr Tait has gone to town,' Miss Weatherbeaten said. 'He had to go, because of work. He went early this morning. He's going to check at the town hall,' she went on. 'He was going to give them your names too, but it'll be wasted effort now you're here. Never mind,' she sniffed, 'you are here and that's the main thing. We were so worried!'

I hadn't meant Miss Weatherbeaten to be worried about me after all that had happened, so I said I was sorry and she smiled. We all started down the hill as if there was no question of doing anything else. Rosie walked backwards holding Mrs Wilson's hand and she kept her eyes on me and let herself be led.

'Miss Weather … ,' I put my hand up in the air, as if I was at school.

'Yes, Lenny?'

'Miss Weather,' I said, trying to sound sensible,

'when is Mr Tait going to be back? What time is it now? I really need to go over there myself. He doesn't know what Mavis looks like and where she might have gone. Don't you think I should go over there too, just in case? Shouldn't I? I mean it's not that far, not really, and if I left now, I'd be back in time for blackout and you could look after Rosie and make sure she doesn't follow me this time, and … when are we going to tell her they're all dead? Her family I mean. She thinks they're just missing.'

'Well … ,' said Miss Weatherbeaten slowly. 'It's not that simple. Rosie's only four. She doesn't understand.'

'But somebody still needs to tell her,' I said. 'It's going to be a terrible shock when she finds out everyone's lying to her.'

'I think accusing people of lying is a bit strong, Lenny,' she said.

'Well, not lying, just … .'

I wondered if it was another of those white lies that my mum said was alright. This one just didn't seem very alright to me.

'She can't understand just now,' said Miss Weatherbeaten. 'She will over time.'

I had Mavis's shoe in my hand again. I hoped no-one was lying to Mavis, or pretending to her. I hoped someone was telling her the truth that our mum was ill in hospital and that I was missing, not dead.

But what if all these grown-ups were lying to me too, pretending that my mum was in hospital with bad legs when really she was dead as a doorpost, dead and gone, under a pile of rubble down our street with her head sticking out, and everyone was just too scared to tell me? What if they knew Mavis was dead too? I twisted the shoe in my pocket and looked at Miss Weatherbeaten. What if the face in the sea of bricks was my mum and somehow I hadn't known it?

'Lenny,' she said. 'What on earth is the matter with you?'

I looked at her long and hard before I spoke. And after, when she answered, I kept a close eye on her so that I could spot if she was lying. Sometimes it's hard to tell with grown-ups, there's so many things they think kids shouldn't see or hear.

'Is Mavis dead?' I said quietly. 'And my mum, is she dead? In a sea of bricks?'

'Oh, Lenny,' said Miss Weatherbeaten with a sigh, the new Miss Weatherbeaten, not the teacher one. 'Poor Lenny!'

She had watery bits on her bottom eyelids and her lip was twitching and she didn't seem to have noticed. I felt a terrible churning in my chest and my legs were ready to give way.

'Your mum is in hospital. We don't know which one, and we don't know how ill she is.' She stopped for a minute to wipe her eyes and blow her nose. 'But we know she went there and that it's the best possible place for her to be. We'll just have to wait and see.'

I nodded to let her know I understood. She seemed to be telling the truth. But I was still thinking, what about Mavis, what about Mavis?

'Mavis could be anywhere,' she said, 'but she's probably safe, being looked after by someone like you.' We both glanced at Rosie, who was watching us.

Miss Weatherbeaten put her arm round my back and gave me a tiny squeeze.

'I want my mum,' I said quietly, 'and Mavis.'

'Of course you do,' she said. 'Of course. The sooner we get you back to your mums the better!' She said this loudly with a smile at Rosie.

It was a great relief for me to hear this from Miss Weatherbeaten, but Rosie didn't have a mum any more. I was irked that Miss Weatherbeaten should be so contradictory. It was a lie but there was nothing I could do.

Chapter 14

Mrs Wilson gave me a little straw hat with a brim that was coming undone and a piece of greying elastic under the chin. There was a pink and yellow stripey band around it and some cloth flowers that had once been purple were stuck beneath the band. It was the kind of hat boys didn't wear. I put it on my head straightaway and she took it off again straightaway in case I got grit into it. She found another dress for Rosie and a pair of boy's trousers for me with a belt to hold them up, and jumpers that didn't match. Her grandchildren were too big now, she said. I wasn't sure about the trousers. My mum would never dream of wearing trousers far less putting me in a pair. But there was no choice.

When we got back down the hill Miss Weatherbeaten and Mrs Mags made us a bath and stoked up the fire in our hut. We closed the curtains with the green leaves and the threads hanging down. After Mrs Mags left, Miss Weatherbeaten shut the door and soon we were snug as bugs in rugs, as my gran says, and the horse galloped over the stove, with a tick, tick, tick against the wall. Miss Weatherbeaten poured a last kettleful of boiling water into the bath, and then went into the little bedroom and left us to it. (We were embarrassed taking our clothes off in front of strangers.)

Rosie and I looked at each other. Suddenly I felt hot and shy and had to pull the hat over my eyes. I didn't want to do this. I wanted my mum. She and my gran and my Auntie May were the only people who'd ever seen me without my clothes on, ever, and Mavis of course.

'I want my mum,' mumbled Rosie. Her little bottom lip was trembling again and she was having a go at that earlobe.

And I thought, I want Mavis. I felt that wrench of not knowing again and the need to hold Mavis and feel not sick and not scared. And there was poor Rosie with no sister or mother left, no father or brother, no goodness knows who else, and I hoped it wasn't all true for me too.

So I started to help her undress and this is what I found: Rosie had skint knees, skint elbows and a smattering of bruises all over her body in the oddest places. She wasn't as thin as Mavis but not far off it. I tried hard not to look but she didn't seem at all bothered by my stares. I found myself checking that everything was there, two hands, ten fingers, both arms the same length and so on. I had to be sure. Mrs Mags had given us a little piece of soap. Rosie kept very still while she let me scrub her back and wash her hair and when I'd finished she leant back in the bath and slunk away down into the small quantity of water that we had and pulled her earlobe, and I wondered what was going through her little head that had no fringe, but was too afraid to ask.

I wrapped her in the rough old towel Mrs Mags had given us and she sat silently on the rocking chair that Mr Tait had sat in, but she didn't rock it at all.

She just hung her hand from her ear and looked at the orange flames dancing in the glass front of the stove. We heard the page of Miss Weatherbeaten's book turn and we heard her sigh, and when the bang, bang, bang of the hammer started again we gasped and looked at the window, even though the curtains with the big leaves were closed and we couldn't see anything.

It's funny how safe a hat makes you feel and I don't mean a hat like Mr Chippie's hat that was made of tin and was shiny and hard. Even an old straw one that nobody but me wanted any more could do it. No-one would dare call me a boy in that hat, even if I had to wear someone's trousers until my dress was dry. I kept it on in the bath, at least to begin with, then I put it with Mavis's shoe on the three-legged stool where I could see both the hat and the shoe, in case Miss Weatherbeaten decided to throw them away. I put my old dress there too.

The water in the bath was already black and grimy when I slipped into it, and it was getting cold, and when I'd finished washing, Rosie poured a jug of cold water over my head to rinse out the soap, just as I had done for her, only she missed most of it so I had to do it again myself, and then the clean water had run out. When I stood up the water round my feet was dark with all the dirt I'd carried with me over those strange long days, dirt from the bombing over the hill at home, shiny black dust out of the coalbin in Mrs Wilson's hut, brown mud from under the rope swing, sticky smears from jammy pieces and stew that I'd eaten and spilt. After my turn with the towel it was black like a miner's rag and full of bits of hair from both our heads.

BANG, BANG, BANG, went the knock at the door. I fell back into the water with a slop. Miss Weatherbeaten ran through from the other room and grabbed the door handle before anyone could turn it. But it was only Mrs Mags with a mirror for us to look at ourselves in.

I reached for my hat again knocking Mavis's shoe and my old dress off the three-legged stool and onto the floor. Mrs Mags opened the door a tiny crack and slipped the mirror through it. A slither of icy air reached round my back in the metal tin bath. Miss Weatherbeaten set the mirror down behind me against the chest of drawers.

'Lenny, you need to have those cuts seen to,' she said. 'Why don't you let Mrs Wilson have a look at them, once you're dressed?'

She tiptoed back next door. A right good seeing-to. Hmm.

The mirror was one of those cut glass affairs that I'd seen in my friend's bathroom, the same friend that had a bed like Mr Tait's new stick. I couldn't see all of myself in it at once so I had to bob up and down and then stick all the bits of me together in my head. Everything was still there but a lot of it was red and I had itchy scabs all down my legs and arms and on my face, and over my left ear there was a bigger cut that had started bleeding again and felt worse than all the rest. Apart from that I looked very like Rosie, with strange bruises in funny places. We stood together, me and Rosie, bobbing up and down in front of the mirror, jostling each other out of the way, then we got dressed in our new clothes that weren't really ours.

Rosie's dress was dark pink, a bit like Mrs Wilson's

hat, and her jumper was light powder blue. My trousers were dark red and my jumper a vivid green, like the green of new leaves in spring, and there was a leather belt that was probably meant for a grown-up, but it had a hole in it made specially for someone as small as me. I rolled up the legs of my trousers, tied the belt tight and put my new hat back on my head.

I felt very sleepy and stiff. Perhaps it was the grit that Mr Tait said I had. But there was a lot of grit in the bath now along with my burnt hair. I saw it when we poured it in bucket-loads into a special hole at the back of the cludgie. I hoped that didn't mean I was going to be a jelly again.

I thought bath-time was over but Miss Weatherbeaten had found a pair of scissors and wanted to sort out my hair.

'There's nothing left to cut!' I said, thinking I needed every bit of hair I had, but she put me on the three-legged stool anyway and got down on the floor on her knees with the scissors. Snippety-snip-snip, she cut off the last remaining wisps which hung down here and there, reminders of how long my hair used to be. While she was down there she had a look at the cut over my ear and said 'Tsk, tsk, tsk!' just like Mrs Wilson the witch had said. Then Mrs Wilson came and had a look. She said that salty water was what my ear needed, three times a day.

'This is going to hurt,' she said, and guess what? She wasn't joking either. She asked me if I had any more cuts that felt like that and I said no although I hadn't even thought about it. But when Miss Weatherbeaten washed it again later that day I showed her the yellow cuts on my legs and she washed them in salt too.

When Mrs Mags and the boys came to take the bath back, bad boy George said an extra bad word. I heard it loud and clear above everyone else's chatter. It was 'bloody'. I couldn't move I was so shocked and excited. He got a thump on the ear for that and was sent to get more water from the well at the bottom of the hill. Good riddance to bad rubbish is what I thought. And then he did it again. He said 'bloody hell' this time. I had to cover my mouth in case I screamed or laughed or said something I shouldn't. Mrs Mags was red in the face either with embarrassment or from carrying the bath, I couldn't tell.

After all that we went to the lookout chair, me and Rosie, to wait for Mr Tait. The lookout chair was a big old thing with only one arm that someone had left on the brow of the hill and we sat on it and waited in silence for a long time, Rosie on my knee. We could see right across the valley, even as far as a farm that must have been Mr Tulloch's, and all the way back down the road towards home. The sun had gone down and a big black rain cloud was where it should have been. We fixed our eyes on the bend in the road so we'd see Mr Tait's bus as soon as it appeared.

After a while some rabbits came out to eat the grass, twitching their little noses. The sun came back out from behind the cloud and made all the raindrops shine. Birds came and sang in the bushes behind us and over by Mr Tulloch's farm there were trees that were waiting for winter to end.

The road was busy with people like us, like me and Rosie and Miss Weatherbeaten and Mr Tait, walking away from danger, walking to keep themselves safe. A big blue van came and parked behind the Halfway

House pub and some people gave out soup. Mrs Mags went down and brought some of those lost people up among the huts and found them a bed for the night.

'Lenny,' whispered Rosie once I'd almost forgotten she was there.

'Mmm?'

'I know my mum's dead,' she said, 'but when is she coming back?'

'She's dead, Rosie, you know … .' That sickness came back like my tummy was pushing up against my heart and my heart was trying to escape out of my mouth.

'I know, but … .'

I didn't want to talk about this, not least because Miss Weatherbeaten would be angry if she found out I had. It was just that my mum had told me not to lie, and so had my gran. It was very annoying because it meant I couldn't, for instance, for talking's sake, take an extra biscuit. I'd be scared of them asking if I'd taken an extra biscuit, because then I'd have to tell the truth and be found out. But then my mum had also told me there were times when little lies were alright. Telling Rosie her mum was coming soon felt like a very big lie, not a little one at all. I thought about what Miss Weatherbeaten had said and I wondered what to say.

'Lenny?' said Rosie.

'I was just thinking that I don't know,' I said. 'I think being dead means you're not coming back.' She jumped slightly. 'But I could be wrong, so I don't know.'

She nodded.

'But my mum always comes back,' she said. 'She wouldn't go anywhere without me.'

'She probably didn't mean to. It was probably an accident that she didn't come back,' I said. 'Lots of accidents happened that night, remember?'

Clearly she did remember because she was pulling at her ear again, vigorously. She was staring into the distance at where the road disappeared but I could tell she was seeing things inside her head too. I wished I wasn't too scared to ask what she saw in there, but I was.

'What did the ARP man say?' I said.

She thought about this for a moment. The rabbits appeared again and sat nibbling a few feet away, pausing every so often to listen.

'He said "Hello, what's your name?" so I told him.' She stopped for a minute and pursed her lips. 'And he said "Why are you wandering about here? Where's your family?" so I told him.' She stopped again to watch the rabbits. Her hand drifted up towards her earlobe.

'What did you tell him?' I said after a bit. She seemed to have got stuck.

'I told him I'm Rosie Tomlin,' she said.

The rabbits were nuzzling each other.

'And?' I said.

'And what?' she said.

'Nothing,' I said.

A hammer went bang, bang, bang again and all the rabbits ran away. The birds in the bushes behind us fluttered in the branches.

'I told him my mum and dad and gran and big sister Rhona were at home,' she said, 'and he said

"Where's home?" And I told him the address because my mum made me learn it. I couldn't find my house.'

'What next?'

'He said "Oh, dear".'

'Oh, dear,' I said. 'He said "Oh, dear" and then what?'

'He said "Who was in your house?" So I told him again.'

'And?'

'He said "I'll do my best".'

'That's all?'

'Well, no. He said other things like "Hold on tight" when he was carrying me, and "Close your eyes" and then he brought me down to the Scala.'

Suddenly I was very angry with Mr Chippie even though none of it was his fault, but then I remembered how kind he had been to me. He'd promised me he'd find Mavis too and instead he found Rosie. I tried wishing again that Rosie would be Mavis but it didn't work. Mavis was a thumb sucker. Rosie tweaked her earlobe.

Something flashed on the horizon at the bend in the road where it disappeared over a hill. We stood up even though we couldn't see any better standing and we watched the sunlight glint off something that was creeping along the road at a snail's pace. After a bit this shiny thing turned into Mr Tulloch and his horse and cart with the silvery milk churns on the back. When he got closer we waved at him, but he didn't see us.

Then Miss Weatherbeaten sneaked up behind us and we nearly jumped right out of our skins. She sat down on our chair and I didn't know what to say again. The sun was making her face glow yellow and her reddish-brown hair glinted with gold.

'I brought you this, Lenny,' she said, 'in case it got lost. I know it's quite important to you.'

It was my old dress with Mavis's shoe still in the pocket. I took it from her and turned it over in my hand. Beside our new clean clothes that were somebody else's, this rag of a dress looked filthy and useless, but I decided to put it on anyway seeing as it was all I had left of my mum and Mavis. I started to take off my bright green jumper so that I could put it on underneath.

'Lenny, I think we ought to wash that first,' said Miss Weatherbeaten.

'Why do you want that old thing anyway?' said Rosie.

I pulled the dress away from Rosie's grasp.

'What do you want to do with it?' said Miss Weatherbeaten kindly.

I couldn't speak. I don't know why. I stood very still, I'm not sure how long for. When Miss Weatherbeaten put her hand on my arm I jumped.

'It's Mavis's, isn't it?' she said softly. 'The shoe?'

Rosie was kicking the grass around the bushes.

I managed to nod my head, but it was like I was all filled up with rain water and when I moved my head it rushed out through my eyes and down my cheeks.

'What if … ?' I said between sobs. 'What if … ?' I pulled my hat down over my face and just stood there sniffing like a baby, like Rosie had done, like I'd seen Mavis do, standing in front of Miss Weatherbeaten with tears and snotters running down my face. I squeezed Mavis's shoe so hard the blood escaped from one of my cuts again and ran onto the dirty blue of the dress.

Miss Weatherbeaten stood up and took the hand that squeezed the shoe and opened it up.

'Tsk, tsk,' she said and shook her head in that way I hate grown-ups doing, but what could I do? Then she put an arm round me and sat back down on the chair and held me in close. I could tell this was something new for her.

'Can I see the shoe?' she said.

She turned it over in her hands like I had done, even though it meant we were pulled close together. Finally, without a word, she put the dress and the shoe on her lap.

'Oh, look!' she said in a whisper. 'Rabbits.' They were back to nibble the shoots under the tree.

Rosie suddenly kicked at the grass and ran at the rabbits.

'Oh!' said Miss Weatherbeaten. Then, forgetting the rabbits she said, 'I've got an idea. Why don't we tie the strap of Mavis's shoe to your belt?'

It felt funny to hear Miss Weatherbeaten say Mavis's name. I half-wanted to take it back and keep it for myself. I know that doesn't make sense.

'And I've got another idea,' she said. 'Why don't I take this dress, what's left of it, and wash it and make a bag out of it for you to keep Mavis's shoe in? You know you have to give these clothes back soon.'

The belt idea I liked, but the dress I wasn't so sure. My mum had made that dress. It was light blue with pink stitching and she had put pink flowers on the collar, daisies or maybe they were lilies, I wasn't sure, and there were more flowers on the pocket, not a lot but enough to make it mine and nobody else's. Except Mavis. Her flowers were purple.

Rosie started yanking up the grass in wet handfuls and throwing them over us.

'Stop it, Rosie,' I said and we ducked, but she kept on.

'Stop it, Rosie,' said Miss Weatherbeaten, but Rosie tossed wet grass over our heads anyway. She was laughing now as if this was the funniest thing ever, and I can tell you it wasn't.

'Stop it, Rosie!' I said. 'Stop it!'

'You stop it!' she squealed.

'Stop it!' I shouted.

A shock of rain hit me in the eye. In my blindness I reached out for Rosie to grab and hold her but a shower of grass like green snow floated before my eyes. Rosie screamed a shriek of laughter. It was sudden and close, like being punched, and I swung my hand back to hit her. Miss Weatherbeaten grabbed my wrist from over my head and held it tight, so that I was helpless, one arm vertical. Mavis's shoe fell from her lap. Rosie plucked it from the ground like another handful of grass and ran off up the hill with it, still giggling in that forced, pretend, lying sort of way. Miss Weatherbeaten let go of my hand and hared after her. She had my dress. It's pocket bounced off her leg as I watched her go and she called out for Rosie. I could only walk stiffly after them, helpless and stupid and bereft.

When I was past the bushes and had a clear view up the hill, I saw the two bad boys, George and Dougie. They had Rosie between them, each holding an arm while she wriggled to get free. Mavis's shoe was not in her hand. Miss Weatherbeaten was striding up the hill towards them, her big old-fashioned coat and my old dress flapping in the wind beside her. I couldn't hear what was said but Miss Weatherbeaten was waggling her finger at Rosie and I hoped the bad boys would do something really bad to Rosie for being a horrible wee besom and stealing Mavis's shoe when she knew perfectly well it was important and the only thing I had left of Mavis, who I might never see again and who might even be dead. I turned round and thumped my way back to the bushes pulling my jumper round my neck to keep off the rain, and although the bushes had no leaves I crouched underneath them anyway for whatever shelter they could give me, and stared fuming at the ground which was strewn with bits of grass thrown up by horrible Rosie.

Chapter 15

Mr Tait's blue Alexander's bus sneaked over the brown brackeny hillside without my noticing. I must have been tying Mavis's shoe, which Miss Weatherbeaten brought back to me, to my belt. What a relief! Being without it had made all those bombs go off inside again. Rosie was back but I didn't want to talk to her.

Mr Tait was the very, very last person off his blue bus, although there were lots more people still on it, most of them peering out of the windows at us. In fact he was so much the last person, I thought he wasn't on it at all and I had taken hold of Miss Weatherbeaten's hand before I realised what I was doing. The bombs fizzing away made my chest feel sore and tight, so I had to stand very still in case I set anything off and my legs would turn to jelly and I'd sink without a trace.

And then he stepped down from the bus and gave us a wave. He put a big suitcase and a carpet bag down on the grey tarmac. Then he went back up again into the bus and came back down with a bird cage with a bright yellow budgie in it. He waved this at us with a triumphant smile.

Oh, goodie! I thought. A budgie. What about my mum and Mavis?

Miss Weatherbeaten went to help him. This left me and Rosie standing with each other. I didn't want to look at her and anyway Mr Tait had gone back into the bus for something else and he was going to need more hands that just Miss Weatherbeaten's to carry it all up the hill so I followed her and left Rosie by herself. I nearly said 'Stay there', but that seemed too mean, even to me, and she probably wouldn't do it anyway. The thing he'd gone back inside the bus for was his very fancy stick that looked like a bedpost. This he waved at us too, but I think it was meant to be friendly.

'Lenny, you're here!' said Mr Tait in a cheery voice. 'Goodness, what a lovely hat!'

I hid my happiness under its brim.

'And what a lovely dress, Rosie!' he said.

I hid my consternation too. That's another word from my dad. It's got nothing to do with stirring, or not much.

'Goodness!' he said, in a different voice.

'Yes,' said Miss Weatherbeaten. 'I know, but there was no choice.'

They were looking at my trousers. I felt my face blush to match their red blood colour.

'It's only until her own clothes are washed.'

'Well, but really? Couldn't she just have stayed indoors?' said Mr Tait.

But I liked the feel of the trousers. They were warmer for a start, even if they were meant for boys, and they covered my skinny legs and the scabs and bruises that were all over them. I was about to point this out but I saw that his face had lost the smile he arrived with even though his voice was still gentle. And what did trousers matter anyway when there was news to be had about my mum and Mavis?

So we set off up the hill to the hut. Miss Weatherbeaten carried the suitcase, Mr Tait carried the carpet bag and I carried the budgie cage. The adults went first, then me, then Rosie.

'It'll be weeks before the factory is running properly again … ,' said Mr Tait. '… devastation is extraordinary, just extraordinary … incredible there's anyone left at all … nothing of the school, no, nothing of any of the schools, I think … .'

They kept lowering their voices so I wouldn't hear. Why do grown-ups do that? I might have been young but I wasn't an idiot. I could understand things and I wanted to know what had happened, what the town was like, who he saw.

'It'll take ages to clear it up,' said Mr Tait. I couldn't hear the next bit, something about unexploded bombs, and then he laughed. How could he laugh at a time like this? What unexploded bombs? Did he mean the ones inside me? Why wasn't he telling me about my mum and Mavis? What if the news was bad, I mean really bad, worse than my mum being in hospital and not knowing where Mavis was?

'Mr Tait … ,' I said, but Miss Weatherbeaten was talking. He held up the stick to indicate I should be quiet. I closed my lips so tight it hurt.

He laughed again and said, 'Well, well, well. They're even tougher than I thought. But really, I do think trousers on a girl is a step too far, even for a girl with grit in her bones.'

So the grit was in my bones. I thought about this. Was I turning into a boy? Hair, trousers and grit? Mavis and my mum wouldn't recognise me. I stopped for a second to think and Rosie bumped into me. It gave me such a fright I fell and dropped the budgie cage and it rolled back down the hill. I wrapped my arms around my head and the pretty hat with the ribbon and flowers was squashed all any old how over my face. I couldn't see anything at all except the ricochet of a blast across a road, and that was inside my head.

Rosie ran down the hill for the budgie. I wished Mr Tait would help me. He knew what to do when that kind of thing happened, but when I opened my eyes he was standing a little way off gazing at the last glimmers of light that were strung across the hills made stripey by the trees. Miss Weatherbeaten wiped the wet fronts of my legs, which were now muddy with falling and bloody too. I could feel the sting in my knees.

The budgie was still alive, which was a surprise, and Mr Tait didn't seem to mind that I'd dropped it. He said its name was Joey, which I thought was a boring name, to say the least, so Rosie and Miss Weatherbeaten set about renaming it. Miss Weatherbeaten wanted to call it Prometheus and Rosie suggested Runaway, and when they asked me I said I didn't care. Names like Nuisance and Stupid came into my head but I thought I better not say them out loud.

'Joey,' I said finally, which stopped all their silly chatter right away.

We arrived at the hut and I could see kids up at the rope swing.

'Goodness, young lady, what a fidget!' said Mr Tait. 'You can go up and have a shot on the swing if you want.'

'I can't,' I said. I held up my hands so he could see the sore bits.

'Ah,' he said. 'I see. Would a pair of gloves help?'

And without waiting for a reply he produced a pair of brown leather gloves, man's ones but not very big. Mr Tait was not very big.

Rosie and I trooped in silence to the swing and sat on the roots of a tree at the edge of the spreading beech while the other kids played on the rope swing.

'Why aren't we going on it?' she said. 'Mr Tait said we could.'

'Shut up, Rosie,' I said.

She touched her earlobe.

'Don't you want to go on it?' she said.

'Shut up, Rosie.'

'Why not?' she said, fiddling now.

I pulled Mavis's shoe round in front of me and held it.

'Why not?' she said again.

Why didn't she just shut up like I told her to?

'Lenny?'

'Don't you even care?' I spat at her. 'Your whole family are dead and all you want to do is go on a stupid rope swing.'

The boys' shouts fell away and the rope creaked against the branch. A bird flapped in the tree overhead and its silhouette slid silently across the deep blue sky. Rosie sniffed. One of the boys jumped off the launch pad and stood, legs apart, in front of us. I didn't know which boy it was. I hid and didn't look.

'Is that true?' he said.

'Is what true?' I said.

'Are all her family dead?'

Rosie was pulling madly at her ear.

'Yes,' I said, looking boldly now at the small bad

boy Dougie. I was fed up trying to explain. 'Every single one.'

'My mum's coming soon,' said Rosie.

Dougie laughed.

'Shut up, Dougie,' said Sandy who was behind him.

'People don't come back when they're dead,' said Dougie.

'Yes, they do,' said Rosie. 'My mum always comes back.'

'You're mum must be a ghost then,' said bad George.

'That's not funny,' said Sandy.

'Does she go "whooo, whooo" in the night, then?' said George.

'Leave her alone,' I said. 'She's only wee.'

'I bet your whole family's dead too,' said George to me and he made a whistle-boom-crash sound just like the bombs we'd all heard, him included.

'They're not,' I said emphatically. 'They're in hospital.'

'Well, in that case they'll be dead soon.' He put his hands together and looked at the sky and pretended to pray. I wanted to punch him in his stupid stomach.

'They won't!' I said.

'Yes, they will, especially your mum,' he said. 'She'll be getting what's coming to her by now, in hell, where she belongs.'

'No she won't! Don't you say that, don't you say that about my mum!' I was shouting now, and remembering the old woman in the street with her bags with Mr Tait. 'Don't you say that!'

'She's a tart,' he said. 'Everyone knows that. That's probably what she was doing when the bombs were going. WHEE-BOOM-CRASH … aaah!' He made kissing noises.

I didn't know what he meant, but I knew it was nasty to my mum, so I shouted, 'She's not a tart! She didn't do anything! She went to the pictures with a nice young man!'

'Maybe you'll be a tart too one day.'

'I won't!'

Rosie had started wailing. 'I want my mum!'

Sandy and Dougie were telling big bad George to shut up and trying to drag him away but he flung his fists at them and they stumbled out of his reach. But now Mrs Mags and Mrs Wilson had come out of Mrs Mags's hut. I didn't wait. I didn't want to hear anything, so I shouted all the way down the hill.

'It's not true! It's not true!' I tried to run with my hands over my ears but it didn't work.

And Rosie came after me shouting, 'I want my mum! I want my mum!'

And then suddenly she stopped.

She was shaking a little fist at them – her other fist on her waist, her legs firmly apart and her head thrust forward.

'I'll get my dad to you!' she said in a little girl's big growl. 'And then you'll know all about it!' She waved that fist at them again and turned to me with her bottom jaw stuck forward and her lips all squeezed together. Then she swung back towards them and shouted, 'And she'll get her dad too!'

She stomped towards me so that I had to get out of the way, and then on past towards our hut and banged into the door. I could just make her out in the half-light fumbling with the door handle in the dark. 'Let me in!' she shouted, so they did.

When I caught up she had wrapped herself around

Miss Weatherbeaten and was sobbing loudly. Joey the budgie was on top of the dresser. Mr Tait was on the edge of his rocking chair.

'Lenny,' he said in his nice soft voice. 'What on earth is the matter?'

He stood up and the rocking chair clattered backwards against the wall. Joey stopped singing just as Sandy and Dougie arrived, which made me leap across the room to Mr Tait who was standing not quite upright, with his wiggly bedpost stick.

'Well, well, well,' he said.

'Sorry, Mr Tait,' said Sandy. 'It was George again.'

'George was it?' said Mr Tait.

'He called her mum a tart,' said Sandy.

'Did he now?' said Mr Tait.

'Yes, sir, yes he did.'

'I think I asked you to look after these two young ladies whenever I'm absent, did I not?'

'Yes, sir, I know.'

'Was it so very difficult?'

Sandy hung his head.

'I shall speak to his aunt, your mother, Mrs Mags, in the morning.'

Mr Tait was bent forwards as if his back was stuck and wouldn't unwind. He was leaning on his stick and his other arm was around my shoulders. I don't actually remember how that came about but I was glad of it. My heart was thumping so hard I didn't even know. My lovely hat with the band and the flowers was round my neck to one side and it was only afterwards that I realised my ear was bleeding again.

Mr Tait seemed to think better of being hard on

Sandy, and I was glad because he didn't seem bad like the other two, like bad George or Dougie who was skulking now behind him.

'Thank you for trying,' said Mr Tait. What he really meant was 'goodbye' and Sandy took the hint and left, taking bad boy Dougie with him.

'Where's my mum?' I said before he could say anything else.

He seemed to stoop a little further. The rocking chair stopped rocking. He lowered himself into it. He looked older than he had in Clydebank. Loose folds had formed under both eyes and his leg seemed to be giving him more trouble than before. His eyes were bloodshot and he had a broad pasty forehead with lots of lines running across it and a broad mouth with pale thin lips.

I stood close to him watching his every move, this bringer of news, watching for a sign: was it good or bad, how good, how bad?

'She's in the Western Infirmary,' he said at last.

He sniffed and drew a clean white handkerchief out of the pocket of his brown jacket. He blew his nose with a great big HONK which surprised me so much I jumped back a step.

'Sorry,' he said, smiling for the first time.

'Mr Tait is very tired,' said Miss Weatherbeaten from the sofa where she had retreated with Rosie. 'Perhaps we could talk about this in the morning.'

'In the morning?' I said, swirling round to face her.

Before I could say any more she directed her eyes pointedly at the top of Rosie's head, which was falling into her lap. I felt all those words bursting up, wanting to fly out of me like little bombs, words like 'They're.

All. DEAD!' And 'Explain!' And strings of words like 'What about me?'

'But … ,' I said instead. Miss Weatherbeaten shook her head and looked away.

I turned back to Mr Tait who was smiling. He held out his hand to me but I kept mine safely by my side.

'D'you know what Lenny?' he said. 'I'm very, very tired. I'd like to eat some of that lovely soup that Miss Wetherspoon has so kindly made for us and then I think I might put on my coat that I brought with me today, and go and sit on that bench, out the back.'

'But … .'

'Rosie looks like she's very tired,' he went on. 'Have you been very busy today?'

'Rosie?' I said.

He took my hand, this time without asking. 'Hmm?' he said smiling. He had a kind face with soft grey eyes with wrinkles round them. He was trying to tell me something. Suddenly I twigged.

'Can I … ?' I said shifting my eyes in the direction of the outside bench.

'Hmm,' he said, and let go of my hand.

'I'll put the soup out,' I said.

Of course what actually happened was Rosie fell asleep right there on the sofa next to Miss Weatherbeaten with the empty soup bowl still in her lap. Her head fell back, her mouth fell open, her hands fell away from the bowl, and the spoon slipped round its edge with a tuneful scrape. Miss Weatherbeaten tucked her arms underneath Rosie's legs and shoulders and lifted her through to the little bunk room at the back. Mr Tait lit the way with the candle and for a brief couple of seconds I was left alone in the pitch-dark except for a tiny glow from the front of the fire. Even the budgie was quiet. The horse above the fire swung soundlessly as if it was running on cushions.

Mr Tait and Miss Weatherbeaten came back into the room and sat down on either side of the stove and me. Mr Tait put the candle back on the ledge beside the stove and leant back in his rocking chair and rocked.

'Your mum, Peggy Gillespie,' he said, as if I had more than one, 'is in the Western Infirmary in the West End of Glasgow,' he said.

I knew that. He'd already told me that.

'She's in ward twenty-seven.'

I nodded in case it might hurry him up.

'She's not very well,' he said.

That sick feeling like a prickly itch inside me started up. I felt very hot and moved back from the fire.

'She's going to be alright,' said Miss Weatherbeaten quickly. 'At least she's not going to die.'

My eyes smarted with sudden tears.

'Well, there's no need to cry,' said Miss Weatherbeaten. 'I've just said she's going to be … .'

'She's going to be mostly alright, in the end,' said Mr Tait. He was right forwards on the front of his rocking chair now, staring at me, but he glanced briefly at Miss Weatherbeaten.

I wiped my face with the sleeve of my jumper.

'Don't … ,' started Miss Weatherbeaten.

'What do you mean?' I said to Mr Tait. 'Mostly alright?'

'I mean … I mean … .'

I held my breath until I was fit to burst. A chill went up my back so I moved in towards the fire again.

'I mean she's lost a leg,' he said. 'Or part of one.'

'Which one?' I said, trying to keep still, and not disturb the bombs.

'Oh, now, I don't know. I didn't ask.'

'How much? How much is … ?'

'I'm afraid I don't know that either.'

'Didn't you see her?' I said. 'Didn't you even see her?'

'No, Lenny, I didn't,' he said.

'She's in there with no leg and you didn't even see her?' I said. I stood up. 'Why didn't you see her?' How could he? She was all alone with strangers in a hospital with her foot … .

'There was a lot to be done today,' he said. 'The factory is still burning. Some of the roads are still blocked. I thought it wiser to use the time when I wasn't at work to collect some of my belongings from the remains of my house.'

The last thing I saw at his house was the head in the sea of bricks. It floated through my head now. I shook myself to get it to go.

'Can we go in the morning?' I said in a whisper.

He took my hand in his again and swung it to and fro.

'Sit down, Lenny,' he said, in his soft voice. 'Sit down and we'll talk about tomorrow later.'

'But we have to go tomorrow,' I said, and I straightened my arm so that he couldn't swing it any more. He let go.

'And so you shall,' he said. 'There's a lot to be done tomorrow too. I'm sorry I can't tell you more about your mother. They had no more information at the town hall, and I gather we're lucky to have that.'

'She's all alone,' I said. 'You said you knew her.'

'I do know her, Lenny,' he said. 'The trouble is … .'

Again he stopped and his wrinkles all sunk over his brow so that I couldn't see his eyes for a minute.

' … your mother doesn't like me very much,' he finished.

When I thought about it I knew that was probably true. She thought he was a bad man with a big stick for naughty kids like me. She had told me that herself, but when I really thought about it, it didn't seem to be true. He was a kind man with a bad leg and a big stick to help him walk.

But I had to listen to what my mother said.

'Why not?' I said. 'Why doesn't she like you?'

Mr Tait was a person who liked to think carefully about what he said before he said it. It could be a bit wearing if you were in a hurry to know something.

'Someone thought she was doing things she shouldn't have been doing at work,' he said, 'and I heard the rumours and warned her. I think the rumours began because the shift organiser likes her and gave her extra shifts to help her make more money. Someone wasn't happy about this – first they invented nasty stories about her and then they made an official complaint. She thinks it was me, but it wasn't.'

'What did they say she was doing?' I said.

'Goodness, too many questions!' he said with a long sigh, shifting back into his seat. 'That's private business and for adults. She'll tell you in her own time if she sees fit.'

'She wants to go to family in America,' I said. 'She and my dad wanted us to. Uncle James lives there. I suppose we can't now, if she's only got one … .'

'Nonsense,' he said, with unusual vigour (my gran's word for what she uses for scrubbing stairs). 'People with legs missing can go to all sorts of places. All you need is a good stick.' He tapped his own which lay against the arm of the rocking chair. 'And plenty of gumption.' He tapped the side of his head. 'And your mother's got plenty of that.'

I got the feeling he liked my mum, even though she didn't like him.

'But … promise … please can we go and visit her tomorrow?'

'Yes, we can go and visit her, if they'll let us in,' again he glanced at Miss Weatherbeaten. 'You know they probably won't let you in, don't you? They don't let children in.'

I saw Miss Weatherbeaten was smiling at me, but there was something funny about that smile, like it was only her mouth doing it and the rest of her seemed to hang, heavy, as if she couldn't move.

'Did you send her a message saying I'm alright?' I said.

'He couldn't,' said Miss Weatherbeaten, coming to life again. 'He didn't know where you were.'

'Oh!' I said. My poor mum. She'd be worried sick. I lost the key, I lost Mavis and then I lost me!

'What about Mavis?' I said. I knew the answer before I asked.

'Sorry,' he said quietly, reaching for my hand again. 'No sign of a Mavis Gillespie. But you know, Lenny, it's chaos down there. Not much has changed since we came away, just no bombers. People got onto buses or went with other people, just like we all did. I'll go back tomorrow and I'll ask for Mavis and I'll tell them where you are.'

The tears smarted to my eyes again. I let them run and I sat there on the three-legged stool and held Mavis's shoe. Nobody uttered a word. Even the horse over the fire seemed to have come to a temporary halt. Mr Tait scraped his rocking chair over the floor and put his arm around my shoulders. He felt solid like an armchair and warm, though his jacket was rough on my face, and he smelled of the fires but also of tea and toast.

'Is it true?' I sniffed. 'Is it true or do you know she's dead and you just won't tell me, to be kind? Do you really know she's dead?'

I sat resolutely on my three-legged stool waiting for his answer, letting him hug me gently. He withdrew his arm from my shoulders and I peered at him through blurry eyes to see how truthful he was being.

'I don't believe in lies,' he said. 'Especially in such matters as life and death. Even with children.'

He glanced past me at Miss Weatherbeaten then back at me. Then he paused.

'Lenny, my dear,' he said, at last. 'You must wipe your tears and save your grief for when you need it, which indeed, you may not.'

He said this kindly, without bossiness or harshness, and he laid his hand on my own hand, in which I turned the shoe that might have been Mavis's, and I let him pull me gently towards him so that I could lean against him and let my sobs subside. Miss Weatherbeaten maintained her silence on the old sofa.

'Now,' he went on. 'Tomorrow … .'

But there was a knock on the door and all heads turned towards it.

It was Mrs Mags and behind her she had a whole crowd of lost people who had come from Clydebank like us. She wanted us to share our hut with them, and seeing as it wasn't ours and they were in the same state as us, we had to, and soon we were stuffed fit to burst with filthy people who smelled of that horrible smell that I didn't want to know about. We tried to make everyone as comfortable as we could but we had nothing to give them except our floor.

Mr Tait slept in the rocking chair, his leg raised on the three-legged stool. Miss Weatherbeaten lay in the bed opposite ours in the bunk room. I clung to Rosie and she clung to me and above us there were two other kids and two more above Miss Weatherbeaten. It was a long awful night. The floor of the stove room was a mass of bodies, arms and legs spread everywhere in a tight space.

In the dim light of the early morning I stole through to Mr Tait who was goading the fire into life so we could drink some hot black tea before our journey to the Western Infirmary, to where my mum was.

'That one's not breathing,' I whispered, indicating a man whose head was half under the sofa. 'He's sleeping the sleep of the ... .'

'He's sleeping the sleep of the absolutely exhausted,' Mr Tait whispered back, 'and we're not going to waken him.'

I watched this man, wanting him to move. His head was on one side and his cheek seemed to have sunk inwards. One eye was slightly open. On the sofa above him lay a girl in a dress that was nearly as ragged as mine. She was bigger than me and had a little kid lying in the crook of her arm, a boy in short trousers with fat stumpy legs and a sudden mass of red curls on his head, his face black.

The grey woollen blankets that I had helped Mrs Mags carry lay over the people on the floor. Some had SA embroidered in red on them. What did that mean? Silly Asses? Sold Already? Sweet Apples? Save Auntie? It was the same letters I had seen on the side of the big blue van that had been in the field behind the Halfway House pub. (Halfway to what?) And what was everyone going to eat?

'Mr Tait?' I whispered.

He handed me some tea. The horse over the stove tapped against the wall as if it was eager to get going.

'Yes, of course we're still going to town,' he said. 'Mrs Mags and Mrs Wilson will look after everyone, and the budgie. Mrs Wilson has more people at her hut and the Salvation Army will be back later.'

Ah, the Salvation Army, hallelujah people in funny hats with trombones at Christmas, except they hadn't had their trombones the day before, only blankets and soup.

We drank our tea until it was time to wake Rosie.

'It's time to get up!' I whispered in my dad's stage whisper. 'Rosie!' I said. 'We're going back today!'

Chapter 16

Rosie and I had to pee in the bushes because the cludgie was in no fit state with so many people. We weren't the first amongst the bracken and the broom either. Mr Tait gave us the last of his bread and we got dressed in our new, clean dresses with the velvet collars that the lady in the town hall had given us. I tied the trouser belt around my waist so that I could hang Mavis's shoe from it and made sure Rosie didn't see. I felt guilty for letting her think she was going to see her mum, but I had to, otherwise she wouldn't have got ready so quickly.

Miss Weatherbeaten seemed to take ages and when we finally climbed into the bus she was silent for most of the way, as if she wasn't really with us.

Rosie and I sat in window seats one behind the other, Miss Weatherbeaten beside her and Mr Tait beside me. So I leant over the seat and tickled Rosie's hair and we watched the green countryside fly past and then the grey streets. There was a church smouldering near the road – the bus had to slow down to get passed it. Some boys were throwing stones at the fire. (Stupid boys, like George and Dougie.) Tenements like ours were black with no roofs and only the sky in their place, and packs of dogs were sniffing amongst the rubble. I wondered if we were nearly home.

'No, Lenny,' said Mr Tait. 'This is Glasgow. They got bombed too.'

He told me we had to go into town and change onto a tram to come back out to Clydebank. We would go to the town hall first to find Mavis, passing the hospital on our way, and then come back to the hospital to find my mum. It seemed daft to me but I took his word for it.

On the tram to Clydebank we pressed our noses to the window to see all the fancy shops. Much fancier than Kilbowie Road they were, and more expensive too according to Miss Weatherbeaten. There were cafes with shiny coloured-glass windows, and people I didn't know walking up and down the street.

'We'll be passing the hospital soon,' said Mr Tait after a bit.

'Will she see me if I wave?' I said. 'I'm going to wave!'

'I'm going to wave too!' said Rosie.

'Why can't I go and see her?' I said.

'She's probably resting,' said Mr Tait.

I realised this was most likely true.

'I'm going to wave anyway,' I said.

'So am I,' said Rosie.

'Couldn't I just go and ask at the front door,' I said. 'I could go and ask if she's alright. Surely I could do that, couldn't I? You could all go to Clydebank, go to work, find Mavis at the town hall and come back here in time for visiting. When did you say it was?'

'That's very organised of you, Lenny,' said Mr Tait, 'but ... .'

'Is that it?' I said. A huge stout building of red sandstone, like the red tenements at home, had appeared beyond some trees. It had pillars and tall windows, a sweeping driveway and deep, wide steps up to the door. 'I'd better get off!'

'That's the museum,' he said, tapping my arm. 'The hospital is over there behind it, but I don't think it's a good idea. They probably won't let you in. Wait and we'll go up at two o'clock together and I'll go and speak to your mum.'

'Can't I see her?'

'I don't think so. They're very strict about children, but I hope they do let you in because then you can tell her I'm not a scary man with a big stick.'

I hid in my hat.

'She might not agree,' he said, 'but you could tell her anyway.'

The tram had stopped, and I realised my heart was pounding. I needed to tell my poor mum that I was alright, and that Mr Tait and Miss Weatherbeaten were going to find Mavis.

'I'm going to tell her you can stay with me in Carbeth until she is better,' he continued. 'That while she is ill you can stay with me and I will provide for you. If she would like me to do that. If she'll let me speak to her.'

He looked very serious. The smile had fallen from his kind old face and deep lines had appeared everywhere. He was worried that she might say no. He coughed lightly and patted his brown hat.

'We're nearly there now,' he said. 'Look, isn't it grand!'

'Maybe they could take a message to her,' I said. 'I mean a message that I'm still alive.'

My heart was beating hard and I gulped for air. But

I couldn't stay on that tram. She was too close to me by then. I had to go, even if it meant sitting on a wall outside waiting in the freezing cold. I pulled my collar up around my neck and stood up.

'Lenny, I don't think … ,' said Mr Tait.

'Lenny!' said Miss Weatherbeaten suddenly, making me jump. 'Sit down IMMEDIATELY and do what Mr Tait says.'

'Lenny, I really don't think … ,' said Mr Tait.

'I'm sorry, Mr Tait, I really have to go. I have to find her. I have to find my mum.'

'Lenny!' said Miss Weatherbeaten.

'Excuse me, Mr Tait,' I said.

After a pause he, too, stood up and let me out of the seat.

'Mr Tait!' said Miss Weatherbeaten. Rosie was silent, pulling at her earlobe.

'I promise I will be there at two o'clock. Sharp,' he said quietly. He smiled a weak little smile, almost a laugh, even though nothing was funny. The he reached up with his big knuckly hand and pulled the cord so a little bell went 'ting' for the driver.

'Thank you,' I said. 'Thank you so much!'

'Lenny,' he said quietly, slipping half-a-crown into my pocket, 'you need to be brave for this.'

'What about Mavis?' I said. 'You will look for Mavis, won't you?'

He looked me in the eye as if he was trying to fill me up with bravery and grit. 'You know I will,' he said. 'Off you go now. Say goodbye to Rosie. Miss Wetherspoon will make sure she stays with us.'

So I stood up on my shaky legs on that big shuddering tram and I said goodbye to Rosie and

Miss Weatherbeaten, and suddenly there I was on the pavement, the great yellow and orange tram pulling the tails of my coat after it in its rush to leave me. Rosie screamed and pressed her face and hands to the window, kneeling on her seat with Miss Weatherbeaten's angry face beside her. Miss Weatherbeaten's hands grasped her by the middle trying to bring her back into the seat. It was the first time we had been parted. I almost wished I'd taken her with me.

Now I had no Mavis and no Rosie. I held Mavis's shoe and looked about me. I didn't even have Mr Tait or Miss Weatherbeaten. I'd have made do with Mrs Mags or even Mrs Wilson at that point, or Mr Chippie, or even Mr Tulloch the farmer. But I knew my mum was not far away and that got my feet going. I watched the tram disappear behind a row of buildings and turned my feet towards the great giant that was the hospital.

Suddenly this didn't seem so easy.

It was immense, gigantic, enormous and much more and it got bigger and bigger as I trudged towards it. It loomed over me and stretched all around like big arms ready to pull me in. There were turrets with little pointy roofs and balconies and chimneys and hundreds of soaring windows, and I thought about all the blackout curtains they'd need and how big each curtain would need to be. There must be thousands of people in there, I thought, and I wondered where they went when the sirens sounded and how they got people like my mum out when they couldn't walk. I thought about all the sick people not being able to move, like the bad boys' granny downstairs in our close who was probably dead. I thought about this big place where all the people were big, and small people, like me, weren't allowed, unless they were sick too. I needed all the grit I could muster so I thought about Mr Tait filling me up in the tram, and then I reached the steps, and when I was ready I stepped up to the door and went in.

Chapter 17

The lady at the desk told me I was too early to visit anyone, that I had to come back later for visiting time, and then she glanced up for the first time and said that children weren't allowed in anyway in case they spread germs. I didn't know what to do so I went and sat on a bench outside and fiddled with Mavis's shoe. Then I went back in.

'Excuse me,' I said. 'My mum thinks I'm dead. We're from Clydebank, you see, and our house burnt down.' I thought I'd better explain in case she didn't know.

She looked me up and down. I hate it when grown-ups do that.

'I thought she might get better if she knew I was alive.' I pointed this out in case she thought I was just making conversation.

'There's a waiting room down the corridor,' she said. 'Some other people like you with nowhere to go are already down there.' She looked me up and down again.

'I have somewhere to go,' I told her indignantly.

But she sighed and looked straight at me at last.

'Then go there,' she said, and went back to writing something in her ledger.

I thought of Rosie shaking her fist at the bad boys

with her chin jutting out and her lips all scrunched up together, but all I could do was slink away in the direction of the waiting room, and as I got close to it I began to smell that terrible smell again, the smell of the bombing, of debris flying about and smoke and unexploded bombs, and I couldn't go in and be back in that hell. There, I've said it. Hell. That's what it was. It's how I'll always imagine hell, and there were no bells, like my dad used to say when he thought no-one was listening, only boom, crash, crackle and roar.

'Hell's bells!' I whispered under my breath.

'I beg your pardon?' boomed a voice.

I dived in the door of the waiting room.

'What are you doing here anyway?' said a tall woman in a suit. 'Children are not allowed in here. Poo, what a stench!'

She had a strange voice, a bit like my dad when he's playing the fool. I half-expected her to say 'Lah-di-dah!' But she didn't. She craned her long neck over my head into the waiting room.

'I'm looking for ward twenty-seven,' I told her. 'I've got an urgent message for someone there.'

'Ward twenty-seven is up those stairs,' she said crisply, her gaze returning to me. 'Can't you read the signs? Give your message to the lady at the desk and I'm sure she'll get it to the individual in question.'

Well, yes, I could read the signs but I needed to notice them first. I didn't say this to her. I just nodded and watched her float off down the hall in her long tweed suit with no threads hanging down, and her shoes going clickety-click on the hard floor. Individual in question? What did she mean by that? What question was the individual, my mum, in?

I did think about going back to the lady at the desk but she didn't seem to understand how important it was that my mum knew I was there, alive and well, even though I'd lost Mavis. So, before I'd even planned it, I ran my eyes from left to right along the corridor then I flew up those stairs faster than the wind, and faster than debris after a bomb, and found myself in a corridor similar to the one I'd just left. There was no-one in the dry silence of its length but ward twenty-seven was on the right-hand side.

There were too many beds to count in ward twenty-seven, probably about a hundred, maybe, and a terrible smell of boiled cabbage and school cludgies. I couldn't see my mum from the tiny crack I'd opened in the door. Nearly everyone seemed to be sleeping and I wondered if they were sleeping the sleep of the … no, I didn't think so, not dead, not there. There were strange contraptions attached to some of the beds, with metal sticking out and things hanging down. There were white bandages around heads and arms and legs and no sound at all, except for some wheezing. It was the biggest room I'd ever seen, bigger even than the school assembly hall, with cool light from some windows high up on one side and a huge fireplace in the middle where a fire glowed. And then I noticed two ladies and a man standing round a bed at the far end of the room, and I mean the far end of the room.

'Give her some … ,' said the man in a plummy voice like the tweed lady downstairs, and one of the ladies nodded. They were all dressed in white. I couldn't make out what they were saying so I started looking for my mum, checking each bed as far as I could see.

But I was disturbed by voices further down the corridor and suddenly I was through the door, and almost as suddenly I was underneath the nearest bed with my hat toppled around my neck again. A snore sounded above me. The floor was smooth, hard and cold. I couldn't see much above the beds but underneath them and further down the line, in amongst the bed legs there were some human legs, those of the doctor and two nurses. One of the nurses was scratching the back of her ankle with her other foot. They shuffled round to the next bed and stopped again.

I shouldn't have been in there. What on earth was I doing? How did I end up in this mess? That's another fine mess … only this one wasn't funny.

'Pssst!' said a voice. 'Pssst!'

A hand dangled off the side of the next bed. It was an old hand with wrinkles and veins, like my gran's, and freckles all up the arm, as far as I could see.

'What are you doing here?' said the voice. 'They'll kill you if they find you.'

I already knew that.

'I'm looking for my mum,' I said to the side of the next bed. 'Peggy Gillespie.'

'They'll kill the bloody sister too, for that matter, which would be no bad thing!' said the voice. 'You're in luck. She's two down from here. Nice girl, your mum.'

'Thanks!'

'Don't get caught,' she said.

Two beds down, having tossed all care to the wind, I found her. I found my mum.

I found my mum!

It was so hard to contain myself and not get off the floor and jump up and down and scream and sing and shake myself all about that I had to cover my mouth with both hands and jiggle on my knees so that my dress bounced and Mavis's shoe slapped at my side.

And then I stopped bouncing and checked to make sure I hadn't been seen. I was on the floor beside my mum's bed, down on my knees and then I noticed the name above the bed. It was a brass plate on the wall with a name on it, like some people have at their front doors, but the name wasn't hers. It was Picklethwaite. It said 'Donated by Mr and Mrs PICKLETHWAITE' and I wondered whether I was at the right bed after all because it wasn't my mum's name up there above her but somebody else's. Mr Tait told me afterwards it was the name of the people who bought the bed and gave it to the hospital.

'Pssst!' said the voice, only I could see her now over the sleeping lady in the bed between us. She was pointing at my mum and at the wall behind her and I noticed another, smaller sign made of card saying 'Gillespie' which was on a shelf behind her head. I looked closer and underneath Gillespie it said 'Margaret' which is another name for Peggy, only I don't know why it had a second 'a' because everybody knows its Margret not Mar-gar-et. You'd think those people would have known. So I had a closer look at this sleeping Mar-gar-et who might be Peggy, my mum, just to make sure.

This is what I saw: she had my mum's lovely brown hair, all clean and shining on the snow-white, crispy pillow, and my mum's soft pale skin on her face with cheeks that were almost without colour, as if she'd put on her foundation and forgotten the rouge. Around her head to one side there was a thick white bandage that was tied above her eye with a safety pin, like my Auntie May's turban hat slipped sideways with a not-so-fancy pin. Her eyes were red and sore but her long eyelashes were as thick as ever. Her lips were pale like ashes and above them was the tiny scar she'd had since she was Mavis's age. A blue bruise was on her neck and her arms were criss-crossed with more bruises and cuts, a bit like my own. She was wearing a plain white nightgown with ribbon ties on her chest, and her hand lay entangled in the ties as if she'd been fidgeting with them when she fell asleep. A sheet and a green blanket were wrinkled at her waist. I followed the contours of her hips and legs and at the bottom of the bed I saw what wasn't there. There was no lump where her foot should have risen like the other one into a sharp peak, and over the end of the bed was a metal cage, I suppose to protect her from anything that might fall on her.

So it was her, it really was, and this horrible thing had really happened. I stared at this gap at the bottom of the bed, horrified, the sickness rising in me again, my stomach full of butterflies and wasps. I was willing it not to be true, willing her foot back and wondering where they would have put it so that we could put it back on, her poor foot that wasn't where it should be. I peered into her face and listened for her breath and watched the shallow rise and fall of her chest. I wanted to ask her where it was, the foot that was missing but not dead, surely not back in the heap I had seen by the road the night we left Clydebank. I bobbed down onto my knees again to hide.

'Mum!' I whispered in her ear. 'Mum! It's me, it's Lenny! Leonora! Mum!'

She lay like an impenetrable castle, spread out before me, there but not there, lost in a mist of her own, giving nothing away. I put my hands over my mouth again in case any of those fizzing bombs went off, or the wasps and butterflies inside me fluttered out, and I checked her chest again, in case she'd died right there in front of me without letting me know. Her chest rose again and fell again and rose and fell and rose and fell, and I put my ear to her nose so that I could feel her breath against it, but still she didn't speak, not even a whisper.

'Mum!' I said again, and I felt the tears of longing slide down my cheeks and I had to fold my mouth inside and hold my breath to stop the cries from bursting out because then the nurses and the doctors would come and throw me out and not let me back in even to ask at the desk, or to leave a message and she wouldn't even know that I'd been there. I put both hands over my eyes now and pressed them so that the tears couldn't get out but they got out anyway and I had to wipe them away on the sleeve of my new coat from the town hall.

'Mum!'

I leant forward to kiss her but my pretty hat with the purple flowers fell in the way and its scratchy rough edge fell onto her smooth pale cheek. I lifted it carefully from my head, ruffling my strange, boy's hair cut and I shoved it under the bed behind the little cabinet that sat there with a glass of water on top. Now that I'd noticed the glass sitting there, and being thirsty, I just had to have a little sip because

I hadn't had anything since Mr Tait's black tea that morning.

When I went back to kiss her a strange thing happened. Instead of kissing her, I leant in along her side, just like we were at home and she was sleeping in our own bed in the alcove. I lay along her side on the bed with only my feet still on the floor, and I imagined Mavis on her other side, wee enough to snuggle into her, while I laid my head in the crook of her arm and slipped my fingers through hers so that the ties on her nightgown became entangled with mine too. I closed my eyes tight and I wished and wished for us all to be alright, for her foot to be back where it belonged so that I wouldn't have to see it in my head, and for her to wake up soon and tell me where Mavis was.

'Mum!' I whispered. And then I remembered about Mr Tait's prayer and I said, without saying it out loud, 'Dear God, Please make my mum better and find Mavis and take us all back home soon. Love Leonora Gillespie.'

Of course, not long after that the doctor and nurses came round to the bed on the opposite wall from Peggy Gillespie's bed and there I was, caught like a rabbit in a trap, all the electric lights on me as if the moon was full and the bombers had me in their sights. Run, rabbit, run!

'She's my mum,' I said, so they'd know it was alright, even though I knew it wasn't.

'What in heaven's name are you doing there?' said a grey-haired woman in white. 'Get down from there, you filthy wee rascal. I'm so sorry, doctor. I don't know how … .'

I didn't move.

'Get down from there when I tell you to!' she said.

'Yes,' said the plummy doctor. 'How is it possible in a hospital of this calibre and in time of war, that urchins of this sort can wander in here without anyone so much as noticing? Extraordinary!'

'I'm so sorry doctor. It won't happen again, I promise. I'll make sure of it,' said the grey-haired nurse. 'Get up then, you! Who do you think you are? You heard what the doctor said.'

'She's my mum,' I said again. 'She doesn't know I'm … .'

'How dare you speak to the doctor!' she said. 'Be quiet!'

She came at me with her big strong hands but I pulled away and accidentally knocked over the glass of water on the bedside cabinet and my back walloped against the bed.

'Children in here indeed!' she said under her breath while she was righting the glass. 'Nurse a towel! How did you let her get past you?'

The other nurse was young with painted eyebrows and dark hair in a tight bun. She stood to attention. Our eyes met briefly and a smile trembled on her lips. She turned away and her feet tippety-tapped across the linoleum floor.

'What were you thinking?' said the grey-haired nurse. 'Coming in here with your germs and such-like. You've probably killed her, you dirty wee midden.' She spat the words out as if they were filth in her mouth.

Was it true? Could I have killed her?

'Look,' she said. 'You've woken the whole ward now.'

No, I haven't, I thought, not all of them.

'Mum!' I said, this time out loud. 'Mum, wake up! You have to wake up!' I gave her arm a shake. 'Mum!'

The doctor was tapping his fingers on the metal end of the bed. Click, click, click went the gold ring he wore.

'I'm losing patience,' he said.

'Out, you!' said the nurse. 'Out, right now!'

'Mum!' I said, louder now.

'Out!'

Click, click, click!

The grey-haired nurse grabbed my sore arm and hoisted me away knocking my foot against the bed end with a clunk.

'MUM!' I screamed. 'MUM!'

'LENNY!' She had woken up!

'MUM!' I screamed again, and wrenched at my arm and kicked at the grey nurse's legs. 'MUM!'

The young nurse came through the door with a towel in her hand.

'What on earth took you so long?' said the grey-haired nurse indignantly.

The young nurse looked at me and then at her shoes.

'MUM!' I howled, but I couldn't get free.

'Take this ragamuffin and make sure she gets back out onto the street and let them know down at reception that they will be hearing from me shortly.'

The young nurse took my other arm and they both wrestled me through the ward door. Then the grey-haired nurse turned swiftly on her heel and left us. The door rattled shut behind us.

'Stop struggling!' snapped the nurse.

'I want my mum!' I shouted. 'I want my mum!'

'Stop it!' she said.

'MUM! MUM!'

'Shut up, Lenny or I'll … .'

'My hat!' I said. 'I left my hat!'

She propelled me back down the stairs past the smelly waiting room, past the reception desk and out the front door where I had the biggest coughing fit since the bombing.

She waited until I'd stopped, I suppose in case I died. 'You poor thing,' she said, and then she went back in.

Chapter 18

Mr Tait arrived at two o'clock on the dot. Sharp, just like he said. But that had left me with a good few hours to reflect on my misbehaviour and to dread his arrival when I'd have to confess. Miss Weatherbeaten and Rosie were not with him.

He had a basket in one hand and his fancy bedpost stick in the other.

'Lenny!' he smiled.

'Hello, Mr Tait,' I said, jumping off the wall I'd been perched on for ages and ages.

'I brought you an orange,' he said, bringing one out of his pocket and handing it to me. I was surprised, delighted and ashamed all at the same time.

'Thank you,' I said, drooling. 'Thank you so much!' But I knew he'd take it back once he knew what I'd done.

It was a blood orange. I hadn't had one before. I peered at it and rolled it in my hand like a precious jewel that belonged to someone else.

'What's that?' I pointed at its strange mottled peel. 'Is it alright?'

'Of course it's alright,' he said kindly. 'I know it looks a bit funny. It's funny inside too.'

It looked like a big bruise to me, a new one, the kind that isn't blue, like the ones me and Rosie had, like my mum must have had too, with veins of red blood through it.

'Thank you,' I said, not sure.

'Don't forget it's an orange, just an orange, and it tastes just the same as an ordinary one,' he said. 'Now, have you asked after your mum? What did they say?'

We sat down on the wall that I'd been on for so long that it felt like my very own wall, and I told him the whole sorry tale.

'Oh, dear,' he said.

'Oh, dear,' I said. It was cold. I was cold. I was waiting for him to stop being the nice Mr Tait with a golden red orange for a present and become the scary man with a big stick for naughty kids like me.

'I'm sorry,' he said after a bit. 'I shouldn't have let you come down here all by yourself. Whatever was I thinking?' I was confused. He didn't seem to be angry.

'At least I saw her, and I saw … .' I couldn't say it. 'You know … .'

'You saw her leg?'

'I saw it under the covers. I saw where it should have been.'

'Oh, dear. What did you think?'

I didn't know if it was alright to say my poor mum's leg was horrible, especially when I hadn't even seen it. I didn't know if it was alright for my stomach to churn at the very thought, for me to imagine the foot I knew so well that I'd tickled and felt on my backside, for me to imagine it to be like the bits I'd seen when the bombs were falling. Things I didn't want to see crowded back into my head. I closed my eyes to make them go away. They didn't.

'Lenny?' he said. 'Lenny!'

'Did you find Mavis?' I said, forcing the words out.

'Miss Wetherspoon has gone to the town hall with Rosie. She'll tell us about Mavis when she gets back to Carbeth.'

'Oh,' I said. It hurt to think about Mavis too. It didn't feel like bombs in my stomach any more. It was like all the bits of me that were usually bendy were suddenly stiff and straight which made it hard to move. Too much grit.

'Let's stick with your mum just now, shall we?'

He had jammy pieces in his basket, and three daffodils. He handed me two jammy pieces so that my hands were full and he stuck one of the daffodils into a buttonhole in my coat.

'Where's your hat?' he said, and when I told him, he promised to get it back.

'Right then, young lady,' he said. 'Can you bear to sit here a while longer and I'll go and see what's what?'

I nodded and he disappeared through the big main door to the hospital and left me warmed with anticipation and reassurance. It was all going to be alright. I tucked into my jammy sandwiches and crossed my fingers that my mum would believe how kind he was.

The next hour felt more like a zillion hours.

At last Mr Tait came back out the same door he'd gone in and took off his cap to wipe the sweat from his brow with his handkerchief.

'Good gracious me!' he laughed. 'Goodness. Gracious. Me! What a lassie!'

'Who? What happened?'

'Let me sit down a minute,' he panted. 'Let me sit! What a nest of she-cats!

'Tell me! Tell me!' I was laughing too, infected by his mirth. (That's another of my dad's special words. Mirth.)

So we sat back down on my wall and he pulled the pretty hat with the pink and yellow ribbon out of his basket. It was wet where some of the water from the glass had landed and it had been squashed flat so that a line ran from the front to the back where the straw had burst. I straightened it out and put it back on my head. He stuck a daffodil on one side under the ribbon.

I hadn't eaten the blood orange. Somehow I couldn't bring myself to do it.

'So, what happened?' I said, unable to wait while he caught his breath.

'Quite a stooshy you caused up there young lady! A stooshy indeed! And your mother's good for a stooshy too.'

So after he'd rested his bad leg for a bit we walked the length of the great sweeping driveway and stood at the tram stop for a tram home, to Carbeth, the closest thing we had to home, and he told me all about it.

This is what happened.

Mr Tait went to the reception desk and he asked for ward twenty-seven. The unhappy receptionist looked at him as if he was a rat and she was a snake under a rock, and she asked him who he was intending visiting. When he told her it was Peggy Gillespie she stopped looking at him like a snake and started moving the papers about on her desk and slamming them down into even neater piles than they were already in.

Finally she told him that Mrs Gillespie was not allowed visitors today due to an 'incident' earlier on.

Mr Tait told her he was a very important person at Singer's factory and that it was 'vital' that he see Mrs Gillespie that day.

The unhappy and prim receptionist snorted, something Mavis and I used to practise a lot, but not normally acceptable behaviour among adults.

Mr Tait produced a blood orange from his basket and tossed it nonchalantly into the air with one hand, watching it rise and fall as he did so.

'What a shame,' he said. 'Now I have too many oranges.'

'I'll not be persuaded with that sort of brriberry,' she said, just like Miss Weatherbeaten.

'Shame,' he said, and he stopped throwing the orange into the air and set it down on the desk in front of her. 'Could you convey a message to Mrs Gillespie? Please tell her that while she is incapacitated, I will care for her lovely daughter, Lenny, at Carbeth.'

The unhappy receptionist eyed the orange then said, of course she could do that and reached out to take the fruit from where it sat on top of the counter.

'Oh, no,' said Mr Tait in his usual mild manner. 'Oranges are only for visits.' And he whipped away the orange from right under the receptionist's greedy little nose and her sneaky little hand. Mr Tait cleared his throat and tossed the orange in the air again.

A nurse hurried by, giving the receptionist enough time to think over the price of her meanness.

Mr Tait replaced the orange on the counter.

The receptionist said the ward sister had been unclear in her instructions and thought the word 'probably' might have been said in relation to whether Mrs Gillespie was to be allowed visitors. Perhaps he'd like to take his chances with her. Ward twenty-seven was on the first floor, down the corridor past the (smelly) waiting room.

Mr Tait smiled sweetly and thanked her very much, leaving the orange on the counter.

Upstairs he found the door to the ward, cleared his throat, straightened his tie, straightened his back, removed his hat and flattened his hair.

'Can I help you?' said the nurse who was at the nurse's station.

Mr Tait explained who he was and asked if he might be allowed to speak to Mrs Peggy Gillespie.

The nurse went to ask and returned with a smirk on her face. She said she was not able to repeat what Mrs Gillespie had said but the answer was 'no'. This was not good news and I found my heart beating on my ribs once more when he told me this. Really, if they'd just let me in none of this would have happened.

'Shame,' said Mr Tait, who assures me that blood oranges would not have worked in this instance nor would they have worked with the ward sister, or with Matron who finally had to be summoned.

Mrs Gillespie, my mum, was refusing to see anyone, least of all Mr Tait, until she had been allowed to see me, yes, me, Leonora Gillespie.

Mr Tait was refusing to leave until he was allowed to see her, Mrs Peggy Gillespie, my mum.

The most almighty row followed because apparently someone, possibly the young nurse, didn't agree that Mr Tait should have to leave. During this argument Mr Tait sneaked in his rumbling way down the ward, swept my fantastic straw hat with the ribbons and flowers and elastic from the floor under my mum's bed, emptied his basket of goodies and daffodils onto the cabinet beside it, being careful not to knock over the glass of water, and told her very quickly about our plan.

My mum then lifted the daffodils and threw them at him saying, 'Bring back my Lenny! Where's Lenny? Where's Mavis? You've done enough harm!' The tears were rushing down her poor pale cheeks.

He reassured her, from a sensible distance, that I was safe and well, and that he and Miss Weatherbeaten were doing all they could to find Mavis, that I was outside eager for news, but Matron and everybody else were determined not to give me any.

And right on cue Matron, the grey-haired ward sister, the young nurse and two others discovered their loss at the door and arrived to 'retrieve' Mr Tait from my mum's bedside. My mum was speechless by this time, but some of the other patients were not and were applauding him for his 'audacity', others booing the ward sister, and some were cheering the nurses for evicting him.

Mr Tait shouted over his shoulder to my mum, as he was guided swiftly to the door, that he would take very good care of me, she wasn't to worry, she still had her job and soon she would have Mavis as well, but she didn't seem to want to hear.

He was escorted to the front door (past the reception desk where a faint whiff of orange hung in the air) by the Matron who was explaining why no children were allowed into the hospital – germs and infections and all that, carried in on air and clothes and things. I don't quite understand it but Mr Tait said the danger on me was dirt we couldn't see but the doctors and nurses knew all about it. He told her that he agreed wholeheartedly with everything she said, but that he, himself, had important things to say to Mrs Gillespie and would be back again very soon.

I was barely breathing by the time he'd finished. I stared blindly out of the tram windows at all the shops passing by and all the people going about and thought about her all alone in that big ward of strangers and the ward sister who was being unkind to her.

'No Mavis,' I said.

'No, no Mavis,' said Mr Tait.

We got off the yellow and orange tram in the middle of Glasgow and onto a blue Alexander's bus for Carbeth and I watched the streets of the north-west of the city flit past. Some of them looked just like Clydebank, with houses collapsed into heaps, but no smoke or fire, just everything black, the stones, the roads, the people all dressed in dark colours and nobody smiling. And as we passed the big houses on the outskirts, the daylight started to go and then the green fields of the country looked cold and the black unclothed trees were like the broken tramlines in Kilbowie Road.

Other people on the bus were travelling with bundles wrapped in blankets, suitcases, pots and pans, brown-paper parcels, kettles and buckets. I turned away and wrapped my coat around me and let the world drift by.

Then the rain came on, running in thick lines outside the window, and on the inside the mist clung to the glass, making my shoulder wet from lying against it. The bus rattled along and shoogled us from side to side, bumping my head off the window pane.

Mr Tait had to hold the handle on the seat in front to keep from falling into the passageway.

The damp seemed to slither up my bare legs, and make my skin creep. I felt myself shrink, like the rain shrinks your jumper if you're caught in a shower. I thought about Mavis and where I'd last seen her, down by the canal throwing dirt in a bad boy's eyes, but I couldn't see her face and I wondered if that meant she was dead. I wished Mr Tait would talk to me so that I didn't have to think like that.

The blood orange that Mr Tait had given me was still in the pocket of my coat, warm and a bit squashed between me and him. When I pulled it out, he smiled and said we could have it later, that he had another one for Rosie.

'Oh, an orange!' said a lady who was going down the aisle to get off the bus. 'This lucky wee lassie's got an orange, no less!' she announced to the rest of the bus.

'Give us a bit of your orange then!' said someone at the back of the bus.

Mr Tait put it in his basket on his knee. Then someone began to sing, 'Don't sit under the apple tree with anyone else but me!' It was a woman with a scarf wound round her head, but someone else cut in, 'I don't like your peaches, they are full of stones,' and then the whole bus joined in, 'I LIKE BANANAS! Because they have no bones!'

Then everybody fell about laughing, which was funny enough in itself, if you're in the mood, but I didn't understand what they were saying, especially the ladies. Mr Tait, who had seemed quite delighted with the singing at first, became quite cross, I think, with his brow all furrowed and wrinkly, and I wondered if he was annoyed because I hadn't eaten the orange outside the hospital. Perhaps he thought I wasn't grateful, which I was.

'Oh, what I wouldn't do for a banana ... ,' and they screamed with laughter, and I couldn't help agreeing.

But by then we had arrived at Carbeth.

Chapter 19

Mr Tait had a terrible time getting up the hill that afternoon because of his leg.

'What's wrong with your leg, Mr Tait?' I asked him. He was using me as a crutch, leaning one hand on my shoulder and the other on his fancy stick.

He waited a very long time before he answered, but then all he said was, 'Nothing much. Sometimes it gets a bit stiff.'

What I really wanted to know was how he'd hurt it in the first place, but then he stopped suddenly and his face twisted up in pain. After a few seconds he patted the bad leg and cleared his throat with a great harrumph and I thought I'd better not ask again.

There was a great hoo-haa going on at our hut, which wasn't really our hut. It was full of people and they were all talking at once. The stove door was open and a fire blazed fiercely in the grate. Someone else was in Mr Tait's rocking chair. The hut smelled that horrible way of smoke and whisky and burnt buildings and it wasn't just ours any more.

So I hid in my hat and sneaked off to the lookout chair as soon as I could, even though it was still drizzling and the light was going. Mr Tait gave me the blood orange before I went, saying I'd braved the ward sister and I deserved it.

So I stuck my thumb in the top of it and peeled off the skin. The segments unstuck themselves with a gasp and I thought about what Mr Tait had said. It was just an orange, like any other orange, so I kept my eyes shut to make that easier to believe. But when I opened them I saw the blood running between the little orange beads in that first segment. I wondered whether that was what I would look like if you cut across the bruises on my arms with a knife. I wondered if my mum's leg looked like that.

'I like bananas,' I sang under my breath as I chewed, 'because they have no bones. Don't give me tomatoes, can't stand ice cream cones. I like bananas … .'

But I had to eat it because Mr Tait had given it to me and because it was an orange, roughly equivalent to a pot of gold, and because it tasted absolutely, miraculously delicious. It seemed to bring my whole body to life with its sharp, sweet tartness.

Tart-ness. Was my miraculous mum full of sweet, sharp, tartness?

I was halfway through, trembling with confusion and dripping with juice down my chin, when Sandy and Dougie came round the bushes. They seemed surprisingly grey in their grey jumpers against the winter brown of the hills, and their faces shone in the twilight.

'It's a blood orange,' I told them.

I could see they were impressed and appalled.

'That's disgusting!' said Dougie.

'How do they get the blood into it?' said Sandy, examining a piece of peel.

'It's not real blood,' I laughed, understanding this properly for the first time.

'What does it taste like?' said Dougie. 'Give us a bit then.'

So I gave them a piece each and then they were covered in pink sticky juice too.

And while we were standing there guzzling, Sandy happened to mention big bad George for no reason, except to tell me that he wasn't allowed out because he'd been swearing again and because he called my mum a tart.

'Bloody hell!' I said, as much to my surprise as theirs and we set off across the wet grass to where the last bus would come.

And then suddenly some other kids ran past, like a flock of birds at the clap of your hands.

'It's the bus!' said Sandy as he charged on ahead. 'Come on!'

'Woo, woo, woo!' I called after them, imitating their excitement, trying to feel it. 'Hello, Mr Tait!' I said as I passed him a little way down the hill leaning on his fancy bedpost stick.

The bus clattered to a halt a few minutes later after a few resounding choruses of 'Why are we waiting?' and amid a round of applause. But this applause soon fell away, shooshed by Mrs Mags and Mrs Wilson who cleared a path for the latest escapees from Clydebank to step down and begin the hard trudge up the hill for a hut, for a night or perhaps longer. I waited for Miss Weatherbeaten and Rosie, and then the crowd thinned and everyone disappeared up the hill. I watched the bus roar away from the side of the road and vanish round the bend and a dread crept over me. They were not there, no Rosie, no Miss Weatherbeaten, and no Mavis.

Sandy, the sandy-haired boy came back for me.

'Did they miss the bus?' he said.

How should I know? I thought.

'Must have missed the bus,' he said, as if this was now an established fact.

How would he know? I thought. Nobody knew, so why say something so stupid? And now I wouldn't know about Mavis until tomorrow. How was I going to get through the night without even Rosie to look after?

'That's a shame. It's the last bus,' he said.

'I know,' I said through tight lips.

I looked up the road after the bus and listened for it to turn round and come back, open its door and let Mavis out, the driver saying, 'Look who I forgot to leave! Aren't I silly?' Then I'd go over and hug her and take her bag, if she had one, and her hand, and lead her up the hill to 'our' hut.

'Mine missed it too,' he said. 'My dad,' he went on, 'he's always missing the bus and then he has to stay at my uncle's. My mum gets very angry.'

'Oh,' I said, not really interested. 'Mmm,' I said. There was a cold chill creeping up my back and it had nothing to do with the weather.

'They'll be alright,' he said.

'How do you know?' I snapped.

He didn't reply. I pulled my hat back down and watched the rain run into the puddles. I couldn't imagine what could have happened to Miss Weatherbeaten and Rosie. It gave me a bad feeling.

'I hope they're alright,' said Sandy quietly interrupting my thoughts.

I fumbled for Mavis's shoe under my coat.

'Better go up then,' said Sandy.

'Yes,' I said. 'Mr Tait will be wondering what's kept me.'

How steep that hill was and how quiet the trees that stood there. And everything was sodden, the grass, our shoes and socks, everything. We climbed the first part in silence and then he surprised me.

'My mum, Mrs Mags, says you'll be going to school tomorrow.'

'What?' I said.

'Craigton,' he said. 'It's very nice. Much smaller than our school at home and there's a big field out the back to play in.'

'I don't want to go to school,' I said. 'I have to find Mavis. I can't go to school.' I stopped on the side of the hill. 'I have to find Mavis,' I said again. Nobody seemed to understand that.

'We sang all yesterday morning,' he said. 'Run, Hitler, run Hitler, run, run, run. No lessons, just singing.'

'Oh, good,' I said flatly, even though I liked the idea of singing all morning, especially if you got to sing the words wrong. Miss Weatherbeaten would never have allowed that. 'I suppose I'll have to find Rosie and Miss Weatherbeaten too now.'

'Won't Mr Tait find them?' he said. We started up the hill again.

'Well, no-one's managed to find Mavis so far, so I'm going to have to do it myself.'

'I'll help you,' he said.

I squinted at him from beneath my hat, which was soggy and sagging. What kind of help could he be?

'My mum, Mrs Mags, says you're going to go into one of the tents too,' he said.

'No!' I said.

'Yes,' he said. 'That's what she said, a tent. Don't know what'll happen now Miss Weatherbeaten's not back. I mean you can't live in a tent with Mr Tait. You're not even related to him. It's not like he's your dad.'

'Yes, I can,' I said, changing my mind. 'I can live in a tent.' I'd never been in one but it couldn't be that hard could it? 'And I'm sticking with Mr Tait until my mum's better. He promised. He promised to provide for me. My mum threw his daffodils at him, but I don't think she meant it.'

I put my hand to my head to make sure the daffodil was still there then sniffed a big sniff and drew my sleeve across the bottom of my nose.

And there was Mr Tait, standing in the drizzle still leaning on his fancy stick.

'Oh, Mr Tait!' I said. 'Sorry I was so long. Are you alright?'

'Yes, Lenny my dear, quite alright really, but I need to go back up and sit down. Where are Miss Wetherspoon and Rosie?'

Sandy and I helped Mr Tait back up to Mrs Mags's hut where we were welcomed with toast and jam and a space was cleared on the old sofa for Mr Tait to sit on. Bad George growled at me and wiggled his hips in a funny way when he thought the grown-ups weren't looking but they were and he was sent through to the other room. Sandy and I sat on the bench I'd been on before.

I told Mrs Mags and Mr Tait all about Miss Weatherbeaten and Rosie not coming back when they were meant to. Mr Tait seemed very angry, which I'd never seen before, so I was glad Sandy and Mrs Mags were there. Perhaps my mum had been right after all. The wrinkles all creased together over his brow and he muttered something to himself but I couldn't make out what, something like, 'Please God, put love in that beaten heart.' And after that the sick feeling came back so I stared at the picture of Izzie laughing over their stove.

The light was gone now and the room was yellow and pale with only one candle. I could barely see at all. Mr Tait and Mrs Mags were talking. Mr Tait was calmer again and the shadows had taken his wrinkles, in fact they'd nearly gobbled him up altogether.

'Do you like my pictures?' said a voice.

'Oh!' I said, jumping in my seat.

'She can't see your pictures, Grandpa,' said Sandy. 'She can't even see you.'

'No, but I saw her looking before,' said Mr MacInnes, the old man in the shadows, Mrs Mags's father-in-law. 'She looks at the pictures more than she looks at the people. Very wise.'

'Matter of opinion, Grandpa,' said Sandy.

'I think they're very nice,' I said.

'See?' said Grandpa Mags defiantly with a chuckle. All I could see of him was the whites of his eyes and his hands on the top of his stick. He was sitting on a chair in the corner behind the sofa, as if to keep himself out of everyone's way.

'Well, she has to say that!' said Sandy.

'No, I mean it. I like them,' I said.

'Which is your favourite? Let me guess, no, don't interrupt,' he waved an arm in the air as if he had a duster to rub me out. His other hand held his forehead between finger and thumb trying to squeeze the answer from it. 'Pah!' he said. 'It has to be the one of my granddaughter up there over the stove. Looks like she's laughing doesn't it? Ha, ha! I always get it, everyone's favourites.'

'Well, actually … .'

'Ah, you're just teasing. I'm always right. Everyone loves that one. Ha, ha!'

'But … .'

'Grandpa, tell Lenny where you got the paper and the pencil,' said Sandy.

'It was Barmy's sister, wasn't it?' said Mr MacInnes.

'Don't call him Barmy, Mr MacInnes,' interrupted Mrs Mags, 'or you'll say it to his face one day.' She threw me a grin and went back to her conversation with Mr Tait.

'Barney, Barmy what's the difference?' said the old man tossing his head at her. Landlords are landlords whatever you call them. Anyway this was Miss Barmy doing the rounds with his lordship one day and graced us with her presence and sat exactly where you're sitting now, and blow me but wasn't she sitting in just that exact same position as you are now, and wouldn't you make a lovely picture just like she did that day? Blast the darkness, is all I can say, but you can come back tomorrow, eh? This day, Miss Barmy was lovely sitting there on the bench with her hat and her bunch of bluebells, so while everyone was talking, I took the liberty of a quick sketch. Now Mr Barnes could quite easily have thought that cheeky, which it was, and he could have put us off the site straightaway, and I think he would have liked to, but she was delighted and gave me a sketch pad and some pencils from her bag.

Turns out she's a famous artist. Talk about coals to Newcastle!'

'Oh!' I said. 'A real artist sitting here!'

'Gave me a shilling for the picture too.'

Sandy snorted noisily.

'Grandpa ... .'

'Stop that snorting, Sandy, it's not nice,' said Mrs Mags. 'You'd like to go to school, wouldn't you, Lenny, dear?' she said, changing the subject. 'Sandy can take you down to Craigton in the morning on the bus. Mr Tait will probably be gone by then, won't you Mr Tait?'

'I'll sort her out,' said George from the doorway to the next room.

'I'll sort you out,' said Mrs Mags fiercely, then she composed herself and George slunk off.

'I'll find Miss Wetherspoon and Rosie,' said Mr Tait before I could say anything. 'And Mavis. I'll go and find out first thing in the morning.'

'She doesn't want to go to school,' said the old man in the corner. 'Don't make her go to school. She wants to stay here and learn to draw with me. We'll look after her, won't we Mrs Mags?'

'Don't be silly, Mr MacInnes, why would she want to do that?' said Mrs Mags.

'Why wouldn't she?'

'Because the law says she has to go to school,' said Mrs Mags.

'We'd all like to stay and learn to draw with you,' said Mr Tait. I think he was speaking for himself. 'But we have to work and study too, to keep this country on its feet.'

'Would you like a lesson or two Mr Tait?' said Mr

MacInnes. 'I've got some fine brushes and paints too.'

'But I can't go to school,' I said, quietly. 'I have to find … .' But no-one was listening. I just knew I couldn't go to school and see all those kids I didn't know and a new teacher who might not be nice, and no-one would even have heard of Mavis or my mum. 'I can't,' I said again.

'Of course you can, dear,' said Mrs Mags, kindly. 'They've got a field at the back to play in.'

'Mr Tait,' I said quietly, 'can't I come with you?'

Chapter 20

But of course I couldn't go with Mr Tait. My fate had already been decided.

And worse, by the time we made our way back to 'our' hut that night, the beds were all full and all that was left for us was the floor. There were two children on the sofa who were made to move so that Mr Tait could sleep there while I lay down on the floor beneath him and put my head on a chunk of firewood and tried to sleep.

It was another long night. The fire was 'banked up' to last all night so I was too hot at first, and then too cold in the early morning, but I pulled my coat up around my neck and pressed my back to the sofa. The stove door was dark. I eyed it suspiciously and fell asleep.

Later I was woken by the girl beside me talking in her sleep. 'It's coming down, it's coming down!' she said. That smell was there again, the smell of unwashed bodies, the smoke and fear seeping out of them. I held my nose and tried to concoct the lovely smell of oranges, but that took me to blood oranges and cut flesh and my mum and Mavis and all the things I'd seen and shouldn't have. I kept my hat with my dying daffodil as close to my nose as I could so that I could smell the daffodil instead, and I put the sandwich that Mr Tait had given me to take to school inside the hat.

In the morning Mr Tait woke me up with his stick by mistake. He was trying to climb over me to leave, but his legs weren't long enough. A cold daylight shifted through the green leafy curtains with the threads hanging down.

'I'll be thinking of you, Lenny,' he said, his voice softer than ever. 'You be a brave girl and have a good day at Craigton. I promise I'll be back on the last bus. I never miss!'

He really was going to go and leave me there. How could he?

'Just remember I promised,' he said. 'I promised you and I promised your mother that I was going to look after you, and it just wouldn't do to be letting you two down, would it? You can tell me all about it tonight. I'll pray for them all, for Mavis and Rosie and Miss Wetherspoon. And you. And your mother.' And then he bent down and kissed me on the top of my head and gave my shoulders a little squeeze. He coughed and cleared his throat as if my hair had tickled him and he tiptoed over the sleeping bodies and gave me a little wave before he closed the door.

I crawled up onto the sofa, into the warmth he'd left behind and wrapped myself up in my coat and let my tears seep out. What if he didn't come back? Now I'd lost everyone. Even Mr Tait had left me now, and all the bad things I'd done came back to me, just like they did the day I'd run away and met Mr Tulloch the farmer along the road. There were so many awful things I'd done, it was no wonder really.

But I didn't get to feel sorry for myself for long

because Sandy stuck his sandy-haired head round the door and in trying to wake me up, woke everybody else up as well, and I trod on a few fingers and toes before I got out, whispering 'sorry' all the way. The damp air hit me first, then the smell of coal fires starting up. Everything seemed very bright and green.

'We've got porridge,' he said when we got to his hut.

'I can't go,' I said.

'Nonsense!' said Mrs Mags.

'But … .'

'She wants to stay with me and draw,' said Mr MacInnes in the shadows.

'Nonsense, she'll have a lovely time,' said Mrs Mags. 'The teachers are lovely, just lovely, a bit stuck-up but just lovely!'

'But … ,' I said.

'And I could do without you putting your oar in,' she said with a glare at Mr MacInnes's dark corner.

Bowls of steaming porridge landed with a smack along the bench and a row of heads bent over them, knees on the floor, as if they were all saying their prayers. Mrs Mags shooed me off to join them.

'But … I don't have my glasses,' I said.

'Glasses?' said Mrs Mags. I don't think any of them believed me, which was very wise because it was a lie.

'Yes, glasses,' I said, not looking at anyone. 'I can't see the blackboard.'

'She'll put you at the front with the wee kids,' said Sandy.

'No, I mean I can only see the blackboard. I can't see the slate,' I said in a panic now.

'We're probably singing anyway,' said Sandy. 'She hasn't made us do any work so far.'

'Better get a move on,' said Izzie, 'or you'll miss the bus and then you'll have to walk and it's miles and miles and miles … .'

'I know,' I said.

So I went to that school with all those kids I didn't know and the two new teachers, and we sang all morning. Well, not quite all morning. The first half was taken up with registration. Our teacher's name was Miss Read, suitably enough, and I wondered if there were two other teachers at that school called Miss Write and Miss Rithmetic. Miss Read called our names out one after the other and when it was ours we had to stand up and say 'Here!' Then she did it all over again. She was a thin woman in a thick blue tweed skirt and lilac jumper. I never saw her in anything else. She had a pair of spectacles which lived alternately in her hand or on her nose depending on whether she was looking at you or a book. When she called my name the second time she said 'Gillespie' as if testing it to make sure it was right. 'Gillespie,' she said with a flick of her hand. She smiled at me and looked me directly in the eye. 'Welcome Leonora Gillespie,' she said. 'Did I get it right?'

'Yes, Miss,' I said. 'Gillespie.'

'And what do they call you? Leonora?' she said.

'Yes. No … .'

Big bad George called out, 'It's Lenny, Miss, like a boy.'

The murmur went round, 'Lenny … Leonora … Lenny.'

'Thank you, George,' said Miss Read. She nodded

her thanks and turned to me. 'Which is it to be?' She smiled. I wondered if she knew what I was thinking, that I could be someone new, someone special and sophisticated, not scared and dirty and lost.

'Leonora,' I said. I caught Sandy's eye and turned my back on George. 'Leonora,' I said again, just to be sure.

'Leonora,' she said. 'Such a pretty name!'

'I've got a sister called Mavis too,' I told her. Everyone always said what a pretty name Mavis was.

'Is she here?' Miss Read put her glasses swiftly onto her nose and looked down her ledger and then took them off so she could see me.

'No,' I said. 'She's … not here.'

'Not yet?' said the teacher.

'Not yet. She's only four. And a half,' I said.

'And dead,' came a murmur from the back.

A gasp rippled round the room. Slowly Miss Read removed her spectacles from her nose. Tears smarted in my eyes.

'George, dear,' she said in the sweetest voice. 'Would you do me the favour of coming out to the front of the class where we can all see you.'

I flushed with horror and delight.

'Now, George,' she said.

Everyone turned in their seats, all eyes on George. He was slumped down in his seat behind his desk.

'Right now,' she said, still sweet.

There was a long awkward silence. Everyone held their breath.

We all jumped when the teacher stamped her heel sharply on the floor but none more than George who jumped right out of his seat, probably before he knew it, and after giving himself a little shake (and me a monstrous sneer) he sauntered over to stand in front of the teacher, Miss Read.

Miss Read turned IMMEDIATELY on her heel.

'Follow me please,' she said, and she left the room. George followed meekly behind her. She returned two minutes later alone and took us all through to the other classroom which had a piano but no George. There were more children in there too.

We sat cross-legged on the floor and listened to Miss Read, who was also the headmistress. She told us we were all welcome and she was delighted to have us there, and she smiled a big smile that showed us all her very yellow teeth, and then she and another teacher took turns at the piano. I sang along as best I could to 'You are my sunshine' and then 'Hey, little hen' and my favourite, 'Run, rabbit, run' (except of course Hitler was the rabbit). But the best of all was 'The quartermaster's stores', including all twenty-nine verses, the most fun being 'There were bears, bears, with curlers in their hair', during which we got quite rowdy and had to be calmed down with 'Bread with great big lumps like lead'. Each time we sang the chorus, 'My eyes are dim I cannot see', I looked over at Sandy and he made a daft face at me. At first I was embarrassed about my lie earlier on, and then I mouthed 'bloody hell' back and he sniggered into his hand.

And suddenly it was lunchtime. We ate our pieces and ran into the playground where the drizzle still hung in the air. I had no idea where George had been but he came out into the playground not long after the rest of us. Two older girls had a skipping rope and were singing a song I knew. They sang, 'Down by the meadow where the green grass grows', and I hung about and sang under my breath, and when the rest of the kids took turns with the rope I took a turn too, and thought about how funny it was that we really were down by the meadow.

But out of the corner of my eye I saw Sandy, Dougie and George sneak round the side of the building to the back, and I wished I was sneaking round with them, even though bad George was there. I remembered Mr Tulloch, the farmer, saying the path to Clydebank was by the school. Now Sandy, Dougie and George were going to steal off to Clydebank leaving me there when it was me who most needed to go.

'Leonora! Leonora! Hello?' the girls were shouting. 'Anyone home? Leonora!'

I dropped the rope and ran round the side after the boys. They were throwing stones at each other across the burn and when George saw me he burst into the brruumm-brruumm of the killer-bee bombers, then ack-ack-ack and whee-boom-crash so I turned back and left them, but not before I'd had a good look at the burn and the path which rose beside it into the trees.

Miss Read came out just then jangling the bell to call us all in and I found myself at the front of the line.

'Leonora,' she said with a smile. 'What a lovely hat!'

'Thank you, Miss Write,' I said.

'Read,' she said.

'Pardon?'

'Miss Read,' she said and smiled.

'Sorry, Miss Read,' I said, and blushed in case she thought I'd done it on purpose.

The afternoon was spent reading. We went round

the class reading a bit each and I discovered that I was better at it than George. Why are boys so stupid? Bad George had to be helped to read by Dougie who was sharing a desk with him, but at least he had the grace to be embarrassed, hiding behind his book. Miss Read sent someone out for sniggering at him and I wondered where she was sending them and why she didn't go round the room with a ruler for people's knuckles like Miss Weatherbeaten did.

And I wondered, with a pang of guilt (I'd forgotten her for a whole morning), whether Mavis would ever come here. I fumbled at my side where I'd tied the shoe onto the belt underneath my dress so no-one would see it. (It made a bit of a lump.)

'Leonora!'

'Yes, Miss Read?'

'Welcome back. We are at the third paragraph on page ten.'

'Yes, Miss.'

She didn't raise her voice, or even scowl. She was sweetness and politeness throughout and when I'd finished reading the third paragraph on page ten she said, 'Thank you, Leonora.' I wished my mum was a school teacher and not a machinist lying in bed with a foot missing.

What a terrible person I was to have thought that, with my poor mum all alone in a hospital bed and not even allowed to have me as her visitor. I wished my hat wasn't out on its peg so that I could hide inside it and think my secret thoughts. Suddenly this nice school with its songs and skipping ropes didn't seem such a nice place to be after all and I wished I was outside climbing up the hill over to Clydebank.

'Leonora!'

'Yes, Miss Read?'

'First paragraph, page seventeen.'

'Yes, Miss Read.'

I got halfway through before the page blurred behind my tears.

'Josie, could you finish the paragraph for us please?'

Miss Read took her glasses off her nose and handed me a clean white handkerchief she had up her sleeve, and even though this other girl read the rest of my paragraph, no-one in the room was paying her any attention because they were all staring at me, George included.

'Let's read the rest of it together. There's only a couple more paragraphs,' said Miss Read. She gave my hand a little stroke, as if I was a cat, and returned to the front of the class, tossing her glasses onto her nose as she went. I managed the last two lines along with everyone else, then she clapped her hands and said 'Home time!' and my first day at Craigton was over.

Chapter 21

But not quite. Miss Read kept me back so that I could help put the books back in the cupboard and by the time I was finished the others had already started up the road. No-one wanted to wait for the bus which wouldn't be there for a while yet, even though it was miles and miles and miles to walk. I could see Sandy and Dougie and bad George up ahead, nearly at the brow of a hill. The stragglers were mostly the wee-est ones.

So I stood on the road where the burn dives under it and wondered which way to go, weighing up Mavis at home over the misty hills, my mum in hospital down the road in Glasgow, and Mr Tait coming back from there to Carbeth.

Mr Tait had promised. He'd promised before and kept his word, so maybe he would keep it this time as well and find Mavis, Rosie and Miss Weatherbeaten and bring them all back to Carbeth with my mum. On the other hand grown-ups were always making promises they couldn't keep. And some grown-ups were straightforward disorganised, like Miss Weatherbeaten who had missed the bus. I didn't fancy being left in Carbeth when Mr Tait missed the bus too. Everything rested on Mr Tait.

Miss Read came out of the school with the other

teacher and made the decision for me. She thought I'd lost my way and very kindly told me what I already knew, that I had to follow all the other kids until I got to the Halfway House pub. Then she waited and watched while I followed her instructions, so I set off for Carbeth.

And then Sandy came back for me.

'I'm not a baby,' I said.

'Thought you might not be able to see to get home.'

I looked at him sideways.

'Without your glasses?' he said.

I stopped. My hat shoogled precariously. I grabbed it quick before the breeze took it. Sandy was laughing so I laughed too and we carried on up the road.

'You shouldn't mind George,' he said. 'He's alright really. He was evacuated last year and he's been like that ever since. He says there was a lady there who had lots of friends and kept funny hours and he had to work all the time.'

'Hmm,' I said. I wished my mum had lots of friends.

'Poor George,' he said.

I couldn't agree less, but I didn't say so.

'Dougie was going to go there too but their mum and dad realised something wasn't right,' he said. 'So they went and brought George back instead.'

'Hmm.'

'He's just as horrible to his mum as he is to you.'

This didn't make me feel a lot better.

'Hates his mum.'

After a few hundred yards we came to a broken-down house I hadn't noticed before behind the hedge. Its roof was caving in and the door was half-open and it smelled of cowpats. Sandy wanted to explore so we climbed the gate, but I didn't like it.

'I don't like it here,' I said. 'I want to go.' I waited by the gate for him to come back. There were sheep further down the field, soggy things with mud on their legs, and crows over the turnip field next door. The sky was grey and the wind was sneaking inside my coat.

'Let's go round the back,' he said, ignoring me, but I stayed where I was and sang under my breath, 'Down in the meadow where the green grass grows, Where Lenny bleaches all of her clothes, She sang, she sang, she sang so sweet … .'

'Aren't you coming?' he called back.

'The wind, the wind, the wind blows high … .'

Then Dougie and bad George came running out of nowhere shouting 'BOO!' and Sandy came back shouting 'Leave her alone!'

So I screamed and landed in a cowpat and the mud that was everywhere and I climbed back over the gate and onto the road.

'Bastards!' I shouted, shaking my fist like wee Rosie. 'Bastards, you're all bastards! I'm telling Mr Tait on you! You wait! You just wait!'

'Shut up! You great bullies! Why did you do that? She's only nine!' It was Sandy and then I heard the thwack and grunt of boys fighting, stupid boys, always doing stupid things, and I wiped my tears back with the sleeve of my new coat from the town hall and banged my feet on the road to get the cow poo off, then ran as fast as I could along the road.

It felt good to say 'bastard' out loud, but scarily naughty so I kept on saying it but only inside my head, in case someone else might hear. But I was saying it so loudly inside my head and banging my feet on the tarmacadam so hard that I didn't hear the bus come up behind me until it was right beside me. It roared past me with a snarl that threw me into the hedge that ran along the roadside and then it came to a crunching halt a few yards up ahead. As if I didn't have enough cuts and bruises already!

A lady I hadn't seen before stepped down and hurried back to me.

'Are you alright, love?' she said and helped me out of the hedge. 'You look like you've been in this hedge before, if you don't mind me saying so!' She fussed about and pulled the twigs off me and straightened my torn hat. 'Nice hat!' she said.

'Thank you,' I said. I stuck my hand in my pocket and found Miss Read's clean white handkerchief which wasn't very clean or white any more but was a lot better than the sleeve of my coat that I couldn't very well use with this kind lady standing there being so particular.

When we got to the door of the bus, I saw Mr Tait standing at the top of the steps with his fancy bedpost stick in one hand, and his other resting on a special handle for people getting off.

'Mr Tait!' I said. And the tears sprung to my eyes at the same time as the grin which spread right across me and through me and lit me up from the inside.

'I did promise,' he said. 'Didn't I? Good gracious whatever happened to you?'

He thanked the kind lady and we sat down on a seat together and it seemed like no time at all till we were standing at the side of the Halfway House pub looking up that big enormous hill to where 'our' hut stood. I told him everything that had happened, apart from me calling the boys 'bastards'. And then it hit me!

'Where are they?' I said. It was an accusation really to us both. I had forgotten all about them, Mavis, Rosie and Miss Weatherbeaten, and he had let me prattle on about silly playground games. That meant he hadn't found them, I was sure, and I crossed my fingers for it not to be true. 'Please?' I said, all my longing squeezed into that one little word.

'Well … ,' he began. 'Well … .'

'Well … ?' I said, helping him on. This slowness was not good news. It meant that Mr Tait was trying to think how best to tell me something that he knew I didn't want to hear. 'You didn't find them, did you?' I said flatly.

'Well, actually … ,' he said, and he put his bottom lip over his top one and blew. Those wrinkles on his forehead squeezed together. 'In a sort of a way I did. Let's walk a little way or we'll never get up this blasted hill.'

Blasted hill? I thought. That wasn't very polite! What had happened to Mr Tait? I thought it better to just wait and see what he might say, in his own very good time.

'Miss Wetherspoon, in her great wisdom,' he said between breaths, 'has decided to go to an evacuation centre to help out – a kind of rest centre.' He stopped briefly and rubbed his back and caught his breath. I held mine, thinking over and over again, what about Rosie, what about Rosie? I bit the fingernail on my forefinger until I pulled a great strip of nail right off all the way down to the quick. He took ages to get going again.

'What about Rosie?' I said in the end, unable to help myself.

He coughed loudly putting a fist to his mouth and then licked his lips a few times before replying.

'She took Rosie to the town hall.'

I put both hands over my mouth.

'No!' I said. 'Oh, no! How could she? Wee Rosie!'

'I know, I'm sorry, I'm so sorry. I'm sure Miss Wetherspoon was doing what she thought was the very best thing for Rosie. It's just not what you or I would have done. Quite extraordinary that she's a teacher, really.' He muttered this last under his breath. It was quite a breach of grown-upness to have been so frank with me and I don't think I was meant to answer.

'How could she? Poor Rosie. Where will she be taken?' I said, and I remembered the town hall ladies saying they'd no idea where she'd end up. Rosie didn't want to go with them. I imagined her screaming and crying, maybe shaking her fist and sticking out her jaw when she found herself betrayed. Perhaps she even thought I'd known? Perhaps she shook her fist at me.

'I'm sorry,' said Mr Tait.

The tears were spilling through my fingers now so I pressed at my eyes to stop them.

'Poor Rosie!' I said. 'Poor Mavis and now Rosie too!'

Mr Tait nodded and his breathing was heavy. 'I'm so sorry. I really didn't expect this. She sent me a message.'

It seemed the whole world was crying. The grey sky

had turned to mist again and the mist had turned to rain and poured down on us with no compassion or kindness.

'No!' I sobbed. 'That's not fair! Poor Rosie! We have to rescue her. We have to get her back. She doesn't want to go to Edinburgh, or anywhere else!' Edimburry, as she'd called it. 'Poor Rosie! What are we going to do?'

'Well, we have to think carefully about this. We don't know … .'

'What do you mean we don't know? We know where she's gone and they'll have a record now of wherever she ends up. We just have to go and find out and get her back, don't we?'

'Lenny,' he said with a sigh, 'it's quite possible Rosie has family somewhere, aunts and uncles or grandparents.'

'She never mentioned them to me,' I broke in. 'I don't think she does. She might not.' A sudden gust of wind lifted my coat and I grabbed it back down, quick as I could.

'Miss Wetherspoon will have assumed I couldn't look after her. The authorities will assume the same. I'm a man! They're not going to hand her over to me, a man who's not even related to her. I'm a cripple without a house.'

'But why not?' I said. 'I'm alright, aren't I and you're looking after me?'

'Well, that's debatable,' he said, but he had his head to one side and a little twist in his mouth. I wasn't sure what debatable meant but I had a good idea. He looked me up and down. 'If they saw you now, if your mum saw you now, she'd be very worried indeed!'

He took me by the hand and we struggled up the

rest of the hill, slipping and sliding in the wet. The rain washed the last of the cow poo off my feet. My hat was sodden and soft and the daffodil was gone. My new coat grew heavier with every step and my bare legs were streaked with mud. We went straight to Mrs Mags who gave us steaming bowls of vegetable soup and hung our coats around her fire. I didn't want to eat. I wanted Mavis and now I had to want Rosie too, who could be anywhere.

Mrs Mags was upset about Rosie too.

'Poor wee mite!' she said. 'What a heartless thing to do!'

'Miss Wetherspoon went to help other poor souls at a rest centre,' said Mr Tait. 'It does seem odd but perhaps she thought it was for the greater good … ?'

'Greater good, my big backside!' was the retort. 'For the greater good a poor wee thing like that who's just lost all her family has to go to God knows where, Edinburgh if she's lucky, the poorhouse more like and all by herself, without even you and Lenny with her.'

Mr Tait and Mrs Mags both glanced at me. She'd named my greatest fear, that Rosie had been sent to the poorhouse, that Mavis might be there too, eating watered down porridge and working twelve hours a day.

'No!' I said. 'No, they wouldn't have taken them there! No!'

I'd been so grief-stricken about Rosie I hadn't had the heart to ask about Mavis too, even though I knew what he was going to say, that he hadn't found her, that she was still missing, that anything could have happened to her – the poorhouse or even missing presumed dead. I howled into my soup.

'It is extremely unlikely that Rosie and Mavis are in the poorhouse,' said Mr Tait in his quiet voice. 'Extremely unlikely. They will both probably be billeted with families out in the country, just like lots of other children.'

'Then why is there no record of Mavis?' I said loudly with a big wet sniff. 'If she was billeted with a family they'd have had to give her a billeting slip and so they'd know.'

'Lots of children went with families in a hurry,' said Mr Tait, 'and lots didn't get billeting slips. They just had to get out, just like we did and sort things out later. You don't have a billeting slip to stay with me, do you?' And he dug into his pocket and handed me a clean white handkerchief.

'No, but … .' I wiped my eyes and blew my nose so hard it hurt.

'I'm sorry I mentioned the poorhouse, Lenny,' said Mrs Mags. 'It was careless chatter.'

'Careless talk costs lives,' I said, even though I knew that wasn't the case here. I'd seen the posters and they scared me, just like I was scared now.

'Lenny,' said Mr Tait, quietly. 'You're starting to be rude.'

I had Mavis's shoe in my hand. I pulled it round to the front of my lap, under my dress, and fiddled with it. I had no hat to hide under because it was hanging up to dry, so I hung my head. The fire crackled and spat.

'Sorry,' I said.

'That's alright dear,' said Mrs Mags. 'You're upset. I understand.' She patted my knee. 'She'll turn up. Don't you worry. I feel it in my bones, I do!' she laughed as if that was that settled then.

Mr Tait and I both stared at her with our mouths hanging open while she sat there slapping the sides of her big round tummy.

'You both think I'm crazy,' she said, 'but I'm never wrong, never wrong. She'll turn up, just you wait and see.'

'Well, I very much hope you're right on this occasion, Mrs Mags,' said Mr Tait.

I very much hoped so too, but honestly, why did grown-ups come out with such things? It wasn't kind, even though it was meant to be. Now I didn't know what to think.

'Where's my boys?' said Mrs Mags, suddenly, as if she'd only just remembered them.

I couldn't tell her the truth.

'They missed the bus,' I said, which was true.

'Why, what were they up to?'

'Um.'

'I see, so you've joined their ranks already, have you?'

'Um.'

'Clearly they're up to no good,' she said.

I was too tired for this, and too wet. She had let me sit very close to the fire on an old wooden box, so that steam came out of my dress and the air was heavy with dampness. My socks were on a nail behind the stove and were soon hard and dry. I rubbed the crispness out of them and put them back on my feet, then ate my soup.

Mr Tait and Mrs Mags started talking about tents then, and it turned out there were tents in Carbeth but other tents on farms nearby too, with people from Clydebank in them. Perhaps even Mavis. But just as

I was about to point this out, Mr MacInnes, the old man in the shadows, came in shaking a huge umbrella behind him and smelling of whisky.

'Damn rain!'

'Mr MacInnes!' said Mrs Mags. 'Language!'

He gave me a wink and sat down heavily on the sofa next to Mr Tait, who bounced slightly. Mr MacInnes threw his head back in a gesture of relief but stayed there so long I had time to look at his tonsils and his teeth, which were few and far between.

'You're the girl who wants to learn to draw,' he said, finally, flipping his head over to look at me. 'Let's see how good you are then.' He pulled a grey canvas bag from his side. The strap hung across his shoulder. 'It's in here somewhere. There you go. That's a good solid soft pencil,' he said. 'And ... here's paper, that's gold dust to you and me. Gold dust! Now you draw whatever you can see and I'll tell you what a fine artist you are! No, no, now, just you go ahead, there's no need to thank me. It's an artist's duty to encourage other aspiring young artists, budding, at the beginning ... .'

Mr Tait was deep in conversation with Mrs Mags by then so I took the precious paper and laid it on a slab of wood Mrs Mags handed me. The pencil wasn't remotely soft but made a very solid black line and wore down in no time. I began a portrait of Mr MacInnes, starting with his knees for some reason which I can't explain. By the time I'd reached his face it had fallen back against the sofa again and I got a second look at his tonsils and gums, so I drew them too.

Meanwhile Mr Tait and Mrs Mags were still chatting. Perhaps I ought to explain about the tents, for anyone who doesn't know. You see, before the huts went up, there were tents in a field a little further out from town. They were owned by the Socialist Sunday Camp who ran summer and weekend camps from April to September every year, and when they weren't there they stored their tents in a hall that they had built beside a stream. They put on shows and concerts in their hall, and dances, and they had a tennis court too and a special cookhouse. At any other time, in any other circumstances, I would have been excited beyond belief to be going there.

'He's given us another piece of ground, rocky, not the best, by the Sunday Camp, with room for probably fifty new huts,' said Mrs Mags.

'I can't build with this leg,' said Mr Tait. 'That's all gone now. When will the Sunday campers be back? We can borrow one of their tents until they come, and then think again.'

'April Fool's Day. First of April, and they're not just Sunday campers. They come every year on April Fool's Day and stay all summer. Where are we now?' she muttered. 'That gives us less than two weeks to build.' She cocked her head to one side, thinking, her face red in the heat.

'Mrs Mags, I can't build. I can hardly get up this hill.'

'There's others here can help you, the boys for a start, if they ever get here.'

'They're not old enough.'

'It'll make them old enough. George especially could do with keeping his hands busy. He's my sister's boy. She'll be coming here with his dad at the weekend. He can help too and my husband will be here.'

'I can't see that they'll want to help me,' said Mr Tait. 'I'm the wrong side of the tracks for most people up here. I'm probably his boss!'

'No, Mr Tait,' she said. 'You're not his boss. But right enough, he'll only be about at weekends, and then if you're lucky. The other men will help, though, I'm sure.'

'I don't like to ask, they've enough to do already.'

'The coal man says he'll lend his lorry for getting the material here, for a small fee. There's an old garage I know that's falling down. You could take that to start you off. You can direct proceedings, just like you do at your work, while the boys do the heavy stuff. It'll be a piece of cake.'

I hadn't really been listening to much of this but at the mention of cake my ears pricked up, naturally enough. There was no cake anywhere to be seen.

'But I'm a gaffer, Mrs Mags!' said Mr Tait.

'All due respect, Mr Tait, but you're not a very big one,' said Mrs Mags. 'Not exactly the biggest fish in the ocean. It depends what you're prepared to barter with.'

'I don't have anything but the clothes I stand up in and the contents of my suitcase!'

'And your position … ?'

'What do you mean?'

Mrs Mags shook her head and glanced at the ceiling. She lifted one of Mr MacInnes's drawings which was pinned further along the wall from the stove. Underneath it was the word BROWN'S printed in big bold black letters.

'Ah,' said Mr Tait. 'From the shipyard. I see. If I come and go with them, and turn a blind eye, they'll come and go with packing cases and whatever else I might need.' He clicked his tongue and all his wrinkles came back. 'I see,' he said quietly, and his eyes flicked left and right.

'Shhh!' said Mrs Mags and she blinked in the direction of Mr MacInnes and myself. Clearing her throat she carried on. 'They're quite comfortable so I'm told, the tents I mean. There's people down there already. Why don't you go and have a look. They have wooden floors and camp beds in the hall too. You might even get to stay longer when they come out in April to open up.'

'I can't share a tent with Lenny,' said Mr Tait. 'It might have been possible with Miss Wetherspoon and Rosie here but ... this is all very difficult really, isn't it? I'm not sure what to do.'

'Don't take me back to the town hall,' I said, leaping off the wooden box. 'Please don't.'

Mr Tait sighed and smiled and took my hand.

'Have you noticed, Lenny, that when I make a promise I keep it?' he said.

'Yes, Mr Tait, sorry, but I just thought that ... I have to tell you ... I won't stay if you take me. I won't stay wherever they send me. I'll do what Rosie did. I'll run off. And I'll get the bus all the way back out here and knock on your tent door. So you might as well plan on keeping me.' I was quite breathless. 'Maybe Rosie will run off and find her way back here too anyway. That'd be good, wouldn't it?'

'Lenny, I'm not taking you back to the town hall,' said Mr Tait. 'I promised you and your mother and I wouldn't take you back there unless you begged me on bended knees. The thing is you may have to live in a tent. What do you think of that?'

'A tent?' I said.

'Yes, a tent. Haven't you been listening?'

Well, no, actually, not properly.

'And then you might have to help me build a hut,' he said.

'A hut?' I said.

'Yes, Lenny, a hut.'

'I can't build a hut!'

Mr Tait had lost his marbles.

'In that case I'll have to ask the boys.'

'I thought you said you couldn't build a hut either,' I said.

'Ah, so you were listening,' he said.

'I heard that,' I said. 'And "a piece of cake".'

'Who'd miss "a piece of cake"?'

We all sat back and laughed and Mr MacInnes shut his mouth with a crack of whatever teeth he had left, then we watched it eek its way open again. Then suddenly it slammed shut again just as the hut door flew open and the three wet boys flooded in, all of them talking at once.

Mrs Mags stood up, arms folded across her belly, mouth tight shut. Her eyes appeared to have shrunk. I looked at these boys and wondered how on earth she thought they would be any help at all building a hut. They dripped great splotches of rain all over the rug and chairs and even down my newly dried dress. But worst of all they had burst lips and blood on their jumpers, even Sandy, and bad George had a graze on his cheek just below one eye. They all had mud from their hair to their shoes and they smelled suspiciously of cowpats.

'Boys!' boomed Mrs Mags finally breaking her

silence. Sandy stopped jabbering. Mrs Mags seemed to be at a loss what to say next. 'Lenny!' she said at last. I stood up.

'Yes, Mrs Mags?'

'Let's test your allegiance, eh?'

Mr Tait shifted in his seat.

'Yes, Mrs Mags.' I wanted to ask, What's allegiance? Was it something to do with intelligence?

'What happened?' she said.

'I don't know,' I said, which was true. None of these burst lips and blood-stained shirts had happened before I ran off.

'Are you sure?'

'Yes, Mrs Mags,' I said.

She dropped her arms and raised her eyebrows. She sounded angry but she didn't look it so I couldn't be sure.

'Honest!' I said.

'Hmm … ,' she said.

Six eyes drummed into me. Mrs Mags tapped her foot and looked at the cobwebs over her head.

'Well … ,' I said, glancing at the boys, but not quite at George.

Ten eyes on me now.

'They were arguing,' I said. 'They were arguing so much they got left behind and didn't notice the bus.'

'I see,' said Mrs Mags, 'and what were they arguing about?'

'Football,' I said. 'And then a sheep came and chased them across a field. I suppose they must have fallen down. That'll be how they got all those cuts and bruises.'

Sandy, Dougie and bad George all nodded, vigorously.

Mrs Mags's arms returned to their former position, folded across her belly.

'Thank you, Lenny,' she said.

She turned back to the boys.

'No offence, Lenny,' she said without looking at me. 'That was a nice try. I was with you until the sheep part, but when did you last see a sheep chase anyone anywhere?'

'I'd never seen a sheep before today,' I said, sheepishly.

Mrs Mags laughed loudly and patted me on the shoulder.

'Right boys, back down to the pump and get the mud off you. Straight back here afterwards, and you can take those buckets with you to fill while you're about it.'

Mr Tait smiled at me. 'It's wrong to tell a lie,' he said quietly, while she shooed them back out the door, and for my ears only, 'but it's right to be loyal to friends, even new ones.'

'What are we going to do about Mavis and Rosie?' I whispered.

Chapter 22

Mr Tait and I slept on the floor of Mrs Mags's hut that night. We shared the room with Mr MacInnes who snored on the sofa. Mr Tait snored too and in the morning he was late for work. He was so late for work he was still there while I slurped hot porridge with Sandy, Dougie and bad George and when I ran down the hill just in time for the bus.

It was Thursday, exactly a week since the start of the bombing, exactly a week since I last saw Mavis and thought I'd lost my mum for ever, but it passed much as the day before had done, only I made friends with the girls with the skipping rope and ignored the boys as much as I could. At the end of the day I hurried up the road ahead of the others. It was windy that day with sun between the showers so I had to hang onto my hat. It was odd to be all alone. It made me feel dizzy and queasy. I hadn't exactly forgotten Mavis and my mum, or Rosie, but we'd done clapping games all morning and writing all afternoon, and I had to share my slate with the girl beside me, so the afternoon sped past with plenty of talking which Miss Read didn't seem to mind at all, as long as we all kept quiet when she was talking. So it was only when I left that I got to thinking about my mum and Mavis at all. Shocking!

When I knocked on the door of Mrs Mags's hut

Mr Tait was there on her sofa with a hot black tea in his hand.

'My, you're back early!' said Mrs Mags, who was sliding bits of carrot into a pot on the stove. 'We're only just in ourselves.' Joey the budgie had taken up residence on Mr MacInnes's chair in the corner behind the sofa.

'Hello, Mrs Mags,' I said. 'What's the news, Mr Tait?'

'Hello to you too, Lenny,' he said. 'We've got a tent. Isn't that good?'

'Oh,' I said, not expecting that. 'Yes, I suppose.' I didn't really want to go somewhere else, even if it was much better than where we were. 'Did you find any news of Mavis and Rosie? When is my mum going to be out?'

'I had to stay here today,' he said. 'So that I could get the tent sorted out. It's very grand, for a tent, and I've put ... .'

'What do you mean?' I said. 'You mean you didn't go? You didn't go to the town hall, or work, or to see my mum?'

'Now, Lenny ... ,' he said.

'You didn't go! You didn't even go!'

'Lenny, that's very rude,' said Mrs Mags. 'Don't talk to Mr Tait like that. Think of all he's done for you.'

'It's alright Mrs Mags,' he said in his quiet voice. 'Of course you want news, but Lenny, the people in the town hall know where you are. Your mother knows where you are. In time perhaps Mavis will know where you are too.'

'But ... !'

'And Lenny ... .'

'No! You didn't go. You don't care!'

'I do care Lenny, but … .'

'No, you don't! I knew I'd have to do this myself.' Immediately I started to plan how I was going to sneak off from the school in the morning. I'd slip round the back of the bus when no-one was looking and off up the hill when they were doing morning prayers.

'Mr Tait cares very much,' said Mrs Mags, interrupting me.

And what did it have to do with her anyway?

'No, he doesn't. He just wants money for billeting me.' That didn't sound right.

'Lenny!' said Mrs Mags with a gasp.

But Mr Tait laughed, laughed, of all things to do! He laughed, and I hadn't found Mavis!

'You're not worth very much, you know,' he said. 'What is it these days, Mrs Mags? Six shillings or thereabouts? Six and sixpence?'

'Oh, no, it's big money now. Ten and six, I believe?'

'Ten shillings and sixpence a week,' said Mr Tait with a nod. 'I'll need to take in a few more then, won't I?'

'Mr Tait!' I said, shocked. 'You think it's funny!'

'I don't think it's funny in the least,' he said, suddenly his old quiet self again. His brow was smooth and he had sat back comfortably on the sofa. 'You want to find Mavis. I want to find Mavis. I want to make sure you have a roof over your head and that you're safe. Hitler may be back. This seems like a good place for you and your mother and your sister to be for the foreseeable future. I have a bad leg. I need to rest it every so often in order to be able to do all the things that need to be done. Mrs Mags has very kindly walked with me today to the Sunday Camp and I have made some arrangements for us, and on the way back, while resting by the road, we met Mr Barnes-Graham, Old Barny himself, and we have now identified a very good site on which to build our hut. What do you say to all that?'

'Now do you see that he cares?' said Mrs Mags.

I nodded. Of course I did.

'But you said you couldn't build a hut,' I said.

Mr Tait drummed his fingers on the arm of Mrs Mags's old sofa.

'I have been persuaded otherwise,' he said. 'Of course I need someone who can draw to help me design it. Do you know of anyone who might be able to help?'

I thought about this long and hard until Mrs Mags pointed out he meant me. She picked up my unflattering portrait of Mr MacInnes, the old man in the shadows (it occurred to me for the first time that she might not be very pleased about my drawing the inside of Mr MacInnes's mouth), flipped the paper over and straightened it out on the board I'd used the day before. Then she thrust paper, board and a pencil into my hands and we all went and sat outside on the old church bench at the front of the hut (for the sake of the daylight) and plotted how we would build our new home.

We'd need a room for me and my mum and Mavis, and another for Mr Tait, and another for the stove, but perhaps Mr Tait could sleep in the room with the stove, or perhaps me, Mavis and my mum could sleep in with the stove. Yes, that sounded good. I knew it wasn't really alright to sleep in the same room as Mr

Tait but seeing as I'd just spent the night on the same floor as him and a hundred other people and was about to move into a tent with him, I didn't really see what the problem was. We settled on two rooms with a stove in one and a big bed in the other. There would be a cupboard and a table in the stove room. The plan was drawn and our new hut was going to be much grander than our real house in Clydebank, and the cludgie would be all ours!

We'd need bricks, and struts, and sleepers (apparently we didn't have enough and these came from the railway anyway), and packing cases for the floorboards, hammers, nails, saws, and shovels. Mr Tait took a small notepad out of his pocket that I hadn't seen before and started to write things down in it.

We were still there when the boys arrived back. Of course they had plenty to say about it all, especially Sandy and Dougie, who suffered from delusions of grandeur (something my Auntie May thought my mum had) about how they were going to help with the building. I looked at their puny arms and knobbly knees and scratched my head. Bad George grunted and kicked the corner of the hut. His jumper was ripped at the elbow, his face scabby from the day before. Mr Tait was small and had a bad leg. I was even smaller. We were a sorry crew.

But after an early tea and a quick shot on the rope swing, we headed over a field towards our plot, dodging the horses that were kept there and skirting the big house that Old Barney lived in.

I needed to get Mr Tait to promise to go to Clydebank the next day but with so many people about and so much excitement it was hard to get him alone. Instead I spent some time with Sandy making squeaky noises through reeds from the burn. We pressed them between our thumbs and blew, tickling our lips which made us squirm. Then Sandy cupped his hands into a hollow and made a soft sound which he told me was like an owl, and I heard them answer him from the trees, rhythmic and gentle. 'Wuh-woo-woo-wuh-wuh,' they went. Mrs Wilson told me the next day they weren't owls at all, but wood pigeons, like the ones you see in town only bigger, and tastier.

Finally we met the road and on the other side of it, our plot. There was bracken all over it and it wasn't flat. We kids stopped and stared at this disappointing scratch of ground and shook our heads. The wind made the trees creak. Someone was working further along the road. 'Tap-tap-tap' went a hammer, then the clatter of wood on wood.

'You see how close we are to the standpipe?' said Mr Tait. He was flushed with excitement, 'and it's quite protected from the wind by these trees.'

'But it's not flat,' I pointed out. 'Won't we slide down the floor?'

'Gracious no!' he laughed. 'That's what the bricks are for, to even up the floor. We'll put the hut here.' He pointed to a bush. 'From here to here,' he said, hobbling past a little tree, which he'd have to take down or it would come up through the floor. 'The door can be roughly … um … here. And if we build it high enough we can have a verandah.'

'A verandah?' said bad George. 'And what would a "verandah" be when it's at home? La-di-dah!' He sounded just like my dad, but not nice at all.

'George!' said Mrs Mags. 'Behave!'

'A verandah is like a balcony,' said Mr Tait, 'like the bit outside our hut, the one Lenny and I were in to begin with … .'

'It's not your hut,' said George.

'… only it's raised higher off the ground – very posh!' said Mr Tait.

Mr Tait went back to the bush and walked, with some difficulty, heel-to-toe from one end of the proposed hut to the other, counting under his breath with each step, then he took out his notepad and wrote something in it, and then he did it all over again at right angles and wrote that down too. A motorcar went past on the road so we all stood and waved at it as if it was the king inside, all except Mr Tait and Mrs Mags who were too busy to notice. The car slowed down at the top of the hill and disappeared.

I thought about my mum and about Mavis, and I wondered what they would think of all this. As far as we knew my mum still didn't like Mr Tait and wouldn't want to set foot in any hut of his, never mind stay in it. I hadn't been allowed to tell her he wasn't bad but good and kind and that it hadn't been him that had clyped on her for whatever she did at work. And if I told her I was living in a hut, she would do what I had done, she'd imagine my uncle's hut with no windows and with tools hanging everywhere, instead of something like the one Mr Tait and I had stayed in first. My mum seemed so far away. How could I explain all this if I wasn't even allowed to see her?

Mavis on the other hand would LOVE it, and everyone here would love her, and she'd have so many friends she wouldn't know what to do with herself.

I could just see her now, swinging on the rope, like Rosie had, with the big ones helping her, or sitting on Mrs Mags's bench with a glass of Mr Tulloch's milk, or scrambling through the woods picking snowdrops like the ones I'd seen on the way over. I gave the shoe a squeeze and remembered buckling it onto Mavis's foot the morning before we all went out to go round the shops in Kilbowie Road.

It was a week ago at exactly that time that she kicked the shoe off into the canal and I fell in. She threw dirt at the bad boys. I jumped out, but she had run off. I chased after her and the sirens went, and I couldn't find her; she wasn't there; she wasn't anywhere; no matter where I looked she wasn't there.

'Lenny.'

'Leonora!' said bad George in a singsong voice.

'Lenny,' said Mr Tait, bending down so that his mouth was close to my ear. 'Lenny, my love, we're going over the hill to the tent. What's wrong?'

I sniffed.

'It's just … it's just … today … .'

'Today?' he said. I could hear him puzzling. 'Ah, today. It's exactly a week.'

I nodded.

'Since you saw Mavis?'

I nodded again.

'Shall we say a prayer?'

I shook my head.

'No,' I said. 'I can't. I don't want to hear it. I don't want it. Don't pray. Not out loud.'

He took my hand. 'On you go,' he said to the others. 'We'll catch you up.' And then he said to me, 'Alright. No praying, not out loud.'

And we just stood there in the middle of the bushes, beside the road and just along from the standpipe, and when I looked at him his eyes were closed. But I didn't want to close mine because I was scared of what I might see, so, remembering that talking kept those pictures in my head all shut up in the dark, I said, 'Mavis is my sister. She's the best sister anyone could hope for and only four, well, four-and-a-half, and she's cute as ninepence, if she's ever allowed to get here, if everything is alright, which I'm sure it is, and she has dark hair like Rosie's but with a fringe and a dress like my old one before it got burnt. I know she'll love it here with all the other kids and the rope swing, and she'll love Joey the budgie too and we can go and find the lily pond that Dougie told me about and swim in the loch when the weather gets warm and … .'

Mr Tait stood on his sore leg and listened to me tell him all the things I'd already told him about my sister Mavis, and he held my hand, and when I looked at him his lips were pursed as if he was trying to lock something in, and his eyes were wet round the edges.

'I will go to Clydebank tomorrow,' he said. 'I promise.'

'Thank you,' I whispered. 'Thank you, Mr Tait.'

'Now, I'm going to sit on that rock over there,' he said in the softest voice ever, 'and you can run up that hill through the trees, straight up mind, don't go sideways, and when you get to the ridge at the top, you'll see the tents down at the bottom on the other side. Mrs Mags and the others will be up there too. Have a quick look then come back down. I think we should stay with Mrs Mags one more night.'

As I ran up the hill, some of the others were already

coming down, shouting about how they wanted to stay in the tents too and how lucky I was. At the top there was a sharp drop, and down below there were tents, white tents and brown tents and green ones, like little houses dotted about amongst the trees. A burn ran through the middle of them and some people had built a fire beside it and were sitting by it with plates on their laps. They looked dark and bedraggled like the lost people in the hut, but I heard someone laugh, and someone else call over to them in reply.

Mrs Mags pointed to a little group of four tents all close together and told me ours was one of them, and I remembered again about the other tents on farms nearby that I'd heard about and wondered whether Mavis might be in a tent too. Then Mrs Mags took my cold shivery hand in her big warm one and led me back down the hill. We went back along the road because the light was nearly gone, and I listened to the wind for killer bees and bombs that went boom-crash.

'Run, rabbit, run, rabbit, run, run, run,' I sang under my breath as I wandered along.

'My eyes are dim, I cannot see!' sang Dougie gustily.

And Sandy joined him, 'I have not brought my specs with me!'

And we all sang, 'I have not brought my specs with me!'

And then we had to climb that big hill again.

Chapter 23

That night we shared the floor with Izzie, a docker, his wife and their three kids, and Joey the budgie, and of course Mr MacInnes. In the morning when I woke up Mr Tait, Izzie and the docker were gone and the rest were still sleeping the sleep of the exhausted.

I was so excited. Mr Tait had done what he promised! Again! He'd gone to Clydebank.

I was sure to have news that night.

Sandy, Dougie and bad George were all wearing identical balaclavas which Mrs Mags had finished knitting the night before. They were the colour of girders with four holes on the front (or the back if you're daft like Dougie), two for the eyes, one for the nose, and a bigger one for the mouth. That's twelve holes in total. Mrs Mags was at pains to point this out. I don't think she likes knitting. The boys thought they were Romans and made swords from fallen branches which they sharpened with penknives and poked the girls, especially me, in fact in George's case, most particularly me.

George surpassed himself that day. That means he beat himself at his own game. In other words in trying to be the biggest nuisance and the baddest boy in the whole school he was a great success, so much so that Miss Read and the other teacher had no time to put him out, or even to give him the belt, or even to take him into the other room, before he had run off anyway, shouting, 'You're all filthy, scummy wee bastards anyway, and you're a stuck-up bitch,' and other terrible things like that. I was thrilled and horrified all at once, so much so I thought I might embarrass myself and be sick right there in the classroom next to my new friend, Senga, who has a back-to-front name.

Miss Read was mostly calm, relieved I think, when he ran off. Her thick round glasses leapt on and off her nose, into and out of her hand to begin with. The other teacher had a face like iron, as if she was wearing one of Mrs Mags's balaclavas too, the skin all tight and pulled across her large bulbous nose.

Then, at the end of the day, Dougie was handed a sealed envelope addressed to Mr Connor (George and Dougie's dad) so we all hid behind the hedge in the turnip field by the ruined house and Sandy, being the oldest, tried to ease the letter out. But the rain made the envelope soft and it ripped anyway. He read it silently to himself, nodding like a grandfather, his lips forming the words, then the envelope landed in the mud, same as me two days earlier.

'Well?' said Dougie. 'Well? What does it say?'

'He's been expelled,' said Sandy, retrieving the envelope.

'Expelled?' said Dougie.

Expelled? What did that mean? Was that something to do with witches? Were Miss Read and the other teacher witches?

'Expelled?' said Dougie again and he asked my question for me. 'What does that mean?'

Just then we heard the bus coming through the

trees by the school and ran out in time to watch it hurtle by without us. The boys swore and pulled their balaclavas over their faces. I yanked my straw hat down over my ears, and we tramped back to Carbeth. We wondered where George might have run to. Clydebank probably, up and over the hill, in my opinion, just like I wished I had done.

The bus was pulling away from the Halfway House pub when we stumbled panting into the crowd it'd left behind. For every human being there seemed to be the same bulk again in baggage. I counted four budgie cages, two cats in orange boxes, two small cupboards, one with drawers, three rolled-up mattresses, countless bundles that rattled with pots and pans and broken crockery, a couple of chairs and five pot plants. Several people were carrying small piles of bricks tied up with rope, and a stack of pale wood with 'John Brown' stamped on it stood next to another that said 'Singer'.

I scanned the heads hurriedly and found no Mr Tait, no Mavis and no Rosie. Perhaps this bus was too early for Mr Tait. He had a lot to do.

Mr Tait thought my poor mum wouldn't be out of hospital for another week or two, which would be enough time for us to build a hut, as long as it all went to plan. Mrs Wilson, who used to be a nurse, said she thought my mum would be in for much longer. Mrs Mags said we should wait and see.

There was no sign of bad George either but Mrs Mags was there to help out, so we all helped out too. It was unfortunate, after what happened to Joey, that I was handed a budgie cage to carry with not just one budgie but two inside it hanging on for dear life and unfortunate too that their owner lived at the top of the hill near Mrs Wilson's hut and the other rope swing. The climb certainly heated me up.

I gave the swing a professional once-over, now that I was an expert, and watched with green envy as five little kids swept across the path to it without so much as entering their hut. Through the window I saw their mum and dad standing by the curtains in a hug. It was like the hug my mum and dad had hugged when he went away just after we moved to Clydebank. They didn't do that sort of hugging very often and only when they thought you weren't looking. I left the budgie cage at the front door.

Instead of going straight back down to Mrs Mags's hut I headed into the woods, beneath the pine trees, behind the big beech tree where the other rope swing was, the main one. I could hear other kids there, and if I was careful I could see them too. There was a log of wood lying there in the grass, damp and slippy and hard to move. I rolled it over as best I could, cold earth slipping up my wrists. I wanted to sit on it. I wanted to be close to the other kids but alone, alone but not lonely.

The thick pines deadened most of the sound (like being wrapped in a blanket) but even so I heard Mrs Mags and bad George shouting.

'Where is Lenny anyway?' shouted Mrs Mags, clear as a bell across the field.

'How should I know where she is?' said bad George. 'Who gives a damn, anyway?'

'Don't you swear at me! Just you wait till your father gets here!'

'Hah! If he ever does.'

'Come back here this minute!' she said.

Bad George swooped past the beech tree. For a second I thought he was going to dive into the trees and find me. I kept as still as I could until he set off along the path towards the two budgies' hut and the other rope swing.

'Lenny!' It was Sandy, calling for me.

'Lenny!' shouted Mrs Mags.

And then I couldn't hear anyone, only 'Wuh-woo-woo-wuh-wuh!' somewhere in the branches above me, and a reply from somewhere far off. 'Wuh-woo-woo-wuh-wuh!' so soft and peaceful, two friends calling to each other through the trees.

'Wuh-woo-woo-wuh-wuh!' I whispered. 'Wuh-woo-woo-wuh-wuh!'

I closed my eyes the better to listen. I don't know how long I sat there.

Then something in the bushes made me jump, and suddenly George was standing by the pines near where I was hiding. He stared at me through pinched little eyes, as if he didn't want to let anything either in or out. His mouth was small and clamped shut. I was scared of what he might do. Then from down below the horn on a bus honked twice, which usually meant 'goodbye'. George made a face and left without a word, so I breathed a sigh of relief and I too started wandering down the hill towards the road.

'Beep! Beep!' I whispered.

Chapter 24

'Get the wheelbarrow!' someone shouted. 'We need a wheelbarrow!'

I hadn't got very far, only as far as Mrs Mags's hut, where a big old wheelbarrow like a bathtub was lying on its side against the back wall. It had long handles and a little rubber wheel and was heavy and difficult to get upright.

'Need a wheelbarrow!'

'Coming!' I muttered. What was all the hurry? A cupboard could wait. So could a stack of pots. It wasn't dark. I had the wheelbarrow standing but every time I tried to lift the handles, it lurched sideways.

'There you are!' said Sandy. 'Where did you get to? You must be so excited!'

About no news?

'Not really.'

He came round behind the wheelbarrow and took one of the shafts and together we wound our way down the path.

'Mr Tait's in a terrible fluster. She won't speak to him,' he said.

'What?'

'Mr Tait. She won't even let him help her off the bus.'

'Who won't?'

The wheel struck something under the grass, jamming the shafts into our stomachs. We both cried out, laughed, righted the barrow and set off again. A man in work clothes came to help us.

'That's my dad,' said Sandy with a grin. 'Dad, this is Lenny.'

'Hello, Mr Mags, Mr MacInnes,' I said, not sure what to call him. He looked nothing like his wife, Mrs Mags. He was tall and thin with neatly combed hair, whereas Mrs Mags was short and stout and had hair like a wild bush on fire.

'Hello, Lenny,' he said. 'Mr Mags is just fine.' He put his head to one side. 'But look at you! So like your mum!'

'Tart!' said bad George who strode past us now.

'Don't you dare, boy,' said Mr Mags. Mr Mags looked nothing like the old Mr MacInnes in the shadows on the chair behind the sofa who was his father, but for a second he looked quite a lot like George with his little eyes and tight mouth. They hissed and glared at each other. I pretended not to notice.

How did Mr Mags know my mum? Perhaps he worked in Singer's too.

When we got down the hill the road was so full of people and their mountains of belongings that I wondered how they had ever fitted on the bus in the first place. People hugged each other and talked and a little brown dog was sniffing their ankles, looking for an owner.

'Make way! Make way!' said Mr Mags, friendly again now. 'The royal throne is here. Make way!'

'She still won't come out,' said Mrs Wilson, who was standing with a group of others. 'Not until Lenny's found.'

'I'm here!' I said. 'Where's Mr Tait? What's going on?'

Mr Tait was by the door of the bus with Mrs Mags. He had his brown hat in his hand and was turning it round and round and frowning at it so that all his wrinkles fell forwards to his mouth. The bus driver, usually a patient man, was explaining that he couldn't wait forever, it would be blackout soon and he really had to go. I slipped my hand into Mr Tait's.

'Lenny, my dear, there you are at last,' he said. 'Your mother is here.'

'What?' I said, tears bursting to my eyes, my heart going bang-bang-bang and my tummy all tight. 'Where?' I didn't understand. 'How can she be? The hospital … you said … .'

Perhaps she hadn't really lost her foot. Perhaps it wasn't true.

'Yes!' he said. 'She's here, a bit earlier than expected. She's on the bus. Go on. You can go in. She won't get off the bus without you.'

Her face floated through the shadowy reflections of the glass, a face I knew so well, still surrounded by the white turban which was held in place by a safety pin. She didn't see me. Mr Tait produced a clean white handkerchief. He patted my tears with it and put it in my hand.

'Lenny's here!' Mr Tait called in through the bus door.

'Don't come in here!' said my mum, when he put his foot on the step.

'She's a bit scared, Mrs Gillespie, that's all,' he said. 'But alright. I'll wait here. Lenny, on you go.'

How could my mum be there? She wasn't supposed

to be out of hospital until we'd built the hut, until her foot was better or her leg, at least everyone said so. I didn't understand. What was going on?

'Lenny?' Her voice was small now.

'Yes, Lenny's here,' said Mr Tait.

So I clambered up into the bus and stood on the top step blinking back the tears, smoothing down my grubby dress and squeezing the shoe at my belt.

'Mum,' I said. I couldn't say more. My throat felt like I'd been strangled. (I knew how that felt because a bad girl had tried to strangle me at school in Clydebank.)

My mum was perched on the edge of the seat behind the driver in her old grey coat. She wasn't as pale as a ghost any more, but she looked tired like she usually did. Two crutches sat on the seat beside her, strange wooden things. She smiled at me, or tried to, and I wondered if it hurt her to smile, the way it had hurt me after the bombing, and then she cried out, like the mew of a cat, and held her arms out to me, like a kid, like Mavis, because she was helpless and couldn't move. Under the seat I saw her leg, what was left of it, wrapped in a pale brown bandage and tied up with another safety pin. She shifted in her seat a little.

'Lenny?' she said, still holding out her arms to me.

I didn't know what to do.

'Mum,' I said.

I didn't know what to do, so I stayed where I was and I waited. I didn't want to be near her leg. There were things in my head again, things I shouldn't have seen, and it was all my own fault. These things were everywhere now, and my eyes flickered back to her foot, her leg rather, the bandage, under the seat, and back to her face and then to the floor. I couldn't look at her. I was so scared I couldn't look, so I closed my eyes and shook my head.

'Down in the meadow where the green grass grows … .' I didn't sing it out loud of course but I wished I could and I tapped my foot in time.

'Go on, Lenny,' said Mr Tait from the ground behind me.

I could see the top of his head again. The grit was all gone. His head was clean.

'I can't,' I whispered and stepped down one. My mum sniffed.

'Go on, Lenny. It's your mum, just your mum,' he said.

Mrs Mags was trying to shoo everyone up the hill. I saw Sandy's head bobbing about in the crowd.

I tried to whisper. I was going to tell him that I really couldn't, really, but my mouth wouldn't work. I was going to tell him how cold I was, too cold to be standing there. I bit the fingernail on my thumb, and I fumbled for Mavis's shoe, but it must have got lost round the back because it wasn't there, so I fumbled all the harder and came down another step. One more step and I'd be on the road. As it was I was the same height as Mr Tait, or very nearly. I left my poor mum up there in the bus with her head in her hands, sniffing and mewing.

'Lenny, my dear,' he said, in his soft voice from close by. 'This is a moment for being brave. You have to gather up all your strength and all your kindness, from the very bottom of your boots and you have to stand up very straight and go and give your mum a little kiss and say "Hello". Then I will come and help you get her off the bus.'

'No, you won't!' said my mum fiercely. 'Don't you come near me!'

'Perhaps the lads at the back of the bus could lend a hand?' He said this loudly so that they could hear him.

'Why are all these people still here?' said my mum. Her words burst out of her, and then she sniffed them back in.

'This is the hardest bit,' whispered Mr Tait, leaning into my ear. 'After this it will be easier.'

Mr Tait left me on the bottom step of the bus and went to ask people to stop staring and move away. I think that's what he was doing. I kept my eyes shut while he did it. I didn't want them to see me. I didn't want Mr Tait to leave me standing there.

'Lenny?' said my mum. 'Lenny, darling … .'

My heart went bang-bang-bang so loudly I thought everyone must have heard and I still couldn't find Mavis's shoe. I suddenly needed to cough very hard. When I opened my eyes and stopped coughing Mr Tait was standing a few feet away. Someone was talking to him but he wasn't listening. He was watching me. He interrupted whoever was doing the talking, Mrs Mags perhaps, I don't know. I didn't wait to see.

In a sudden rush all the grit came up from my toes, from down inside my boots (except I only had sensible t-bars like Mavis's) and I hopped up the two metal steps with a clunk-clunk, and without looking down at anything I didn't want to see, I went to my mum and took her head in my hands and kissed her cheek and held onto her neck.

'Hello,' I said, just like Mr Tait had told me to do.

'Hello, Lenny, my darling Lenny!' and she put her arms all around me like a huge warm blanket by the fire. She sniffed and sobbed and shook so much it took me a while to realise I was sniffing and sobbing and shaking too. Then she stopped and ran her hand across the top of my forehead and along the side of my cheek to my chin, just like she's always done since I was a baby, and she put her hand to her mouth to stop the cries coming out again. 'Thank God for you!' she said, and the skin on her forehead wrinkled up with trying not to cry again. She wiped her tears away with the heel of her thumb, just like Mavis does and then she wiped mine with the top bit of her thumb, just like she does when she doesn't have a hanky. I gave her Mr Tait's nearly white handkerchief and she wiped our tears all over again.

She tried to take my lovely hat off, and I tried to stop her, but she took it off anyway and saw no hair, or hardly any, and lots of little scabs, the big one over my ear. Her eyes darted backwards and forwards between mine and around my face trying to understand what had happened to me. I put the hat back on.

'Lady, I need to get this bus moving,' said the driver. 'How about you boys in the back give these two a helping hand?'

'I lost Mavis!' I said. 'I'm sorry.' I hugged her all over again. 'Sorry,' I sniffed. 'Sorry.'

'Lenny,' she whispered back. 'I don't believe Mavis is lost.'

'Mr Tait's going to find her. He's nice, I promise. He brought me an orange and it wasn't even my birthday.'

She made a face like bad George and I wondered how I was ever going to persuade her? The boys at the back of the bus were hovering about us like nervous rabbits ready to run. They didn't look much older than Sandy or bad George, but they helped her anyway which meant I didn't have to. When I got to the bottom step of the bus Mr Tait was there. I smiled at him so he'd know I'd done what he said and he stepped out of the way so my mum could get down with one of the back-seat boys helping her. Another passed her crutches down to Mrs Mags, and somehow an ordinary wooden chair, like the one Miss Read sat on at school, appeared by her side and she plumped down on it and sighed.

'Thank you, thank you so much,' she said in her voice that was different from everybody else's because we weren't from Clydebank or Carbeth.

I figured if I stayed right beside her all the time I wouldn't have to look at her foot, or her leg, so that's what I did, I stood right beside her, with my hand on the back of her chair. She smelled funny, a hospital smell I suppose, of disinfectant and ether, which is what Mr Tait said it was. I suppose they must have used the same stuff on my mum's cuts as the lady with the fur coat at the La Scala. But my mum smelled of bombs too and misery and fear. Perhaps it was stuck to her handbag, which she was gripping tightly on her lap. Its blue leather was ripped at one end but it still bulged like it always did only now it smelled of boom-crash.

The bus roared off. The crowd thinned out. Mr Mags and another man were talking to Mrs Mags and a woman who looked just like her only smaller, all in a huddle. Mr Tait was some way off, wrinkly again and standing with Sandy.

'I don't know what to do, Lenny,' said my mum suddenly. She still had Mr Tait's handkerchief. I didn't tell her it was his.

'What do you mean?' I said.

'They needed the bed,' she said, 'and I had nowhere else to go, the hospital I mean, but I thought you had somewhere to stay here. Mr Tait told the nurse he had a hut, in fact he called it a chalet in the hills and it sounded lovely. He told me there was a nurse here who could look after my leg, and I don't believe it now for a second. And then once they'd let me out and we were on the bus he told me he hadn't built his chalet yet. I don't know what to do!'

'There is a nurse,' I said, 'and we didn't think you were coming for another week or two.'

'They might have kept me in longer if Mr Tait hadn't turned up,' she said.

She was fiddling with the clasp on her bag, clipping it open and shut, open and shut. I put my hand over hers. It shut with a brisk snap.

'He's nice, Mum,' I said quietly, 'and so's everyone else here. They opened all the huts, even the ones that were locked and the owners weren't there, and they let the people from Clydebank in. The Salvation Army were here giving out blankets and food, and Mrs Mags, that's her over there, gave us stew and baths. I've been to school too. Not my school, Craigton school.'

'I can't accept any help from Mr Tait,' she said, through tight lips. 'He's a nasty, evil, little man. We'd be in America now if it wasn't for him.'

I looked at wrinkly Mr Tait with his fancy bedpost stick. He had taken off his hat again and was wiping his forehead with another of his clean white handkerchiefs, even though it wasn't hot at all.

'Umm,' I said.

'What are we going to do?' she said.

'There are some tents … .'

'Tents?'

'Yes, Mr Tait and me, we were going to stay in one until we got the hut built. I was going to help seeing as he's got a bad leg.'

'You and Mr Tait in a tent? That's ridiculous! I'm not going in a tent and neither are you. How could I with only one … ? Where are these tents anyway? That's what I want to know.'

I started to point down the road, but Mrs Mags was coming towards us, smiling a big smile.

'Mrs Gillespie!' she said. 'Welcome to Carbeth! I'm so glad to meet you at last. Lenny's been an absolute pleasure to have around. She's a lovely girl!' I blushed under my hat. 'Very adventurous, she is, and not afraid of anything, aren't you not, darling?'

'Eh?' I said.

'I'm Mrs MacInnes,' she went on, 'but everyone calls me Mrs Mags. That's my husband over there and my sister, Mrs Connor, and her husband. But you'll be wondering where on earth you've come to.'

'Well, yes,' nodded my mum.

Mrs Mags bent down so that their faces were very close together and I couldn't hear what they were saying. I caught Mr Tait's eye and shrugged my shoulders. He shrugged back.

And then Mrs Mags told the other grown-ups they

were all to wait while she and my mum went into the hall.

I haven't told you about the hall yet because I hadn't been in it before then. It was near the bus stop and was used for dances. I think my mum needed a wee. Mrs Mags took her to the toilets in the hall and I tiptoed along behind them, not sure what to do with myself, but making sure I didn't look down. I kept my eyes on the back of her head.

When we came back Mr Tait had borrowed the chair to rest on for a minute. He stood up straightaway. My mum looked at him sideways but wouldn't say a word. Poor Mr Tait who meant no harm. Poor Mr Tait who had been so kind to me. I wanted to go and slip my hand into his but I thought I'd better not.

'We don't need the wheelbarrow,' said Mr Mags. 'We can lift her in the chair. You grab the other side.' The other man took hold of the other side of my mum's brown wooden chair.

'OH!' screamed my mum as she was lifted vertically and nearly thrown over backwards onto her head.

And I screamed too. I'd only just got her back. I didn't want her hurt again and to have to go back to hospital.

The chair landed with a ker-thump on the road.

'Wheelbarrow!' said the men. 'Ha, ha, ha!' They seemed to think this was very funny. My mum didn't agree, and Mr Tait was jumping around as if he had ants in his pants, as my Auntie May would have said.

'You keep out of this!' said my mum to Mr Tait, then, 'Lenny?' she said in her small voice to me. 'Lenny, you stay right beside me. I don't want to lose you.' I said I would make sure that I did.

So they put the chair in the wheelbarrow, not with my mum still on it of course, and she stood up and put the crutches under her arms to support herself. I stood right beside her, just like she said, and she swung her crutches forward and hopped on her one leg. She managed all the way to the Halfway House pub which was probably the length of four buses, and then they took the chair out of the wheelbarrow again so that she could sit down a minute. She was trembling all over with so much hard work and exertion.

'You're all very kind,' she said. 'I'm sorry to be so much bother.'

Mrs Mags said she was no bother at all, and not to be so silly. She said we could all stay in her hut because the boys, Dougie and bad George (she didn't call him 'bad' but I suspect she would have liked to) would be staying in their own hut now that her sister and her husband (their parents) had arrived for the weekend.

'I'll leave you here then and go to the tents,' said Mr Tait.

Mrs Mags fussed and fussed and tried to insist that he didn't go to the tents but came along with us, such a long way and it was nearly dark, and I hoped and wished that he would change his mind and come to Mrs Mags's hut instead. Then my mum would see I wasn't lying, that Mr Tait was kind and good and didn't clype on her at Singer's factory. But she was silent as the grave, as my gran would say, staring straight ahead of her at the great hill she had to climb.

Mr Tait said he was quite sure he wanted to go to the tent.

Even though I didn't want to and I knew my mum

wouldn't be pleased, I had to say goodbye to Mr Tait. I didn't want him to go. I needed him to tell me what to do next.

'I'll come over in the morning,' I said. 'I'll bring Sandy and Dougie too and we can start on the hut, first thing. I promise.'

'Let's just wait and see what happens, shall we?' he said. 'Your mother needs you to help her. I think she must get first shout.'

I didn't want to help my mum. I wanted to stay with him. Wasn't I awful? I wanted to stay with him in the tent and build the hut in the morning and play on the rope swing whenever I could.

'She's like the orange, Lenny,' he said. 'She looks a bit funny, a bit scary, but she's just your mum, the same old mum you last saw a week ago going to the pictures.'

But I thought that was years ago, even though I knew it wasn't. It felt like years ago and Clydebank felt like miles away even though it was only over the hill. I looked at the hill now, for a clue, and so that no-one would see me bite my lip.

'Good night, Lenny,' he said. 'No doubt I will see you tomorrow.' He bent down and gave me a little hug so that I could smell the smoky fire on his jacket, and he hobbled away from us along the road all by himself with the trees looming in on him from either side.

Suddenly I was very cold and very tired and the hill seemed very, very big.

Chapter 25

'Stop it, you two!' said Mrs Mags. She was talking to Mr Mags, her husband, and the other man, George and Dougie's dad, Mr Connor. They had lifted my mum out of the chair and were trying to position her in the wheelbarrow. Even in the falling light I could see my mum's face redden under the white turban and I could see her wince with pain. It was a question of dignity, she told me later, as well as comfort and practicality, which seemed difficult to achieve under the circumstances. Finally they settled for pulling the wheelbarrow up the hill behind them rather than pushing it, while she sat propped up on somebody's bundle with her feet, her foot, dangling over the back but as the hill got steeper she began to slip and they had to stop.

Everybody stood about scratching their heads and wondering what to do next and my mum apologised until she just couldn't any more and then sat staring firmly back at the road. And while we were all standing there with the wind blowing around us and the sky threatening rain, again, I heard Mr Tait of all people calling us from the road.

'I've borrowed a bogey,' he said, 'from the hall, for Mrs Gillespie, if you'd care to come and get it for her.'

He didn't mean ghosts or snotters. He meant a

trolley on wheels. It had a cage about a foot high all round for her to lean on and not fall out, and enough room for her legs, or leg, to stretch out. Good Mr Tait. Now she'd see.

Mrs Mags and her sister, Mrs Connor, went back down to get it while the men held the wheelbarrow. I gave Mr Tait a big wave and he disappeared along the road again. Then the men lifted my poor mum out of the wheelbarrow while the women rearranged the bundle in the bogey for her comfort. Then my mum was lowered into it. I couldn't breathe. I couldn't watch. I paced up and down and looked and looked away and thought I'd be sick at any moment. I could tell she was being brave, but I could tell it hurt too and she was scared. I didn't like her to be scared.

Mrs Mags and her sister walked on one side carrying the crutches and Sandy and I walked on the other. I held my mum's hand as I climbed the hill and stared straight ahead or to the side but definitely not down at the leg. And I didn't know what to say to her.

Up above us the men talked about things I didn't understand and people I'd never heard of, about organising and bosses, overtime and beer and things that had fallen off lorries. Maybe all the lorries had been bombed too and were in bad shape, but lots of things seemed to have fallen off them.

'I was so worried,' she said. I thought you were … .'

'I know. Me too.'

We couldn't talk any more, not really. The ride was too bumpy and she had to concentrate to stay safe and not hurt and every so often she'd cry out in pain and I'd cry out too or hold my breath and bite my lip. Mrs Mags scolded the men for not being more careful and took her other hand and told her how brave she was, and I thought maybe I should tell her something like that too, but I couldn't think what. In fact there were lots of things I wanted to say, but none of them seemed to fit, perhaps because they were old things now, things that I'd thought I'd want to say when I was dreaming about her arriving. I'd wanted to say 'I'm so happy you're here!' and 'Everything is going to be alright!' but neither of those things were true now, and it felt so much like they should have been.

She squeezed my hand so I tried to smile, but it hurt.

'It's going to be alright you know,' she said. 'We're going to be just fine, just as soon as I've got the hang of these crutches, and then they're going to give me a new ... .'

'No!' I said. I didn't want to hear. What did she mean, a new foot? One from the pile? Somebody else's? No! I let go of her hand and put both hands over my ears.

'I've heard they're very good now,' said Mrs Mags. I heard her through my palms, even though I didn't want to. 'They've come up with all sorts of new ideas. They have to, there's so many people losing limbs, with this war and all that.'

I squeezed my hands harder over my ears. My mum shouted 'Stop!' and the men stopped. She tried to pull my hands away but she couldn't get at me from the bogey so Mrs Mags came round to where I stood and tried to as well.

'Lenny! Lenny, stop this,' said Mrs Mags. 'What on earth is the matter? Aren't you pleased to have your mum back?' And then she tried to laugh, even though we all knew none of this was funny. 'Of course you are!'

I was ashamed of all the things I felt. None of them fitted. Mrs Mags let go of my hands so I put them back over my ears and she went back to talking to my mum again. I took my hands off my ears but not so anyone would know.

'We don't actually know what Lenny saw,' said Mrs Mags, 'but she's been a bit upset, not naughty exactly but … Mr Tait's been very protective. Apparently he's been through something similar before, you know, in the last war, so he understands a bit. Wilful, on occasion, I suppose is what you'd call it, and desperate to find you and your wee Mavis.'

The bogey moved again and I took my hands off my ears. Sandy and I stayed to one side. Mrs Mags seemed to have lots of things to say to my mum so I kept out of the way and left them to it.

As we got nearer to the hut we could see Dougie up at the rope swing although it was nearly dark. Sandy and I broke into a run but he got there first. He told the other kids I was to get first shot and bugged the life out of the boy who was on it. But I didn't really want special attention. I just wanted my place in the queue, and for my mum to be alright and this day to be over, to be left alone to hide in the trees and to help Mr Tait build his hut.

So I left them and sat against Mrs Mags's hut so I could listen to the grown-ups through the wall, feeling guilty for being on the outside, not inside close to my mum.

'He's still a gaffer,' said Mr Mags. 'We don't want gaffers here. How are we going to get huts built with him about? And I know what you're saying, the man's a cripple, no offence Mrs Gillespie, but he's a bit of a mover as far as I can see, and straight as a die. We'd never get anything past him.'

'Aye, he's trustworthy alright,' said the other man, Mr Connor, 'but he's not dishonest, not as he'd see it. He wouldn't turn a blind eye for long but his conscience would get the better of him, and we'd all be sunk. He's a gaffer, for God's sake! It's not worth his while. Not worth ours.'

'Well, he's only just a gaffer,' said Mr Mags. 'Wee in both status and stature but still a gaffer.'

'He's a gaffer because of his leg,' said Mrs Mags. 'What else was he going to do, coming back with a leg shot to bits? No-one would have him at the shipyard would they? He's never risen above supervisor level, you know, and he's a capable man. I'm sure he could have risen higher in all that time. He's only trying to survive and do the right thing, like the rest of us.'

'Och, away you go,' said Mr Mags. 'He's still a boss, so he's not to be trusted.'

'You've not seen him here with our Sandy,' said Mrs Mags. 'Or your Lenny, Mrs Gillespie.'

'He shouldn't be anywhere near my Lenny,' said my mum. 'He's nothing but trouble. So I've heard.'

Nobody spoke, as if they didn't want to speak about that, whatever it was that had happened. But I did. I wanted to tell them he didn't do it, he told me so himself. I wanted to know what my mum was supposed to have been doing. Perhaps they didn't know anything about it, but their silence suggested they did.

'I've heard he has an eagle eye for things going missing and things going on,' said my mum.

'Would you like more soup?' said Mrs Mags.

Soup? I thought. I'd love some soup. My tummy rumbled so loudly I thought they must have heard me.

'I've too much to do to be helping him,' said Mr Connor.

'You've too much to do to be helping anybody,' said Mrs Mags smartly, but I think she was joking. 'And if your George is going to be off school, I'm not keeping an eye on him. Mr Tait can get the use of him and keep his hands out of mischief. I'm sure he'd teach him a thing or two and not just about carpentry.'

'I know he's a problem, our George, I know that.'

'And I'm sure it's a great relief to you for him to be out here,' said Mrs Mags flatly. 'He's needing a father about.'

'What can I do?'

'Send him to Mr Tait,' said Mrs Mags.

'He's strict, right enough,' said Mr Connor.

'Strictness is a good thing,' said Mrs Mags. 'Everybody knows where they are with strictness.'

'You're starting to talk like a boss now yourself, Mags!' said Mr Mags.

'Och, you men, you don't know a thing!'

Was Mr Tait strict? I didn't think so. He'd always been very kind to me but fair, not to mention helpful, and always there. He'd promised to provide for me while my mum was in hospital, and he had. He'd even brought me an orange. I wanted to be expelled from school too so that I could help him with his hut and learn a thing or two, and not just about carpentry.

Sandy and Dougie came screaming down the hill so I leapt out of the darkness and frightened the living daylights out of them, and then we went inside and had soup with big lumps of chicken in it and jammy pieces.

My mum was wearing different clothes. Mrs Mags had lent her a pair of dungarees so that I couldn't see the bandage where the foot wasn't. She still had her white turban and a new pink cardigan that I hadn't seen before, like the pink clothes Mrs Wilson wore. I went and stood next to where she was sitting on the end of the bench.

'There's my Lenny!' she said smiling. She put an arm round me. 'Where have you been?'

'The rope swing,' I said.

'She's really good on the swing now,' said Sandy.

'Am I?' I said.

'I'm Sandy,' he said.

He threw me a big smile and I wished I had a big brother.

'Your mum tells me you've been looking out for Lenny,' she said. 'Has she been good?'

Sandy looked at his feet and I squirmed.

'You'd need to ask Mr Tait that,' he said.

'Of course I've been good,' I said quickly. 'I'm always good.'

'I'm sure you're a great help to your mum, Lenny,' said Mrs Mags. 'She's certainly going to need you now until she gets a hang of those crutches. How long have you had them?'

'Two days. Not long, but I don't think I'll ever get the hang of them.'

'Of course you will. Look at Mr Tait. He's

managing,' said Mr Mags. And I wondered why Mr Tait would have needed crutches; perhaps when he first hurt his leg, perhaps he had a stookie. Mr Mags must have known Mr Tait longer than me.

'Mr Tait, Mr Tait,' said my mum, suddenly angry. 'Do all roads lead to Mr Tait?'

I wished the ground would open up. I wished my mum wasn't so rude. You could have cut the air with a knife, as my gran used to say when my dad was home last year. I knew what that meant now.

'Sorry,' she said at last. 'I'm so sorry. It's the pain. I'm so tired.'

'Mr Tait's nice, Mum, honestly,' I said quietly.

'That's alright, dear. I think we're all a bit tired,' said Mrs Mags, standing up. 'Let's see if we can sort a bed for you and Lenny. Don't you worry about a thing.'

I had temporarily and completely forgotten about Mavis, although obviously there was no news of her or someone would have told me, I was sure, or was I? Perhaps I ought to check.

'Mum ... ,' I said, once Mr MacInnes senior was snoring on the sofa and Dougie and his mum and dad had left us for their own hut, which really was their own.

'Yes, Lenny?'

But she had shrunk, somehow, so I thought I'd wait until the morning to ask her about Mavis, because I knew really what the answer was going to be.

Chapter 26

That night we slept, the two of us, on the floor by the stove in Mrs Mags's hut, snug as bugs with the wind roaring through the trees all around us and the old man snoring on the sofa. I asked my mum what she thought of the huts, and weren't they fantastic and not like huts at all.

Yes, she said, what an adventure I'd been on, staying with such lovely people in such a beautiful spot.

Well, but it wasn't really like an adventure, not really because everyone thought I was a boy to begin with and not everyone was nice, George for instance. And I didn't know where she and Mavis were.

Sorry, she said, of course it wasn't an adventure. Probably very scary really not knowing anyone and not knowing where she, herself, was.

Yes, very scary, because Miss Weatherbeaten had been there.

Miss Weatherbeaten?

Yes, Miss Weatherbeaten, I said. Didn't she know Miss Weatherbeaten had been with us and had gone now to look after a rest centre and had taken Rosie back to the town hall.

'Rosie? Who's Rosie?' she asked.

'Rosie was lost,' I said, 'and came to Carbeth with us.'

'Didn't she like it?' asked Mum.

'Yes, she did,' I replied, 'but Miss Weatherbeaten thought she'd be better off at the town hall.'

'She might be right.'

I said I didn't think so and that I would have looked after Rosie myself, and so would Mr Tait, who was very angry with Miss Weatherbeaten.

She didn't say very much at all then, for a little while, lying beside me in the darkness. I couldn't lie close because of her leg. If my own foot had given it even the tiniest little dunt with its tiniest little toe I would have hurt her. I didn't want to hurt her and I didn't want to touch the foot, or the leg, or whatever. So I lay close but not right up against her as I would have liked, as we always did at home in our bed in the alcove. It was like the night before when I slept on the floor with Mr Tait and the other family that I didn't know, keeping a respectable gap between us all.

I asked her if she was comfortable, as comfortable as she could be and whether she needed anything else, a glass of water, or some of my 'pillow' (my coat bundled in a roll).

She said she'd barely slept for a week with the pain and with worrying about me, but she felt as heavy as lead and thought she'd sleep fine. We could worry about tomorrow when it came. I stroked the bit of hair that stuck out beneath her turban and tickled her neck. And she sang, 'Golden slumbers kiss your eyes, Smiles await you when you rise,' just like she did when I was wee, just like she's always done for Mavis and me. 'Sleep pretty Lenny, do not cry, And I will sing a lullaby.'

A drop of her tears hit my palm before I realised my

own were soaking the coat. There was no need to ask about Mavis.

Into the long night we journeyed together, drifting on a sea of dreams and nightmares, waking each other with cries or shudders, dodging falling bricks and shooting flames, stepping over things we shouldn't have seen or shouldn't have lost, together but apart, apart but together, and always with Mavis crouched somewhere in the shadows.

Chapter 27

You see, what I'd really been hoping for was this: Mr Tait would build his hut, with help from me and the boys and perhaps some of the men, and while he was doing this he would visit my mum every so often in hospital and win her over with daffodils and oranges (perhaps not the daffodils – he'd already tried that) and then she'd come to Carbeth. By then the hut would be finished and she'd have seen Mr Tait for the lovely man that he is and we'd all live together in his hut until the war was over. Naturally Mavis would have turned up by then and Mr Tait and my mum would be the best of pals. The best thing would be that she loved Carbeth so much she'd change her mind about going to America and Uncle James, and we'd all live happily ever after. This is what I dreamt about when I wasn't having nightmares.

My plan wasn't quite working.

That morning I was woken by some kids shouting outside the hut. Others were hiding behind it, dragging their bodies along the outside where I'd been hiding the night before, and then they were gone. There were birds cackling in the trees and Joey, Mr Tait's budgie, was still on the dresser with a cloth over him to keep him quiet. Poor Mr Tait could probably have done with his company.

I got up to light the stove, which had died in the night. My mum lay sleeping the sleep of the dead, her face smooth and restful and her breathing soft like a distant whistle. There were old copies of the *Daily Worker* behind the coal box. I scrunched a couple of sheets into a ball and pushed them into the stove, piled some coal on top and whisked a match to light it. Then I closed the door, adjusted the vents, and crossed my fingers that it would work. I put the kettle on the floor by the water bucket and scooped in the water with a glass, then heaved it onto the stove where it rasped and spat at me until the heat silenced it.

And still my mum slept.

The kettle wasn't long in boiling, even though I was watching it. I made tea and warmed my hands on the cup. Mr MacInnes was breathing rhythmically on the sofa, like my mum, but to a different tune. I tiptoed outside to a chair and fumbled for Mavis's shoe.

But Mavis's shoe wasn't there.

It really wasn't there. It didn't matter how I tried to turn the belt, which was still there, or lift my dress right up past my waist (it was an emergency), the shoe was not there. I couldn't remember when I'd last seen it. But I had to find it quick before someone else did. Bad George for instance.

So I gulped back my tea, then ran three steps up the hill and six down before I decided up was best. But no-one at the swing had seen the shoe, not even Dougie and he was searching for something too. He was searching for bad George.

'He didn't stay at Mrs Mags's,' I said.

'No?' he said. 'I was just coming down for him.

My dad wants a word, if you know what I mean. I'd scarper too if I were him.'

I really didn't care.

'Do you think he went to the ruined cottage?' he said. 'Or an empty hut? Maybe he slept out under the trees. He might have died of the cold! He'll be frozen to a tree trunk with his eyes staring at the sky.'

'I don't think there are any more empty huts.' Who cared anyway? Where was my shoe?

But he hadn't seen Mavis's shoe and he was being nosey, so I left him by the swing and began to retrace my steps, first to where the wheelbarrow had been and then down our zigzaggy route to the road and along it, the length of four buses, to the bus stop. No shoe. It wasn't in the cludgie in the hall either, and when I came out Dougie was standing there. He said we should ask Jimmy Robertson. I hadn't met Jimmy Robertson then so I didn't know what he was talking about.

Jimmy Robertson, who, by the way, was rumoured to have built the dance hall near the bus stop with the toilets that my mum had used, Jimmy Robertson owned a shop that was next to the bus stop that was next to the hall, just on the brow of the hill, four bus lengths up from the Halfway House pub. But this was no ordinary shop. This was a shop in an old bus, and it had a tree growing up through the floor and out of the roof. There were baskets and boxes piled high and old newspapers stacked against one wall. I'd never been somewhere like that before. Dougie said I should wait outside if I was scared so I kept very close behind him when we went in.

Jimmy Robertson was very interested in Mavis's shoe (he made me explain why it was so important), but he hadn't seen it. He got me to describe the shoe in great detail even though it was just an ordinary shoe, and he nodded as if he was writing himself a note inside his head, and said he'd keep an eye out for it. My dad told me once that you could take your eye right out of its socket and look behind you, but I don't think it's what Jimmy Robertson meant. I was glad he was taking Mavis's shoe so seriously.

When we stepped back down from Jimmy Robertson's shop-bus, Dougie told me in a loud stage whisper that Jimmy Robertson lived in the bus too, in at the back of it amongst the boxes of cabbages, and he took me to the end of the bus and pointed to some dusty old curtains across the back window to prove his point. It didn't seem very likely to me that a grown-up would live in a bus, even if it was also a shop, but Jimmy Robertson was watching us so I didn't like to argue.

There was no sign of the shoe and no sign of George.

'Does it really matter?' said Dougie. 'She's bound to have another pair by now.'

Well, yes, I had to concede this was probably true, but it wasn't really the point, was it?

We went back to Mrs Mags's hut.

'Lenny!' my mum beamed.

I plumped down beside her and eased into the space under her arm.

'Bad George has … I mean,' I said. Whoops! Oh, dear.

Old Mr MacInnes let out a snort.

'What has bad George done now?' said Mrs Mags with a rub of her very round tummy.

'He's gone missing!' broke in Dougie.

'Missing? Oh, dear,' said Mrs Mags with a pat to the tummy. 'Well, that's peace for all of us.'

Dougie was not happy. I could tell. His eyes looked like his brother's, small and sharp. I hadn't seen him like that before, not even at the canal.

'We think he might be under a tree somewhere,' I said. 'Or maybe in another hut.'

'You're the expert when it comes to sneaking into huts!' said Mrs Mags.

'Oh?' said my mum. 'Why?'

So while Mrs Mags was explaining things, I went hunting for Mavis's shoe.

Soon I was lost among the paths behind the rope swing. Clouds slid over the sun and a harsh grey coldness hung about me. The sun was not burning its way through the haze but suffocating behind it instead. I didn't know where I was and then I hit a road. There was a wooded area to the right which was thick with the sound of bang-bang-bang and other building noises, and a bit further on, a few yards, maybe a mile, was a lorry and some men. (I still hadn't got the hang of distance but reckoned I'd covered at least twenty miles that morning already.)

Mr Tait was so well camouflaged in his brown tweed suit that I didn't notice him at first, leaning against a tree trunk with a tin mug in his hand.

'Mr Tait!' I said.

'Lenny! Hello there!' he said. 'You are always full of surprises!'

'George!' I said.

He had been hiding behind the tree where a tiny bonfire was burning. A battered old saucepan was sitting over it astride some bricks.

'Hi, Lenny!' he said in a friendly voice. 'Fancy a cuppa? We've got milk. Mr Tulloch the farmer came by and said he knew you.'

This was too many surprises at once.

'They're out looking for you,' I told George. 'Even Jimmy Robertson's looking for you, in his bus.'

'Ah, yes,' he said, giving his little fire some extra special attention it didn't need. 'I stayed with Mr Tait last night, in his tent. It's great! There was a huge bonfire by the burn and lots of ... .' He suddenly stopped speaking and a frown spread across his face. I think he'd forgotten he hated me. 'I'm glad you weren't there,' he said weakly.

'So your mother didn't actually send you down here to help, did she?' said Mr Tait slowly in his quiet voice.

'Well, no, not exactly,' said bad George, 'but she would have done if she noticed me at all, which she doesn't.' He was muttering now and neither Mr Tait nor myself could make him out.

'You've got bricks!' I said.

'Yes,' said Mr Tait, 'not many but it's a start, and a shovel, on loan from our nice new neighbours. I can't really dig of course, but I've marked it out, you see? There and there and there?' He pointed with his fancy bedpost stick. 'I've marked where it needs dug. The men down there at that lorry said they'd help as soon as they've got time. Very nice lads, I must say, very nice, and I've got George here.'

'His mum's frantic,' I lied.

'Is she?' said bad George. He seemed very pleased about this, which I didn't think was very nice. Of course I'd no idea whether she was frantic or not; it was a lie and probably not a white one like my mum said was alright. And, like Mrs Mags, George's mum might well have been delighted at his disappearance, for all I knew.

'Well, no, I don't really know, but Dougie is, was.' The truth was Dougie and Sandy had probably forgotten all about George, and for a second I was tempted to tell him that. Mr Tait saved me from my deliberations.

'How's your mother?' he said. George handed me some tea in a jam jar, with milk.

'I don't know,' I said. 'I need to get back to find out. I've been away for ages looking for Mavis's shoe. I lost her shoe last night and I haven't found it yet.' The smoke suddenly blew sideways into my eyes. 'I need to tell my mum what happened.'

'Is it hard having her back?'

'It's wonderful,' I said. I moved out of the smoke which had decided to persist in my direction. I wiped my eyes with my trusty coat sleeve.

'But strange,' he said. 'It's not quite how we planned it, is it?'

I looked at him in surprise. Good Mr Tait. He'd understood.

'I'm going to tell her everything that happened,' I said, 'so she knows you're kind. She just doesn't know it yet. She'll change her mind when she knows what you did, I'm sure of it. She won't listen just now at all, not even to Mrs Mags; she won't even hear it. But she'll be worried sick that I'm not there. Thank you for the tea but I'm afraid I can't drink it. I'm so long away already.' I tried to give George back his cup of tea, but Mr Tait shook his head and wouldn't let him take it.

Instead Mr Tait said, 'Excuse us a minute would you, George? Why don't you run down to the lorry and see if they need a hand.' George threw the dregs of his tea manfully into the bushes, set his cup by the fire and swaggered off down the road. Mr Tait seemed to have taught him a thing or two already.

Mr Tait sat himself down on an old chair that was beside the little stone fire and I sat on a log a couple of feet away.

'Can I come back over here?' I said.

But before Mr Tait could answer me, George came swaggering back up the road. 'I suppose you better have this,' he said. 'It was behind my Auntie Mags' hut.' And he thrust Mavis's shoe into my hand as if he was a big gruff man shaking hands with another big gruff man. Into my palm it went, thwack! And he strode off.

'Thank you!' I called after him as he swayed back down the road. I turned the shoe over in my hand to make sure it really was hers.

'Goodness gracious!' said Mr Tait. 'Wonders will never cease. I had no idea.'

'All I need now is Mavis.' She was all I needed and perhaps the return of her shoe was a lucky omen. I wanted to strap it back round my middle IMMEDIATELY, as Miss Weatherbeaten would have said, but that would have involved wheeching up my dress, so I couldn't.

'I think you'd better go straight back to your mum and see what's going on over there. As far as I'm concerned, you can always come back down here, but your mum is in charge now.'

'What did you do to George to get him to stop being horrible?'

He told me that George had come over after dark saying his parents had sent him to help build the hut, but he had suspected George was avoiding some sort of trouble at home. I told him George had been 'expelled' from the school and Mr Tait nodded slowly.

'Mrs Mags thinks he should be here anyway,' I said, 'so you can teach him about building and other things. Looks like she's right.'

'Yes, it does, doesn't it?'

He laughed a little and swayed backwards into the old chair and I noticed his foot for the first time – his bad foot which had no sock and seemed to have something sticking out of it, something I didn't want to see, something I shouldn't have looked at. But I did, so it was all my own fault.

Chapter 28

Mr Tait had a wooden leg! Mr Tait had a wooden leg! I was utterly unable to speak for five whole minutes.

I should have left straightaway and not stayed to chat with Mr Tait when my poor mum was stuck in Mrs Mags's hut with strangers. I should never have stopped.

It was either a wooden leg or he had a very serious skin condition, because what I saw was dark brown, shiny and smooth with no hairs, unlike my dad's legs which had lots of dark hairs all over them like bits of bristle from a brush, or like the stuff that was coming out of Mrs Mags's sofa. Mr Tait had none of that. In fact he had a dent in his leg, and unlike the dents that frequently happen to my legs, this dent was paler on the inside than on the outside.

The only conclusion I could come to was that *this was not a real leg*.

I had a kind of sick feeling, with prickles up the back of my neck. I think I may have become temporarily deaf because I didn't hear a word Mr Tait was saying. I stood up and, before I knew it, I had picked up a brick and was positioning it roughly where we'd agreed the corner of the hut would be. I think I may also have become temporarily blind because it wasn't long before I'd built a short tower, two bricks one way, then two bricks the other until I had about six or seven layers, but with no idea of what I was doing. Sandy says you call that automatic pilot.

'There were legs, legs, made out of wooden pegs,' I sang inside my head. A brick slipped from my grasp and landed heavily, narrowly missing my foot. My pretty hat slipped down over my eyes. I left it there.

'Whoops, careful,' said Mr Tait. 'Very good, Lenny. That's exactly how we'll do it, but we need a bit of cement to stick them all together and we need to dig too, so that it sits right down into the ground. I need someone else for that though because of my bad leg.'

I wanted to say to him that it wasn't a 'bad' leg; it was a non-leg, a leg that didn't even exist, either as a good one or a bad one, and he hadn't even told me about it in all this very long time that I'd known him, which of course was only eight days in total, but felt more like eight months.

'Lenny?' he said. 'What's wrong?'

'Nothing,' I lied, only a little white one. I slipped Mavis's shoe into my pocket. 'I really need to go. My mum will be so worried.'

'Lenny … ?'

'Bye, Mr Tait! Thanks for the tea!'

'Lenny, perhaps you could bring Joey … .'

I pretended I hadn't heard. That was a white lie too wasn't it? Or was it a black one, a black lie? I shook my head as I ran, to keep out the pictures of horrible things. I ran, heavy of heart. There were people all down the road, back a little among the trees, doing what Mr Tait was doing, building huts. They were mostly men but up the hill a bit there were women and kids. Bonfires smoked here and there. I wondered if any of them knew about Mr Tait's leg, if I was the only person in the whole world who didn't know about Mr Tait's leg, if everyone else had been let in on the secret, everyone except me.

'Bye, George!' I said as I ran past the lorry, my hand on my head to keep my hat on. I'd forgotten too that we hated each other, but he had found and kept and returned Mavis's shoe.

He had two legs; that seemed important.

I had two legs; that seemed important too. I listened to my two feet tap-tapping on the road and remembered what Mr Tait's feet sounded like when he was on the road, his one foot, his wooden foot, and his stick. It was more of a tappety-tap, tappety-tap, and his body rocked as he went. It was just an old person's sway. I couldn't have known, but surely he could have told me. Now images of a stump filled my head, but was this stump below the knee or above it? How far above it, or how far below? Was it round and smooth, like the wood at his ankle, or flat like a tree branch that's been sawn off?

'The animals went in two by two, hurrah, hurrah!' I puffed and took my hat off. 'The elephant and the kangaroo... .' Who was the elephant and who was the kangaroo? 'And they all went into the ark for to get out of the rain.' And they all had the proper amount of legs, and nobody had any secrets, and everyone was everyone else's friend.

How could he not have told me?

Mr Tait had lied! He'd told me his leg got a bit stiff sometimes when really it was completely and totally solid.

I had to slow down to consider this (I was running

out of breath). Was it a white lie, to be kind, to save me being upset, or was it a black lie, designed to cheat? Did he pretend to be my friend when actually he wasn't?

The road came to an end. I turned left into the main road. Jimmy Robertson's bus was up ahead and people were milling about with milk bottles and loaves of bread. Jimmy Robertson glanced up as I passed so I pulled Mavis's shoe out of my pocket and waved it at him. He gave me a quick thumbs-up and went back to his customers. The length of four buses and I was at the bottom of the hill, relieved to be on familiar territory.

I was exhausted.

When my mum laughed it sounded more like extra big hiccups, almost sore. It was high and sharp, a bit alarming if you weren't expecting it. Sometimes people stopped laughing themselves and stared at her, to make sure she wasn't choking before carrying on with their own laughter. My gran, on the other hand, was like a donkey; a long husky intake of breath followed by a single honk, and my dad was different again. He was a straightforward Ha … Ha … Ha, slow and rhythmic like the beat of a waltz, but somehow airy. I used to worry he'd run out of breath.

It was my mother's laugh that assaulted my ears as I rounded the curve of the hill, somewhat breathless myself. Laughter was not what I'd expected and not, I felt, quite right somehow. She was sitting on an upright chair, wrapped in a coat with a tartan blanket tucked in around her knees and her crutches lying on the ground, one on either side of her as if she'd dropped them and fallen into the chair.

'Lenny!' she said, still laughing. 'Hic! Where have you been? Hic!'

Mrs Mags was on another chair beside her, rolling from side to side. She was a silent laugher. Clouds burst from both their mouths. Mrs Mags struggled to compose herself.

'Where have you left the boys, Lenny?' said Mrs Mags.

I collapsed onto a stump of wood, panting, then rose again to get some water from the bucket inside, thumping back down on the stump again, cup in hand.

I told them I'd found bad George at Mr Tait's hut, that wasn't a hut yet.

'Oh, good!' said Mrs Mags. 'When you've caught your breath you can go and tell his mum. She's frantic.' (So I was right.)

I didn't really want to. I wanted to be with my mum.

'You went to Mr Tait,' said my mum as if this was a simple statement of fact.

'Yes, sorry,' I said. I didn't really think I had to be sorry because going to Mr Tait had been an accident, but I was sorry I'd gone, sorry I'd seen his ... I took a deep breath.

'Mr Tait has a wooden leg,' I said. 'I saw it this morning by mistake.'

'Does he, now?' said my mum.

Mrs Mags said she knew that. She thought everyone knew that. Didn't I know that?

No, I hadn't known, obviously I hadn't known.

My mum said she'd heard about his leg but thought it was just a rumour.

'He lost it in the last war,' said Mrs Mags, 'or so he said. Blown up by a mine or something like that. What did you see?'

'Nothing,' I said, and I pulled my lips tight inside my mouth so that nothing would fall out.

But they weren't having it, especially Mrs Mags.

'You must have seen something,' she said. 'What was it like?'

'I don't know,' I said. 'Brown, I suppose. I don't know.'

'Brown,' she said. 'And which bit did you see?'

'Nothing,' I said, squirming now, because what I saw was an ankle without a foot, torn and ragged, blood drying on a dark pavement, a pavement covered with glass and glittering like rubies. 'Nothing.'

'Nothing indeed!' said Mrs Mags

'Nothing,' echoed my mum, not laughing now.

'I saw nothing,' I said.

'Well, nobody else has ever seen Mr Tait's leg so you're a very lucky girl,' said Mrs Mags, and she did her silent laugh. 'I only know because I asked him. It's nothing to be ashamed of after all. He's a hero, he is.'

I stood up. I needed to move so I hopped from foot to foot. My head felt hot and my throat was dry. I started to cough, just like when I was down at the bus the night before, and while I was coughing I was singing, inside my head of course. I sang my favourite skipping game: 'The wind, the wind, the wind blows high, Out pops Mavis from the sky, She is handsome, she is pretty … .'

I could hear Mrs Mags and my mum behind it all, somewhere far off. They were calling my name, and then Mrs Mags went back inside the hut and brought me some more water from the bucket and my mum was telling me to 'Come here!' and trying to get out of her chair to get to me.

'Lenny!' said Mrs Mags so loudly it made me jump. 'Stop that!' She took my hand and put a tin cup full of water into it and practically forced me to drink. I took a big gulp, which made me cough all over again.

'Lenny ... ,' said my mum half out of her chair, reaching for her crutches.

'Mrs Gillespie, sit back down! You're going to fall!' said Mrs Mags. She sounded just like Miss Weatherbeaten for a second.

We both lunged forward in time to steady my mum. She sat back on her chair and I rearranged her blanket, tucking it in around her waist, but once within her reach she wasn't letting me go. She kept a hand on my elbow in case I tried to run. When I'd finished tucking her in and wiping my eyes and nose, she slipped her arm around my middle and gave me a squeeze, and I leant in against her.

'You mustn't upset your mum like that,' said Mrs Mags, sounding more and more like Miss Weatherbeaten every minute, only she was breathing heavily as if she'd just climbed the hill too. 'I thought you had more sense than that, Lenny. Really, running off over the hill when you know your mum needs you.'

'She's alright,' broke in my mum, 'aren't you, Leonora? She's just a bit scared, like Mr Tait said. Isn't that right?'

I nodded, and felt those coughs coming on again.

Mrs Mags said she thought she'd take a little walk over to George's mum, and perhaps check up on the boys on the way. She meant Mr Mags and Mr Connor. They were working on someone else's hut a little further over the field. She told me to take good care of my mum, which I always do anyway.

I had a conversation then with my mum like nothing I'd ever had before. She told me what had happened the night of the bombing. She had met her friend down near the docks and no sooner had she met him but the sirens went off. They had laughed and shrugged it off as just another false alarm, which is what most people did to begin with. It was what I did, except I didn't laugh because I'd already lost Mavis by then. But suddenly he said he had to get back to his wife and family and he left my mum standing there in the middle of the main street all by herself and ran off down a side street, which made him a not very nice young man.

My mum ran through the tunnel under the canal and up over the railway bridge calling out for me and Mavis, but the bombers had arrived by then and no-one would have heard a thing, so she had to keep looking, looking, looking, peering through the smoke and the dust, but seeing nothing. And then she heard a bomb with her name on it and ran down a close to get away, but the bomb really did have her name on it and that's when she was buried for hours and hours and hours. She was only down our street on the other side of the road. We'd looked in the same places but missed each other.

'I lay there in the dark and listened,' she said. 'When the bombs stopped for a bit I tried to shout again but it hurt. I shouted your name, Lenny, but no-one heard for ages and then a man called in to me and said they were coming back; they were going to get me out. After that it got very cold, even though the fire would have been raging above me, and all I could hear was the bombers flying backwards and forwards and the bombs dropping.'

I was standing beside her with my fingers pressed into my eyes, little gulps coming up from my tummy as if I was going to be sick.

'Oh, I'm sorry, sweetie,' she said. 'I didn't mean to … I thought you'd better know.'

'I had better know,' I told her, although I wished I didn't have to. 'I do want to hear.'

'Sit down, Lenny,' she said, 'so I can see you. I've missed you so much! Here, sit beside me.'

I didn't want to do that either, but it was alright, I'd laid the blanket over her so that it went all the way to the ground. I pulled Mrs Mags's chair over a bit closer and sat down. I still had my hat on, my pretty hat with the yellow and pink ribbon and the purple cloth flowers. She took it off and sat it on her knee, fiddling with the pretend violets while she spoke.

'I don't actually know what happened next, just that I miraculously woke up in hospital with bandages all over me and no … .'

'I know!' I said, interrupting. 'I know what happened next. Mr Tait was there. He was there when they brought you out.'

'Was he?'

'He said you were speaking.'

'Was I?'

'He said you wouldn't go in the ambulance because you didn't know where me and Mavis were.'

'Wouldn't I?'

'He said your legs were in bad shape, but not, you know … .'

'Not that I'd lost a foot.'

'No, not that.'

'I see.'

We sat a minute in silence. I flicked my bottom lip with my finger so that it went pop, pop, pop against my teeth.

'They said it was gone,' she said, 'when I arrived, and that … .'

'No, no, no, no!' I shrieked.

'Oh, Lenny, I'm sorry.'

'It's just that I saw it,' I said.

'Saw it?' she said.

So I told her how I'd seen it further up the road when I'd been running through the bombing with Miss Weatherbeaten; I'd seen her foot and I'd seen some other stuff too that I shouldn't have seen, because Miss Weatherbeaten made me promise not to look but I'd broken my promise, like I knew I would when I made it.

'No, Lenny, no it can't have been. They said … they said it was there. Still attached but … no use. They had to … .'

This hung in the air between us, this unimaginable thing that I didn't want to think about but couldn't help trying. I put my hands over my ears and screwed my eyes tight shut and hummed, 'When Mavis comes marching home again, hurrah, hurrah!'

'Lenny! Lenny!'

I heard her through my palms.

'When Mavis comes marching home again, hurrah, hurrah!'

She held my elbow again and I could tell she wasn't going to let go. The tears were pouring down my cheeks, so that I couldn't see. Her hand squeezed on my arm, like the rhythm of a heartbeat, and she reached over as far as she could and wiped the tears from my cheeks with her thumbs, just like she always does, and I saw that big tears were pouring down her cheeks too.

'They said I'm lucky to be alive,' she said, when I took my hands off my ears.

'I know.'

And for the first time I considered the possibility of her not being alive, of my being like wee Rosie with no mum or dad, and that took the breath out of me all over again.

'Mr Tait said he had to tell them who you were,' I said, after a bit.

'He must be lying then because I had my bag,' she said. 'I still had my bag when I woke up in hospital. And guess what?' Her voice fell to a whisper. 'I still have all the papers, the birth certificates and the photo of your dad and me on our wedding day, and the America money! What a relief! Thank goodness I did what the government said and kept it with me all the time.' She sniffed loudly and laughed a loud 'hic'.

'Oh, good,' I said, not convinced. I didn't want to go to America to family and I didn't believe Mr Tait ever lied. He just sometimes forgot to tell me he only had one leg.

'Though God only knows if we'll ever get there now,' she went on.

'Mr Tait says you will,' I said. I was annoyed now. Mr Tait was my friend. 'He says you've got gumption, like me. He says I've got lots of grit, for a girl, and that people should listen to what happened to me and how I survived. He says I'm the bravest little girl he's ever come across. And he says you are too and all you need is your gumption to get you to America.'

'Leonora,' she said, a bit sharp now. 'When you're a big girl I'll tell you what Mr Tait did and why I don't like him. You're too young to understand, just now.'

I stood up and grabbed my hat from her lap and trembling, stuck it firmly back where it belonged, on my head.

'I'm not too young!' I said. 'I don't know what you did, but I know that Mr Tait didn't clype on you. It was somebody else. He said so and Mr Tait doesn't lie! He promised me he'd come to the hospital at two o'clock sharp and he did. He even brought me an orange, and … .'

'Alright, alright!' she said. 'Goodness! Alright, Mr Tait is not a liar. It was someone else. Alright!' She waved both hands in the air as if to shake off all the bad things she'd been thinking about him.

I didn't know whether to mention what George had said, about her being a tart and all that. Perhaps not. I sat back down on Mrs Mags's chair. We sat there so long in our silence that the rabbits came out and started nibbling the grass again. It was a beautiful clear sunny day at last, and I had my mum at last, and I didn't want either of us to be upset any more. We watched the rabbits until a gang of wee kids came rushing up the hill and chased them away with their noise.

'So tell me what happened to you and how you got through the bombing,' she said.

So I did, I told her all of it, all that I've told you,

about the bad boys and losing Mavis and the bombs and Mr Chippie, the fur coat lady, Annie and the dead baby and on and on and on. I told her about Miss Weatherbeaten and Mr Tait and walking over the hills, and Miss Weatherbeaten slapping me, and Mr Tait's sandwiches and his blood orange, and poor Rosie losing all her family and then going back to the town hall.

I told her about sneaking into the hospital, that I hadn't meant to sneak in, I just had to see her so that I knew she was still alive, and I had to tell her I was alive too.

'Of course you wouldn't be allowed in,' she said. 'What on earth was Mr Tait thinking of letting you go up there on your own?'

'That's what he said,' I said.

She looked at the treetops and shook her head.

'Poor little you!' she said, finally. 'You've been so brave! I hate to have to say it but Mr Tait is right! You are the bravest little girl in the whole world!'

Which wasn't quite what Mr Tait had said but I thought I'd let that pass. And I hadn't been brave. I'd been terrified. I'd survived but I'd lost Mavis.

'When you came into the hospital that day they were not nice to me, the nurses. I mean I do understand, they didn't want you bringing in mumps and measles and whatnot, but it wasn't my fault. It wasn't your fault either. If the trumped-up little tart on the reception desk had been kinder she would have taken a message for you.'

(It still didn't seem like the moment to ask. About tarts.)

'I'm only saying that because that's what everyone said about her, a nasty little busybody who thinks she's too good for the shoes that she's in,' she said. 'One of the nurses, a young one, said so. She was lovely.'

She said she hadn't actually seen me getting hauled out of the ward because the doctor was in the way. She'd given him and the grey-haired monster nurse a piece of her mind afterwards and very nearly got put out of the hospital for her trouble. Then Mr Tait had arrived with his daffodils and his basket, fumbling about and coming in when she'd expressly said she didn't want to speak to him, not without seeing me first. It was just like Mr Tait had said.

'I know,' I said.

'You do?'

'Yes, Mr … ,' I said. I paused a moment. 'Sorry. He told me. He said it was like a nest of she-cats in there and that you and I caused a stooshy.'

'Mr Tait said that?' she said. 'He's right.'

'Mmm … .'

'I should still be in hospital,' she said. 'How am I going to learn to use these crutches in the middle of a wet field? The bottom just cuts right through the grass and disappears. If we were even by the road I could practise on the road.'

I couldn't say 'Mr Tait's hut is by the road' so I couldn't say anything at all. I moved my chair a bit closer to her and leant my head on her shoulder.

'I'm trapped,' she said. 'Completely trapped and helpless. I can't do anything for myself. I can't even make tea or go for a wee!'

'I'm here, Mum,' I said. 'I can help you.' I put my arm around her shoulders.

'I know, love,' she said, patting the top of my head with her hand. 'I know.'

But I wasn't going to be enough.

We watched the wind stir the trees and some birds flitting in and out. A man walked by with a hammer in one hand and a toolbox under his arm. He waved to us and passed on up the hill.

'To have to depend on strangers … ,' she said.

'And me,' I said.

'And you,' she said.

'And if they needed help, wouldn't you help them, these strangers?' I said, stroking her arm.

'Of course I would, Leonora, it's just that I'm not sure how I would help anyone now. I can't pay anyone back for their trouble.'

'Not now,' I said. 'Maybe some other time.'

'I won't even be able to look after you or Mavis.'

So I told her I could look after Mavis, and I could look after her too until she was better, until she'd got used to the crutches. And while I was about it and feeling a tiny bit braver, I told her we could stay in Mr Tait's hut and she could practise walking on the road and he could make sure she still had her job when she was better. She didn't need two good legs, did she, to test sewing machines?

But apparently she did. What about lifting and carrying and working the foot pedals and so on? And no, she wasn't going to stay in a hut with Mr Tait, or grovel and ask him for her job. Sorry, but no.

Shame. It seemed like the perfect solution to most of our problems, but she didn't seem as angry with him as she had been, so I allowed myself a tiny smile, which she wouldn't have seen because I still had my head on her shoulder.

Three rabbits came out of their burrows again and

hoppity-skipped across the grass until they found a patch they liked and settled down for a good nibbling.

'Mum,' I said in a loud stage whisper. I didn't want to disturb them. 'Mum, what about Mavis? Mr Tait's the only person who can go to Clydebank and look for her.'

'Nonsense!' she whispered back. 'What about Mr Mags?'

'Mr Mags won't get the time away from his work. Mr Tait's a boss. He can leave whenever he wants, can't he?'

'Not really. He's not a very big boss,' she said, and I remembered the grown-ups' talk the night before. 'Big enough to get me into trouble but not big enough to save my job, I'm sure. Okay, okay!' She threw her arms up as if she was defending herself from an attacker. 'He didn't get me into trouble.'

I didn't disagree.

'Alright, I'll go,' I said. I forgot to whisper so the rabbits scurried off into the bushes.

'No, you can't. I've heard there's still terrible things to be seen there. They'll be clearing up for ages.'

'Are there?' I said.

She ran her hand down my hair and began to stroke it even though there wasn't much there, and no long bits to twiddle round her fingers.

'What are we going to do about Mavis?' I whispered, even though all the rabbits had gone.

Chapter 29

By the time Mrs Mags arrived back with Sandy and Dougie, my mum and I had fallen asleep where we sat. We were woken by the boys' laughter.

'You boys are in no position to laugh!' roared Mrs Mags. 'Sorry to waken you, Mrs Gillespie.'

They were as filthy as boys ever were, except after the bombing, and had clearly had an exciting morning. Sandy's jumper was thick with mud from cuff to shoulder as if he'd stuck his hand down a rabbit hole and their boots squelched.

'Off with the boots!' shouted Mrs Mags. And off the boots came, along with the trousers and the jumpers. I didn't know where to look and neither did my mum. The door slammed behind us but the row was probably heard at the other end of the field. After a while they reappeared, clean in old clothes they'd outgrown and were too big for, and Mrs Mags holding them both by the wrist. She tramped off up the hill with them towards Mrs Connor's hut. A heavy silence fell.

My mum needed a wee.

Such a small thing to need, and obviously I knew she did wee because I'd seen her at home with the pot under the bed when it was too dark and cold to go to the cludgie on the stairs, but this was different. I'd never had to help her do it before, and cludgies were built for one. I had to be her modesty screen, to prop her up and to undress her all at the same time so that by the time she finally landed on the seat she couldn't look at me. I closed the door for her and felt all the grit in me sink back down into my shoes. And she was right about the crutches: straight through the grass they went, sinking three inches down in some places and refusing to come out. By the time we were back at the front step we were both exhausted, and she was very quiet.

Then Mrs Wilson came. She looked harmless enough in her blue, white and grey Aran knit and her pale grey-blue coat, but looks can often deceive, as my gran often says, and although I hadn't been right when I thought she was a witch, I wasn't entirely wrong either. I know she came to help and she was just what my mum needed and I know it had to be done but I couldn't bear it, not for a second. After all, I'd spent so much time making sure the blanket was all the way down to the ground.

Anyway, she helped my mum indoors so she could 'tidy her up'. I brought Mrs Mags's chair in and Mum sat on it with the blanket over her knees by the window for light. Mrs Wilson closed the door. I stoked up the fire and boiled some water. I even helped undo the bandage round her head, holding the safety pin between my teeth while I did it, like Auntie May does with the baby's nappy pin.

'Off you go, Lenny,' my mum had said. 'You don't need to be here for this.'

'Nonsense,' said Mrs Wilson. 'She needs to learn how to do this so she can do it herself when I'm not here. It's not difficult.'

And when the bandage fell down around her neck I saw that on one side of her head the hair was greasy and flat like it hadn't been washed in weeks, and the other side had no hair at all. None whatsoever, only what looked like hair but was actually a line of black stitches with the ends of the thread sticking up. The skin beneath it was rose pink and the rest was white like window putty but with stubble like my dad's chin.

The safety pin fell on the floor. My head felt hot like it might burst and I swear I could hear my own pulse, even see it in the room which suddenly seemed very bright. I noticed a jam jar that had fallen behind the stove and the spider that was hanging from its lip, and the boys' muddy boots down there too, and when I looked back at my mum's head the wound was still there, bulging round the thread.

'That's a beezer of a cut,' said Mrs Wilson, 'but it looks quite clean. Lenny, pass me the first-aid tin will you please. Lenny?'

But I was backing away towards the door. The bench jabbed into my leg and I fumbled for the door handle until I had it and had turned it and opened the door and fled, flinging it shut behind me. And I ran round the back of the hut and hid behind a bush, but after a couple of minutes I couldn't keep still and I thought I ought to go back in. Then I heard them calling me so I changed my mind and ran through the trees and up behind all the other huts and the rope swing where there were loads of kids and through the pine trees into my clearing, and then I sicked up the tea and bread and honey that I'd had earlier on and I thought I'd never stop.

Because I knew what would be happening next in Mrs Mags's hut.

I knew they'd be pulling back the blanket and rolling up the dungarees and ... and I was sick all over again just at the thought of it, except there was nothing left in my tummy to be sick with. And having felt so very hot at first, I began to feel cold as if it wasn't a sunny day at all but a cold winter one with icicles.

I had one of Mr Tait's clean white handkerchiefs in my pocket so I took it out and wiped my mouth and bundled it up and stuffed it back in again, then went and sat down on the log of wood that I'd found when hiding there before and I rocked myself and cried and hummed and tried not to think about what was underneath the bandage beneath the dungarees.

I plucked at the shoe in my pocket, which for some reason I still hadn't shown to my mum, and I laid it on my lap and had a good look. I know this seems odd but I hadn't really looked before, hadn't followed the indentations and wrinkles, the crease around the toes, the shiny worn bit on the leather made by the buckle pin, or the stitching round the heel. I hadn't even undone the buckle except to tie it onto the belt at my waist. I untied it then, and put my hand in and tried hard to remember what Mavis's foot looked like, what her toes were like, what those nobbly bits at her ankle were like, but I couldn't. I couldn't even see Mavis's face, and it made me wonder whether Mavis had lost a foot too. And I felt ill again at the thought and shook the shoe off my hand so that it jumped across the clearing and fell into a patch of stingy nettles. Then I wrapped my arms around myself and cried like there was no tomorrow.

I didn't hear George shuffle into the clearing until it was too late.

'What are you doing here?' I snarled.

'What are you doing here?' he snarled back.

'This is my bit,' I said. 'Go away!'

'This is my bit,' he said. 'You go away! If you come back here I'll … I'll throw that shoe in the loch.'

I ran to grab it from the nettles but he got there first.

'Give it back!'

He whacked me about the shoulders with it so I kicked him hard in the shin and he laughed and said I wasn't a bad fighter for a girl. He grabbed my pretty hat with the ribbon and the flowers and flung it in the nettles where the shoe had been, so I tried to kick him again. He dangled the shoe over my head so I couldn't get it.

'You're mum's a tart!' he said. 'My mum said so and your sister is dead.'

'No, she's not!'

'Dead as a doorknob!'

'Stop it!'

'Dead!' He held it high so I jumped and caught the front.

'No!'

'Dead!' He swung me towards the pine.

'Give me it!'

'Dead!' The nettles brushed my leg.

'Bastard!' I screamed.

'Ha, ha! Yes, probably that too!'

Some bracken caught my ankle.

'She's dead!' he shouted, as I fell into the nettle patch.

'Dead!' he said leaning in at me.

So I grabbed some nettles and rubbed them in his face, just like Mavis had done with the gravel down by the canal, and while he was hopping from foot to foot I picked up Mavis's shoe where it had fallen and hit him hard across the back of his head then ran out of the trees as fast as I could.

My hands were red and white and sore. They were like the toads I'd seen one morning with Sandy and Dougie, all lumpy and mottled, just a different colour, and they were hot as if there was cheddar cheese baking inside them. By the time I arrived at Mrs Mags's they were throbbing, whoomf, whoomf, whoomf.

But the sight that took my breath away was Mr Tait, sitting on Mrs Mags's chair talking with my mum, who was listening to every word he was saying and nodding in agreement. She had the blanket over her legs, all the way down to the ground so I couldn't see if Mrs Wilson had 'tidied it up', and although my mum wasn't actually looking at Mr Tait, I knew she was listening because her eyebrows were very close together in the middle and because if she hadn't wanted to hear him she would have sent him away and thrown daffodils at him, if he'd brought her any. Above their heads a strip of bandage was strung like Christmas decorations across the front of the house, clean and dripping, to catch the breeze.

Which is what my hands were doing over my own head, trying to catch a breeze. Bits of nettle were dangling from my elbows too. And no hat, so my stumpy hair was there for everyone to see. I drew down my arms and showed them my palms.

'Lenny!' said Mr Tait. 'So George found you then?'

'Look at my hands!' I wailed and for a moment I wasn't sure who to go to.

I went to my mum and she went into a tailspin (Sandy told me that one – it was something to do with bombers) but she couldn't actually move, so the tailspin was more of an agitation, which was my gran's word. (She cured them with a nip of whisky.)

'Dock leaves!' she said. 'Get her some dock leaves!' Mr Tait was already on his feet, his real one and his wooden one, and pulling gigantic leaves out of the ground, two or three times the size of my hands.

'Let me see,' he said in his calm, quiet voice. 'Oh, dear, that looks very sore.'

Well, of course it was sore and now that the shock of seeing them together had worn off, the pain in my hands was worse.

But inside me my heart was singing with joy as if it was soaring in the sky like the rooks I had seen on the way to the school, and when my mum was fussing about trying to find her crutches a little later I gave Mr Tait a huge big smile.

They took a hand each and rubbed the leaves into my palms. I let my hands go limp and surrendered myself to them. There was nothing else I could do. I stood leaning against my mum's good leg, and every so often she turned her face up to mine and smiled quietly.

'Big George forgot a thing or two,' I told Mr Tait.

'Yes, I see that,' said Mr Tait. 'He did, didn't he?'

'He said Mavis is dead,' I said, 'and he said … .' But I didn't like to mention what he called my mum.

'Mavis is not dead,' said my mum. 'I'm her mum and I should know.'

Mr Tait nodded. 'I'm afraid George is not very well behaved at the moment, Mrs Gillespie, not at all. I will do my best to keep him out of your way. He seems to behave better over at the Cuilt Brae where my hut is.'

'Is it up yet?' I asked.

But Mr Tait just laughed, and suddenly I was angry with him again.

'Mr Tait,' I said. 'Do you have a wooden leg?'

'Lenny!' said my mum. 'Don't be cheeky!'

The smile fell from Mr Tait's face.

'You lied!' I said.

'Lenny!' said my mum. 'Stop it!'

'I didn't lie,' said Mr Tait, in his kind voice. 'I just didn't think you needed to know, at least not until you'd seen your mum.'

'Of course I needed to know,' I said. 'I thought you were my friend. Friends know everything about each other, don't they?'

'Do they?' he said. 'Would it have made a difference? Would you still have stayed with me? You were scared of me to begin with anyway. How could I have made friends with you if you'd known about my leg? Hmm … ?'

'It was a lie. A black lie.'

'Lenny!' said my mum. Her mouth was hidden behind her hand as if it was her saying all these terrible things.

'It wasn't a black lie,' he said. 'It was a white lie, so that I could be your friend. The rest of me's all flesh and blood. Pinch me and I squeal.' He pinched himself and squealed. 'Tap me and … .' He tapped his knee with his knuckle and there was a hollow 'toc, toc'.

'No!' I said, putting my hands over my ears.

Gently he took them and he bent down so that his face was close to mine.

'It goes all the way up to here,' he said indicating a point halfway up his thigh. 'If I'd shown you that you'd have run a mile. I had to find out how bad your mum's was,' he said with a nod in her direction. She was still hiding behind her hand. 'There was no point in frightening you with something worse or you'd have worried yourself sick. You probably did anyway, so perhaps I should have told you.'

'That's very kind,' said my mum, coming out from behind her hand. 'Thank you for being so kind. Lenny, apologise to Mr Tait for being rude.'

I looked from one to the other and wondered how the world came to be on its head. She should have been apologising to him, not me; well, perhaps me too.

'Sorry, Mr Tait,' I said.

'That's alright, Lenny,' he said.

My mum went back to rubbing the dock leaves into my hand. They were pulp now and my palms had turned green as well as white and red.

'Good girl,' said my mum, and when she looked up at me I glared at her. She stopped rubbing my hand for a second and looked away. I coughed. She let go of my hand.

'Mr Tait,' she said. 'Lenny thinks I should apologise to you for thinking you were to blame for the trouble at work.'

'What do you think?' he said, letting go of my other hand.

I held my breath. My mum rearranged her blankets.

'I think I may have misjudged you,' she said at last. 'I'm sorry.'

'You have no need to be sorry,' said Mr Tait. 'It was an entirely understandable mistake. I'm delighted you have seen the light! Let's say no more about it.'

'Oh, Mr Tait!' I jumped up and hugged him and then my mum, who mumbled something about there being no need for public displays of affection.

And then they got boring like grown-ups always do just when something exciting is happening and they talked about people from Singer's factory who I'd never heard of, and I wanted to ask Mr Tait if my mum was going to be able to test sewing machines any more or if there was another job he could give her. So I went off again, this time round the back of the hut where I heard Sandy and Dougie having a carry on.

They didn't see me at first, and they didn't see Mr Tait either when he sneaked up behind me. Dougie was sitting in a chair I hadn't seen before.

It was an old chair made of dark brown wood with a straight back and two curved arms, so it was like lots of other old chairs you might see anywhere, a bit bashed and dusty looking and not very comfortable. But this chair had wheels, two big ones at the back and two smaller ones at the front. All four were brown with rust, but as Sandy and Dougie were demonstrating, they all turned. It was a fully functioning wheelchair, of a sort.

'Oh, Lenny!' said Dougie, in a silly voice. He had one leg tucked up behind him. 'What am I to do? No-one will want me now I'm Peggy the peg leg!' He rolled in the seat and howled with laughter. Sandy, who had been pushing the chair, now pulled his leg up too.

'Hop, rabbit, hop, rabbit, hop, hop, hop!' sang Sandy, until he fell onto the grass, helpless with laughter. 'Don't let the farmer get you with his ... mop!'

'Boys!' shouted Mr Tait at the top of his voice, and I jumped and threw myself to the ground as if a bomb had gone off, then I scurried back to my mum before another word could be said. I didn't tell her what had happened, but vowed never to talk to boys again, ever.

Having sent the boys off somewhere, Mr Tait brought his creation round for my mum to see. She sat very upright where she was and stared at this odd chair.

'You didn't have to ... ,' she began. 'I can't ... I don't want ... .' She put both hands to her face. 'Thank you,' she said at last. 'Sorry, I'm so rude. Thank you so much. So many surprises! It's hard to know what to do!'

Mr Tait and I didn't say a word.

Chapter 30

After Mrs Mags came back with George, and after another terrible row, and after the boys apologised to everyone they had upset and bad George had been sent back up to the clearing in the pine trees to bring back my pretty hat; after Mr Tait and my mum rubbed dock leaves into George's hands and turned his face green too, and the other boys fetched water from the pump down the hill, and Mrs Mags had given us all a big bowl of soup with bread toasted at the fire and dumplings floating in the top; after Mr Mags, old Mr MacInnes and Izzie and George and Dougie's mum and dad had all come back from working on other people's huts, and everyone was friends again all squashed up in the tiny hut; after all of that, Mrs Mags started shimmying. She was standing in the only space available, in front of the stove, in her dungarees with her big tummy wobbling about and a red scarf wound about her head and tucked in at the top.

Old Mr MacInnes was tut-tutting on his chair behind the sofa until Mr Tait began an earnest conversation with him, probably about sketching. Bad George was applauding loudly but not meaning it, until his dad, Mr Connor, roared at him to stop. Sandy was trying to stomp a beat for his mum to dance to, and then Mr Connor reached into his pocket and brought out a mouth organ and played a jig I hadn't heard before and everyone clapped along.

'Come on, Mags!' said Mr Mags. 'We've got to get that baby going somehow!'

'Mr Mags!' was the shocked reply, but she was red and happy even though we could hardly see now that the light was going and no-one had lit a candle. 'What a thing to say in company!' she said.

My mum stopped clapping and looked at all the faces, then she laughed and carried on.

The girl in the drawing chattered away above the warm stove, just as her real self was doing in the room, when a noise arrived at the door. The clapping stopped, Mr Connor's moothie stopped, and in came Bella and the two little kids. She smiled at me so I smiled back, even though she'd thought I was a boy that first night.

Outside the door stood a woman I didn't recognise and behind her I could hear more people. They were on their way to a dance that was happening that night down in the hall and they wanted us to come too. Mr Mags went outside to talk to them and I heard them all laugh and then they all left, like the tide at the beach that I'd seen at Ayr.

So we were left with Mr and Mrs Mags, Mr and Mrs Connor, Mr MacInnes, Mr Tait, my mum and me, while the boys and Izzie ran down the hill to the dance at the hall behind Jimmy Robertson's bus.

'Mrs Gillespie,' said Mr Tait quietly. 'Would you like to try your chair?'

Mrs Mags had stopped shimmying and was in the other room taking off her red scarf.

'It's nearly dark, Mr Tait,' said my mum. 'I don't think it's such a good idea in the dark. Perhaps tomorrow.'

'It has been well tested by young George and some of the other lads over by my hut,' he said.

'I'd slide right out of it, the seat is so smooth,' she said.

'Perhaps we could tie you in somehow,' he said. 'I hadn't thought of that.'

His fingers drummed the top of his fancy bedpost stick.

My mum hung her head and looked miserable.

'There's enough of us here to carry her down,' said Mr Mags. 'Only kidding!' he added when he saw my mum's face.

'It's the getting back up that's going to be hard,' said Mr Connor.

'Yes,' said my mum. 'That's what I'm worried about too. I'll just stay here with Lenny.'

'But … ,' I said.

'What we need is a belt,' said Mr Tait, 'one that's big enough to go round Mrs Gillespie's waist, if you'll pardon me, and round the back of the chair.' He drummed his fingers on his lip.

'I've got one!' I said, delighted but also guilty to be so treacherous. 'I've got one!' The belt was under my dress so I flew into the other room to where Mrs Mags was. 'Sorry, Mrs Mags,' I said as I rummaged around under my dress for the belt which was so big it was wrapped around me twice. The shoe was still in my coat pocket.

'Here it is!' I handed it to Mr Tait.

'Thank you, Lenny,' said my mum, and I could see

she didn't really mean it. 'But it's dark. We'll end up in the bushes.'

'I'll be scout!' I said. There was no stopping me now.

We were all standing about in readiness, in almost pitch darkness, all but my mum who was still sitting at the far end of the bench. Someone lit the hurricane lamp which hung on a nail by the door.

'Just you go on,' she said.

'How sure are you of this contraption?' asked Mr Connor. 'The hill is a steep one.'

'But a short one,' said Mr Mags.

Which was quite patently not true. It was a very big hill.

'It's a lot of fuss,' said my mum.

'Are there handles on the back, Mr Tait?' said Mr Mags.

'I'll just stay,' said my mum.

'Of a sort,' said Mr Tait. 'I strengthened the back with a board; you could probably hang onto that, and there's a very rudimentary braking system, which runs against the wheel, very rudimentary and I'm not sure how effective, so be vigilant.'

'Lenny can stay with me,' she said. 'Lenny?'

Loyalty required me to sit down beside her on the bench, but I watched the men eagerly and wondered whether 'rudimentary' had anything to do with being rude, and I hoped that Mr Tait would somehow manage to make everything alright. My toes and fingers curled into little knots but, just in case, it seemed sensible to do a bit of extra wishing: 'Dear God, please make my mum go to the dance. And bring Mavis back to us. Love Lenny Gillespie.'

'Well, let's have a look at it,' said Mr Mags, lifting the hurricane lamp from its nail. Shadows lurched across the wall and all the drawings jumped and raced in the breeze from the open door.

'And a practice shot too, to be on the safe side,' said Mr Connor. Mrs Mags and her sister, Mrs Connor, and Mr Tait followed them out.

'He seems to know what he's doing,' said Old Mr MacInnes, from his chair in the corner. We couldn't actually see him because our eyes had become accustomed to the light of the hurricane.

'He's a sewing-machine-testing supervisor, not an engineer,' said my mum gruffly.

I watched them through the window. Mrs Connor was in the chair tying the belt around herself. Mr Mags and Mr Connor were behind it. It was Mrs Connor who had told George my mum was a tart. Maybe I should have asked her what she meant.

'We'll have to get you down there somehow,' said old Mr MacInnes from the shadows. 'It's that or the wheelbarrow.'

'And why?' said my mum.

I peered into the darkness to see the man who dared tell my mum what to do.

'Well, you can't stay here,' he said, as if this was obvious.

'Why not?' she said.

'Because you want to go to the dance,' he said.

'No, I don't,' she said.

'Yes, you do, and so does young Lenny here,' he said.

I couldn't deny it.

'You'll both be miserable if you don't and you'll

go on being miserable when we all come back with stories of what went on,' he said.

'They don't want to be bothered with me,' she said.

Then Mrs Connor in the wheelchair shrieked outside; it was a laugh like my mum's.

'Okay, let's try her up the hill now,' I heard Mr Tait say.

As they turned the chair round I saw the board he had put across the back of it to make it strong. It was a board from Singer's factory where he was my mum's boss and it said 'SINGER' in big bold letters right across the middle of it, and I thought 'That's my mum's chair,' because she so liked to sing. She sang when she was happy and sometimes she sang when she was sad so that she could be happy again. I knew that because it's what I do too and, as you know, I even sing inside my head sometimes when I'd be in trouble if I sang out loud. I wondered whether my mum did that too, so I pointed out the board to her but she couldn't turn far enough to see it.

'I think they do want to be bothered with you,' said Mr MacInnes. 'Maybe I'm wrong, maybe I'm wrong,' he said vaguely, and he waved his hand to indicate the conversation was over.

'I can't go,' she said, addressing me. 'Of course I can't go. This is silly.'

I didn't reply.

But finally she had no choice because Mrs Mags came in and declared it not exactly comfortable but safe as long as Mr Connor and Mr Mags paid attention to what they were doing and didn't get tempted into the kind of silliness their sons were prone to. Mrs Connor stayed outside.

She was scared, my mum, and embarrassed, and she tried to protest just one more time, but no-one was leaving without her, so in the end she wobbled to the door on her crutches and lowered herself into the chair with Mrs Mags's help. I tied the belt around her middle, even though she wouldn't look at me she was so scared, and she grabbed my elbow.

'Stay beside me,' she said.

'I'm right beside you, Mum,' I said. 'Not going anywhere.' I took her hand. 'It says Singer on the back, you know,' I told her again, 'so you'll have to sing.'

She didn't answer me.

I didn't press it.

Down across the wet grass we went, past some other huts and bushes of yellow broom like flames in the dark, with our hurricane lamp to light the way (which we shouldn't have had because of the blackout). She gripped my hand so tightly there was very little feeling in it by the time we arrived at the road, just like wee Rosie had done in Mrs Wilson's hut. I thought she might be pig-headed and want to walk the length of four buses to Jimmy Robertson's hall but she didn't. She sat in silence, as she had done the full journey down the hill.

The rain had started again, the kind that doesn't fall but seems to hang in the air and seep through your clothes. Some people were standing under the eaves of the pub waiting for the bus which was late and would be creeping along the narrow road with no lights to see by. They were a sober crowd, huddled and worrying in the dark mist, and by the time we reached them we were pretty sober and cold too.

'I can't,' said my mum. 'I'm sorry, but I really can't.'

I tried to take my hand back but she wouldn't let go.

'Mum!' I whispered loudly. 'You can't say you can't. They've brought you all the way down here.'

'I'm sorry but I can't. The chair is lovely. Thank you, Mr Tait,' (he was up ahead with Mrs Mags and her sister and didn't hear) 'but I ... .' Her voice cracked and I knew what she meant. She couldn't go socialising and celebrating and relaxing without knowing where Mavis was. I knew this to be true, and I knew this to be true for me too, but it didn't stop a flash of anger that Mavis was lost, that she'd run off, that she was four and didn't have any sense, that my mum's foot really was gone and that we weren't going to the dance.

Dougie and bad George were yodelling further down the road outside the hall, and I was furious with them too for being nasty by the canal. The sound of a squeezy box came and went with the opening of the hall door. Mr Tait, Mrs Connor and Mrs Mags slipped inside.

'Come on, Mrs Gillespie!' said Mr Mags. 'It'll do you good. Off we go then!'

'No!' she said, rather loudly. 'Sorry,' she said. 'I really can't. Take me up now and you won't need to worry about me later. Please.'

As some people were going in, Sandy stuck his head out and gave me a cheerful wave. The door banged shut behind him. I could feel my ears burning and was glad of the dark. How could she? How could she? But of course she could, and of course she wouldn't want to go. She'd already said that many times in the hut. I just didn't want to face the truth, same as I didn't want to see her leg that I knew, really, some day I'd have to see.

'Well … well … ,' said old Mr MacInnes as he passed us, as if he had something to say, but instead his words hung in the air unspoken, unformed like the mist that was clinging to us.

So they pushed her back up the hill.

Nobody spoke, not a word. They left us. I lit the candle, fed the fire, made tea, helped her to the cludgie, made a bed on the floor for us, tucked us in, blew out the candle and waited in the silent darkness for the chattering in my head to stop, waited for the explosions to die down.

By the time I heard happy voices growing louder as revellers flocked back up the hill, I had a plan.

Chapter 31

In the pocket of my coat, along with Mavis's shoe, there was a silver half-crown, the one Mr Tait had given me when I went to find my mum at the hospital. In the other pocket I stuffed the 'piece' Mrs Mags had given me for my lunch – two chunks of bread and dripping. Along with the silver half-crown and Mavis's shoe I had the picture of Mr MacInnes's gums, on the back of which were the plans Mr Tait and I had drawn up for the new hut. I tore off a piece and scrawled a message. I still had a pencil, the same soft one I had used for drawing, which I had sneaked from Mr MacInnes's bag the night before and hadn't had a chance to return. The message read:

'Please tell. Gone for Mavis. Back soon. Sorry. Len … .'

The lead ran out before I could finish my name.

It was Monday morning. Mr Mags, Mr Connor and Izzie had left on the early bus to go back to work for the week. Along with all the other kids, I was in line at the school door. Miss Read was beaming happiness and order from the front step. I slipped the message into Sandy's pocket and said I needed to go, you know, to the cludgie. But really I just needed to go. I didn't want to go; I'd much rather have stayed and recited my nine times-table, but I knew there was no alternative. No-one else could do what needed to be done, that was clear. It was down to me.

So while they were all saying prayers in the hallway, as we did every morning, I sneaked up the burn beside the school as fast as I could scamper, which wasn't very fast at all because this hill was even bigger than the hill at Carbeth. They were singing 'There is a green hill far away' practising for Easter, and I sang 'The wind, the wind, the wind blows high … .'

When I got to the top of the hill I saw the big beech tree that we had sat under when a big bomber killer bee flew over us a week-and-a-half earlier. Carbeth was hidden in the valleys now, tucked up safely amongst the trees.

I was sorry to upset everyone, especially Mr Tait, but I really needed to find Mavis. The day before and the night before that, when everyone had gone to the dance except us, had been unbearable, intolerable, suffocating. My mum had cried all night and we hardly slept a wink and I knew I had to find Mavis for her. The next day I had been unable to speak to anyone, not even Mr Tait. It all had to stop. I had to do something. Even the simple act of walking over the hill made me feel better. Mr Tait would be busy with his hut. Mrs Mags would look after my mum. No-one would miss me until school was over.

I thought about how worried my mum would be with me gone but how pleased she'd be when I brought Mavis back. I wanted to bring Rosie too, but that might have to wait.

Ten days had passed and there was still smoke over Clydebank. It was drifting in from the west (from the same oil tanks, as it turned out, that had been hit at the beginning of the bombing, guiding the killer bees to us.) I walked towards the town, getting hotter with every step, although the big sun that was rising above me was no more use than a light bulb. If there was still smoke, there must still be fire. What on earth would I find? My mum had said there were still terrible things to be seen in Clydebank and I started to worry about the things I'd already seen that I shouldn't have seen.

A man passed me, hurrying to work. I told him where I was going and he wished me luck and sped off down the hill in great lollops. There was something that looked like tents over by a farm – bedraggled looking things hanging all loose and any old how with some kids playing out in front of them. Cows wandered across the path, eyeing me and eyeing the tents, interesting new inhabitants of their field. I eyed the tents too and wondered. At the big flat rock, the one we'd sat on before, I washed my hands in the burn, not because they needed it (my mum made me wash them the night before) but more for luck, which seemed in short supply. I sat on the wide flat rock and looked out over Clydebank. I couldn't see much from that distance except something white and square which might have been the La Scala picture house where I had spent most of a night.

Perhaps my planning had not been complete. Perhaps I needed a plan for what I could do if I saw things I didn't want to see, which it seemed likely that I would. What had Mr Tait said I should do when I got a fright, because it would be a sort of fright, wouldn't it, to see things I didn't want to see? He said … I tried to hard to remember, squinting into the morning sun, ignoring the cows on the other side of a stone wall, munching, nodding their heads. He said … don't be scared, we're safe in Carbeth. Well, that was no use; I wasn't in Carbeth any more, was I? And he said … this jumpiness will pass, being scared will pass, even though I hadn't told him I was scared. It would pass.

'Excuse me!' said a voice.

I threw my arms about my head and rolled onto my side.

'Sorry, love,' said the voice. 'You alright? I didn't mean to give you a fright.'

It was a man in a dark-red knitted hat with a ripple of bright orange hair around the sides. He was wearing a jacket that stretched over his tummy so that the last button looked like it might ping off at any minute.

'Mr Tulloch?' I said breathlessly, rubbing my shoulder. I'd only seen Mr Tulloch in the dark. Perhaps he had orange hair and was tubbier than I remembered him.

'Do I know you?'

'Oh! No,' I said, peering at him, 'but you look like Mr Tulloch. He gave me a lift on his cart.'

'That would be my brother. We sound the same, don't we? He's got a farm over Carbeth way. I'm the brainy one.' He smiled.

'That's him. Yes, you do sound the same.'

'Well, I'm sorry to bother you; sorry to give you a fright, but I wondered if you could fill this bottle for me, from the burn, save me climbing over the wall? Phew! You've been roughed up a bit. What happened?'

I nodded towards the town.

'Oh, yes, of course,' he said. 'Are you coming or going? To the town?'

I nodded at Clydebank again. 'I've got to find my sister. She's four. I lost her.'

Mr Tulloch, this new Mr Tulloch, asked if there wasn't a grown-up that could look for me, to save me going, and I told him there wasn't. I filled his bottle for him and handed it back. He had a tin cup in his hand.

'Fancy some milk?' he said.

I nodded. And then to my surprise he slapped the nearest cow on the behind and he bent down behind the wall for a few seconds where he and his cows were and came back up with a cup full of frothy milk.

'Straight from the cow,' he smiled. 'It doesn't come any fresher than that.'

'Thank you,' I said, taking the cup, but it was warm from the cow's body and I couldn't drink that!

'Go on, then,' he said. 'It won't do you any harm. Goan.'

I didn't really want to drink it, not really at all, but I knew it was a very special present, this foaming cup of warm milk, even though the very thought of it made me feel sick.

'Goan,' he said, just like his brother had said to the horse.

And this will pass too, I thought. This will be over soon too. So I flung the milk down my throat with a gulp, gulp, gulp and smiled a big thank you to him.

'There now, that'll set you up for the day,' he said. 'Better um … ,' and he pointed at his top lip and peered at mine so I wiped the milk moustache off it with the back of my hand.

I thanked him and hurried on my way down the path.

'Good luck!' he called after me. 'I hope you find her.'

'Thank you!'

'What's her name?'

'Mavis,' I said. 'And Rosie. Rosie's my friend, same age as Mavis.'

'I'll look out for them.'

'Thank you!'

'I'll ask at the tents!'

I stopped and went back. 'Tents?' I said.

'Tents isn't exactly what they are. More like make-shift bivouacs.'

'Bivouacs?'

'Made of sheets and sticks and bits and pieces. Next to my barn in the calfing pen.'

'Who's in them?'

'Oh, now, there's a load of people all ages. Yes, there's a few kids with them. Maybe even your Mavis and Rosie.'

What was I to do? I thought about it for a minute, my hand on the shoe in my pocket, and then red-haired Mr Tulloch scratched his chin and shook his head making his red hair wobble. Then, like his dark-haired brother, he told me what to do.

'I think you should keep going where you were going, the town hall I'm guessing, and I'll ask my wife for you. She's the one who knows about the tents. I can see there's no time to be wasted.'

'Will you? Thank you!'

'What's your … ?'

'Lenny,' I said as I started down the hill. 'Lenny

Gilliespie.' And I hurried away from him as quickly as I could mainly because I needed to go into a bush and go 'Yuck, yuck, yuck!' about the milk.

I stole in behind some yellow broom, in amongst the spiders and the beasties and I rubbed my tummy, imagining that I felt sick. And actually I did feel sick but it was nothing to do with the milk. It was the thought of going back to Clydebank and what I might find. I thought about going over to the bivouacs instead, with red-haired Mr Tulloch, but he was a stranger so I couldn't do that, or back over the hill to wait again for grown-ups to find Mavis, but so far that hadn't worked. So I thought about grit and being brave, which wasn't how I felt, not at all. I felt more like that jelly I didn't want to be, with no grit at all. I took Mavis's shoe out of my pocket and rubbed its leather, hoping for the genie of bravery and grit to put in an appearance, or just an ordinary genie to grant me three wishes: Mavis is alive, Mavis is with me, Mavis and I get home safely. But after all that wishing I still felt sick.

Another man came over the hill so I waited until he'd passed and then crawled out and followed him down across the fields, until at last we came to a road. The man was far ahead of me now where the road turned down towards Clydebank. There it became Kilbowie Road, the main road that ran near my house, so I followed on down, Mavis's shoe still in my hand.

At the junction of Kilbowie Road and Great Western Road, which is the big road that runs all the way into Glasgow and marks the very edge of Clydebank, a huge crater had opened up, a big deep hole. It was deep enough for four of me all standing on top of myself and as wide as the baths at Hall Street. It was full of pipes and mud and rocks and water. I peered in half-expecting a giant beetle to wave its snappy claws at me. There was another hole a little further down Kilbowie Road, just as deep and just as wide. It too was full of rocks and mud and pipes, and over in the field to my left there was another one and mounds of grassy earth were scattered everywhere, even onto the road where I was standing. The houses on the right of the road had holes in them too, and great mounds of rubble were spread up the streets with broken furniture and glass everywhere. It was just like before, just like our street, just like all the other streets I'd run through on those two terrible nights, only with the cool daylight from the big shimmery sun spread all over it, so you could see everything.

There were socks and little girls' dresses, forks and teapots, tablecloths and bedpans, potted plants and bent budgie cages, all sprinkled with the glitter of broken glass. Most of the houses had no glass in their windows or only fragments that were jagged and treacherous. Some were roughly boarded up with bits of table or loosely covered over with old curtains. There was an odd quietness, few chimneys with smoke and hardly any people in the street, and those I passed were silent, or whispering closely to each other, as if afraid to disturb the peace.

'Mavis,' I whispered. 'Mavis, Mavis, Mavis.' And then, 'The wind blows low, the wind blows high, Out pops Mavis from the sky.' And then I had to hold my nose and sing inside my head because there was a smell. It was different from the night of the bombing because the houses weren't burning any more, only the oil tanks. It smelled of burnt oil, like cars, but it smelled of other things too, rotten things and toilets, old meat and churches, and cold, dark places where you don't want to be.

It's a difficult thing trying to look all about you and not look at the same time, especially when the world has been turned upside down and everything is in the wrong place. It was like someone had lifted up each house and turned it over so that all the contents had fallen out, including all the roofs and floors, then set them back down again exactly where they'd been. How else could these things get so mixed up?

I tiptoed past the first big hole and then the second one and the holes in the fields and the broken houses with roofs missing, and then I tiptoed past a whole lot more broken houses, and then some more, until I wasn't sure where I was because nothing looked familiar any more, except that I could see the La Scala, big and white up ahead. Before the La Scala, where the high tenements should have been, there was a long pile of rubble with metal girders sticking up at one part like the outline of rooms. At another there were girders like doorways from one pile of muck to another, but they weren't doorways because doorways are made of wood, everyone knows that. I don't know what they were. Behind the pile of rubble was the back wall of the buildings that should have been there. You could see the sky through the windows, and the haze drifting in from the oil fires. The shops from our window-shopping day out were all gone and so were their fancy goodies that no-one was going to buy now, and above me some tram-wires still ran from their posts, spindly across the street.

There was another big hole in the road. My school was beside it, but a lot of it was missing. A row of sinks was on the outside and the playground was full of sandstone. My heart beat fast. Beyond the big hole in the road I could see the church. There were people at the entrance, going in and out, and I thought I might know them, so I skirted the hole, shaking, careful not to fall in, and asked.

Some of them knew my mum, and some of them even knew that she'd gone to the hospital, and one even knew she'd lost her foot; but no-one knew where Mavis might be except that she might have been in a shelter at number thirty-two, down our street. So after I'd asked everybody in the crypt (they were having sardine sandwiches and tea) and I'd told them we were in Carbeth with Mr Tait from Singer's factory, I crossed the road beneath the great gaping hole that was there and stood at the beginning of the side street that went towards our house.

I tugged my coat tight about me. I held my nose with one hand and Mavis's shoe in the other. I closed my eyes and waited for my heart to stop thumping but when I realised that it wouldn't I opened them again and stared. If Mavis was up there, I thought, I'd never find her. It was a mountain of rubble as far as I could see and dogs were sniffing about it, skinny dogs with scabby legs and hungry looks who turned their big eyes on me when I took my first step.

Perhaps it was the dry spring air, or the dust or the smoke that made my throat so rough but I felt those coughs coming up, like gulps and barks at the same time, so I swallowed hard until I couldn't swallow any more and coughs came bursting out of me. Some dogs came tripping over, I don't know how many, five or six, all sizes.

'Leave me alone!' I said, and I pulled myself all tight while they sniffed at my knees and my pocket and at Mavis's shoe. I was shaking, crying, wishing someone was there, like my dad for instance, or a passer-by, and then suddenly they all went away and left me standing there on top of a pile of bricks.

'Mavis,' I whispered, trembling with cold. 'Mavis. I've got to find Mavis.' I tried to breathe properly but I was all shuddery and sore. 'Mavis,' I said louder. And louder again, 'Mavis!' Her name echoed off the buildings. The dogs stopped and gazed back at me. 'Mavis!' I shouted, and one of them barked.

Some of the buildings were full height but empty inside and some were hardly there at all. 'The wind, the wind, the wind blows high … ,' I sang under my breath.

'Mavis!' I called her name into doorways and up to the rooftops. 'Mavis!' I said.

I tripped over the foot of a table, trying not to see its brown curves and caught my fall with my hands. 'I like bananas because they have no bones, ow-ow-ow. Don't give me your peaches, don't like ice cream cones … Mavis!'

My palms were bleeding now, new cuts by the old, and they were black like when the bombs fell, like the day after, and the day after that.

'Mavis!'

There was nobody to be seen down that street and

all the buildings were black. Tenements lined the road, high ones of four or five floors a least with holes for windows and nothing inside. The road had been partly cleared so that for some of the way I could walk up the middle and it wasn't difficult, but for the most part I had to clamber over things I didn't want to see. There was an odd rotting smell like the damp moss that I'd smelled in our first hut at Carbeth, only it was different, sharper and foosty, sweet and clammy, a smell I didn't like. I wanted to hold my nose again but I needed both hands, one in case I took another fall and the other to hold Mavis's shoe.

'Mavis!' I shouted at the top of my voice, and it echoed back to me this time as if lots of little Mavises were hiding out there and I had to stop and cough and got scared that the buildings might fall down. Maybe there were unexploded bombs in them, like the ones inside me, and that was why all the other people I'd seen were being so quiet, so as not to explode the bombs. But nothing moved except the dogs so I stayed there for a moment and looked all about to make sure the buildings weren't going to fall on me.

But in amongst the writhing debris there were things I couldn't help seeing, things no-one should see, things that shouldn't have been there, a teapot for a head, a drainpipe for a leg, a shoulder of rubble, eyes of glass winking. The wind suddenly rushed through me, funnelled by the tenements. It lifted the sleeve of a jacket caught in a window and threw my straw hat over my shoulder.

A rat shot out in front of me, and another and another, hundreds of them, whistling and screaming across my path.

'Go away!' I shouted. 'Go away!' And I heard my own breath pumping through my mouth, pumping in my chest, pump, pump, pump and I thought I was going to run out of air and the rats were going to run up my legs under my dress, under my arms, onto my head, and I nearly dropped Mavis's shoe. But instead I wrapped the shoe and my jittery hands around my head and pulled all my bravery up from my t-bar shoes and I jumped as far as I could right over the stream of rats and didn't look at any of the houses or the mess in the rubble, even though I could see things moving in there. I ran on and on down the street and round the corner, with the sudden sound of all the dogs barking behind me in excitement over what they had found.

But my street was even worse and I couldn't find number thirty-two where Mavis might have been because there were no numbers, and I didn't want to go round the back of the tenements because I might find a lady in a sea of bricks and I knew exactly where one of those was and I didn't want to see her again or anyone else dead for that matter.

I began to tap out a rhythm on my side: dah-dah-di, dah-dah-di, dah-dah-dah-dah-dah, and then I hummed a tune to it. I hummed my way over the mess until I came to our house.

Our house was exactly like all the other houses, black and windowless and cold, but I knew it was ours because the house over the road was gone.

And there I cried so hard I thought my body would just break into pieces, and I crumpled down onto a piece of the baffle wall and wished it all not to be true.

But it was. It was all true. I knew it was because

the stone I was sitting on was the same one Mr Chippie had put me down on before the second night of the bombing. Dah-dah-di, dah-dah. And I knew I couldn't leave there until I had checked for Mavis. And lots of horrible things passed through my head clear as daylight as if it was all happening again, and all the bombs were raining down and the people were running and screaming and lying down dead, and one of them might be Mavis. 'The wind, the wind, the wind blows high … .'

So like a ghost I stood up and started looking for bits of our life, things from before, the teapot, the clock, the bed, my dad's chair perhaps, checking for things that might be useful, things that were ours. We didn't have much that was ours. We hadn't had much even then, but every little counts. All we need is Mavis. Out popped Mavis from the sky, She is handsome, she is …, I thought. I clutched my hat on my head, squeezed Mavis's shoe back into the pocket of my coat, and took a step towards our close. Glass crunched beneath my feet and a mouse ran under the stone. A couple more steps and I was in.

It was oddly dark and light. Anything that could have been burnt, had been, everything that fire could gobble up. Even the white walls of the close were black and through the jambless door of the downstairs flat where all my neighbours had been sheltering there was a black hole that stank, no tables or chairs or beds, just stone and bedsprings, twisted and jumbled under a blanket of dirt. There were no neighbours and no bits of neighbours but there was a stove like our stove with a big iron kettle on it, set back into the stone wall underneath the chimney.

There were no floors in that house or any of the others, but up above in the stone wall was another stove with the curve of a kettle, like our kettle, just visible over its edge, and another up above that. And above that only sky and some birds fighting over the top spot on the gable, flapping across the space where the roof should have been.

'Mavis,' I whispered. 'Please don't be here.'

Something moved behind me, glass falling through the debris. I wanted to run but I had to stay.

'Mum,' I whispered, and I wished she was there, and the birds flapped at the sky and I wished I was in Carbeth with the wood pigeons and not in this dark, scary place with my blood pumping in my ears and every foothold so shoogly. I started up the stone stairs, sliding on the mess, but needing to go up and fast.

The door to our house was gone and there was no floor, only a drop all the way down to the bottom that reminded me how sick I felt. Our stove was there too, crouched in the wall beneath the chimney, with my mum's cup sitting by the chimney pipe and the kettle next to it. The iron poker lay along the foot shelf at the front waiting for my mum to lift it.

Our window was gone and through the gap I saw a billow of black cloud from the oil tanks and beyond it a deep blue sky. There was nothing else left in our single end flat: no sink, no draining board, no cupboard underneath. The silence boomed in my ears. I looked and looked, trying to put the bed back, the floor, my dad's chair, the patchwork bedcover, the rag rug, the sink, the space under the bed. Where we'd have died if we'd been there.

A little brown bird suddenly landed in the window,

clutching the blackened stone with its little claws. It fluttered silently to the stove and sat on the edge of my mum's cup. Two more came in after it and together they swooped around the space where our room should have been, chattering to each other, then rushed out the window again. I heard them over my head but couldn't look up because my legs were shaking and I might get dizzy and fall into the big hole that went all the way down, down, down into the basement below the bottom flat.

Something moved behind me up the stairs and I got such a fright I nearly did fall down that big hole, but instead I ran and fell and slid down the stairs, just like I had done when the bombs were coming down and it was killer bees and not little brown birds up there, and I arrived panting at the bottom. But instead of going back over the rubble to the street, I went through the close, like the wind did, so that I could look in the back court in case Mavis was there, but sure, somehow, that she had not died there.

The ground was full of holes and bricks, and further down the street there were buildings missing. There was nothing of our life in the back court, no bits and pieces that had been flung through the window, no pegs on the drying line and no line. Nothing – nothing at all but rats and little brown birds and big black crows up in the sky, and a dog howling, like I wanted to howl out over the rest of the town.

Back out the front, I ran down the road telling myself it was a good thing Mavis wasn't there, and not wanting to look anywhere else in case she was somewhere nearby. I couldn't find number thirty two and anyway time was running out and I had to get to the town hall. A little further on, I passed the building my mum had been buried under and the place where the nasty old lady with the bundle had told me she had seen Mavis, but I carried on over the railway bridges which had more gaping holes on either side of them, and under the canal. It was the same way I had walked after the first night of the bombs only in the other direction. I wished Mr Tait would suddenly appear, just like he had then, and I wished I'd let him in on my plan so that he could have come with me.

Chapter 32

The road outside the town hall was heaving with people. There were vans serving food and crowds of people milling about, waiting for their turn. Inside the town hall their voices echoed off the stone floors and the high ceilings as if they were all in there and shouting, so I hid behind a pot plant in the hallway and watched them through the door. I didn't know what to do and the noise frightened me after the strange silence of our street.

Then a big man in a suit came over and asked me why I was there.

'I'm looking for my sister, Mavis,' I said. 'She looks like me only she's four.'

He pointed to a counter in the corner and told me to ask there.

'I'm looking for my sister,' I said. I was suddenly tired of this.

'Your sister?' said the lady there. She had bright blond hair in a tight little curl which hung over her forehead, pink rouged cheeks, and a purple jumper with blue diamonds on it. She looked at me over the counter.

'Yes, my sister,' I said. 'Mavis Gillespie.'

'If you go and wash, I'll tell you where to go,' she said, and she wrinkled up her nose, which was very small. 'Yes, wash,' she said, when I stayed where I was. 'Have you been playing in the bombsites?'

'No,' I said, which was true. I hadn't been playing.

'Hmm,' she said, and her mouth squashed up sideways.

So I went anyway, down a corridor, and washed my hands and came back again. It was a very clean town hall and I hadn't realised how filthy I was or how badly my hands were cut, again.

'Hello again, Miss Gillespie,' she said. 'It's through that door there.'

I went through a huge dark door, about twice as high as Mr Tait. There were two ladies at desks with telephones and papers and ledgers (like the one at school for roll call). Pots of ink and jars of pencils sat at the front of each desk along with a gas mask. There was another desk beside them across the corner opposite the door. A large dark-green ledger was on top of it. 'DECEASED' was written in heavy black letters that were barely visible across the front of this ledger. Deceased. I knew what that meant. It meant dead. It seemed like a book I might want to have a look at.

I glanced at the two ladies. One was licking her pencil. Her brow was knotted with concentration. I don't think she knew I was there. The other sat back in her chair and stretched her arms behind her head and stared at something on the ceiling that I couldn't see. I didn't think she knew I was there either until suddenly she spoke.

'You're Peggy Gillespie's girl, aren't you?'

'Yes,' I said. 'Yes, I am.'

'She's not missing is she?' she said, flinging her arms down into her lap and leaning across her desk at me. Her face was almost the same pasty colour as her fawn-coloured jumper, like old potatoes.

'No, she's not,' I said.

'Thank goodness for that!' she said. 'She's always good for a laugh, your mum. Always ready with a shoulder if you need one.'

I wasn't sure what she meant but she seemed to like my mum so I smiled.

'Why are you here?' she said.

'I'll deal with this,' said a voice I'd heard already. The lady in the hall with the curl on her forehead and the pink cheeks was looming large behind me. 'Sit down, Miss Gillespie.'

The other lady was suddenly hard at work just like her workmate with a pencil in her mouth.

I sat on a chair next to the desk and she sat on another one at the other side, leaving the door behind me open to the hall. The seat was hard but when I sat in it I thought I might fall asleep I was so tired, but all of me ached with worry and fear for what I might be told. I looked at the Deceased book, and wondered whether it didn't mean diseased instead. I wasn't very good at spelling.

'Do you think she might be dead?' asked the lady with the curl, seeing me look.

I gulped. 'Yes.'

'What's her first name?'

'Mavis. Mavis Gillespie.'

'Age? Date of birth?'

'Four. Um … .'

'Four?'

'Yes, four. And a bit.' I didn't think she liked Mavis being four. 'Twenty-third of December.'

'Nineteen thirty-six.' She was a very fast counter.

I nodded though I'd no idea.

She picked up the deceased book and balanced an odd pair of glasses on her tiny little nose. They didn't have anything to go over her ears, no arms so I wondered why they didn't fall off.

'When did you last see her?' she said over the top of these glasses.

'Just before the bombing, by the canal. We were ... .'

'Who was she with?'

'Me, but ... .'

'You, but ... .'

'I lost her.'

'I know that.'

I gulped.

'What were you doing?'

'Um ... .'

'Never mind. Doesn't matter. Why do you think she might be dead?'

'Because nobody knows where she is.'

'Where are your parents? And your family?'

So I told her the whole story that I've told you, only not quite so much of it because she kept interrupting with questions. She seemed very busy. Then she looked through her Deceased book and the only thing I could hear was the tick of a clock which sat on a mantelpiece beside a sign that read 'Dig for Victory!' I'd seen that sign before. Digging for victory seemed different now, not about carrots and onions any more. It meant digging down into the rubble and finding my mum not so very long ago, and I hoped it wouldn't mean the same for Mavis.

Suddenly the pink-cheeked lady with the curl who didn't tell me her name shot out of her seat.

'Excuse me, Miss Gillespie,' she said, and she left the room without further explanation.

Her shoes went clackety-clack across the marble floor and mingled with the voices of the crowd.

I did wait for a while, for her return; I didn't do it immediately, but the deceased book was lying open where she'd left it, so I tried to read the names upside down. The names were just squiggles of grown-up handwriting in pencil and ink but next to it was a column with numbers which seemed to be ages and dates of birth. I had to twist my head to see. Mavis's shoe bulged in my pocket. The two ladies at their desks were still concentrating, one on another similar ledger, the other on the ceiling. I stood up very slowly, checking them, checking the book.

And then I saw a big four, bigger than all the other fours and I was sure as sure it was her, and my heart was beating in my mouth again, but I had to be really sure and I couldn't read the name. So I grabbed the book with both hands and in one fell swoop I was under the desk that the lady with the curl had sat at.

It was one of those huge heavy desks with drawers on either side and a tunnel in between for legs. I squashed myself in there and held my breath and waited for the two desk ladies to call me back out again, but they didn't.

Quickly, quickly now, I told myself. The name next to the big four was not the name I was looking for. I gave myself a two-second break then carried on down the number column. I was nearly at the end when the lady with the curl came back in. She had someone with her.

'I'm sorry,' said the voice. 'I didn't mean to come in snivelling. How stupid of me! I just wanted to report in, from the rest centre.'

'Sit down, Debbie, it's alright,' said the lady with the curl. 'Where did the girl go?' she said in surprise.

'The girl?' said the woman with the fawn face.

'The girl, where did she go?'

'I'm afraid I didn't notice.'

'Didn't notice?' She made a sound a bit like Mrs Wilson, who wasn't a witch. 'Tsk, tsk.' Then she told the two ladies at the other desks to go and check whether the afternoon post had arrived, yes, both of them, and leave them in peace for a minute. And while they were at it to look for that daft wee girl (me).

Underneath the desk I was quaking. I knew that voice, the voice of Debbie, and I knew those shoes that nearly tapped me with their toes, and the ankles, and the bottom of the not-very-clean coat that dangled over them; I knew that coat had fur round the collar and Miss Weatherbeaten's face would be sticking out above it.

'Go on then,' said the Curl. 'Tell me.'

'It was awful (sniff, sniff),' said Miss Weatherbeaten. 'Just awful! I don't think I've slept for five days, not in a bed, not even properly lying down, only in a chair in the corner of the kitchen, and once on the you-know-what.'

I couldn't help feeling it served her right for leaving us and for taking Rosie, but she went on.

'There was a woman who gave birth in the headmaster's room in one of the other centres and I kept thinking it was going to happen to one of our pregnant ladies. We had quite a few. I mean I didn't see the worst of it. They had gas rings to cook on by the time I got there. They'd had nothing for three days – just a few sandwiches and a huge pile of carrots and turnips. And the WCs. Ugh, you wouldn't believe them! Sorry, it's so selfish of me to complain. At least I'm not there any more. I'm not anywhere!' There was a loud honk as she blew her nose, and the foot which had been crossed (and nearly tapped me) slid down onto the floor. Her elbows thumped onto the desk over my head.

'It all sounds horribly inefficient to me,' said Miss Curl.

'Oh, it's not, Jinty, really it's not. Everyone's trying so hard but there's hardly any billets to give them and there was no food for ages, or not much, and no blankets or mattresses and all the workers are run ragged. I feel so guilty for leaving but I just couldn't do it any more.'

'Are you going back?'

'Well, no. Of course I'm not going back.'

'I see.'

'And people keep losing each other. They keep sending buses to take people away but some of the men have gone back to work and the women won't get onto the buses for fear of losing their men. There's been some terrible scenes. I just can't describe it!'

'If you went back you'd have somewhere to go. You're in the same boat as them, I suppose.'

'How extraordinarily unfeeling you are!' said Miss Weatherbeaten. The tears had gone from her voice.

'I'm not unfeeling,' said the lady with the curl. 'I can't put you up if that's what you're meaning.'

'Well, I had hoped … .'

'We've got almost all my nephews and nieces and my … .'

She stopped suddenly. Nobody spoke. I held my breath. Had I been discovered?

'Robbie died,' said Miss Curl in a whisper.

'Oh, my goodness. I'm so sorry!' said Miss Weatherbeaten. 'How awful.'

Miss Curl was behind her desk now and plumped down sharply onto the chair which grated backwards under her weight.

'My mother's distraught. He was her favourite, even though she never said so. She's just … oh, it's too awful this, just too awful! And we still don't know where Alasdair is, and me sitting here all day taking other people's names, everybody trying to find somebody, and I have to tell them their somebody is dead, when … .'

'Oh, dear! I'm so sorry,' said Miss Weatherbeaten again. 'I wish there was something I could do. I suppose at least you have your mother. I don't have anyone.'

'We don't even have windows. The rest of the house is alright, well most of it, but … .'

'I'm sorry,' said Miss Weatherbeaten.

'I keep putting too much rouge on because I can't see in the candlelight,' said Miss Curl. 'Isn't it silly to fuss over such things when there's so much to be done. We really must keep going. There are too many people who need us. This war is making fools of us all.'

'I can't go back,' said Miss Weatherbeaten in an odd husky voice.

'I know,' said Miss Curl. 'I'm sorry I even suggested it.'

There was a pause that was so long I was sure I'd have to breathe and be found out.

'Do you remember little Rosie that I brought to you?' said Miss Weatherbeaten.

'Yes, I do,' said Miss Curl. 'Cute little thing. Poor soul.'

'Where did she go? Where did you send her?'

'Oh, dear. She sat on that chair you're on now while you left. She had no idea you had gone. And then, after about twenty minutes, when she still hadn't twigged, I had to leave the room. I told her to stay where she was but when I came back she had gone. I've no idea where.'

'Oh, no! That's terrible. I knew I shouldn't have left her!' Miss Weatherbeaten's voice shook and her feet jumped off the floor for a second then fell back down.

'I'm sorry, but, you know, it's not my fault if the little mite won't stay where she's told.'

'No, I didn't mean that. It's just that she never stays where she's told, not if you tell her. I was going to come back and get her, seeing as neither of us have anybody now. I saw some poor little things at the rest centre. If I'd had a home to take them to ... .'

'You can't take them all home.'

'I only wanted one, just Rosie. It's not a lot to ask. You're younger than me. You'll have your own children.'

'But you've nowhere to take her. Don't be ridiculous. You don't even have a house with no windows. You have nowhere to go yourself.'

'Thank you, Jinty. I'm aware of that.'

'What are you going to do?'

'I don't know, perhaps … .'

'You know it's odd,' said Miss Curl. 'I had another little girl, a bigger one, probably about nine or ten who was in here looking for her sister. She also just upped and disappeared when I left the room.'

'Was she upset?'

'Not specially. Filthy little thing, she'd been playing in the bombsites.'

I was desperate to come out now, mainly because my neck was so cramped against the underside of the desk, but also because I was most definitely not playing in the bombsites. I was looking for Mavis and it had been horrible.

'Do you think you'll go back to Carbeth?'

'I'd love to go to Carbeth but I don't think they'd have me after bringing Rosie back here, especially if they ever find out she's lost again.'

'Maybe she went back there herself.'

'Unlikely. It's a long way, a straight road from here but too far. They're right, of course. It was unforgivable. I just didn't think I could leave her with Mr Tait, being a single man, of course. It's particularly bad because of Lenny, the wee girl who … .'

'Lenny?'

'Yes, Lenny. Why?'

'She was here. That's the girl … what was the surname?'

'Gillespie.' They said this together.

I think we all three gasped at the same time.

'Looking for Mavis,' said Miss Weatherbeaten.

There was another long pause. I was sure I'd been found out. I was grateful for a sudden hullabaloo in the hall.

'Did you find her? Mavis, I mean,' said Miss Weatherbeaten.

'I hadn't finished look … hang on, she's taken the deceased book! Oh, Lord! Oh, my good Lord! No! What on earth am I going to do?'

Miss Curl's legs straightened as she stood. So did Miss Weatherbeaten's and I heard things being shifted about up on the desk.

'What did I do? Did I have it with me when I went to the hall? Did I have it … maybe it's … ?'

I nearly came out straightaway and confessed. Instead, when they went back out to the hall to look for the book, I leapt out from my hiding place and flung the book onto the desk of the fawn potato lady, then dived back under.

The fawn potato lady came back into the room immediately afterwards with her companion and said loudly, 'How did that get onto my desk, I wonder?' and dumped it back onto the desk over my head. 'Oh, look what I've done!' she went on. 'I've dropped my cardigan.'

Her face appeared round the end of her desk. She looked at me across the cold floor and pursed her lips, trying not to laugh. Then she disappeared again.

Miss Weatherbeaten and Miss Curl came back.

'Goodness, look how I'm losing my marbles!' said Miss Curl seeing the book. 'What a fluster. That's not like me at all. I'm so sorry.'

They started going through it together, and then through other ledgers of people missing or billeted, and every so often one of them would say 'Here's one, oh, no, sorry,' and it would be Mavis something else, or some other missing four year old.

And slow, slow, slow! I couldn't bear it. And then they'd stop and talk about someone I'd never even heard of until finally the time had come. I had to get out. I put one hand out on the floor.

'What's that?' said the fawn potato lady.

'What's what?' said Miss Curl. 'We're very busy. Can't you see?'

'I thought I heard a child's voice. In the hall. Maybe it's that girl. What was her name?'

I pulled my hand back in. Miss Weatherbeaten nearly trod on it.

'Don't be ridiculous. How can you tell in all that noise?' said Miss Curl.

'There it is again!' said Miss Fawn.

Miss Weatherbeaten shot out the door, followed closely by Miss Curl.

'Out, quick!' whispered Miss Fawn. She went to the door. 'Out! Now!' She beckoned me with a pudgy, fawn hand. 'That way, that way! Now!' And she shoved me out into the busiest part of the crowd. I bent double and sneaked out the door and round the corner of the street as fast as I was able.

'Lenny!' I heard in the distance. It was Miss Weatherbeaten. 'Lenny darling, where are you? I'm here looking for Mavis. Lenny! And Rosie too! Lenny!'

A big corporation bus squealed to a halt just over the road. It said 'DEPOT' on the front. I didn't know where Depot was, but it was heading in the right direction for Glasgow and the Carbeth bus. It was only when I found my seat on the bus that I realised I'd lost my pretty hat with the pink and yellow ribbons and the purple cloth flowers.

Chapter 33

My lunch sandwich with the dripping that Mrs Mags had given me had been squashed into a blob like a dumpling. I ate it anyway; I was starving. Mavis's shoe was still there too, rammed in the other pocket, but I couldn't bear to touch it and sat instead at the upstairs window of the bus looking out over the devastation that used to be Clydebank.

Work gangs of men crowded round houses with walls missing or bomb craters, reminding me of flies swarming on old rubbish tips. Even their lorries piled with stone looked small and useless beside the wilderness of mess and the insides of people's homes that were on the outside now. Streets like my street stretched off up the Kilbowie Road hill and more of them off Dumbarton Road, black and crumbled and dusty, and when we got to Partick (or Depot I suppose) they put everyone off the bus so we could get a tram like always into Glasgow. Even the tramlines were damaged in Clydebank.

I half-expected to find Mr Tait once I was on the Carbeth bus. Instead I found a woman with a chicken in a box. She was wearing several layers of clothing although it wasn't that cold, and she smelled funny, or maybe that was the chicken. I sat as far away from her as I could at the back of the bus.

By now it was late afternoon, late in March and I was alone on a bus, which under normal circumstances would have been very exciting, but I didn't want to be alone that day, not even on a bus heading towards Carbeth and my mum and Mr Tait and Mrs Mags. I didn't want to be on my own because I needed someone to talk to so that I wouldn't have to think about our house with no floors and no roof, and the little brown birds fluttering around in it without a care in the world. I didn't want to think about the rats and the mice and the rotten stench that clung to your nose no matter what you did, and I didn't want to think about all the things sticking out from under the rubble in the street. I didn't want to wonder about the names I'd run my finger down in the deceased book, names I'd seen without seeing and which came back to me now, names which I might have known but wasn't sure, next to addresses that seemed familiar. All these things floated about uninvited in my head, like the bees buzzing inside my jam jar last year.

But worst of all, I hadn't found Mavis. I sank down into the seat, like my heart sank into the pit of my tummy. 'Run, rabbit, run, rabbit, run, run, run,' I sang under my breath, and I peered over the window's edge for rabbits hiding in the hedgerows or the fields. There was a farmer ploughing amidst a cloud of seagulls, and a cart like Mr Tulloch's at a gate, the horse snorting white puffs into the air. There were snowdrops under the hedges and sheep dotted across the field behind the school which was up ahead. Miss Read was in her garden digging, still in her violet jumper, and the sun spread out over the turnip field on the other side of the road. And in the trees above the field behind the school I saw a deep-red hat with a rim of orange hair bouncing through the dark branches of the trees: orange-haired, red-hatted Mr Tulloch number two.

And I remembered the bivouacs.

'Stop the bus!' I shouted. 'Stop! Stop the bus! I've got to get off!' I threw myself down the aisle banging off the chair backs as I lurched to the front.

One last chance. It was still daylight. Mr Tulloch number two might be coming with news and if he wasn't, I could walk back to the bivouacs with him.

'Stop the bus!' I shouted. We were past the school now, almost at the ruined house.

'Alright, alright, keep your hair on!' said the bus driver. It was the same driver who had been driving when my mum came to Carbeth.

'Stop, stop, stop!' I said, and 'Thank you, thank you, thank you!' when he did.

'Oh, it's a pleasure, believe me,' he said, making the door open. The chicken squawked in its box and the smelly lady muttered something I didn't care about.

I had a long way to run back, at least a mile, maybe two. I couldn't see him on the hill any more. There were too many trees in the way.

'Mr Tulloch!' I shouted. 'Mavis!' (Pant, pant.) 'Rosie!'

My feet barely touched the ground and my heart worked like a steam engine. A family of little birds leapt out of the hedge as I passed and I just missed a fleeing fieldmouse.

'Mr Tulloch!' I shouted.

Miss Read lived in a house next door to the school.

She had stopped digging and was standing by the gate to the path that Mr Tulloch was on, spade in hand.

'Afternoon, Miss Read!' I said, turning up the path.

'Leonora!' she said. 'What are … ? Goodness, is everything alright?'

'Yes!' I said. 'Mr Tulloch's brother is coming over the hill with news.'

She followed me up. 'Are you sure?' she said.

'Yes, yes, I'm sure!' I said, although I wasn't.

Suddenly there were rabbits everywhere scurrying into the bracken by the burn, and now that we were in the open field, there were only sheep and no red-haired Mr Tulloch on the path, never mind Mavis or Rosie.

'Mr Tulloch!' I shouted, scanning the field which seemed to curve away from me in all directions as if I was standing on a gigantic ball. The path rose up before me, familiar now because it was only that morning I'd climbed it. A pair of magpies cackled at me, gossiping about things that didn't matter, and the burn gurgled round the stones.

'Maybe he stopped by the tree,' I said. 'Maybe he dropped something and had to go back. Maybe if I just go a bit higher. I think it's harder to see from here than it is from the road. He might be lost.'

'Leonora, Mr Tulloch walks over here all the time,' said Miss Read. She was panting too. 'Are you sure it was him?'

'Yes, it was him, I know it was,' I said. 'I'm going up.' I left her there with her spade. The spring grass soaked my shoes. Up, up I went until I was dizzy with the effort and dizzy with the height, looking down on the roof of the school, the treetops at the back of it, the outhouses, the farm over by, back along the road. But there was no-one at the big beech tree and no-one on the path which stretched off into the distance, only a woman with a donkey.

'Mavis!' I whispered, not understanding. 'Where did you go?' I sat down on the same root I had sat on to eat Mr Tait's sandwiches, and let tears of frustration flow down my cheeks, out there on the hillside where the wind was straight, penetrating and impossible to hide from, even behind that tree.

Miss Read caught up with me. Her shadow joined the shadow of the beech and stretched long and cold across the field warning me the light would be going soon. 'Stop it, Mavis!' I whispered. 'You have to come back to me.'

'There's nobody here except that woman,' said Miss Read.

'They might be at the tents,' I said. 'Mr Tulloch said he'd ask his wife.' I stood up. 'I'm going to go and ask her myself.' I took a deep breath and gazed across at the dark hill where I thought their farm would be, but there was only hill and more hill, no farmhouse or tents.

'I don't think so Leonora,' said Miss Read.

'If I go back to the flat rock I can find it from there,' I said, but I knew I couldn't. I must have walked a hundred miles already that day and everything hurt. I plumped back down onto the tree root and Miss Read came down beside me.

'Come back tomorrow,' she said, 'and you can go over there in the morning instead of school.'

So we sat there a little longer until I found the strength to go back down the hill with her. She gave me a bowl of hot soup in her kitchen and a chunk of chocolate, and went back to her digging while I started for home.

I sucked the corner of the chocolate to make it last longer and to stop the sobs that were threatening to burst out, and because I was shaking so badly my mouth wouldn't work properly. I had no way of stopping the thoughts that ached like bee stings so I walked slowly, thwacking my feet off the tarmac like the day I'd met Mr Tulloch number one and his cart.

'Mum. And. Mav. Is,' I said. 'Mum. And. Mav. Is,' and I pulled her shoe out and bumped it against my leg in time. And then I sang, 'The wind, the wind, the wind blows HIGH, Out pops Mavis from the SKY!'

After a short while I was disturbed by the sound of hooves behind me on the road, and I thought I'd better sing inside my head instead.

'She is handsome, she is pretty.'

Although I was tired, I didn't want to meet anyone, not even Mr Tulloch who had been so kind before and might have given me another lift to Carbeth. I thought if I saw another kind person I might dissolve into jelly again, so I went as fast as I could. But quite soon the noise of the cart was so loud it seemed like he'd catch me up if I didn't get out of the way. So I stepped onto the verge and disappeared behind a bush. Mr Tulloch and his cart came clattering round the corner, the horse's hooves hitting the road hard. Clearly Mr Tulloch was in a hurry. But his hurry seemed to leave him and he began to slow down.

'Woah!' he said, and he pulled back on the enormous reins, just like I'd seen him do before, and the horse and cart came thundering and clattering and snorting to a stop a few yards up in front of me. He was talking to someone I couldn't see who was sitting at the front, hidden by the milk churns.

Suddenly he started to shout.

'Lenny, Lenny!' he shouted. 'Where are you?'

'Bother!' I muttered to myself, he'd seen me, but I stayed where I was, even though there was rain-water dripping down my neck from the bush.

'Linny!' I heard, and 'Lenny!' and 'Linny, Lenny, Leonora!'

'Leonora?' said Mr Tulloch, who hadn't known my real name, then 'Leonooora!' His voice sang out across that beautiful sheltered valley, clear as a bell.

'Liiinny!'

'Leeenny!'

'Leonoooora!'

I tiptoed out from my hiding place.

'Mavis?' I whispered.

The cart was shoogling about all over the place now and the churns were clanking against each other as if they were excited too.

'Mavis?' I said, louder, a bomb jumping up into my throat and making my eyes hot.

'Linny!'

A head appeared above the milk churns, and then another one. They had identical hair except one had no fringe and when I got closer I saw that one had blue eyes and one had brown, and one had her thumb in her mouth, when she wasn't shouting 'Linny!' and the other was rubbing her earlobe as if it might come off.

'Mavis!' I shouted, 'Rosie!' and I ran to the cart and climbed up onto it as if it wasn't there at all and I hugged and hugged them both, and then I stopped and looked at Mavis to make sure it really was her, my very own Mavis, two eyes, a nose and a mouth.

'Hello, Linny!' she said. 'Why are you crying?' She looked worried and scared and leant back against the seat of the cart but I grabbed her little hand and pulled her back to me.

'I'm not crying,' I said, wiping the last of my tears away. 'Don't use that silly baby voice. It's Lenny, not Linny.'

'Linny,' she said, trying very hard.

'No, Lenny,' I said.

'Li-nny,' she said.

'No, Le-nny,' I said.

'No Le-nny,' she said.

'That's better,' I said.

She shifted away from me and stared, her little eyes darting about my face.

'I look funny, don't I?' I said. 'But it's still me inside.' Her gaze stopped at the tufts of hair on top of my head.

'Mum's over there in amongst those trees,' I said, and I pointed across the valley to where the huts were hiding in the bushes. 'But she's not the same … .'

Mavis squinted over the valley. Then she coughed as if she was very thirsty.

'Why didn't you tell them at the town hall where you were?' I said. 'We've been looking and looking.' She stared up at me, worry wrinkling across her brow.

'She was in a tent on my brother's farm,' said Mr Tulloch. 'She was with a neighbour from Clydebank, I think.'

'I stayed in a tent too,' said Rosie. 'Miss Weatherbeaten forgot to take me with her.'

'Tents?' I said, ignoring Miss Weatherbeaten for the time being. 'Lucky you!'

'Did my mum come yet?' said Rosie, her eyes lit up with hope.

'No, Rosie, your mum isn't coming, but Miss Weatherbeaten is. I'm just not sure when, but she will. You wait and see.'

Mavis frowned.

'She's not scary,' I said. Mavis knew I wasn't keen on Miss Weatherbeaten. 'She just makes mistakes.'

Rosie was considering this and nodding sagely.

'And Mr Tait's not scary either although he does have a stick.'

'Mr Tait?' said Mavis.

'He lives in a tent too and he gave me an orange,' I said, sidestepping the fact that she knew him as the scary man with the big stick for naughty kids like us.

'An orange?' she said.

'Yes, an orange,' I said. 'Imagine that! A whole orange just for me, except I gave some to … .' Oh, dear, the bad boys by the canal.

Mavis twisted a strand of hair round her finger and stuck it into the corner of her mouth along with her thumb.

'I don't know if he has any more.'

'Lenny,' said Mr Tulloch, 'If you sit down, if we all shift along a bit, then we can get moving. It's cold and the light's going.'

The horse was shifting on its feet, the churns were singing behind us, and my heart was soaring again right up into the sky. I slipped in between Mavis and Rosie and put an arm round each of them.

'Goan,' said Mr Tulloch.

'Goan,' I said too, and the big horse with the steaming sides lurched forwards making us all scream and laugh.

The sun had slipped behind the hill again and Mr Tulloch started to sing.

'My eyes are dim I cannot see!'

And Rosie and I joined in. Mavis kept her thumb in her mouth and gazed at me as if I was from the moon.

But while we were singing the 'Quartermaster's stores' I looked down at her and checked that she had both her feet, which she did, and both her shoes, which she did, and I very nearly chucked the shoe in my pocket over the side of the cart, but thought better of it.

'There were kids, kids, wearing dustbin lids, in the store, in the store!' I sang, and I nudged Mavis in the ribs but only Rosie sang it too.

And then I just sat and held onto their little four-year-old bodies, poking my fingers into their sides and stroking their necks while we sang about fleas with hairy knees, and gravy, enough to float the Navy. If I'd been a cat I'd have been purring.

Just before the Halfway House pub, Mr Tulloch stopped the cart.

'It's back here, isn't it?' he said, and I had to tell him that it was really along there, next to the pub. I think he knew that already.

He jumped down at the bottom of the path that led up to the huts, his big boots scratching on the gravel, and he helped Mavis down. Mavis had both her arms, all her fingers, all her hair, and both her eyebrows, but she had bruises on her dirty little legs and scabs everywhere including on her face, some of which she'd picked open so they were red and dirty. She stared up at me, standing there under the eaves of the pub where my mum had demanded to be taken up the hill again, and I gazed back at her.

'It's me, Lenny,' I said. But she only stared, so I got down close beside her and whispered. 'The wind, the wind, the wind blew high. Out popped Mavis from the sky.'

And I slid my arms around her and we stood quietly waiting for Rosie.

'You shouldn't have run off,' I told Mavis.

She was quiet.

'Don't ever go anywhere again without telling me first,' I said.

Not a word.

'Not even the cludgie,' I said. 'We all do that here, tell each other, I mean.'

And she looked up at me, in surprise.

'Yes, even the grown-ups,' I said. 'Even Miss Weatherbeaten.'

Rosie came and leant against us, which was a nuisance, but poor little Rosie didn't have a big sister any more. She didn't have a wee sister either, so I put my arm around her too.

Mr Tulloch left us there, promising to visit us the next day so he could tell my mum how he came to have Mavis and Rosie on his cart. We thanked him and waved him a cheery goodbye. I could hear him whistling in the dark but I couldn't make out the tune.

It was a long heave up the hill but there were plenty of people to tell on the way.

'Rosie's back!' I called, like the town crier. 'This is my sister! This is Mavis! Look everyone, it's my sister!'

'Well done, Lenny,' said a lady near the bottom.

'Mum!' I shouted. 'Look, it's Mavis! Mrs Mags! Sandy! Look! Mr Tait! Look everyone. I found my sister!'

I did a cartwheel UP the hill and nearly broke my neck, and Rosie did somersaults that misfired and turned into backwards ones that took her halfway back down to the road.

'I want my mum!' she shrieked in joy and delight, springing back onto her feet, and taking the wind out of me.

'Mum!' squeaked Mavis, breathless, puffing up the hill beside me, her hand firmly in mine.

Rosie and I collapsed onto the wet grass, puffing and laughing at the sky and waiting for the grown-ups to find us. But Mavis just stood there looking all around her at the huts and the trees and the yellowy green grass, like I had when I first arrived.

'Where's Mum?' she said. Her voice was soft as if she had a frog in her throat, then she put her thumb back in her mouth and looked at me.

'She's here,' I said. 'I told you, didn't I? I told you she was here, but … I didn't want to tell you, in case you didn't notice, but … she lost a foot.' I waited for this to sink in. Mavis's big brown eyes didn't leave mine, except briefly when she glanced down at my own feet. 'She can't walk properly. She has to use crutches, like the man we saw last year … the soldier? No, you wouldn't remember that. Wooden things to hold herself up with.'

'I think my mum has those too,' said Rosie.

'No, Rosie,' I started. 'No, I don't think so.'

'Yes, she does,' she said.

'No, Rosie … .'

Rosie stood up suddenly and stuck her nose in the air, as if she didn't care to have anything to do with someone who didn't believe her about her mum.

But Mavis was still staring at me. She had smears of dirt down her cheeks and a storm brewing on her brow. I shouldn't have told her about the leg and a little bomb went off in my tummy because of it. I was worried too because she'd been so quiet, hardly saying a word and all the time her big brown eyes shifting about watching everything in a way I'd never seen her do before.

'Come on, Mavis, and I'll show you.' I said, and I took her by the hand.

Rosie lost her huff and came and took my other hand.

'This is it,' I said, outside Mrs Mags's door.

Rosie pulled at her earlobe. Mavis slouched to one side with her thumb in her mouth. Her other hand held mine.

I knocked. No-one came. I turned the handle and peered inside. No-one was home. Rosie pushed past me but kept my hand.

'Mrs Mags!' she called. 'Mum!'

'They're not here, Rosie,' I said.

Mavis dropped my hand and took a step back.

'Mavis!' I said.

Her eyebrows shifted lower over her eyes. She stuck her free hand into her armpit and turned away from me.

'Mavis!'

She got down on her haunches and started picking at the grass.

'Alright then! Stay there!' I said.

'You're lying!' she said quietly as if she was talking to the ground.

'I'm not lying!'

She turned further from me.

And Rosie chimed in too. 'Yes, you are!'

'I'm not lying. Let go of me!'

Rosie wouldn't let go of my hand. I had to force her fingers off mine. They were white with holding on, and her face was red, her bottom lip trembling.

'Stay there!' I said as if I was biting the air, but of course Rosie couldn't stay there and Mavis wouldn't be left outside on her own. Rosie and I shuffled into Mrs Mags's hut with Mavis close behind, only dimly aware of someone following us up the hill.

I was looking for my mum's dress which she had been persuaded by Mrs Mags to swap for dungarees, the better to cover her leg and her foot that wasn't there. In the pale light my hand found its well-rubbed cotton on the back of the bedroom door, hanging from a nail.

'There you are. See!' I said.

Mavis sniffed hard.

She had the sleeve of my coat tightly grasped. I took her hand, clenched tight just like Rosie's had been so many times before, and I put it on my mum's dress.

'Oh!' she said, and she leant into the jumble of coats and scarves that our mum's dress was muddled up with.

Rosie wanted to touch it too.

I stroked its familiar material, strangely cold without the warmth of my mum's body.

'See?' I whispered. 'She's here. I promise.'

I took Mavis's hand again. It was sticky with sweat and bogies but softer. She had her thumb in her mouth and was resting her head on my mum's dress, as if she'd fallen asleep.

'She won't be far,' I said, and we stood there, all three of us, leaning against my mum's dress, made soft by other people's coats and scarves, huddling into it, even little Rosie who didn't have a mum any more; and we stayed there for a minute or two, tired by our journeys and the hills and hope and longing.

We were still standing there when the boys arrived.

Mavis screamed and disappeared into the coats.

'Go away stupid boys!' said Rosie.

'I found Mavis!' I said, jumping away from the dress. 'Look! I found my sister! And look, it's Rosie!'

Sandy stood grinning and nodding, pleased and understanding. 'Where is she then?'

There came a muffled snort from behind me.

Rosie stepped forward and shook her fist. 'My dad's going to get you!' she said, mainly to bad George.

'You're dad's d … ,' began George, but Dougie and Sandy kicked him and shoved him out the door.

'Your mum sent us,' said Sandy as he grappled with George. 'We're at Mr Tait's. My mum's time came when she wasn't expecting it.'

'Her time?' I said. Was Mrs Mags dying? She wasn't old enough to die. My heart was pounding now. No! I liked Mrs Mags. She was nice as long as she didn't do a Miss Weatherbeaten.

I dragged Mavis and Rosie from behind the

bedroom door. There was a ripping sound as the dress was torn from its hook.

'Wait!' I said. 'What do you mean, your mum's time has come. She's not, you know, dying, is she?'

Sandy looked as if he'd never thought of that, as if I'd made him think about it for the first time. Bad George seemed to know a lot more about what was going on, so once he'd thrown Dougie and Sandy off the step he explained things to us, sitting grandly in his Auntie Mags' chair with his legs apart like the men I'd seen in 'our' hut. We lined up in a row on the step with my mum's dress across our laps.

So it turns out Mrs Mags was having a baby right at that exact moment right in the middle of Monday afternoon teatime, except of course she wasn't making the tea or she'd have been there in her hut. I wasn't sure what 'having it' meant, and George didn't know either, and no matter how hard I tried to understand what Mrs Mags having a baby might mean I couldn't figure out whether I should be excited or worried. (I had heard sometimes people died when they were 'having babies' but usually people were pleased and excited.) George said he thought the baby was inside Mrs Mags but he couldn't tell us how it was going to get out.

And if my mum was helping her 'have' her baby, I wondered how she could possibly do that when she couldn't even go for a wee by herself. And I began to worry because, of course Mr Tait couldn't help either of them with either of those two things, having babies or going for wees.

'We have to go over there as quick as we can,' I said, 'right now.'

'That's what Mr Tait said,' said Sandy, suddenly remembering, 'and bring the ... what was it?'

So we lit the hurricane lamp and collected towels, and bread and cups and disinfectant. Actually I didn't do any of it. I couldn't. Mavis and Rosie were so firmly attached to me as to make all movement impossible unless it was in a straight line down a hill, past the Halfway House pub, and past Jimmy Robertson's bus. There was a candle burning inside his bus – I could see it through a crack in the curtain. He pulled back the curtain and I shouted, 'I found my sister!' I waved Mavis's shoe at him and pointed to Mavis who was trying to get my waving hand back. 'Hold the lamp over Mavis!' I said, but Dougie was too intent on making ghosts of the bushes with it. 'She's here!' I said, and Jimmy Robertson gave me the thumbs up and I gave him the thumbs up back and nearly dropped the shoe.

'When Mavis came marching home again, hurrah, hurrah!' we sang, and we sang it for Rosie too, and Peggy my mum and Mrs Mags (also known as Mum and Auntie Mags). It kept Dougie's ghosts away, and it kept our feet moving through the dark. Then Rosie wanted to add some names of her own, names she'd never said before, Chrissie and Colin and Rhona, and I added the names of my friends at home that I might never see again. And we sang Miss Weatherbeaten. But Mavis didn't sing anything at all. She just stayed close in beside me, as silent as the cold dark night.

And then the shadow of a ghost appeared in front of us and we all crouched together in the middle of the road and listened to it hobble down the road towards us.

'Tap-tappety-ketap! Tap-tappety-ketap!'

'Mr Tait!' I shouted. 'It's Mr Tait! I found Mavis! Look, Mr Tait, I found Mavis! That's Mr Tait, Mavis. He's not a bad man with a big stick for naughty kids like us, honest Mavis, he's not, he had oranges. Tell her, Rosie. Tell her he's Mr Tait. He's ... look Mr Tait, isn't she just so ... so beautiful ... so perfect! Oh, Mr Tait I found her! And I found Rosie too. I found them both!'

I fell into his arms and sobbed and sobbed as if I was going to be sick but I knew I wasn't going to be sick. I was just going to sob and sob until all the sobs that I'd been storing up had sobbed themselves away. Mavis held onto my hand even though it was away round Mr Tait's side. I could hear her starting to whimper to herself, saying my name with her baby voice, 'Linny.'

'Well done, Lenny! What a clever girl you are!' he said as he stroked the back of my head. 'Your mum is going to be so, so happy!'

I was so, so happy too because I wanted my mum to be as chuffed as I was to have Mavis back, Mavis who'd got a piece at somebody's door, just like everyone said she would.

Rosie took Mavis's hand in a helpful big sisterly sort of way and said, 'Mavis, this is Mr Tait. He's nice.' But Mavis wasn't so sure and shifted right up against me again.

'Hello, Mavis,' said Mr Tait in his soft quiet voice. 'I didn't mean to give you a fright and I'm afraid I don't have any more oranges. I don't even have any dinner, and I bet you're all starving.'

We all hummed our agreement and bad George

said they'd brought what he'd asked for and Mr Tait rubbed his hands and took one of their bags.

'Hello, Rosie,' he said. 'How lovely to see you again! We were a bit worried about you.'

Rosie was sticking to her story that Miss Weatherbeaten had simply forgotten her, and it seemed to me, in a funny way, to be true.

Chapter 34

I carried Mavis most of the way to Mr Tait's hut, perched on my hip with her long, four-year-old legs waving about and her arms around my neck, and then I set her down and we walked the last bit to the front steps, Rosie and I shouting 'Mum!' all the time.

Mr Tait's hut had a roof! The light from the hurricane slithered down it and along its walls too. Some of the walls were missing and none of the windows were there, but only because they hadn't been put in yet, not because they'd been bombed out. There were blankets across them instead, just like in Clydebank. I clattered up the steps dragging poor Mavis behind me, and wee Rosie stumbled along after her.

'Mum!' I said, 'Look! Look who's here! Look! It's Mavis!'

My mum was standing holding the wall.

'Where is she?' said my mum, and she fell with a thud onto her knees on the hollow floor and held Mavis by her shoulders, their heads at exactly the same height, and Mavis finally let go of my hand and wrapped herself around my mum, and my mum hugged and hugged her back. I got down there and hugged them both too.

'Where have you been?' she said, meaning Mavis,

and 'Where did you find her?' she said to me, but she didn't really want answers just then; she wanted to squeeze Mavis, and she wanted to squeeze me, and I couldn't have answered her anyway because my mouth was full of sobs even though I was so happy because we were all three together again and we had Mavis back. Mavis was crying too in the airless, snivelling way that four year olds do, as if she was shivering with the cold. Her little body was trembling under my arm. Rosie stood beside us patting Mavis on the head with one hand and pulling on her earlobe with the other. I took her hand, the one with the earlobe, and pulled her in beside me.

My mum did what I had done; she examined Mavis from top to bottom to make sure she was all there. She ran her hand round her chin, counted all her fingers (not out loud but I knew what she was doing) and she checked her feet. Mavis was still wearing the dress my mum had made for her, the blue one like mine but with purple embroidery. Mavis had cuts on her hands, bruises on her legs, filthy broken fingernails, and lots of little scratches all over her face, but nothing was actually missing.

'Quietly, now,' said Mr Tait to Sandy, Dougie and bad George. 'On you go in.' They tiptoed into the hut in the way only boys can do with ill-fitting boots, kicking the steps and elbows banging off walls.

And through my tears I saw Mrs Mags sitting on a chair in the corner, all wrapped up in a blanket. Her face was pink and yellow in the firelight and her red hair was loose about her cheeks. She looked excited and ill at the same time and I wondered what on earth could be wrong with her. But of course she'd 'had a baby' – perhaps that was it, and I wondered where this baby was and what type of baby it might be.

A fire glowed in a metal tub set on some bricks. Sparks flew from it at an alarming rate and disappeared up the brickwork chimney above it. The room was busy with yellow shadows. Mr Tait stepped through it in his caramel brown suit and we helped my mum up off the floor and back into her fantastic new wheelchair which was sitting in the corner.

'What a happy day!' I heard Mrs Mags say with a laugh. 'Congratulations, Mrs Gillespie!' She had Sandy on one side, Dougie on the other and George was shifting from foot to foot in front of her.

'Out the way, George!' said Sandy. 'I can't see him. You're in the light.'

And George did get out of the way, which was a surprise really, with him being so bad and whatnot; I thought he'd stay right where he was and annoy everyone by blocking all the light from the fire. But he didn't, in fact he asked Mr Tait for a candle, which Mr Tait quickly produced, and they all peered in at Mrs Mags and I couldn't see anything at all from where I was, leaning against my mum's good leg.

Mavis climbed up into my mum's lap and laid claim to her for the rest of the evening. She was the cat that got the cream, my little Queen of Sheba, sucking quietly on her thumb, great drops of tears falling down her smudged cheeks. She didn't seem to notice my mum's missing foot, the space where her foot should have been but wasn't, and even though there was a brand new baby less than four feet away there was no way she was shifting.

But after a while curiosity got the better of me and

I unfurled Mavis's fingers from mine and tiptoed over for a look.

He was no bigger than a doll. His face was like a turnip and he was made of wax. There was a tiny streak of blood under his chin and something white was stuck on his head. He was just two hours old and I was worried about him because he was fast, fast asleep even though we were all poking at him and talking and jostling to get in there to see him in the yellow glow of the candle. Mr Tait was moving the candle about so that we could see his ears and his nose and his little toes which seemed far too long for such a small person. I pulled on Mr Tait's sleeve and he bent down so I could whisper.

'Is he dead?' I said. 'He's not moving.'

Mr Tait laughed lightly, kindly, so that I knew it wasn't true.

'No,' he said. 'He's just exhausted from getting here. He's sleeping the sleep of the … .'

'How did he get here?' I said, thinking suddenly how exhausted I was too from my day's journeys.

Mr Tait took a very long time to answer, so I knew it was something important he was going to say, and something that was difficult to explain. When I looked into his face I saw that it was red, and I wondered whether he was very hot from the fire.

'Mavis, come and see the baby,' I said, but she shook her head.

Mr Tait still hadn't answered my question but just then there was the tiniest whimper, like the puppies in Ayr when we went there, Mavis and me, at the beginning of the war, only it wasn't puppies; it was the baby.

'Mavis, you have to come and see,' I said, but she

shook her head again and I saw her fall softly into my mum's shoulder.

The whimper suddenly became a cry.

I squeezed my head in between Sandy and Dougie so that I could be sure the baby was alright.

'Lenny, a little privacy for Mrs Mags, please,' said my mum. 'Boys!'

Mr Tait and the boys clattered down the steps outside while she explained what breastfeeding meant. I tried hard not to look, but you know me! Rosie stared too.

When Mrs Mags was finished and Mr Tait had come back in, we tried to quiz Mavis about where she had been. She didn't want to talk but she told us a little and Rosie helped with the rest.

'I went to the hills,' said Mavis.

'To the tents,' said Rosie, 'except she slept in the barn with the cows at the beginning.'

'Who were you with?' I said. 'Who took you there?'

'I don't know. The lady who was singing in the shelter.'

'That'd be Mrs Brand,' I said. We had been in their shelter once or twice before and Mrs Brand liked to lead the singing, which was just as well because her daughter couldn't sing for toffee (which didn't stop her trying).

'Yes,' said Mavis. She shifted on my Mum's lap and turned her back to us.

This is what happened, as far as I could make out, and it took ages to get this much: Mavis had gone up into the hills after the first night of the bombing. She had walked most of the way but was allowed to sit on Mrs Brand's granddaughter's pram sometimes too. She heard the bombs, and she heard people cry but she closed her eyes when she was told to and had hidden in Mrs Brand's voluptuous bosom (what my mum says my Auntie May has and Mrs Mags has one too). But when they arrived at the hills there was nowhere to go, so she stood on the flat rock with Mrs Brand and lots of other people until they were taken to a farm (which turned out to be red-haired Mr Tulloch number two's farm). She had been there ever since. There were so many people in the barn, there was hardly space to sleep and everyone smelled bad, especially Mrs Brand. She said the farmer and his wife were kind people but they got very angry sometimes because there was no food or tea or beds. And then some tents arrived and some sandwiches.

The first night was cold because they had no blankets so she slept very close to Mrs Brand and they covered themselves with straw. That was the night we walked over the hills and my mum was in the hospital.

The next day Mavis and Mrs Brand and her family were given soup, but it was cold because there was nowhere to heat it. I had slept most of that day and ate Mrs Mags's rabbit stew at midnight.

The day after that was the same, only another farmer brought them carrots so they had raw carrots with sandwiches that some ladies had left for them. The Brand family made a 'tent' and filled it with straw to sleep on. That was the day I didn't want a bath, the day I ran away to try and find Mavis, seeing as no-one seemed to want to help me, and Rosie and I went to the witch's hut. Miss Weatherbeaten found us in the morning and we had a bath anyway.

The food on Mavis's farm didn't improve that day

either and our hut was overrun by other people from Clydebank (put there by the Salvation Army).

That was also the day Mrs Brand and her daughter and grandchildren were billeted with a Duntocher family and Mavis was left behind on the farm in the hills. Mrs Brand said she was very sorry and asked another family to keep an eye on her, but then they were billeted too, and Mavis shared her straw bed, in a tent under a tree, with four other kids.

The following morning, having slept on the floor, we got on a bus to Glasgow and I caused a stooshie in my mum's hospital and I cried in the bus on the way back.

But Mavis couldn't tell us what happened to her that day or the rest of the days she spent at the farm, in fact she wouldn't talk at all, no matter what we did. She stuck her thumb in her mouth and coueried into my mum.

Rosie took up the story.

'When Miss Weatherbeaten forgot about me I tried hard to remember where we had been, you and me and her and Mr Tait,' she said. Mr Tait was sitting on the floor against a wall. I could hear the boys playing bombers outside. 'I came out of the town hall and went straight up Kilbowie Road, all the way and then another road which I wasn't sure of and then I came to the flat rock. Mr Tulloch found me on the flat rock, because I didn't know which way to go after that, only it wasn't Mr Tulloch, it was another Mr Tulloch with red hair and a red hat, and he told me I could stay on his farm if I wanted until you, or Mr Tait or Miss Weatherbeaten came for me. So I did. Mrs Tulloch gave me honey.'

Rosie seemed pleased as punch with herself.

'Two days after that all the blankets disappeared and some other things too and everyone thought it was me.'

Mavis turned herself right into my mum's neck. Her feet were all scrunched up together, the toes rubbing against each other.

'No!' said Mavis, sniffing.

Rosie stopped.

'Go on, Rosie,' said my mum. 'Well?'

'Mavis had them. She had all of them, everything that was missing, even the old ladies' teeth and Mr Tulloch's pipe.'

'Oh, dear!' said my mum.

'They were all in her tent. There was no-one in her tent but her, but you could hardly get into it because of all the stuff she'd stolen.'

'I didn't steal it!' said Mavis, suddenly fierce.

'Yes, you did! She didn't get anything of mine.'

'I didn't!'

'I didn't have anything,' said Rosie.

'Did you give it all back, Mavis?' I asked.

She nodded, and I saw it was hard for her, giving everyone back their bits and pieces, all by herself in her tent with no-one of her own to keep her warm at night. I thought about the shoe, her shoe, and how important it had been to me, but when I searched my pocket it was gone, and so was the drawing of Mr MacInnes and his blunt bit of pencil. I found all of it later in Mavis's coat pocket.

'She came into my tent after that,' said Rosie solemnly. 'With the other kids and the lady, and then today red Mr Tulloch took me and Mavis over the hill and put us on his brother's cart. And then we found Lenny on the road.'

'Poor Mavis!' I said. I gave Mavis's hand a little squeeze and she sniffed but didn't squeeze back.

It was too late and too dark to go home to Mrs Mags's so we bedded down on that rough wooden floor, the whole lot of us with coats borrowed (not stolen) from Mr Tait's new neighbours.

Sleeping on floors was what I did every night, only this time I had my mum and Mavis so I didn't care where I was. We were like sardines in a tin, me, my mum, Mavis, Rosie and then Mrs Mags all in a row, sandwiched together, and beside Mrs Mags was the new baby, then Sandy, Dougie, and bad George. Good Mr Tait was by the door. Apart from Mrs Mags who fell asleep (and snored) straightaway, we nodded off in reverse order as if sleep was seeping in under the door. Mr Tait went first (even his snores were gentle), then the boys, then Rosie, Mavis, my mum and lastly me. I was too excited for sleep. All my wishing had come true, except for my mum's foot and Mavis being so quiet, and I must confess that I cried and cried and cried, quietly, all to myself, that night, the silent tears of deepest joy. But even I fell asleep in the end, deep and peaceful, almost completely content, only missing Mavis's laugh.

I cried the next morning when I told Mr Tait that Miss Weatherbeaten wanted to look after Rosie and I cried when he left to go and find her. And I cried when, before he went, he stood outside with me and I saw in full daylight what a wonderful hut he had built.

It sat on eight towers of brick, like the one I had made

without thinking the day I saw his wooden leg. On top of the bricks there were big, dark railway sleepers, massive chunks of wood that smelled of factories and oil. On top of those there were floorboards and on top of that there were walls. The roof came down from its ridge among the branches and over the front door and it stopped a few feet in front of the windows. This left a covered area so that on a hot day, or a wet one, you could sit outside and watch the world go by or listen to the birds. 'Wuh-woo-woo-wuh-wuh!' And the windows were so big you could see all the way down the road in one direction and all the way up it in the other.

Mr Tait showed me, while I cried, how he could make an extra room for me, Mavis and my mum, just like we had planned, along one side, and he showed me where he could build another one like it for Rosie and Miss Weatherbeaten, if she came back to us and if she chose to stay with Rosie. He said we could all be safe until the end of the war if we stayed in Carbeth.

In my head I was shouting, 'Yes, yes, yes!' but the tears still ran like rivers down my cheeks. Mavis was with me – there were few times over the following weeks when she wasn't attached to me in some way or other. She was staring up at me, thumb in mouth.

'Yes, Lenny, yes!' she whispered. And Rosie copied her only louder. 'Yes, yes!'

My mum appeared in the front door at the top of the steps. Her face was red and she was struggling with her crutches.

'Mr Tait!' she said, and we all looked round. 'Mr Tait!' she said, towering over us on the top step and swaying slightly. She was not happy, I could tell. 'Mr Tait!'

'Mrs Gillespie,' said Mr Tait, in his quiet voice. 'Is something wrong?'

'I would appreciate it, Mr Tait, if you would not put silly ideas in these girls' heads,' she said.

One of her crutches landed at the bottom of the steps, then the other.

'Silly?'

'Yes, silly,' she said.

Holding the rail that Mr Tait had erected, she edged closer to the rim of the step and hopped down from the top onto the next step. We all moved closer. Rosie grabbed my sleeve. Mavis came in closer.

'How silly?' asked Mr Tait. He glanced at me briefly and smiled, nodding his head as if to say, 'Here goes!'

'We can't possibly stay here,' she said, hopping down another step.

'No?' said Mr Tait, moving closer.

'Well, no, of course not,' she said. 'After all that's happened, after … and we have a perfectly good place to stay at Mrs Mags … .'

'Mum … .'

'… and then I'll go back to the town hall and ask for somewhere for us to live … .'

'Mum … .'

'There's bound to be somewhere.'

'Mum … .'

'What is it Lenny? Don't interrupt.'

'But … ,' I said.

'But … ,' said Mr Tait. We glanced at each other again.

'We can't prevail on you any more … .' She landed heavily on the ground, still clutching the railing.

What did she mean?

Mr Tait tried to protest that it wasn't a question of prevailing. It was a question of survival, so she told him she could survive very well, thank you very much, at Mrs Mags's until she got herself, and us, back to Clydebank.

'But Mum … ,' I said.

'You can't walk well enough yet,' he pointed out, handing her the crutches. 'You need … .'

'Thank you, Mr Tait. I know what I need, and I know what my children need.'

'Mum,' I said. 'The houses are all broken in Clydebank. There isn't anywhere.'

'Look, the windows will be here in a couple of days' time,' said Mr Tait. 'And that wood … .'

He pointed to a pile under a tree.

'It's for our room!' I said.

'It'll only take a couple more days,' said Mr Tait.

'We could have two sets of bunk beds,' I pointed out, 'like our first hut, with enough room for Rosie too!'

'But … ,' said my mum.

'Yes,' said Mr Tait. 'Yes, we could, until we see what Miss Weatherbeaten wants to do, I mean Miss Wetherspoon.'

'It's going to be there,' I said, dragging Mavis and Rosie with me and indicating the side of the hut.

'Lenny, we're not … ,' said my mum.

'A little further back, I thought,' said Mr Tait, following us round. He pointed with his stick at the space he had left for the door. 'Further back would give you the privacy of being behind this bush, you see. There would be a window.'

'No, there wouldn't,' said my mum. 'Where would you sleep?' she said. 'There'll be talk, you know. And there's already been enough of that.'

Well, wasn't that the point? Talk? Someone to talk to? Someone to help out?

Mavis and Rosie were crouched down peering under the hut. They'd lost interest already, although Mavis held on to the bottom of my coat.

'My room would be at the other side,' said Mr Tait. 'There's space there.'

'And another room at the back for Miss Weatherbeaten,' I said.

'What would a teacher be doing living in a hut with us?' said my mum.

Mr Tait and I glanced at each other again. There was so much to explain.

'You see what kind of nonsense you've put in her head?' said my mum. 'No. No, I'm afraid not. Come on Lenny, Mavis. We have to help Mrs Mags back to her hut with the baby. Where are the boys? Come along everyone.' I could hear the boys, Sandy, Dougie and bad George playing Tarzan further up the hill.

'Come along!' she said. 'Lenny, you'll have to push the chair.'

'No!' I said. 'I'm not pushing your bloody chair!'

'Lenny!' said my mum.

Mr Tait, Mavis and Rosie gasped.

'You see the kind of nonsense?' said my mum.

'I'm not pushing it!'

'Lenny,' said Mr Tait, in his quiet voice. 'Swearing is ... .'

'No!' I put my hands on my hips to show I meant it. Mavis and Rosie scuttled back to my side.

'Behave yourself or … ,' said my mum.

'You can bloody push your own bloody chair!'

'Mrs Gillespie,' said Mr Tait, as if I hadn't spoken, as if I hadn't sworn, three times now. 'I didn't do it.'

'Didn't do what?' she said, shaking her head.

'I didn't tell stories about you,' he said.

'What's that to do with anything? I already told you. I misunderstood.'

'In fact I was shocked by how quick they were to do it, shocked by how nasty it became.'

'Who? Who did it?'

'And the stories they told.'

She stood up as straight as she could with her crutches and didn't answer. Mr Tait waved a hand at me like a stop sign so that I wouldn't speak.

'I didn't believe a word of it,' he went on, 'about you and men, all that stuff.' His eyes flickered towards me then back to her. 'You're a hard worker,' he told her. 'You put others to shame with your work rate. People get jealous. You're an outsider and your good man is gone. They were like dogs with a rabbit. I don't like that.'

The boys clattered through the trees, and down the road I noticed old Mr MacInnes wandering towards us. Mrs Mags was nursing the baby in the window.

'I think the shift organiser had intentions,' said Mr Tait, 'if you know what I mean (I didn't) and I must state now that *my* only intention is for you and the girls to be happy and safe.'

Mavis slipped her hand round my back and gripped my coat.

'Mrs Gillespie,' said Mr Tait, 'it would make such a difference to me if you would stay here. If you like I'll build you another hut, if they'll allow it, one just for you and the girls, so that you could all be close by.'

His voice was trembling. I took a step forwards, the better to see him. Taking a perfect white handkerchief out of his pocket he mopped his wrinkly brow, and when he looked at me I saw that his eyes were rimmed with red.

'There's the standpipe, and the road for walking,' he said. He stuffed the handkerchief carefully back in his pocket and took one step towards her. She took one step back, more of a hop. 'I'll stay in the tent,' he said. 'We can see how it goes, see how you like it.'

My mum started to tremble like an autumn leaf on a tree. She shifted slightly on her crutches so that he wouldn't notice.

'Mrs Gillespie,' he said in the quietest voice ever, his head bowed. 'Mrs Gillespie,' he said again.

We waited. I knew he was going to say something important because he took so long about it. It's what he always did, and annoying though it was, it was always worth waiting.

'I'm going to miss Lenny terribly if you go to Clydebank,' he said, 'terribly.' And he shook his head as if to say 'No, no, no.' He held out a hand to me which I grasped as I stared up in wonder at kind Mr Tait with red rims to his eyes who was going to miss me. 'And I'll worry,' he said. 'There's some terrible things to be seen in Clydebank,' and he shook his head.

Rosie pulled her ear. Mavis sucked her thumb. I held my breath.

'And now I really must sit down,' he said, 'before I go over there for Miss Wetherspoon.'

Bad George and Sandy brought the wheelchair and a tree stump so my mum and Mr Tait both had somewhere to sit.

'Lenny,' whispered Mavis, and she pointed at where my mum's foot ought to have been. 'Yes,' I said. 'I told you already.'

'Will they get her a new one?'

'I suppose they will,' I said. 'Mr Tait has a wooden leg.'

'Yes, Mavis, it's true,' said Mr Tait. 'Listen to this.'

He tapped his hip, 'toc, toc, toc'.

'Go on Lenny, you do it too.'

I didn't really want to, not really, but I knew he wanted me to, to show Mavis he told the truth, so I reached out and went 'toc, toc, toc' on his leg, and Mavis stopped hiding in my coat and looked. Rosie had to have a go too.

'My, this is a fine hut!' said old Mr MacInnes, suddenly arriving, breathless from his journey. 'I think you made the right decision there, Mrs Gillespie. Glad you saw sense in the end.'

'But … .'

'Now, where's my Mags?'

So we stayed a few days, and then a few days more, and then a few days more again, just to see how it went, to see how she liked it.

But the very next day when I was crawling about under the hut with Mavis and Rosie, I saw the floorboards from underneath. I saw the roof too when I was up there with George that afternoon fixing the roofing felt. Both roof and floor were covered with the words 'SINGER' (my mum and Mr Tait's factory, remember?) and 'JOHN BROWN' (which is the big shipyard in Clydebank that the Germans missed with their bombs). It seemed that Mr Tait had developed a blind eye in addition to his wooden leg, and I noticed such words on other people's huts too, particularly Mrs Mags's hut. There were other names as well, like 'Auchentoshan Distillers' and 'Clyde Boilers'.

But Mr Tait said he hadn't seen anything of the sort.

The End

Notes on the Clydebank Blitz and the Carbeth Hut Community

Clydebank

In 1941 Clydebank was a medium-sized industrial town close to Glasgow in Scotland. It had a population of well over 50,000 most of whom were employed in the local John Brown's shipyards or Beardmore's Diesel Works and related industries, or making sewing machines in the Singer factory or whisky in Auchentoshan and Yoker. The people of Clydebank had a long tradition of socialist conviction and a close sense of community and belonging.

On two consecutive nights in 1941, the 13th and 14th March, Clydebank was savaged by the worst episode of bombing to take place in Scotland during the Second World War. The Clydebank bombing had certain characteristics that indicated planning and precision on the part of the Luftwaffe, and expertise learned from experience. Prior to the bombing, an enemy plane flew over at height taking reconnaissance photographs. Then on 13th March, the night of the full moon or 'bombers' moon' as it became known, the Luftwaffe checked the weather, and while most of Britain lay under cloud, Clydebank saw a glorious sunset followed by a beautiful clear night sky. Guided by the silvery moonlight which glanced off the River Clyde, advance bombers made their approach along Great Western Road, the road that runs out from Glasgow, past Clydebank to the West Highlands and lovely Loch Lomond. They dropped their first cargo of bombs on Singer's timber yard and Yoker Distillery. The beacons of fire which this created drew further enemy aircraft to their target, and the town was set on fire.

Over the two days of bombing, 439 bombers dropped over 4,000 bombs including 2,411 incendiary bombs; 35,000 people were made homeless with 4,000 houses completely destroyed and only 7 remaining untouched; more than 600 people were seriously injured and over 500 others killed, although many estimate the dead at much more than this.

Carbeth

North of Glasgow and Clydebank and with close connections to both, Carbeth is a hut community which sits beside the West Highland Way. Nestling amongst the lowland hills and woodlands, its history of temporary dwellings dates back to the late nineteenth century when the Clarion Cyclists established their Sunday Socialist Camps. These lasted into the 1960s and boasted, in addition to tents, concrete plinths with removable wooden floors for the tents to sit on, a community hall in which to hold entertainments, a tennis court and a cookhouse.

The first huts went up after the First World War when the benevolent landowner of the day, Allan

Barnes-Graham, allowed a shell-shocked soldier to build a hut on his land. More followed, an outdoor swimming pool was built, and the numbers gradually rose until the Second World War when many children were evacuated there or, like Lenny and her friends, sought refuge there after the bombing in Clydebank. Barnes-Graham assigned another piece of land to the hutters at that time to accommodate these people, and so the community grew. By the 1960s, six double-decker buses regularly arrived at the Halfway House pub (now the Carbeth Inn) on a Sunday evening to take the hutters back to their homes in the city. Other people walked to and from Milngavie where trams left for Glasgow, while 'Bankies' from Clydebank would walk, as Lenny did, over the Kilpatrick Hills via Craigton.

The area is a paradise for children, offering the kind of outdoor freedom that is no longer possible in other places due to the soaring number of cars. The rope swing tree still stands with its rope swing an ongoing enticement to the children of each new generation. The various paths are popular with Sunday strollers and more serious walkers pass by on the West Highland Way.

The huts themselves are temporary homes designed for holidays and weekends. In the past they offered many an inexpensive escape from the filth and toil of the industrial areas. There is no electricity supply and no mains water allowed, although attempts have been made to subvert the supply from the standpipes. The land has always remained the property of the landowner while the hut belongs to its owner.

While a benevolent and generous man, Barnes-

Graham also laid down strict rules and strolled regularly round his land making sure they were upheld. The current generation of Barnes-Grahams have sought to change his ethos somewhat and there is now a buy-out underway by the hutters. Their website can be found at http://www.carbethhuts.com.